THE DEAD AND THE DAMNED

". . . Anyhow, Fehler panicked and, instead of going to ground, blew his brains out. And there was no way to put the lid on it. Fehler was bad enough. But a few days later, General Wendland, Gehlen's old Number Two at Pullach, disposed of himself with a pistol. About the same hour that day Admiral Ludke used a shotgun on himself in a hunting lodge in the Eifel. The next week, Schenk, a high official of the Ministry of Economics, hanged himself in his Cologne home."

"I remember. The German press called it the 'October of the Suicides.' What about you, David? Did you think Fehler's death was suicide?"

The moment of truth, he thought. Or untruth, depending on your needs. "I thought the Germans"—he paused—"or somebody, had given him early retirement. It might have been suicide, though. The Roman kind, where they put a Luger on your desk and tell you they'll step outside while you think about alternatives."

Belknap got up from the table. He'd had enough. He went to the living room and parted the drapes. The unmarked black van was still there. Paranoia, he thought, national pastime of the damned.

"CHESSPLAYER"

WILLIAM PEARSON

PINNACLE BOOKS NEW YORK

"CHESSPLAYER"

Copyright © 1984 by William Pearson

A Pinnacle Books edition. This edition published by arrangement with Viking Penguin Inc.

Viking edition/May 1984
Pinnacle edition/July 1985

ISBN: 0-523-42558-9
Can. ISBN: 0-523-43503-7

Printed in the United States of America

PINNACLE BOOKS, INC.
1430 Broadway
New York, New York 10018

9   8   7   6   5   4   3   2   1

For you, Greg, for a hundred different reasons. And as sidebar, that distant music you hear must be, has to be, the *Marseillaise*

Lenin to Trotsky:

Now this is the truth, and I can refer you to many authorities. When Catherine Second and her royal entourage sailed down the Dnepr in 1787 to view the New Territories, the Field Marshal Potemkin created sham villages of cardboard and other devices along the river bank to give the distinguished visitors a false impression of reality. We want no more Potemkin villages.

Trotsky to Lenin:

On the matter of the Potemkin villages I must disagree. They were real, and this is the truth, for which I can cite many authorities. The illusion that they did not exist was created by historians, who are the source of most of our illusions about the past.

Lenin to Trotsky:

Dear Comrade, what does it matter who was responsible, my Field Marshal or your historians? In either event, somebody was rudely deceived.

—Pre-Revolutionary Correspondence, Lenin–Trotsky, Volume I

1

BRDNOWSKI HAD DROPPED a passenger at the Cannon House Office Building off Independence Avenue and was cruising north on First when the man hailed him from the mall in front of the Library of Congress. Brdnowski pulled to the curb and leaned over to open the rear door. "I'm suburban. Can only take fares going across the D.C. line."

The man was fiftyish, balding, and carrying a leather briefcase. "National," he said hoarsely, and began to cough.

Brdnowski banged his flag. "Sounds like you got a cold."

"I'm in a hurry. That's the main news."

"Right." Brdnowski eased around a stalled van with its hood up. The driver, a man in brown twill coveralls, was hunched over the engine checking wiring. Brdnowski half-turned in his seat. "Catching a plane or meeting someone?"

The passenger, who seemed to be waving casually at a pedestrian farther down the mall, leaned forward to study the TD permit and tiny photograph on the sun visor. "Is your name Brdnowski?"

"Right."

"I figured it probably was. I have this kind of talent for reading TD permits."

Okay, wise apple, Brdnowski thought, I don't have to talk to you either. The tip was going to be lousy, he knew that now—about enough to buy a hamburger · at 1930

1

prices—but on the return trip he'd bag a live one. It was written in the stars.

"What airline?" he said two stoplights later. The man didn't answer. Brdnowski glanced in his rearview mirror, saw the man was dozing. Eyes closed, mouth slightly open as though ready to snore, and chin resting in wattles against the knot of his tie.

Brdnowski slammed his horn a few times to wake Sleeping Beauty. When the man didn't respond to the atonal wake-up call, Brdnowski flipped the switch of his two-way. Ernie was dispatching today, and Ernie had a voice to cut through sleep—or even thunder, if it came to that—the way a hot knife cuts through butter. Brdnowski endured a few foghorn blasts from Ernie, directing his troops to all the wrong hotels ten minutes after waiting customers would have built their own taxis from spare parts, and then glanced hopefully in the rearview mirror again. "What airline? I mean, National isn't Pocatello. It's got so many terminals, even the terminals got terminals." This was more or less a lie, but it was the first one today. "So, what airline? It'll be just between you and me."

The passenger didn't respond. Brdnowski drove in sullen silence until he came to another stoplight. Leaning back, he put his big hand on the passenger's knee, pulled on it, and shouted, "Hey, wake up! I need to know the airline."

Brdnowski was strong, and the man's legs and body came toward him, unresisting. The man's head fell sideways against the door, and it was then that Brdnowski, with a start of terror, knew. His passenger was dead.

Brdnowski had been driving cabs eleven years, ever since he got out of the Army with nothing worse than company punishment for two AWOLs and a head injury from a bean ball he'd stopped in its tracks during a baseball game for division championship. In the course of his cabdriving career, he'd been robbed four times, caught in police cross fire during the riots of '68, and tossed about in two bad crashes, one of which had left him with a game leg, but never had he encountered a situation like this.

He was about to raise Ernie on the two-way to get advice, but the hint of a groan, a sound of some kind from the rear seat, changed his mind. St. Albans was closest; he made a screeching U-turn, scattering oncoming traffic like autumn leaves and hoping, in the process, to roust a prowl car that could give him siren and lights to the hospital.

He tried to weave through occasional holes in the clogged lanes ahead, but nobody was giving an inch, this Tuesday morning or any other morning. It was the code of the road. "I'm taking you to the hospital," his said over his shoulder. This is your pilot, he thought, I'm taking you to London, Paris, Amsterdam.

It was a dumbo game Brdnowski sometimes played. He'd always wanted to be a pilot, but had dropped out of high school in the spring of his junior year to try out for one of the Florida farm clubs, and when they cut him early, his friendly neighborhood draft board invited him to an immediate shotgun wedding with the Army. So now he was thirty-one, with a twenty percent disability pension because he'd once stopped a bean ball cold, and a winning ticket on the next Irish Sweeps. Winning? Oh, Brdnowski, he thought, you idiot optimist.

He turned down the ramp leading to St. Albans Emergency. A black Cad owned all the entrance curbing, and behind it was a vending-machine service van plastered with inspirational logos for Pepsi, Nabisco, and Kraft. Brdnowski parked behind the van and ran toward the plate-glass doors, limping slightly from the old crash. A big, bulky man in a soiled dark-green shirt and baggy chinos, bearded, pale, and sweating.

The young woman in charge of the reception cubicle was lecturing a distraught little hunchback who'd long ago kissed seventy good-bye but couldn't produce his Medicare card. Behind him four other nonpersons waited to approach the throne and state their business. A gray-haired woman covered with hospital sheeting, plastic tubes running from her nostrils to a bottle suspended above her, lay on a gurney. The vending-machine salesman, loading sandwiches and small milk cartons into the maw of one of his robots, idly patted the rump of a passing nurse.

"Hello, Harry Murphy," she said gaily. "What's good on the canteen menu today?"

"For you, doll, raw meat. Arff!"

Brdnowski was baffled and angry. Hospital emergency rooms weren't like this on TV. On TV there were always eager white-jacketed attendants asking to be of service, and where was the patient? Brdnowski decided to act. He took hold of the nearest wheelchair and started pushing it toward the entrance doors. The young woman in the cubicle called out, almost in panic, "Did you want something, sir?"

"I got a patient outside. Heart attack, I think."

"But you can't take a wheelchair outside." She sounded desperate. "It must be done by staff."

Then, miraculously, a woman in starched whites caught up with him. "Where's the patient?"

"In the cab." Brdnowski reluctantly surrendered the wheelchair.

The woman was stronger than she looked. She made the transfer from cab to wheelchair almost without help. Brdnowski hurried after her into the hospital. She made a smart left turn with the wheelchair and started down a tiled corridor. "You can't come in here." She gestured toward the cubicle. "Get him checked in. We'll let you know."

Brdnowski took out his handkerchief and wiped the perspiration on his face. He walked to the vending machine. The salesman was still loading milk cartons. "Can I get a Pepsi from that thing?"

"Not yet, buddy. It won't take no money till I lock it up again."

"Well, how about me giving you a quarter and you giving me one of those milks?"

"Against company policy. All the money's got to go into the machine."

"Okay, I give you the quarter, you give me the milk, and when the machine's ready, you put the quarter in the machine."

The salesman gave him a pitying look. "Then I get a carton of milk out of the machine, and I don't want no carton of milk."

"Listen," Brdnowski said, "I just about had a guy die on me."

"Yeah, well, what you do then, you go down that hallway, take your second right, go by the telephone booths, take your third left, and there's another machine. Only it don't have no Pepsi."

Brdnowski felt a headache coming on again. It was part of what they paid him the disability for, but some of them were pistols. Split vision, dizziness, nausea, and sometimes three or four days off work. He went back to the reception cubicle and resignedly got in line. "Miss," he said when he'd worked his way to its head, "let's make this snappy . . . I got a job I got to get back to."

"I can certainly appreciate that," the receptionist said, and Brdnowski had the feeling he was listening to a recorded announcement being replayed for the hundredth time. "But you do have to check in your patient. That's required."

"He isn't *my* patient. Never saw him before today."

She frowned. "Oh, you must be the one who brought in the J.D."

She made it sound like a disease, but he knew damn well he hadn't brought in any J.D. or V.D. or even T.B. "J.D.?" he challenged her.

"John Doe. The orderly inventoried his wallet. No identification in it. So temporarily a J.D. But I'll bet you can straighten that out. What's his name? First, last, middle initial."

"Look, I'm a taxi driver. All I did was pick him up off the street."

She pursed her lips. Brdnowski had the feeling his answer confused her. She chewed thoughtfully on the eraser of her pencil. "Well, has he ever been a patient in this hospital?"

Brdnowski decided he was going to lose his temper after all. "How the hell would I know?"

She looked up at him, startled, and went on the offensive. "Well, he asked you to bring him here, didn't he?" She snapped the words as if they were wishbones. "He must've said something. Where'd you pick him up?"

"The Library of Congress."

She wrote it down. "Where was he going?"

"National Airport."

She wrote it down. "What airline?"

Exasperated, Brdnowski wound up and fired off a spitball. "Eastern. The shuttle. He was making a connection with KLM for Amsterdam. That's Holland. I got the idea he'd something to do with diamonds."

She wrote that down, too. "How's he doing?" Brdnowski asked.

She said triumphantly, "I'm afraid we can only give that information to next of kin. And you aren't exactly that, are you?"

Up yours, too, Brdnowski thought.

"But I'll need your name," she said. "For the records."

"Right."

She waited. "So what is it?"

"Harry. Harry Murphy. No middle initial."

"And where do you live, Harry?"

"I'm in the Y this week."

"And occupation, cabdriver. What company?"

"Yellow. We're the best."

"I'm sure. Well, that should do it. Wasn't too painful, was it?"

"Not for me. And I want you to know, you run a very human place here. Not like some I've seen." Brdnowski about-faced before she could get off a zinger and went out to his cab. When he saw he'd left his flag down and the meter was reading thirteen dollars eighty, he almost had apoplexy. He gave the flag an angry upward whack, gunned the motor, and was about to burn rubber on the exit ramp when he heard someone shouting from the entranceway. It was the vending-maching salesman, hands cupped to lips. Brdnowski wound down the right window. "Yeah?"

"I said, you can have that Pepsi now."

Brdnowski rewound his window. A day that starts like this, he thought, has nowhere to go except up.

He drove to the front of the hospital, scouting fares, but everyone coming out seemed to be a visitor with his own wheels. Pulling into the main drag, he decided to check in with the dispatcher.

"This is Double-O-Seven," he said. "What you got for me?"

"Cut out that crap on the air, Brdnowski," Ernie said. "Where the hell you been while ten thousand people been begging for rides, even with you? And if it ain't a military secret, where are you now?"

"In a holding pattern at three thousand. Am I cleared to land?"

"You gonna tell me where you are, or am I gonna put you on the list and send you out first every time some old biddy wants to drive two blocks to the grocery store?"

"I'm near St. Albans. I've been having kind of an experience. Some guy gets in and—"

"This ain't a talk show, Brdnowski. There's a double at the Wexford Arms. They'll be waiting in front. They want to go to National."

Oh, Christ, Brdnowski thought, not again.

He was a block from the Wexford Arms when he remembered the briefcase. He craned his neck. It was still on the floor of the back seat. He pulled to the curb, reached for the case, and placed it on the front floorboard. He'd turn it in at Lost and Found when he got to the garage.

2

"HI, MYRT," BRDNOWSKI called. "I'm home."

"Why?" she said from the kitchen.

Oh, boy, Brdnowski thought, one of *those* nights. "Because I love you, you crazy broad."

She came padding into the living room, a plump, black-haired woman of thirty with eyes about as green as you could get. He could tell she was on the warpath, or only a few steps away from it, because she was wearing her faded red bathrobe and her scuffed mules with fur the color of wet string. She looked at the briefcase he was carrying. "What's that?"

"A briefcase."

"Oh. I thought it was one of those new electric spinning wheels."

"Ho, ho, ho," Brdnowski said. "A fare left it in the cab. When I got to the garage, Lost and Found was closed. So I brought it home."

"What's in it?"

"Fifty thousand in small bills. Old currency. Untraceable."

"Come on, Brdnowski. What's in it?"

"It's locked."

"The story of our life." She sat on the arm of the overstuffed in front of the TV set. "I made twenty-two bucks in tips today. The Greek pinched my ass once, no, I think it was twice."

"Hard sometimes to remember," he said philosophically.

"He owns the joint. His privilege. More than I get from you, anyhow."

"I've been tired lately, Myrt."

"Yeah, who hasn't? There's hash for dinner."

"Sounds good," he lied. "I'll open a couple of beers."

"Sure you're not too tired?"

In answer, he gave one of her breasts a squeeze as he traveled by. "Wow, my Romeo," she said, and laughed. "Brdnowski, how'd I ever land in your bed, anyhow?"

"I don't know," he answered from the kitchen, "but I'd say it was a very happy landing for me."

"God, that's almost poetic. How do you think of those things?"

"They come to me sometimes." He returned with two foaming beers and handed her one.

She switched on the TV, saw she had a commercial, and turned down the sound. "I've been wondering," she said to her beer glass.

"Yeah?" he said cautiously.

"Like, say, when are we going to get married? I mean, all the hot air aside. This year? Next year?"

Brdnowski took a statesmanlike pull on his beer. "Gee, Myrt."

"Don't *gee, Myrt* me, Brdnowski."

"Well, I'm thinking of the long haul."

"Sure. All we have to do is wait until there's thirty thousand in the bank, find the right location, and get a loan, some fat chance of that."

"We got a chain letter."

"Yeah, but how much are you dropping on the horses every month?"

"I'm even with the horses all spring. Maybe a little ahead."

"The Home Run," she said. "It's sure one screwy name for a burger joint."

"It's not going to be just a burger joint," Brdnowski said, defending the dream. "What it's going to be is a place you get the biggest burgers in town. In the whole goddamn country. Every one a home run."

Slumping on the sofa the fairy in the next apartment had unloaded on him for thirty bucks when he moved in with his boyfriend downstairs, Brdnowski massaged the back of his neck. "I got one of those headaches coming on. Probably won't be working tomorrow. Maybe not the rest of the week." He morosely watched the silent TV screen. "This guy who owns the briefcase. He almost died on me."

"I'll turn up the sound," Myrt said. "It's that new game show where they use the live rattlesnakes."

Jesus, Brdnowski thought, *nobody* wants to know about it. "Myrt, don't you understand? He almost died on me."

"Who are we talking about?"

"The guy who owns the briefcase."

"You're kidding."

"Listen, I thought I'd a dead man on my hands. I took him to St. Albans. Had a clunker the company hasn't switched to electronic metering and I left the fucking meter running. Thirteen dollars and eighty cents."

"How'd it happen?"

"I forgot to put the flag up."

"No, how'd he almost die on you?"

"How do I know? Maybe he *is* dead. They wouldn't tell me at the hospital."

"And now he owes you thirteen eighty?"

"Plus the tip. But he wouldn't have been good for warm spit there."

"So the company's into you for thirteen eighty?"

"Less my cut."

"Brdnowski, you'd try the patience of a saint. You want your money back, hock the briefcase. It ought to bring ten, maybe twenty dollars."

He thought about it. "If I knew he was actually dead, I might try it. The nurse said he didn't have any I.D."

"What do you think's in it?"

"A bomb."

"Atom, or just old-fashioned dynamite?"

"Atom, the way my luck's been running today."

She lifted the briefcase. "It's not too heavy."

"They make bombs so light these days they fit in envelopes. I saw it once on 'Mission Impossible.'"

"I got a question for you, Brdnowski. A guy's carrying a briefcase costing, what, seventy-five bucks maybe, and yet he's got no I.D. Does that make sense."

"If he's a mad bomber, it does."

"Aw, get off this bomber stuff. Supposing it's drugs."

Brdnowski blanched. "Drugs I want nothing to do with. No way."

"You're not getting the point. Drugs, there'd be a reward from the narcs."

Brdnowski was impressed. Myrt was always surprising him. The chain letter had been her idea too. "I'll get us a couple more beers."

"And I'll get the key to my sewing machine."

"Now slow down, Myrt," he said. "I want to think it through."

Three beers later he'd thought it through, but the sewing-machine key didn't work on the briefcase lock. He got his toolbox from under the kitchen sink. He took out pliers, wire, and a small screwdriver. He asked Myrt for a bobby pin.

"You ain't exactly an expert," she said after ten more minutes of his tinkering. "Why not take it over to Columbia Road? He'll still be open."

"Who will?"

"That locksmith opposite the Safeway."

"We can't have a locksmith opening it."

"Just get him to make a key."

"We'd be getting in awful deep, Myrt."

"Well, doesn't your fare owe you thirteen eighty?"

He nodded and, with beery bravado, said, "If I'm not back in an hour, phone Perry Mason."

"Tell them you won't take the test."

"What test?"

"The one they give you when they pick you up for three beers too many."

As he started toward the door, she stopped him with a voice like a brick wall. "Brdnowski, you dumb Polack! Look at your clothes! That crummy green shirt. The pants. Those crazy cowboy boots. You walk into the locksmith's like that, he'll figure you mugged somebody to get the briefcase."

He had to hand it to her. She didn't miss a trick. "I'll change."

"A shower and a couple of bars of Lifebuoy wouldn't hurt either. Then you'll be all pink and sweet and warm for me." Her laugh, as he headed for the bathroom, followed him like a cheer from the bleachers.

After showering, he put on plaid trousers, a yellow shirt, and a lightweight sports coat with natty blue checks. He even struggled into a tie, though it was against his principles. The last touch was a porkpie hat with a small red feather in the band. The hat was actually too hot for a June evening—he wore it only to Redskin football games—but it dressed him up a bit. "How do I look?"

She admired him a moment. "You look like a fucking U.S. senator."

"Well, I feel like hell. My head."

"I'll have the hash ready when you get back."

"That'll be nice."

He put a lot of tipsy caution into driving his old Chevy the six blocks to Columbia Road and, with drunken luck, somehow managed to reach the Safeway without hitting anything that moved. As he pulled to the curb beside a fire hydrant, he spotted the locksmith's, squeezed between a run-down Cuban café and the iron grillwork guarding a secondhand clothing store.

When he entered, a bell tinkled over his head, lifeless curtains parted at the rear, and a gnome of a man came out wearing what looked like a shoemaker's apron. His ancient face was splotched with red and purple patches, each one a little map of a different country.

Brdnowski laid the rectangular briefcase on the linoleum countertop. "Lost the key to this. I need another."

"Naturally." The locksmith brought a claim check from lower depths. "I'll have it tomorrow afternoon. What's your name and address?"

Brdnowski hadn't anticipated a day of waiting, though now he realized he should have. You had to stand in line for everything nowadays, especially in hospital emergency rooms. "Well, there's a problem."

"So tell me the problem."

Brdnowski hesitated. Then, on the theory two strings to the bow were better than one, he said, "I brought this home from the office to get ready for a meeting tomorrow. Other thing is, the papers in it are confidential. I'm not allowed to let it out of my sight."

"You government?"

"No, computers."

"I thought you were maybe FBI," the Gnome said sarcastically. He put on a pair of cracked glasses and gave Brdnowski a more thorough inspection. He pointed to a sign on the wall, where large block letters said: SHOP TIME—$10 PER HOUR, $10 MINIMUM. "It'd be time and a half."

Brdnowski was taken aback. The fare was into him for thirteen eighty. If there were drugs in the briefcase, he might get a couple of big ones from the narcs. If there was nothing except papers, he probably couldn't hock it for enough to cover the thirteen eighty plus key charges. Still, there comes a time when you have to fish or cut bait. "Go ahead."

"Must be a very important meeting." Lips pursed, head

cocked sparrow-fashion, the wizened locksmith studied the briefcase. "What's your name?"

"Name?" Brdnowski remembered. "Harry Murphy. No middle initial."

"Mine's Finemann." He went to a key rack. Brdnowski guessed there must be a thousand keys and blanks—for cars, houses, and who knew what—on the hooks in the vertical pegboard panels. The locksmith gave the rack a vigorous spin, vigorous beyond his years. Brdnowski was worried for him.

"What's your company, Murphy?"

"IBM."

The locksmith introduced the back of his hand into the circle the panels were traveling. The rack came to a stop. His hand swooped like a hawk on a key at the bottom of the nearest panel. He put it in the lock. Brdnowski, amazed, heard a click. The locksmith started to undo the clasps. Brdnowski slapped down hard. "It's all confidential, Finemann."

"Gratitude ends where success begins."

Brdnowski didn't quite understand the reply, but he didn't want to stay around for explanations. He brought out his wallet. "What's the damage?"

"Fifteen dollars, naturally."

"Fifteen dollars!"

"Plus tax. I told you it was time and a half."

"But Jesus, that was for *making* a key. You took one off the goddamn *rack*. In less than a minute at that."

"You're paying for know-how, Murphy. Put it on the expense account."

It hurt—his pride as much as his wallet—but Brdnowski fished out two tens and took back his change and a little more experience about life. The locksmith opened the door for him. That surprised Brdnowski—it was the kind of old-fashioned courtesy you didn't see much anymore—especially after the unpleasantness of a moment ago. Maybe Finemann was trying to apologize. It was a crazy world.

* * *

Brdnowski had never considered himself strong on willpower, but he did manage to get back to the apartment without stopping to look at the contents of the case. Not that he was about to give himself a medal for the achievement. It'd be safer inspecting it behind locked doors, and anyhow, he wanted Myrt around to hold his hand if the case had nothing except papers.

"Hi, Myrt," he called, momentarily overpowered by the smell of hash and burnt onions. "I'm home."

She came out of the kitchen like a bull-legged ballet dancer, and it didn't take a detective to see she was more than a beer up on him. Somewhere she'd lost one of her mules, but she was full of boozy good cheer. "In the nick. I was about to phone Perry Mason."

He sailed the porkpie into the bedroom and gave the briefcase an affectionate slap. "It's unlocked."

"The suspense's killing me. What's in it?"

"Diamonds. From Amsterdam."

"Don't play games, Brdnowski, or you'll get a hot-grease shampoo."

He grinned. "Let's take a look." He put the briefcase on the sofa.

"It's drugs. I can feel it. No I.D. The guy was playing foxy in case he got picked up."

Brdnowski knelt in front of the briefcase, depressed the latch, and released the clasps. He raised the lid and stared an eternity at what he saw. "Oh, Jesus," he whispered. He looked up at her, panic-stricken. "Myrt, what are we going to do?"

3

In one of the stately restored townhouses adjoining Lafayette Square, two men sat opposite each other on velvet plush sofas separated by a circular marble coffee table, bare except for an ornate French clock enclosed in a bell jar. An air-conditioning unit whirred beneath one of the second-floor windows, but otherwise the room was exclusively the property of the nineteenth century. Most of the furniture and bric-a-brac were Victorian, and the paintings of rural English scenes, whatever their provenance, atrocious.

Belknap, who had a fair eye for art, wondered how Malkin could stand working out of such a place.

"I want to thank you, David," Malkin said with his wonderful boyish smile, "for getting here so quickly."

Belknap gave the order man a wry look. "I didn't have much choice. Some S.O.B. almost broke down my door at five in the morning. In the confusion, I even forgot to pack a toothbrush."

"Well, we can certainly take care of that. And more besides. How is New York?"

"They claim it's surviving. Sometimes I wonder."

"And your wife?"

"We parted after a few months." Belknap hesitated. "Almost amicably."

"I'm sorry."

Belknap shrugged. He was sure Malkin had known before he asked. It was the kind of detail Malkin's radar always picked up. He'd worked under Malkin briefly in

16

Moscow and then in Bonn during and after the Fehler affair, and later in London, but Fehler was another lifetime ago, and now Malkin must be nearly sixty-five. And plainly flourishing. His hair had gone from gray to silver, but the elongated face beneath it, chiseled from patrician marble, was remarkably unlined. Belknap, having reached the magic age of forty himself, the age where a man is said to have earned the face he lived in, wished he were carrying those same intervening years as comfortably. Belknap didn't like mirrors anymore.

"I saw you briefly on the news last night," Malkin said. "You looked in a bit of a huff."

"Well, I testified before that subcommittee two hours yesterday afternoon. In two hours you ought to be able to say a lot about the difficulties of combating sophisticated industrial espionage, but not when half-informed congressmen are interrupting every few minutes with irrelevant questions. That's why I probably looked irritated when the TV crews boxed me in. I had to be back in New York by six and they were going to make me miss the shuttle."

"I wish I'd known you were in town. We could've had lunch at the Sans Souci. Or did you come down with one of your associates?"

"I was alone."

Malkin nodded vaguely. "What did you think of the Brandt affair?"

The question was a quantum jump from lunch at the Sans Souci, and it took Belknap a moment to grasp what it was he was being asked. The Brandt affair, like the Fehler affair, was history too, but more recent. Behind Malkin's rambling, though, there had to be a purpose. "It was a shock. But Brandt faced the music and danced off the stage with better style than Nixon."

"Extraordinary that a fellow like Günter Guillaume, with all that East German background, could get so close to the chancellor without anyone's tumbling to him."

Extraordinary? Was this Malkin speaking? The skeptic

supreme? Belknap decided it would be prudent to be noncommittal. "It seems to be endemic with the Germans. There was Heinz Felfe."

"Yes, Heinz Felfe. Ten years of spying for the Russians from an office almost next door to Gehlen's. The sixties were an awkward time for our German friends." In Malkin's amber eyes, Belknap saw that familiar hint of mockery. "I suppose you and I didn't help any when we dumped Erich Fehler in their laps."

That wasn't quite the way it had happened, but as a historian Malkin had always been a bit of a revisionist.

"David, I'm sorry to have gotten you down here in the fashion I did. But as you'd know, there was a reason. The balloon has gone up."

The balloon has gone up. Belknap wondered how many times in his former career he'd heard the phrase. The crisis-makers and crisis-managers thrived on their clubbish private conviction that each new crisis was without parallel in the memory of man, and only next week's crisis, not yet born, would persuade them otherwise.

"At this moment a meeting's starting in the Cabinet Room. Across there." Malkin, his expression faintly bemused, gestured beyond Lafayette Square, as if to make clear to a slow pupil he wasn't talking about the Elysée Palace or Ten Downing.

"Have the Russians invaded Florida?"

"Don't be too facetious yet, David. It's a very sticky business. A very dirty business. And whenever they have some very sticky, very dirty business, they send for me."

"And then you send for me."

They both laughed, Belknap not comfortably.

"Ah, David. You were always my favorite. We'll have coffee shortly. In the meantime, let me fill you in. The meeting over there's connected with something called Operation Beowulf or Project Beowulf." Malkin touched up the sentence with another brushstroke of simulated vagueness. "Something on that order."

"I see the people who think up code names aren't getting more original as times goes by."

"Don't be too harsh on them, David. As code names go, it has rather a nice ring, I think."

"What is it? Beowulf."

"I can't tell you exactly."

"You can't, or you won't?"

"A little of both." Malkin always enjoyed himself at these moments. "What I can tell you is, Beowulf involves oil and the Middle East, and in the wrong hands its details could blow that area of the world apart. And possibly our area with it. I can also tell you Beowulf's not an operation anyone tends to mount tomorrow. Beowulf's simply part of normal contingency planning, the kind designed to provide the president with appropriate options should certain unfortunate events take place down the road."

"Such as somebody turning off the oil spigots again?"

"Ah, here's our coffee. Come in, Mrs. Pruett, come in."

Mrs. Pruett was a stout, gray-haired woman with rosy cheeks and a brisk stride that fairly shouted of the outdoor life. She pushed the service cart ahead of her in the bluff, no-nonsense manner of a governess pushing a pram out of the rain.

"This is my old friend David from New York," Malkin said in that earnest, engaging style Belknap remembered so well. "He'll be with us awhile."

"We're delighted to have you, David, dear," Mrs. Pruett said.

"Mrs. Pruett looks after me from dawn to dusk. She's secretly British, but grew up Chevy Chase, Bryn Mawr, that sort of thing. Got to London during the war, the big one you were far too young for, David, and did the Red Cross bit. We go back a long ways."

"Thirty-plus years, give or take a decade," Mrs. Pruett said. "I've got croissants this morning, George. I hope you're not dieting."

"In those thirty-plus years, give or take a decade, Sybil,

have you ever seen me dieting? David, do you prefer sugar and cream, or just cream? It's clumsy, I know, but I've forgotten."

Belknap doubted that. "Just cream." He noticed the fine Irish linen draping the service cart and the splendid silverware and the eggshell china. "This is different from Bonn."

"Oh, the outward amenities, yes. But not the basics. Except the stakes here are usually higher. Sybil, I hope you'll keep Vanessa standing by."

"I'll do my humble best, George, dear."

After Mrs. Pruett had closed the door, Malkin served coffee and offered a choice of English marmalades. "I must say, David, you're looking fit. And your face as you push on—forgive me for saying it—into the middle age is developing more character. You used to be, well, almost too good to be true. I like the cragginess. I like the lines you're getting. Smile lines, they called them in my day. And that intriguing scar on your right cheek. People who didn't know might think it came from dueling . . . mysterious hint of a romantic past."

"I keep trying to forget someone almost broke down my door at five this morning."

"I know. I'm being too long-winded and devious. Old habits are hard to break." He fished for his glasses case, polished the lenses with a silk handkerchief he took from the breast pocket of his blue seersucker, and daintily placed the wire stems on his ears. "Let's see, where were we?"

"The balloon had gone up, and we were wandering around the edges of Middle East oil politics and you were talking in riddles worthy of the Sphinx and I was wondering why I was here and what the hell you meant when you told Mrs. Pruett I was going to be around awhile."

"The same old delightful David. I'm glad that hasn't changed."

"And the wise men were meeting in the Cabinet Room."

"Yes, exactly." He buttered a croissant and added a

dollop of ginger marmalade. "You see, David, at one this morning a Postal Service clerk-sorter working in the Barrow Annex found a package addressed to the White House, to the president, to be precise. It was roughly two feet by a foot and a half, clumsily wrapped in heavy brown paper, then tied with kitchen string, and the postal clerk thought there might be a bomb in it. The Secret Service and the Metropolitan Police Bomb Disposal Squad were notified and arrived about an hour later to check the matter out. The police brought along one of those German shepherds that sniff for bombs or drugs, and the dog rejected the package. But one of the Bomb Squad technicians, using a metal detector, got indications of a substantial metal mass, so the police experts and the Street Service adjourned to a parking lot to open the package. Well, there wasn't a bomb, there was a rectangular leather briefcase. And in the briefcase, among other things, were seventy or so Xeroxed pages containing the most current planning for Beowulf."

In his astonishment, Belknap almost dropped his coffee cup. Malkin waited tolerantly for him to recover. "The Secret Service agent who actually opened the briefcase knew nothing about Beowulf, but the first thing he saw when he raised the lid would have wonderfully concentrated his mind. A stapled clutch of papers whose title page carried the letterhead of the National Security Council." He reached into his seersucker and produced a single sheet of paper he passed across the marble coffee table.

Belknap stared at the typewritten title page. It took effort to control the involuntary tremor of his hand as he started to read:

REVISED DRAFT FOR
OPERATION BEOWULF

UTMOST TOP SECRET

WARNING: By virtue of NSC Memorandum 75-17,
             utmost-top-secret clearance is not by itself

> sufficient for access to Beowulf material, and all persons previously cleared for access are now removed from the list unless specifically granted new access by written authorization from the President under the procedures set forth in NSCM 75-17. Unauthorized access to this material, which contains information affecting the national defense of the United States within the meaning of the Espionage Laws, is a crime punishable as provided by *Title 18, United States Code*.

Finally Belknap looked up at Malkin. That took effort too. "Yes," he ventured, "it would have wonderfully concentrated anyone's mind."

"Beowulf planning," Malkin continued, accepting the return of the title page, "has always proceeded under the heaviest possible security. When the final draft was completed a month ago, access was restricted, as you saw, to those with specific authorization from the president. Ten people altogether. And there were only three copies of the draft. One was lodged with the Joint Chiefs, another at Langley in the director's safe, and the last with the National Security Council. So the initial assumption is that we, like Brandt, have a Günter Guillaume in our midst, and that this person—call him Mr. X—delivered Beowulf to an agent of a foreign power."

"Then why was Beowulf returned?"

"Ah, David, if we knew that . . . Who knows anyone's motives, who knows what's truth, what's illusion, in the game of nations? But I could offer a theory. The Beowulf material in hostile hands—let's hypothesize Russian—could trigger a preemptive Russian entry into the Middle East. Iran, say, or Afghanistan. So why not, if you were the Russian chess player, send the material back to us to signal the plan had been compromised? We'd then be expected to understand that if they did go into Iran or Afghanistan and we responded with anything more than pro forma protests, along with a few obligatory restrictions on exports of grain, computer hardware, touring college glee clubs, they'd justify their action before world opinion by releasing the details of Beowulf. And by sending the material back to us, they'd also be signaling that if we ever tried to implement Beowulf, they'd—"

"Except that by sending the material back, they alert us to the existence of Mr. X. Then the hunt is on, the hounds are loosed."

"You've a point. On the other hand, consider what would happen if the existence of Beowulf were suddenly revealed, say, in a speech at the United Nations—to the indescribable embarrassment of the United States. The revelation would create a situation of unprecedented danger in the Middle East for *all* interested parties, not just the United States. Given that premise, a percipient government into whose hands the papers had come might decide it was more prudent to return them, even if it put their Mr. X at risk, than to embarrass us before world opinion."

"No government would put at risk an agent as strategically placed as Mr. X must be. There has to be another explanation. What about the men in the Cabinet Room, what are they doing now?"

"Wringing their hands and trying to create a structure of plausible deniability as to any personal knowledge of Beowulf by the president if the whole plan suddenly appears on the front page of *Al Ahram* in Cairo or the *Times* here, or if Ambassador Dobrynin suddenly asks for a meeting in the Oval office. A structure a little difficult to create," Malkin added dryly, "in view of the smoking gun smoking its way across the title page."

He wandered a moment longer in the labyrinths of the unthinkable. "And then some kind of decision has to be made immediately about the ten men who had Beowulf access." From a sterling silver bowl, he carefully measured two helpings of sugar with a sterling spoon. "Each of them, of course, is now under suspicion—I told you it was a sticky, dirty business—but if they were to be cut off from other sensitive material while the Beowulf investigation was in process, it'd be almost impossible for them to carry out everday responsibilities. A significant part of the governmental machinery would be paralyzed. The chairman of the Joint Chiefs had access. Out of the question to quarantine him, yet where do you draw the line? The president will have to decide."

"Is anyone with Beowulf access at the meeting?"

"Yes, and those who aren't will know before noon that it's been returned. That's what Washington's all about."

"How does the Beowulf access-mechanism work?"

"I'm familiar only with how it works at NSC. A reading room adjoins a walk-in vault. To get material from the vault, you first log in with a guard, identifying the folder you want by its file number. The guard then takes you to the files, removes the request folder, and leaves a marker card in its place. Material carrying special restrictions, such as Beowulf, can be examined only in the reading room. When you finish your reading, the vault guard again goes to the vault and exchanges the material for the marker card."

"Not exactly a foolproof system."

"You have to remember the system was designed primarily to prevent unauthorized access, secondarily to prevent carelessness by those with access. Individuals authorized to use vault material have such high clearances that theft by any of them was never a serious consideration."

"Is there a Xerox machine in the reading room?"

"Yes, but only the guard can operate it, and only when the documents have a classification permitting copying. In addition, the machine's electronic counter can't be reset. It keeps numerical track of all copies produced, and all such copies have to be accounted for in the guard's log, which is audited at the end of each day by the watch officer."

"Would a person be under observation in the reading room? Closed-circuit TV, for example?"

"No, but there are usually other people working there."

"Still, under the right conditions, a person could slip seventy pages of typewritten replacement material into the Beowulf folder, then give the replacement material to the guard, who'd automatically return it to the file."

"It'd be risky."

"Not if the switch were made near the end of the day—just before the vault was closed—with the borrowed material returned as soon as the vault was opened the next morning."

"That'd be rather amateurish, David, and we're certainly not dealing with an amateur."

"I realize that. But the person with whom you are dealing wouldn't have expected the stolen material to be returned through the mails, either. So he wouldn't have worried about what the log would show. Anyhow, it might not be one of the ten men with Beowulf access. The vault guards, who are they?"

"Army personnel on detached duty. Specially selected, specially trained."

Belknap smiled. "Like that sergeant who ended up at the Armed Forces Courier Center at Orly in sixty-two and peddled NATO cosmics to the Russians. Well, all right, where do the CIA and FBI fit into the marching orders?"

"We'll have the resources of both. But one copy of Beowulf, you must remember, was in the CIA director's safe, and two other people over there had access."

"No, that's too preposterous."

"Of course. Still, when Otto John was head of the Office for the Protection of the Constitution in Cologne, nobody suspected him until he went over. And then the Fehler affair. Nobody suspected Fehler. Nobody." Malkin offered his cigar humidor, and when Belknap declined, lit a slender Montecristo and drew on it delicately. "Yes, it's going to be a dirty business, and everybody's suspect. That's one reason, David, you were brought in from outside. Whatever else you can be accused of"—Malkin let the words hang on improvised gallows—"you can't be accused of this."

"I didn't know I'd accepted."

"You will. The enormity of the theft, the immensity of the challenge, those are things you can't resist."

"I thought I was on the blacklist."

"The business with the diamonds and our friend in Jordan? I never believed you were responsible, you know that. In fact, I hoped you might feel"—Malkin hesitated diplomatically—"you owed me a favor because of what I did for you in that unfortunate situation."

"George, I'm astonished. You're blackmailing me before I've even finished my croissant and coffee."

"Nonsense. I'm just reflecting on times gone by."

"Why would you want me, anyhow? I've been out of it over two years now."

"It'll give you a fresher viewpoint. And we both know how good you are at this kind of thing. We've got an office for you. An assistant. Vanessa Holden. You'll meet her shortly. A good staff, all with field experience. And you'll have access to the resources of all government agencies and the Metropolitan Police. My brief comes straight from the Oval Office, and the president'll back you anytime you encounter foot-dragging. I'm wearing two hats these days, David. I'm coordinator of security for the National Security Council and I'm in charge of counterespionage Ops Liaison for what you used to know as the Forty Committee, which is where Beowulf was born. So any way you slice it, what's happened has happened in my bailiwick, and I'm not about to go into retirement with a failure of this magnitude as my memorial. I need you, David. It's as simple as that."

The speech was vintage Malkin, as measured in its flourishes as coronation pageantry. A little discreet blackmail, a little muffled patriotism, a little of the old school spirit, and a little tug at the heartstrings to wind it up. And

Belknap knew he was once more being manipulated. That was another thing that hadn't changed.

"And you," he said, "did you have access to Beowulf?"

Again that wonderful boyish smile, innocent as a waiting shark's. "That's the David I remember, too. No, I had no access." His eyes were twinkling. "Still, I'm as much part of your brief as anyone."

"Which end would I be supposed to work? Finding who stole the material, or finding who sent it back?"

"Finding who sent it back is more immediately vital, because we have to know how far down the pipeline it went, the kind of distribution it got, and why it came back. As to finding who stole it, well, now that we know we have a mole, it's simply a matter of proper tatics to find his burrow. We can work together on that."

"When you find this mole, you'll have on your hands a bigger mess than the British did with Philby."

"You only have a mess, David, when you have publicity. We don't expect to call a press conference, thank you, when we find him."

"How would you suggest I begin?"

"I think you begin by assuming someone delivered Beowulf to an agent of a foreign power."

"There're a lot of foreign powers."

"Well, you can eliminate the Israelis."

"Why?"

"It wouldn't be in their interest to compromise Beowulf."

Belknap stood up, uncomfortable from the enveloping plush of a low sofa. He caught a glimpse of his face in the ornate mirror over the fireplace and turned away. He thought about his crooked nose and thinning hair, and then about the Israelis. "If I can eliminate the Israelis, and if a copy of Beowulf went to the Joint Chiefs, Beowulf must mean a military action the Israelis would favor. What is it, a parachute drop into one of the Arab countries? Libya? Eighty-second Airborne secures the oil fields. Marines come in from the coast. What is it, George? I need to know."

Malkin examined the glowing tip of his cigar. "Unfortunately, there's far more to it than that. But you can work with your hypothesis if you like. It gives you an idea."

"It gives me an idea somebody's monkeying with nuclear war." Belknap, lanky and stooped, hands clenched in anger, walked to the windows overlooking the square. He could see the north portico of the White House. The wise men.

Malkin reached toward a cluttered table at the end of his sofa and pressed a buzzer. "Let's have Vanessa come in, shall we?"

She was thirtyish, blonde, and the top of her head came to about his jaw. She had a smile ready by the time they met in the middle of the room, like Stanley and Livingstone in that famous clearing in Africa, and then there was Malkin fussing over them, making introductions and those quaint little jokes nobody except Malkin understood.

"David has a very successful industrial-security business in New York." He beamed at Vanessa. "We worked rather closely in Bonn and London."

"George was my boss."

"I thought of David as a son"

It was one of Malkin's favorite lies, and Belknap winked at Vanessa. "Does he think of you as a daughter?"

Vanessa laughed. "Do you, George?"

"I know what I'd like to think of you as, but I'm too old." He escorted her with extravagant gallantry to an uncomfortable antique chair. "The coffee should still be warm."

She shook her head, then studied Belknap a moment as he studied her. Her hair fell loosely about a full round face, and her eyes, surprisingly, weren't blue. Black, perhaps, or some dark color.

"David'll be using LaRue's old office," Malkin said. "I've sketched the package incident for him. Is there anything new?"

"Sybil says the Secret Service says they'll have a lab prelim around eleven."

"Good. They're doing all the obvious things, David. Dusting the wrapping paper and the briefcase and the seventy or so pages, hoping to raise prints. A little complicated with the pages, because we can't have the technicians, can't have anyone, in fact, reading the material, but the experts finally worked out a system. The wrapping paper itself was Safeway shopping bags. Somebody had scissored them down the sides, then reversed them so the Safeway logo was on the inside. The White House address was block-lettered with a grease pencil. The presumption is, the package had come off a conveyor belt in the Barrow Annex only minutes before it was discovered at one o'clock. Uncanceled stamps on it in the amount of four eighty, small denominations. Probably very few mailboxes in Washington that have pickups in the hours just before and after midnight. Vanessa, have you queried the Postal Service yet?"

"They'll furnish any such locations and the names of drivers making the pickups to the bureau's Washington field office as soon as possible."

"The other presmumption is, the sender of the package walked up to the loading dock and placed the package on the conveyor belt himself . . . it's not a secured area. The trucks go through an alley to the dock, park alongside, unload, and drive off. What else? Oh, yes. Xerox machines, I'm told, have individualized signatures, just like typewriters. So the Secret Service is furnishing sanitized excerpts from the material to experts at the Bureau. One of the assistants you'll have, Tony Armstrong, is arranging to collect Xerox samples from machines anywhere near the various repositories in the Pentagon, Langley, and the EOB."

"You've been busy."

"Well, it keep us out of mischief. The briefcase, incidentally, is garden variety, purchasable almost anywhere, but it does have the remains of a claim on the handle. In it, along with the papers, were a dopp kit containing an electric shaver, toothbrush, toothpaste, and an unlabeled bottle of pills, as well as two white shirts, underwear shorts, a horseshoe—apparently our substantial metal mass—and a model of a sailing ship in a glass bottle."

"Horseshoe? Ship in a bottle?"

Malkin shrugged. "Our psychiatrist is preparing a profile of the person who sent the briefcase. Maybe he can tell us what those items mean. Vanessa'll give you the list of the ten people with access to Beowulf. By noon, summaries of FBI field investigations of each any time he got a clearance should be on your desk."

"What about my own clearance?"

Malkin smiled in paterfamilias fashion. "It's up to date. I always keep all my old boys up to date. You never know . . ."

The bastard, Belknap thought. He did know about the divorce. And never wrote a letter, or even gave him a call.

"So you're the headhunter," Vanessa said as she was leading him to his office at the rear of the townhouse.

"I don't know what I am," he said, thinking about Malkin and deviousness. "Most of us in this business are pawns on a vast chessboard. We don't know the rules and there are no winners. So to coin a phrase, what's a nice girl like you doing in a place like this?"

She laughed easily, he was beginning to notice, and also that she had a gap between her two front teeth. And that she was a little heavy around the waist. "Well . . . Oh, here's your office. Not large, but comfortable."

"Not if it has all that junk Malkin has in the spider's parlor."

She took a key from a pocket of her powdery blue dress. "You don't like Malkin?"

"Are you one of his spies?"

She forgot about the key she was putting in the lock. "I resent that crack, Mr. Belknap."

"I'm sorry," he said, and meant it. "To answer your question, I've a healthy respect for him, and I know he believes in peace, freedom, and rational accommodation among competing great powers, but I wouldn't expect him not to sell me down the river if it suited his convenience—or rather, the convenience of the mysterious powers that be who move the pawns in this murky half-world you and I seem sentenced to live in."

"That's quite a mouthful, Mr. Belknap. I think I'll need time to digest it." She turned the key, and when she opened the door the first thing he observed was the dust. It was on everything.

"How long has LaRue been dead?"

"What makes you think he is?"

"Vanessa, we're going to get along well, but you've got to give me credit for a few things. Such as reading signs—the kind Indian scouts blaze on trees. Was it a peaceful death, or a lonely one in a far place?"

"The second." She put the key away. "He was nice. He was very nice. He didn't want to go."

"Nobody ever does. Except a few fools who think they're Errol Flynn." He catalogued the room with a professional eye. The wall safe was a good one, but he could've expected that. The metal filing cabinets behind the steel desk were obviously fireproof, as they should be. The few padded leather chairs for visitors weren't much, but the chair on his side of the desk was almost new; it swiveled, and it looked comfortable enough to sleep in. The carpet was threadbare, but he didn't have to look at the floor. The walls were nicotine yellow—LaRue must've been a three-pack-a-day man—and there was, thank God, at least one window. It had a view of a cobblestone courtyard, behind which was a nine- or ten-story building with a rust-colored façade.

"Government offices. Our overflow occupies two floors. We've also the townhouse adjoining on our right, not to mention two underground levels, the lower of which was excavated during the restoration." She indicated the instrumentation under the telephone stand. "They'll hook up the special lines this afternoon. You'll have a direct connection to your liaison at Langley, the FBI, and the Metropolitan Police. The scrambler works from those first two switches, the ones with orange coding. Do you know the positions?"

"Well, it's a new breed from the ones we used to have. But planned obsolescence makes the country tick. Who else besides me gets the combination to the safe?"

"Sybil Pruett."

"That'll have to be changed."

"She'd never go into the safe. It's just in case of emergency."

"It'll still have to be changed."

She examined him a long moment, gaze unwavering. "You don't trust anyone, do you?"

"It isn't a question of trust." He was irritated with himself for even feeling the need to explain. "By the way, does Malkin have the combination?"

"I've never thought about it. I suppose he must have access to all the safes."

"Where did LaRue die?" he said suddenly, so suddenly it made her jump.

"Bangkok."

He noticed her wedding ring for the first time. "Was he your husband?"

"No, of course not."

"Boyfriend? Lover?"

"God, you're a rude, insensitive bastard."

"A lot of people have told me that, you'll be pleased to know. What're we going to do about this dust?"

"Fast Eddy'll take care of it."

"Fast Eddy?"

"He's the janitor. Electrician. Plumber. Chauffeur." She hesitated. "Occasional bodyguard."

"A man of parts. Does he crack safes?"

"You could ask him. We've booked a room for you at the Hay-Adams. Perhaps you'd like to shower and unpack. Eddy'll have the office ready by the time you get back."

He looked at the dust and grime. "He must be very fast indeed." He leaned against the edge of the desk, folded his arms. "You were going to tell me how you happened to get into a place like this."

She pushed hair from her eyes. They were brown, he decided. "I came aboard when this department was established. I happened to know George Malkin. To be more exact, my father did."

"Your father? How did he happen to know Malkin?"

"They were both Oh So Secret in World War Two."

Belknap considered it. "And so Malkin kind of said to himself, I wonder what my old OSS buddy's daughter is doing these days. I think I'll give her a call, see if she wants a top-secret job."

"Why do you put it in such a disagreeable way?"

"I didn't realize it was disagreeable. I'm sorry."

"That's the second time you've said 'I'm sorry' in as many minutes. Is it an acquired habit, or a personality defect you were born with?"

Brimstone, he thought. "Maybe we should start over. Look, Vanessa, my stock in trade is asking questions. I—"

"I know. You're an industrial-security expert. Very successful, Malkin says, and Malkin should know." She smiled sweetly. "I have this mental picture of a man with, oh, maybe gold cuff links . . . sending a chauffeured Rolls to meet the client at the airport . . . sending orchids, sending champagne . . ."

He looked self-consciously at his gold cuff links. "I'm not talking about that trade. I've worked in some dark and scary places, but even when I'm in the sunlight, I look behind me and all around me. You're my assistant, and I know your business. But that isn't enough, not for me, and I don't care how many clearances you've had. I want to know who you are and what you are. People don't end up in this place on somebody's whim. I don't know Fast Eddy from Adam, but I'll bet my bottom dollar he's an ex-Marine who's been in the trade the last ten years. About you, I'm not so sure. Is it asking too much to ask you to give me a reading?"

"All right." She sighed and sat in one of the tatty visitor's chairs.

"Don't sit in all that dust. You'll ruin your pretty blue dress."

"To hell with my pretty blue dress." She stared off. "During the interregnum after the war, my father returned to the quiet academic life in Hyde Park, but when Truman appointed Bedell Smith to head the CIA in nineteen-fifty, Smith asked Dulles back, and Dulles asked my father back. I grew up a CIA brat. It's a club, like being an Army brat, and I wouldn't wish it on my worst enemy. In time I got a husband, and he was CIA, naturally. But it was love all the way." She paused. "They've a policy over there, sometimes, of pulling the wife in. We ended up in West Berlin."

"When?"

"Sixty-eight."

"You were there during the Fehler affair?"

She nodded. Her hands wer tightly clasped in her lap. The knuckles were very white. "Gil, my husband, was running an agent, a White Russian supposedly. God knows what he really was. One night, in an argument over a payoff in an alley, the Russian stabbed him. He died. He bled to death like a stuck pig. In a goddamn alley in Germany."

"All right," he said gently. It was a story he knew as well as his own name, and there was nothing you could ever say.

"There's more. They brought me home. I made a career of feeling sorry for myself. I married again, badly this time. Got divorced, went onto the couch. He was a wonderful doctor and put me back together. I began working in advertising, an executive secretary they call it, but I soon realized I was drifting again. No basic goals, except not to get married if I could help it, and no challenges, unless you consider peddling soap and headache remedies one. My father, who was retiring from the CIA about then, thought something in his line would fit both needs—he has a parochial view at times, but he was on the mark in my case. He touched base with a few old friends. George Malkin was one of them."

The story did somehow ring true, but Belknap knew he had to put one more question; the answer would be less important than the reaction. "Your father's retirement . . . was it a real retirement or a—"

"Oh, you mean that old notion of once a spook, always a spook . . . Well, yes, my father occasionally works as a consultant; evidently they still value his advice. But this doesn't have a damn thing to do with us."

"I know, I know," he said placatingly.

She looked up at him expressionlessly. "Sometime you can tell me how *you* got into this business. A nice boy like you."

4

BRDNOWSKI LAY IN BED, one eye shut, the other watching a fly on the ceiling. When he opened two eyes, he saw two flies, though by squinting he could bring them back to one. The signs were bad; it didn't look as if he'd lick the headache by evening. His mouth felt as if it were full of porcupine quills, and he could hear the subway rumble of stale beer shifting in his stomach. Groaning, he lay there thinking about last night.

He had to hand it to Myrt. They'd argued like hell, but if it hadn't been for her, he would have done the dumbo thing straight down the line. First he'd wanted to burn the damn papers that were in the briefcase and throw away the other junk, and she'd talked him out of that. Then he'd wanted to mail everything anonymously to the cops or the FBI, and she'd talked him out of that. And she'd been right. If the papers were as secret as that first page said they were, nobody except the man in the White House ought to see them.

Myrt was the one, too, who'd thought it would be a classy touch to send the president something personal just from them, so she'd included that ship in a glass bottle she'd won on the Boardwalk the weekend they'd done Atlantic City, and for luck had added the rusty old horseshoe he used as a paperweight for his back copies of the *Racing Form*. If it did as much for the president as it'd done for him, the country was in for trouble.

And when they finally had the package wrapped, she was

the one who remembered about fingerprints. So they unwrapped it and she went over the briefcase and its contents with a rag. They hadn't disturbed the papers earlier, they'd been afraid to, so she left them alone. After retying the package, she used the rag on the Safeway wrapping. Then she wrote the address using her left hand instead of her right. Clever old Myrt, and she'd been drunker than he was.

There'd been another argument about mailing it. Brdnowski wanted to wait until morning, but Myrt wanted to unload fast. So they drove to the nearest postal substation to buy stamps, but it had no twenty-four-hour section. Myrt remembered the substation near the Greek's had one, because she'd been there last week to rent a box for the chain letters, so they tooled off again through the sleeping city. They walked into the twenty-four-hour section, weighed the package on the tinny scale chained to the wall, and fed dollar bills into the change machine until they could buy enough postage from the stamp dispenser to get the package through the mails without a side trip to the dead-letter office.

Outside the substation, they'd fought a losing battle with one of the mailboxes. The package fit through the big slot in front, but it was too large to make the final turn and drop into the box. So there it was, half-in, half-out, and they started arguing again. Two noisy drunks, it was a wonder somebody hadn't called the cops. Brdnowski wanted to leave the package hanging there, but Myrt said somebody with no character might steal it.

Then down the street came a mail truck on its way to somewhere. Brdnowski stepped off the curb to flag it down, and when the driver realized it wasn't a holdup, he slowed. Brdnowski gave him the package; everything was taken care of. But what a pistol it'd been!

"Hey, Brdnowski, you still among the living? How you feel?"

He came out of his reverie. Myrt was in the bedroom, dressed for work.

"Lousy," he said bravely. He could've said he was dying. He took a deep breath. "Did you phone the Greek?"

"I ought to have my head examined, but I did. Told him I'd be a couple of hours late."

He relaxed. He'd been afraid she'd back out.

"It's crazy," she said.

"It isn't crazy." She was going to try to back out after all. He talked fast. "We've got to know whether the guy's alive or dead, and the fucking receptionist over there won't tell *me*, but she'll tell you if you do it the way we agreed. If he's alive, I've had it. I've not only stolen a briefcase from a government agent, I've stolen *secret papers* from a government agent. He knows my name, that's the worst part. Read it on my TD permit. Myrt, they give you twenty years for a caper like that. And try to tell them we never read the stuff, there'd be a big ho, ho, ho."

"What you tell them is, you never saw the briefcase. Stick to the story one of your fares must've taken it. Besides, a guy with no I.D. who has secret papers isn't a government agent, he's a spy."

"If he's a spy, it's worse. He knows my name. He'll find me. He'll kill me. I'm a goddamn witness. I mean, spies, they don't mess around."

"Well, you get protection from the FBI."

"Sure. I walk in, tell them about the guy in the hospital who's going to kill me, and they say, oh, no, he's one of our agents. But we're glad to know you're the buster who stole his secret papers, right this way, please, and it's into the tank for Brdnowski." He was having split-vision again; there were two Myrts out there. He tried to bring them into focus. "Our only hope is, the guy's dead. Then, government agent, spy, anything else you want to call him, our troubles are over. That's why you've got to find out. Let's go over it one more time. The receptionist in Emergency's about twenty. Hatchet face. No boobs."

"Trust Brdnowski to catch that."

"That's why I go for you, Myrt." He meant it too, in a way, and he could see her kind of softening up. "Now, she's got this thing about next of kin, so you've got to be next of kin. Only, you couldn't get away with being his wife or sister or daughter." It wasn't a tactful thing to say, but it was true. "What you are, you're his son's wife's cousin, that'll stop Hatchet Face cold, and his son's in Amsterdam, in the diamond business, right?"

"If you say so, Brdnowski."

"Now this receptionist, she's also got a thing about filling out forms. She'll 'form' you to death, and the first thing she'll ask is, what's his right name? What do you tell her?"

"Harry Murphy."

"No, goddamn it, that's my name." Suddenly suspicious, he said, "You're trying to be funny at a time like this? His name's Joseph Smith. There's only about three million of them, she won't be able to check it out. Anyhow, all you do is learn whether he's alive or dead, then split."

"Okay, I'm off." She bent to give him a smoocher. "If you don't hear from me by one o'clock, phone Perry Mason."

Brdnowski slept awhile. At least he thought he slept. His mind was playing tricks on him again; he was reliving last night, reliving ancient adventures on the sandlots of Hoboken, and throughout he couldn't be sure whether he was dreaming or simply seeing the crazy pictures he saw when the headache was bad.

But the knocking on the apartment door was real, he was fairly sure of that. He slid out of bed and pulled on yesterday's chinos. Bare-chested, groggy, he made his way to the door.

Two men were standing in the outside hall. They said in unison, "Mr. Brdnowski?"

Brdnowski squinted, discovered there was only one man.

Early thirties, balding. He was short, heavy, and breathing hard after climbing four flights. His complexion was pasty, and he was about two sizes larger than his jacket and trousers.

"Mr. Brdnowski?" he said again.

"Right."

The man produced a wallet, then flashed it open and shut in the fast, tricky way a magician shows a card from the deck. "Detective Rosenbaum, Metropolitan Police. Can I come in?"

Brdnowski was embarrased. The living room looked like hell. Still, you have to get along with the Law. "Why not?"

Rosenbaum came into the living room like a landlord taking inventory. "That TV set hot?"

Brdnowski was pretty sure it wasn't, because Myrt'd been gone a long time. But he walked over to the set and held his hand over the vents at the rear. "No, it's not hot."

"I mean, stolen." Rosenbaum seemed a little nonplussed. "Is it stolen? That's all I'm asking."

"I got it at Ward's," Brdnowski said. "I think I did. No, I'm sure."

"Mr. Brdnowski," Rosenbaum said, and Brdnowski could tell he was unhappy, "I work Crimes Against Property. Burglary, theft, arson, all the rest of it."

"Right," Brdnowski said, puzzled.

"You still want to tell me the TV isn't hot?"

"Stolen, you mean?"

"Yes," Rosenbaum said resignedly, "stolen."

"No, it isn't stolen. I can set your mind at rest there."

"Does the name Finemann mean anything to you?"

"Finemann?" Brdnowski felt the name was familiar, but he couldn't place it. "No, I don't know any Finemann."

"How about the name Harry Murphy? Mean anything?"

Suddenly it all came back. Finemann was the locksmith, and Brdnowski was the asshole who'd given his name to Finemann as Murphy.

"Draws a blank," he managed to say.

Rosenbaum scratched his crotch. "Let's take it a step at a time. I level with you, you level with me, and you still come out of this in one piece. I'll give you the bottom line. I'm married to a very wonderful girl."

"I know what you mean." Brdnowski wondered if Rosenbaum could see his legs trembling.

"I got only one complaint. I'm married to a very wonderful girl whose grandfather is a fruitcake. Like, he thinks he's God's gift to law and order." Rosenbaum took out a package of gum. "His name's Herbie Finemann."

Brdnowski wondered if the building would collapse. But he knew he wouldn't be that lucky.

"Herbie phoned me at home last night. Smack in the middle of the game. Fifth inning, bases loaded." Rosenbaum sounded bitter. "I'll give you his exact words. 'Another dude just came in, Joey, smelling like a brewery and offering me time and a half to unlock a hot briefcase, and a song and dance about being Harry Murphy from IBM. He got so rattled when I started to open it, I figured the goods inside were hot too.'" Rosenbaum chewed his gum with a faraway look. "I was noticing you've a slight limp."

"An old auto accident. Doesn't' bother me much."

Rosenbaum nodded. "Herbie said the dude had a limp, too. Herbie also got a make on the license plate. I promised I'd run it through DMV in the morning. It didn't cash out Harry Murphy."

"Things are beginning to come back to me."

"I'm delighted to hear that. Where would you like to begin?"

"Can I put on my shirt first?" Brdnowski asked, needing time to organize a halfway believable explanation.

"Not unless you want me to march you right down to the station. Which reminds me, are you a fence, or just retired on stocks and bonds? I mean, here it is the middle of the day and you aren't even dressed, for God's sake."

"I'm sick. I get these headaches . . ."

"And you sure as hell don't work for IBM. What do you do?"

"I drive a cab."

"So why'd you tell Herbie you were Murphy from IBM?"

"I guess because I'd had too many beers, and I'm kind of a practical joker anyhow. You can ask my dispatcher. I call in, tell him I'm Double-O-Seven. Drives him nuts. Only with that locksmith, I said I was Murphy. But I didn't even remember that much until a moment ago. It's happened before when I get these headaches . . ."

"Sure, I understand. Memory loss. I run into it all the time." Rosenbaum smiled bleakly. "Let's get to why you offered Herbie time and a half, and why you didn't want him to see what was in the briefcase."

"I was too embarrassed. I'm even too embarrassed to tell you."

"Don't be. I'm very understanding."

Brdnowski hung his head. "There were dirty pictures. Awfully dirty pictures."

Rosenbaum produced a sigh that could have blown out a candle at ten paces. "Well, that certainly clears everything up, and I was stupid not to figure it out myself. You got some dirty pictures locked in the case, so you do what anybody'd do in that situation. Most natural thing in the world. Pay a locksmith time and a half to open it."

"It wasn't the pictures I was really after."

Rosenbaum closed his eyes. "I can hardly wait."

"It was my handicapping books I was after. I wanted to get some bets down today."

"Okay, one step at a time. Forget the handicapping books. Where are the pictures now?"

"I threw them in a trash can. My girlfriend made me."

"All right, I'm a glutton for punishment. Where are the handicapping books? Let me guess. In the Potomac?"

"No, they're right over there." Brdnowski walked to the table by the window where he stacked his back copies of the

Racing Form, no longer kept in some degree of parade-ground order by the horseshoe given to the president last night, no return favors asked. He picked up the three books beside them and took them to Rosenbaum for inspection. "The one on top's best."

"And these came from the briefcase?" Rosenbaum asked wearily.

"Right."

"So where's the briefcase?"

"Some guy made off with it while my girlfriend and I were arguing in a bar."

"A story impossible not to believe." Rosenbaum scratched his crotch again. Brdnowski wondered what he had wrong down there. "But impossible as it is not to believe, you don't mind if I have a look around? Not that you have to consent. You can stand on your rights, I want you to know that, and then we can just run you down to the station and come back with a search warrant and tear the place apart, plank by plank, brick by brick."

"You have my consent," Brdnowski said graciously.

Myrt tried to understand why she was doing it. It must be because she loved the clod, she thought. Or else didn't want him to get away. Because she'd a funny feeling that at the far end of this crazy adventure there'd be wedding bells.

She sailed through the entrance to St. Albans Emergency in a swirl of girlish fantasies. Brdnowski walking down the aisle of an old country church in a tony set of rented tails. Hired limousine waiting outside. Honeymoon in Paris on a stolen credit card. Togetherness trips to jewelry stores and lingerie boutiques. In time, a first child, a girl, gurgling in her bassinet. On a certain day the gurgling would stop and the baby's first words on the planet would be, "Brdnowski, it's you!"

Myrt laughed to herself as she plowed like an icebreaker toward the reception cubicle. And when she faced the receptionist, she had to admit Brdnowski was right about the boobs. Count on Brdnowski, rain or shine, when it came to basics.

"Yes?" the receptionist said.

Myrt took a breath. "I got a funny situation here. I put my cousin's husband's father into a cab yesterday morning. In front of the Library of Congress. He was flying to Amsterdam to meet his son, who's in the diamond business. Last night I got a call from my cousin—that's the son's wife—who said he hadn't arrived, and naturally we began to get worried."

The receptionist already had a glazed look, and Myrt hit her stride. In a nonstop singsong she reeled off the facts. She'd checked with the cab company and they checked their records and gave her names of drivers who might have been near the Library of Congress about that time yesterday. Finally she found a driver named Murphy, and he said he'd brought a passenger to St. Albans Emergency. So she thought she ought to look into it, and here she was.

The receptionist was excited. "I know exactly the passenger you mean!"

"Oh, thank God," Myrt said. "Is he . . . alive?"

"He was yesterday. When he left."

"Left!" Myrt felt a stab of panic.

"They took him into the main hospital. He was still unconscious."

Myrt was able to breathe again. "Is it . . . very bad?"

"I really don't know. You'd have to go to admissions and get his room number. Then you could go to the nursing station for that room." She took a form from her desk. "Now that you're here, we can straighten out our records. We've got him as a John Doe. What's his correct name?"

Myrt knew then she was home free. If they still didn't know his name, anything would fly. "Joseph Smith."

"Does he have Blue Cross?"

"I think so, but it'd be in Idaho."

"And his address in Idaho?"

."Pocatello. General Delivery." It had been Brdnowski's idea and not a bad one. "Lives on a farm. Comes in twice a week for mail."

"Phone number in Idaho?"

"Crazy guy doesn't even have electricity."

At Admissions they told her the room was 510, and on the fifth floor she talked to the head nurse. The patient was in a coma, but its cause was still undetermined. No visitors were allowed. Myrt asked if he'd live.

"Would you like to talk to Dr. Matthews?" the head nurse replied. "He's in the hospital somewhere."

Myrt said she'd phone later and took the elevator to the lobby. She walked briskly, heels clicking smartly in the long corridor leading to Emergency. As she stepped into the sunlight, a police cruiser, siren wailing, came roaring down the ramp and skidded to a stop behind Brdnowski's old Chevy.

Myrt's first impulse was to run, but the two officers had already seen and could easily catch her. She stood there helplessly, wondering where she'd made her mistake.

The officer on the passenger side of the cruiser hit the pavement on the double and disappeared into the hospital. He came out in moments with a stretcher. The other officer opened the rear door, and the two of them lifted a sobbing young black onto the stretcher. He was handcuffed, and his bright blue shirt was soaked with blood. One ear was a mangled pulp.

Myrt, feeling nauseated, stumbled to the Chevy and leaned over the hood. Finally the nausea passed, and she got in the car. Then she discovered she was boxed in, the cruiser behind her, a Volkswagen ahead. She fished in her purse for cigarettes, turned on the radio, and waited, foot tapping nervously to the music, for the officers to return.

When the cigarette was half-smoked, she stubbed it out impatiently, took her purse, and went into Emergency. One officer was talking to the receptionist. The other was staring dazedly at nothing. When Myrt tapped him on the shoulder, he spun around as if she'd given him an electric shock. Her purse went flying, and her compact, lipstick, wallet, keys, cigarettes, lighter, and comb spilled in all directions.

"Golly," the officer said, "I'm sorry." He was very young and very pale, and he reminded her of her poor kid brother. He bent over and began collecting the scattered articles.

As she bent to retrieve her purse, she said, "I was just going to ask if you could move your car. I can't get out."

"Sure." He smiled awkwardly. "You startled me. Here's your wallet and things."

"Thanks." They went outside together. "What happened to that man you took in?"

"Liquor-store holdup." He escorted her to the Chevy and opened the door. He looked at her uncertainly. "I shot him."

She suddenly realized his hand, resting on the window frame, was trembling. Intuitively, she said, "First time?"

He nodded, eyes far away "I'll move the cruiser for you now."

5

THE MAN WHO ENTERED Central Park at 72nd and Fifth carried a small bag of bread crumbs he occasionally tossed to the squirrels. At the Conservatory Pond he watched the children sailing model boats and then walked south to the Children's Zoo, adjusting his pace so as to arrive at two minutes past one.

He sat at the north end of a slatted wooden bench and placed the hand carrying the bag in his lap. The other hand rested on the end of the fourth slat, not far from his buttocks. His fingers, concealed by his body and a nearby tree, felt beneath the slat for the key to an East Side Airlines Terminal locker that should have been attached there with a thumbtack within the last ten minutes by someone he hoped never to meet. Finding no key, he resumed his stroll, feeding the squirrels as he went. At two minutes after two, he was back at the bench, and once more searched for the key.

Forced to concede it wasn't there, nor going to be there, he walked to Fifth Avenue, caught a downtown bus, and got off at 42nd Street.

The failure to find the key at the post office in Central Park was the third failure since yesterday, and though he didn't know the person who should have delivered it, his capabilities or weaknesses, he did know the seriousness of three such failures. There was considerable likelihood the key wasn't there because his unknown colleague had been arrested. It was time to use emergency procedures.

He entered a phone booth and placed a call to the Soviet United Nations Mission on 67th Street. He asked the switchboard operator in English if he could speak to Mr. Kirill Yasakov. The operator said there was no Mr. Yasakov attached to the mission. He apologized and hung up.

The young switchboard operator, in accordance with standing instructions for the handling of inquiries about nonexistent mission employees, asked her supervisor if she could be excused to deliver a message to Counselor Glukhov. The supervisor, even better versed in the minor stratagems used to frustrate FBI wiretappers rumored by wits in the mission to be headquarterd in the synagogue across the street, granted permission, and the operator went to Ivan Glukhov's third-floor office and told him a man had phoned asking for Kirill Yasakov.

"Did he speak Russian or English?" Glukhov inquired.

"English."

It seemed to her that her reply troubled Glukhov. It was the first time she'd been in his office, and she thought him quite attractive. Rumpled black hair, sensitive eyes and mouth, jutting chin . . . and now a hint of melancholy because of what she'd told him. "Accented English, however," she added, hoping this might reassure him. "But better than mine."

"That I doubt, Irina," Glukhov said gallantly. It both pleased and surprised her he knew her name.

"Are you enjoying New York, Irina?"

"Oh, yes." She regarded him innocently. "But it's often lonely at night."

Glukhov nodded, but his melancholy gaze was far away. It was obvious his mind was unfortunately on the first message she'd given him, not the second.

Glukhov wrestled the problem almost thirty minutes, but in the end he knew he'd have to alert the Center. He rode the elevator to the offices of the Referentura on the top floor.

At the outside door he pressed the buzzer, waited for the click, and stepped into a small room where a guard ritually inspected his identification and had him sign the log. A second guard, watching through a peephole in the steel door on the far side of the room, admitted him to the Referentura proper.

Glukhov entered the Referentura's library, sat at the conference table, and drafted his cataclysmic message:

JUST INFORMED EDGAR FAILED TO MAKE THREE DIFFER-
ENT RENDEZVOUS SINCE TUESDAY. TO DATE, NO STORIES
IN PRESS OF AN ARREST. ADVISE. GLUKHOV.

The draft completed, he enciphered it and walked down the musty corridor to the code clerk's cubicle. Because all windows in the Referentura had long ago been sealed with special materials to frustrate electronic eavesdropping, no East River breezes ever circulated, and Moscow Center, for either security or budgetary reasons, had refused to authorize air-conditioning. Worse, some anonymous bureaucrat had issued an edict prohibiting smoking within the sacred confines. So in the Referentura, at least in June, you worked, perspired, and dreamed of cigarettes and a change of underwear.

Glukhov, bemusedly wondering whether Irina, with her saucy figure and knowing eyes, had been extending her unsubtle invitation as Irina the switchboard girl on the make or Irina the KGB girl on the make, handed his message to the code clerk. The clerk, a colorless timeserver with relatives in the right places and sweat stains in the wrong places, nodded judiciously, rather as if he were an intermediary between gods above and man below. Which, Glukhov reflected dourly, he in a sense was.

Glukhov watched as the clerk activated the elaborate encoding console that would transcribe the message to tape in a series of random numbers the radio room would eventually send into the ether in a scrambled "squeal" lasting less than half a second. If the ubiquitous NSA fishermen seined it from the atmospheric seas, they could play it forward, backward, and sideways on any instrument in their orchestra until Labrador went Communist and still not produce the sweet music they wanted to hear. At least, that was what the experts in the 13th Department of the First Chief Directorate modestly claimed, and even experts in the 13th Department were sometimes right.

Cryptography was a fascinating business, and Glukhov was happy he knew almost nothing about it. The care and feeding of agents was another fascinating business; about this Glukhov unhappily knew more.

Upon graduating in 1963 from the Institute of International Relations after five years of U.S. and German area studies, he'd planned to apply for the diplomatic service, but a classmate whose uncle, Vladimir Semichastny, had been appointed by Khrushchev to head the worldwide KGB apparatus at the astonishing age of thirty-seven—more astonishing in retrospect because it was an age one year younger than Glukhov's own age now—recommended him for recruitment. Glukhov, cursed or gifted, he wasn't sure which, with instinctive skepticism even a professional devil's advocate might have found disabling, couldn't help wondering whether the classmate's recommendations was a gesture of friendship or, more poetically, a Byzantine act of revenge by the loser in their recent ridiculous scuffle over the favors of a compliant Intourist guide named Lydia.

Nevertheless, Glukhov the pragmatist listened respectfully to the proposals made by the recruiter from Dzerzhinsky Square as they dined at one of Moscow's better restaurants, the Praga. Glukhov wasn't familiar with better restaurants, but he knew you didn't walk in and order Dover sole and French wine unless you'd made special arrangements. The Dover sole and wine, in fact, had been delivered that morning from the KGB Club. Expansively waving a magnificently aromatic Cuban cigar, the recruiter enumerated other perquisites of employment by the Committee of State Security of the Council of Ministers.

Glukhov faced a dilemma. The KGB looked with suspicion on the citizen who stepped forward seeking to become one of its officers, but it looked with even more suspicion on the citizen who, offered that honor, declined. Glukhov was sure that no matter how gracefully he made his excuses, no matter how many names he supplied of splendid classmates gifted in languages, karate, and sexual acrobatics, all of them longing to dine on Dover sole and join the *Komitet Gosudarstvennoy Bezopasnosti*, rejection of the offer would, at the very least, forever bar him from the diplomatic service and any kind of travel abroad.

Ivan Glukhov the pragmatist agreed to become an officer candidate. The recruiter rewarded him with a photograph of Chairman Khrushchev. Glukhov, like an idiot, had expected a box of magnificently aromatic Cuban cigars.

The training lasted two years; near the end there were remarkable seminars at which Rudolf Abel and Gordo Lonsdale spoke with touching candor of the psychological problems the illegal faces in the United States and England. Glukhov, who had enough psychological problems just being Glukhov, was very glad then he wasn't in one of those scattered Moscow apartments where the Center individually trained future illegals.

In 1966 Glukhov was posted to England as an exchange student at the London School of Economics. The Center, always patient, kept him dormant his first six months; he wasn't even required to clip interesting doomsday items from *The Economist*. Somebody at the embassy probably subscribed anyhow.

Finally he was given a few textbook exercises. He retrieved plastic bags from lavatory cisterns in Waterloo Station, cased Hyde Park for new dead-letter boxes for Center postmen, and at the docks one foggy night stuffed five-pound notes wrapped in a wool sock into a crack in a warehouse wall. He was informed he was a support officer for an illegal code-named Falcon, but instinct told him it was all a dry run concocted by his instructors, and training told him he was followed by no one from M15. The only person who ever tried to follow him was so obviously Russian, Glukhov was sorely tempted to lose him, but this would have been not only embarrassing to the tail but also dangerous to himself; he didn't want to establish an overnight reputation as a good man to send into bad places.

When he returned to Moscow at the beginning of 1967, he was surprised to learn he'd played a peripheral role in the escape of the celebrated Russian spy George Blake from an English prison. He wondered which of the fool's errands on which he'd been sent meshed with the master plan. But his superiors, evidently pleased with his performance abroad, confided that he'd soon be given special training. In the meantime work would be found in Moscow, work he'd probably find not too interesting, but everything would change for the better as soon as the next special class began. Until then, he was asked to be patient.

Patience was what he needed. He was assigned to translate and analyze syndicated political columns in various U.S. newspapers, because the writers of these columns, a superior informed him, reflected the views, though sometimes deviously camouflaged, of the political leadership. It was merely a matter of separating what a particular columnist wrote from what the particular politician who'd been his source had had in mind. Like peeling an onion, Glukhov suggested brightly.

Actually, it was more like cleaning a window with a mudball. Most of the columns, he discovered, were obsessively concerned with casting the 1968 presidential election, and though each columnist was a god unto himself, they all seemed to patronize the same astrologer. It astounded Glukhov men could make a living writing such drivel. Either Nixon or Romney was going to get the Republican nomination, unless Rockefeller decided to run, in which case New Hampshire would tell the story.

President Johnson would get the Democratic nomination, unless Senator Robert Kennedy decied to run, in which case Governor George Wallace's decision to bolt or not to bolt the Democratic Party would tell the story. Glukhov dutifully churned out critiques of all this weighty nonsense, vaguely hoping that through some monumental clerical error one of his better efforts might be read as a state paper before the Presidium. But he'd never been as bored.

Feeling he'd been forgotten by his superiors, he began to drink too much. At one drunken party, a reunion with classmates from the Institute of International Relations, he engaged in a black-market transaction involving certificate rubles. It was foolish and dangerous, getting involved with the *farshirovshchiki*, and Glukhov knew it. He decided to reform.

One month of almost pure living later, he learned that the special training was about to begin. First, however, the KGB major who gave him the news wanted him to handle a minor courier exercise in Paris. Glukhov was delighted to be back in the swim. On departure night at Sheremetyevo International, the major, a little tipsy, took him aside and produced a surprising amount of French francs. He wanted Glukhov to bring back perfume and ladies' wristwatches.

On his return Glukhov delivered the smuggled perfume and wristwatches. The major treated him as a Hero of the Soviet Union. Vodka was opened. The major apologized for not having a dacha he could invite Glukhov to visit on his first free weekend.

And the special training began. Glukhov felt he'd been over the terrain before, but wise in the ways of bureaucracies, he recognized that mere completion of the course, shown on his record, would be a passport to greater responsibilities.

After graduation in early 1968 he spent his leave on the Black Sea with a girl to whom, in Sochi's bracing sea breezes, he almost proposed. She was studying to be a biochemist at the Academy of Life Sciences and their future could have been idyllic, except she detested oral sex. When he returned to Moscow, he was asked by another major to deliver priority documents to Stockholm. The major gave him kronor and asked him to bring back, *na levo*, nightgowns, size 36, and a Hasselblad with telescopic lenses. Word was getting around, Glukhov thought, or else this kind of illegal activity among the *vlasti* had been going on forever and he'd been too naïve to recognize it.

He came back from Stockholm with the major's shopping list fulfilled, and one of his own besides. Plus a yearning to own a Volvo. The following morning he was told to report to the North American Department of the KGB's First Chief Directorate. Glukhov was simultaneously alarmed and excited. He was entering the main arena. They had observed and tested him over a period of years, and now he knew he'd not been found wanting.

He was correct. A major he'd never met congratulated him on his achievements in training and in the field. He was the exemplary Soviet Man. Glukhov had the decency to blush. Because of his record, the major continued, he was about to be entrusted with a matter so important his instructions would come, could only come, from the deputy director.

"Ivan Glukhov! *Tovarishch*, are you ill that you cannot hear me?"

Glukhov came out of his reverie.

"I must take your message to the radio room. It is not permitted that you remain in this office when I am not present."

Glukhov bowed slightly to the Referentura's agitated code clerk. "Comrade, you remind me of a hero in this country named Paul Revere, who many years ago had a mission not unlike yours today as you make the perilous journey down the hallway to the radio room."

"Ivan Glukhov, you are as crazy as I always thought."

"Perhaps even crazier. Godspeed!"

6

"THIS IS HATHAWAY," the voice at the other end of the line said. "Can you go on the scrambler?"

"One moment." Belknap covered the phone and said to Vanessa Holden, sitting to the side of his desk with a note pad on her lap, "Can you get this damn device activated?" To the two men sitting across from him, he said, "It's our FBI liaison. Hathaway."

"He's an A.D. over there," the one named Armstrong said. "Be very nice. They don't like people poaching in their preserves, and poaching's what we're surely doing."

"Yes, Mr. Hathaway," Belknap said. "I'm ready."

"We've found the mail-truck driver who got your package. A man hailed him about twelve-thirty as he was driving past the Ellis substation and gave him a package matching the description. The driver was on a run to the Barrow Annex."

"What'd the man look like?"

"Street lighting was poor. The driver knows he had a beard and thinks he had a limp, but can't be sure, because the man seemed drunk and might've been staggering. In his thirties, the driver thinks. Big."

"You'll give the driver an artist and an Identikit?"

"We'll try. I don't expect much. One other thing. He thinks somebody was with him. On the sidewalk, in shadow. Thinks it was a woman."

* * *

"Something must've gone wrong," Belknap said, taking a first bite from the sandwich Vanessa had placed on his desk thirty minutes ago. "The man was in a state of panic. Otherwise he wouldn't have been on the street at midnight with his package, and he wouldn't have flagged down a mail truck, either."

"Hmm," Armstrong said. The other one, Tiffany, puffed on his pipe and looked wise.

Belknap was trying to size up the two men. Armstrong must be forty-five, and his crew-cut hair was graying, but he had the scrubbed good looks of a newly commissioned ensign. Tiffany was his opposite, rumpled and professional, with a nice thatch of prematurely white hair. You could parachute him into almost any small college, along with his calabash pipe and pouch of Balkan Sobranie, and they'd make him chairman of the English Department on the spot.

Belknap turned to Armstrong. "The shirts and underwear shorts and contents of the dopp kit bother me. Panic or not, why didn't he take those personal items out of the briefcase before wrapping it?"

Armstrong shrugged. "Misdirection perhaps. The shirts, the underwear, the electric shaver, the toothbrush, the unlabeled bottle of pills. Midnight hailing of a mail truck by a supposedly panicked man. With a package conveniently containing enough tantalizing little clues to send us barking up all the wrong trees in Christendom."

"You could be right, Tony, but at this stage we've got to run with what we've got. You said you had a preliminary report from our housebroken psychiatrist?"

"A joint one from the medical team. The man who mailed the package has a thirty-eight-inch waist, sixteen-inch neck, thirty-four-inch sleeve." Armstrong looked up from his notes. "I could've told you that by measuring the waist of the shorts and the neck and arms of the shirt, only I wouldn't be able to charge as much. A microscopic examination of the toothbrush shows remnants of dried blood. Conclusion: the man has bad gums."

"Certainly narrows the area of search. What about the pills?"

"Not analyzed yet. A microscopic analysis of the whisker particles in the shaver shows some are brown, others gray. Conclusion: the man's middle-aged and has graying brown hair, unless he's bald. The absence of a brush and comb in the dopp kit suggests he's bald."

"The mail-truck driver says he's in his thirties."

"I guess it comes down to a question of which med school the driver graduated from. Then we decide which opinion we go with. Now the psychiatrist. He says the sailing ship in the glass bottle is intended as a threat."

"Why's that?"

"The ship, in the sender's disturbed thinking, is a symbol for the ship of state. Since it carries a miniature U.S. flag, it represents the U.S. government. Since it's enclosed in a glass bottle, it represents the fragility of the ship of state, or by analogy, U.S. leadership. A mere blow with a hammer would destroy it. I'm not making this up. It's all in the report. Want to hear about the horseshoe?"

"Why not?"

"We shouldn't be misled by the fact a horseshoe in our culture is considered a symbol of good luck. Instead, we should consult a cultural anthropologist to find what societies, what countries, consider a horseshoe to be a symbol of bad luck. The chances are good the sender of the package is a national of one of those countries."

Belknap swiveled in his chair. "We're on the wrong track."

"How so?" Armstrong asked with polite disinterest.

"We've been assuming, because of the shirts and underwear and toilet articles, the man who mailed the package was an overnight visitor to Washington or else a Washington resident on his way to some other place, at least for overnight. But if either assumption's correct, the man would need those items. Ergo, he wouldn't have included them in the package. Throw in the fact some whisker particles in the shaver were gray, while the man who mailed the package is supposed to be in his thirties, and there's a case for arguing he's someone other than the person who owned the personal stuff. We're dealing with two men, not one."

"Don't forget the woman, old boy," Tiffany said, brandishing his pipe.

"All right, and perhaps a woman." Belknap turned to Armstrong. "What about the Xerox samples your people were to pick up at Langley, Joint Chiefs, and NSC?"

Armstrong shook his head. "None of the samples match the copy that came in the mail. It had to have been made on an outside machine. Or on a portable hand-carried to one of the three Beowulf repositories."

"Not three," Tiffany said and, inclining his head toward Belknap as though bestowing absolution, added, "I know you haven't had a chance to plow through all that mishmash on your desk, but there's a late item there from the miracle workers in the lab. It seems the copy of Beowulf that came in the mail was reproduced from a carbon." He puffed earnestly on the calabash. "Now, the final Beowulf draft consisted of an original and carbon. The original went to Langley, a Xerox of it went to Joint Chiefs, and the carbon went to NSC. So whoever waltzed off with the crown jewels didn't do it at Langley or Joint Chiefs."

That helped, Belknap thought. One repository to worry about was better than three. "All right, our target's the NSC reading room. Since the package got into the postal system about one this morning, let's assume Beowulf was stolen no earlier than last Friday . . . whoever stole it would surely want to unload quickly. We need to check the NSC reading-room log, by date and time, for persons who might have claimed Beowulf access from Friday through Tuesday."

"I'll put somebody on it," Tiffany said. "We'll get names and duty shifts of the vault guards while we're at it."

"Pull their security-clearance files, too." Belknap tapped the stack of FBI summaries on his desk. "And I'll go through these to get a feel for the ten men who had Beowulf access."

"Are you going to drink that milk?" Vanessa said. "It's only been sitting there two days."

"Delicious," Belknap said, dutifully taking a sip.

There was a rap-rap on the door, and Mrs. Pruett blew in like a south wind. "Beware of Greeks bearing gifts!" She placed a sealed envelope on Belknap's cluttered desk. "It just came. By courier. One of those charming boys who wears an attaché case chained to his wrist."

Belknap tore the envelope open and scanned the twenty or so lines. "They use a courier for this! It could've been done by telephone in half a minute."

"It wasn't for this they used the courier, David, dear. The courier had just taken Beowulf home again. The lab's through with him; now he's tucked away with his half-brother in a nice little NSC vault."

"It's a summary of the fingerprint work," he told the others. "Each sheet of the Xeroxed material was negative. Same with the Safeway wrapping paper. But they got a partial print from the briefcase. They're going to use computer enhancement to do a simulation study. What the hell does that mean?"

"Ah," Tiffany said. "A very fascinating, very mysterious business, old boy. All kinds of esoteric permutations and combinations and fancy mathematical footwork. When they have a partial print, they use a computer to develop mathematical models for all the possible configurations of the genuine article. The bloody computer even produces a visual display of the missing whorls, swirls, and curls. Then the boffins patch into the computerized FBI fingerprint file, the two companies chat each other up, and lo! out pop the weasels."

Armstrong was all right, but Tiffany and his shopworn Briticisms were beginning to get to Belknap like a hairshirt.

"He also brought this," Sybil Pruett said, depositing a

briefcase on the desk. "Yes, David, dear, the very one that came through the mails."

It was rectangular, shaped from good leather, and fairly new. Part of a green claim check was taped to the handle. Malkin had said the briefcase was garden variety, but garden-variety products were sometimes coded to indicate the factory run, and from the factory run a manufacturer with good records could sometimes determine the city, even the store, to which they'd been shipped.

"That claim check ought to be easy to trace," Armstrong said. "There're only a few printers in the area who handle that type of work. We locate the printer, we can get the name of the customer who placed the order."

"Okay, if the FBI isn't already working that street, have them see what they can dig up. As well as from the manufacturer of the briefcase."

Vanessa got out of her chair to examine the claim check. "Announcement," she said, directing a slight taunting smile at Belknap. "This comes from the Library of Congress. It's what's used if you walk in with a package or anything similar. You check what you're carrying, and on your way out you reclaim it with your stub."

Belknap deflected the smile with a look of meek admiration, because suddenly things were falling into place. A textbook exchange. Two men enter the Library of Congress, minutes apart. Each checks an identical briefcase and receives a claim stub. Separately they go to a lavatory and occupy adjoining stalls. Neither ever sees the other, but a password establishes bona fides. Claim stubs are switched by sliding them along the floor beneath the partition, and a different man reclaims the briefcase containing Beowulf. Or maybe there was only one briefcase, the one belonging to the man who owned the shirts and underwear and dopp kit, and it was the Xeroxed stolen material itself, not a claim stub, that had been passed beneath the partition.

"Tony, have somebody interview the checkroom employees over there. It's going to be hard to jog their memories, probably too many people every day with briefcases, but—"

"We're doing a lot of poaching in FBI preserves," Armstrong said happily.

"Yes," Belknap said, "I feel badly about it too."

He was starting his second hour on the FBI summaries when Vanessa came in with a large street map of Washington. They worked together to mount it on the nicotine-stained wall behind his desk. He used a red marking pencil to print the initials MWP at the address of the Ellis post office. With a green marking pencil, he plotted four small circles in a scatter pattern around the MWP.

"What are you doing, David?"

"The circles represent the four branch post offices with stamp dispensers open round the clock and nearest the Ellis branch office and Man With Package. There were almost five dollars in stamps on the package—far more than most people keep on hand. I'm assuming he went to Ellis to get stamps, and chose it because it was the branch office nearest his home. If we split the distance between Ellis and each of the other four branches, we can draw a lopsided closed figure with Ellis as its center and speculate he lives within the area bounded by it."

"Intriguing."

He glanced at her quickly, suspecting mockery, then marked in black the lines that completed the closed figure.

"Do you like it?" she said.

"Like what?"

"This line of work. A nice boy like you."

"Not when I think about it. But I try not to think. Listen, why don't we declare a small truce? I apologize for this morning."

The phone rang, tinny and insistent. Vanessa took it. "Your fingerprint report." She moved a switch on the scrambler and pointed to the computer terminal on his desk.

"You punch in the numbers he'll give you, which'll tie you into the closed-circuit TV. That way he can put any visual material he has on the screen of your terminal."

He shook his head. "Can this gadget also cook and do the shopping?"

"Give them a few more years. But in the present state of the art . . ."

It turned out they'd developed two configurations from the partial print on the briefcase. "Both individuals have rap sheets," the voice on the phone said. "The first's coming on your screen now."

Belknap watched, mentally capsulizing the highlights: *Emil Karl Hustvar, born in Budapest, 1935, fled during '56 uprising, admitted to U.S. as refugee in '57; private, U.S. Army, Psychological Warfare Detachment, Fort Bragg, '59–'61, naturalized, '62.*

Then the rap-sheet highlights: *Robbery, Los Angeles, 1967, charges dropped; hijacking of refrigerated meat truck, Pasadena, 1969, three years' probation; probation revoked, 1971, for assaulting probation officer, sentenced to two years in Folsom, paroled after twelve months; arrested on suspicion of receiving, 1973, charges dropped. Weight, 190, height 6', hair, brown. Identifying features: appendicitis scar, lame left leg. Occupations: bartender, patio salesman, bill collector. Last known residence, San Diego. Aliases, none.*

"There's nothing in FBI Counterintelligence files or Defense Intelligence Agency files that adds significantly to what I've fed you."

"What would a twenty-four-year-old Hungarian refugee be doing in a Psych War outfit at Fort Bragg?"

"Listening to the Hungarian radio. Place was a melting pot for half of Europe's displaced persons. Linguists were a dime a dozen."

"Any mug shots?"

"You could get one quickest from Folsom. They could put it on the wire. Okay, the next one's a woman."

Her name was Myrtle Dora Bessmeyer, born in Gary, Indiana, daughter of a steelworker, and she was thirty. Her rap sheet was the diary of another born-again loser: *Arrested 1966, New York City, for shoplifting in Macy's. Nightgown, three girdles, and bottle of perfume in her booster bloomers. Charges dropped. Arrested 1968, Des Moines, for using stolen credit card to buy TV set. Credit-card owner, her former common-law husband, refused to sign complaint and paid for TV set. Arrested 1969, New York City, for shoplifting in Bloomingdale's. Skirt, girdle, nightgown, brassiere, and can of precooked ham. Probation for one year. Arrested 1972, Chicago, for embezzling $72 from her employer, restaurant owner. Eleven months in Cook County jail. Weight, 145, height, 5'6", hair, black. Identifying feature: mole on right cheek. Occupations: go-go girl, nightclub photographer, waitress. Last known residence, Cleveland. Aliases: Myrt Ballinger, Alice Jones, Dora Dollson, Dolly Farmer, Dolly Madison.*

"Get it all down?" Belknap asked Vanessa.

The voice on the phone said, "FBI Counterintelligence and DIA show zilch on Bessmeyer."

"Mug shots?"

"Try Cook County Sheriff's office. They'd be most recent."

Belknap put in a call to Hathaway at the FBI.

"And so this Hustvar has a limp?" Hathaway said skeptically.

"I know what you're thinking. But never underestimate the possibility of simple solutions."

"Okay, we'll put San Diego on it, see whether he was in San Diego, Washington, or Timbuktu last night."

"Even if he wasn't in Washington, his fingerprint on the briefcase requires explanation."

"If it's his. What about the woman?"

"Well, she seems to have itchy feet. Why don't you start with Cleveland and follow her trail since then?"

"Believe it or not, I know the routine."

This was what Armstrong had meant. The poachers were suspect; the poachers were a large pain in the ass to the people in the Bureau, who'd acquired a lock on internal security many hundreds of years ago and thought everybody else in the intelligence community was out to steal their empire. They knew Washington, and what happened when the camel got his nose in the tent.

Belknap, remembering he was supposed to be nice, set about mending fences. Finally he was able to ask Hathaway how long it would take the Bureau to get five hundred copies each of Emil Hustvar's and Myrtle Bessmeyer's mug shots distributed, along with descriptions, to police departments throughout the Washington area.

"The photos we could have by morning. Blanketing the area's harder."

"Well, we could call on manpower from the Metropolitan Police."

Hathaway didn't like that either.

"It's the urgency of the thing," Belknap added conciliatorily.

"I know about the urgency."

Hathaway knew about the urgency, but what he didn't know, and it was probably one of the burrs he had in his saddle, were the actual contents of the briefcase and why the midnight mailing of a package had him working overtime. *Beowulf* was a word Malkin, in his infinite wisdom, was keeping locked in the bosom of his little family.

By six-thirty Belknap had finished studying the summaries. He sat back wearily. The hallway was quiet; the others must have left.

He thought of the first time he met Malkin, at the

embassy in Moscow. It was the fall of '62, and there was something in the wind; it was obvious even to someone as green and junior as Belknap, but he didn't know what it was, and nobody chose to enlighten him.

Until Malkin, one evening, took him to a Kremlin diplomatic reception in St. George's Hall. They ascended a staircase covered with red carpeting and passed a huge portrait of Lenin before entering the great hall itself, once a ballroom for the czars. There were hundreds of names written in gold on the white walls—soldiers who'd been decorated for bravery. On a stage, black-booted members of the Red Army Chorus were chanting folk songs. Buffet tables everywhere. Most of the Presidium were present. Cosmonauts. Reigning ballerinas at the Bolshoi. Pomp and circumstance and caviar, Belknap thought, and about as proletarian as the Rockefellers at Bar Harbor."

Malkin introduced him to a pensive middle-aged Russian, who exchanged banter with Malkin in mellifluous Oxbridge English. "Dmitri passes as a journalist," Malkin said when Belknap asked about him later, "but he's really from Dzerzhinsky Square." His smile was musing. "We had a nodding acquaintance in Spain. When we both were very young."

"The Civil War?" Belknap said, surprised.

Malkin nodded. "I got out of college with a marvelously worthless degree in English literature. Finally landed a job on a WPA writers' project. After a year of that, worked my passage to Europe on a cattle boat. Bummed around France, Italy, Austria . . . picked up food and lodging money writing articles. In thirty-six, I was about to go home, try something, didn't know what, when war broke out in Spain. I got accredited as a stringer for several stateside papers. Papers not big enough to send a correspondent but big enough to want to look as if they were. An exciting time, David. Horrible as well, of course. And that's how I met Dmitri. He's quite a decent fellow. Or used to be. We all change for the worse, I'm afraid."

"How long were you there?"

"Until Bilbao fell in the summer of thirty-seven. I was captured."

It was a strange story to be hearing in St. George's Hall a quarter of a century later. Apparently the captain who'd interrogated Malkin at Bilbao decided he was a spy left behind by the retreating Loyalists and ordered him shot. But a British correspondent covering the Franco forces for the London *Times* and evidently on good terms with the captain intervened on his behalf. Malkin was jailed for two months instead and then expelled from Spain.

Belknap, intrigued by this picture of Malkin as a young man about to face a Spanish firing squad, wanted to hear more, but someone else had come up. Malkin conversed with a dozen people before they left: a Polish trade expert, a cultural attaché from the French Embassy, a Swiss businessman seeking orders for pharmaceuticals . . . Belknap never quite catalogued the rest. But all the conversations were in English and seemed innocuous—commiserating exchanges about the approach of winter, jocular exchanges about the present size of Khrushchev's waistline, the whole olla podrida spiced with the latest gossip making the rounds this week in the diplomatic colony.

When they returned to the embassy, Malkin said in an off-hand, slightly donnish way, "Well, the Russian freighter *Poltava*, carrying lorries on the top deck, Panther-class nukes below, is now passing through the Baltic on its way to Cuba."

He waited expectantly, and Belknap knew then that Malkin, the man of almost perfect control, was nevertheless showing off, and that he wanted Belknap to ask how it had been done, and under their hosts' very noses—was it in the numbers bandied about in the guesses about Khrushchev's waistline, or was it in the Pole's salty comments about a certain ballerina's sexual aptitudes? And so Belknap did ask, with proper admiring wonderment, and Malkin bathed him in that wonderful boyish smile and delightedly said nothing. It was the moment Belknap first realized that Malkin was one of those men for whom espionage was a game like chess, a game in which the moves had, for the true believer, a life and beauty of their own. It was also, of course, the moment he learned there was going to be a Cuban missile crisis.

But from that brief time in Moscow, Belknap remembered most clearly the George Malkin he encountered the evening of the Beirut assignment. Mid-January of '63. Malkin was shuffling through embassy cables when Belknap entered his office. The coal briquettes in the little grate produced a fitful flame. The exuberant *"Questa o quella"* aria from *Rigoletto* was playing on a small phonograph, which also contained a special wizard package for jamming Russian electronic surveillance. Malkin decanted a bottle of sherry.

"You've heard of the name Kim Philby, David?" he said without preamble.

"The British MI6 officer supposed to have been the third man in the Burgess-Maclean defection?"

"Exactly. Except he *was* the third man."

"I thought he was cleared in a parliamentary statement by Harold Macmillan."

"Indeed he was. Eight years ago. After which he went to the Middle East. Ostensibly as a correspondent for *The Observer* and *The Economist*, but retained by SIS on the side. Recently a Polish defector—the same one who tipped the British to George Blake—provided some missing links, and Philby was blown."

"So where is he now?"

"Beirut." Malkin tasted his sherry. "It's a delicate situation. The British don't want to bring him back forcibly to London to stand trial, because they've troubles enough at this time with a cabinet minister named Profumo, who's involved with a call girl who herself's involved with a Soviet naval attaché. Sounds like the plot of a penny dreadful, doesn't it? But whisperings of that scandal have already found their way to Fleet Street, and the whole story could be on the front pages any day. Nor do the British want to have Philby disposed of in Beirut. The Brits become queasy about such things when it involves one of their own. M16's decided to solve the problem by frightening him into defecting. They gave him a rough interrogation in Beirut some months back.''

Belknap was puzzled as to why Malkin was confiding the story. He learned quickly enough. Washington, Malkin went on, was opposed to M16's solution, in part because Philby had been the M16 liaison in Washington about a decade ago and nobody yet knew the extent of the damage he'd done, nor how much he could still do in Moscow. Washington had therefore decided to take Philby out of Lebanon in a covert operation and temporarily let the British believe he'd defected. A team was already on the scene, but difficulties had arisen, basically because Philby was too experienced a hand to place himself in a vulnerable situation.

Belknap wondered what would happen to Philby after the interrogators had pumped him dry. It was a thought too disturbing to pursue.

Malkin must have read his mind, because he said, ''Times have changed, David. Since the Powers-Abel swap, every KGB agent knows that if he gets in the bag, he'll sooner or later be ransomed. I imagine that after Philby's been squeezed for everything he's got, he'll be kept on ice until the Russians grab one of ours. And Kim, of all people, understands the rules.''

''You know him personally?''

''Ah, David, life's full of such strange turnings.'' Malkin blinked a few times, moved the lamp on his desk so his face was in shadow. ''Kim Philby was the British correspondent who saved my life in Spain.''

He stood up and poked the fire. ''You'll be going to Beirut with a message for Kim from me. The message will ask him to come with you to meet me in Byblos on a matter of utmost importance. Byblos is an old Phoenician port about twenty miles north of Beirut, reached by a coastal road with hairpin turns and tunnels. The ambush will take place en route . . ."

Belknap was stunned. "I'm to be the Judas goat?"

"No, David," Malkin said wearily, "I'm the Judas goat. But I've my orders, and you've yours."

"But it doesn't make sense. Why would an agent as experienced as Philby believe me, let alone come with me?" Anger pushed him into insubordination. "Why can't *you* go? You're the one he knows."

Malkin turned from the fireplace. His manner was apologetic, and he spoke almost by rote. "I can't go because I'm too well known to the British and Russians in Lebanon. I can't go because I'm needed here for crucial matters about to come to a head. But yours is a fresh face, and Philby will trust you because you'll give him this." He slipped a ring from his right hand and offered it to Belknap. It resembled a wedding band except it was obviously not gold. There was an inscription on it in Spanish.

"What is it?"

"My cell mate at Bilbao gave it to me. The night he was executed in the prison courtyard. He'd been a sheepherder before he became a soldier. And what this illiterate sheepherder said to me just before they took him to the courtyard was, 'In your journey through life, wear this ring and sometimes think of me, because if I live in your memory, I am yet alive.'" Malkin was silent for painful seconds. "When I was released for deportation to the States, I was processed through Salamanca, then Franco's headquarters and thus the place the foreign correspondents spent most of their time. It wasn't hard to locate Kim. All the correspondents knew and liked him. Kim and I drank to many things, but expecially to my liberation. He was touched when I told him about the ring. Kim's an exceptionally sentimental man."

Malkin returned to his desk. His face was drawn. "When

Kim sees the ring, he'll believe you and he'll go with you to Byblos."

"But why me? Why am I the messenger?"

The look Malkin gave him was not unsympathetic. "Because, David, you're the right man in the right place at the wrong time." He went through the motions of consulting a folder. "You'll leave the day after tomorrow on the Paris flight. You'll be taken to our embassy, where you'll get your new identity and a detailed briefing. The route into Beirut will be roundabout, but with luck you'll be there by the end of the third week in January. Philby won't be hard to find. Shows up at the Normandy Bar for drinks and mail about noon every day, I'm told. Have you ever been to Beirut?"

Belknap shook his head.

Malkin sighed. "They call it the Paris of the Middle East. I'm sorry you won't be there long enough to enjoy it."

Belknap was still resentful, but he wasn't insensitive to what Malkin must be feeling. Behind the mannered detachment was a man who, if you pricked him, would bleed. And Malkin was surely bleeding now.

"Have you seen Philby since Spain?"

"In England during the war. He headed M16's Iberian section and I was plowing the same field for OSS. Unfortunately I also ran into him in Washington just before the Burgess-Maclean business."

"Unfortunately?"

"After Burgess and Maclean scampered, everybody who'd ever had contact with Philby was debriefed." Malkin's voice was frayed. "That's how my encounter with him in Spain got in the files. That's why you now have the ring." He hurled his sherry glass into the fireplace. The flames jumped slightly. "Well, you'd better hurry along. Say good-bye to that luscious Russian girl the KGB's been aiming at you, because our plans for her are now aborted. I doubt that you'll be returning to Moscow."

Belknap started for the door.

"David?"

Belknap turned.

"It's enough to make the angels weep. But Ecclesiasticus was right. There is a time to every purpose under heaven."

"I don't want to disturb you," Vanessa said, "but it's awfully late."

Belknap slowly brought himself back from long ago.

"Do you always work this intensely?"

"I wasn't working," He moved his hands in unconscious supplication. "I was remembering."

"Remembering?"

"My youth. My ignorance. My innocence." He laughed defensively. "It was a long time ago."

"You're not that old, David."

"Depends on point of view." He listened to the sounds of silence. "Everybody gone?"

"No, Malkin's in chambers listening to Beethoven's Fifth."

"With, I'd bet, a decanter of sherry on one side, cables from the world's dark corners on the other." He put the FBI summaries and other loose material in the safe, rigging the pile out of long habit in case little mice visited during the night.

He walked with her to the guard's desk opposite the tiny hallway elevator. The guard was monitoring the second and third floors and the downstairs guard on a closed-circuit TV. Belknap heard faintly the surging music of the Fifth as he bent to sign the register and wondered if Mrs. Pruett was there with Malkin, the two of them sipping of sherry and coded cables. He fell in behind Vanessa as she descended the marble staircase, one hand traveling the balustrade, the other clutchimg a blue purse, and he had a pleasing view of her fine rear as it swayed. Her legs were solid, built for many things.

They signed another register at the guard's desk in the

lobby. His TV sets were monitoring the downstairs area and the upstairs guard. Belknap was sure neither of them had ever had to draw his gun in anger. The burglar-alarm system would be tuned to the perfection of a Stradivarius.

The guard unbolted the front door. A brass plaque announced this was the LAFAYETTE RESEARCH INSTITUTE, HOURS BY APPOINTMENT ONLY. They stood on the sidewalk in the vast sweltering sea made by the lifeless evening air, an undefined awkwardness filling the space between them. Belknap impulsively took her arm. "Let's find a quiet place to eat."

As he hailed a cab, he was conscious of her watching him in an intent yet curiously impersonal way, as if he were a butterfly in a specimen case shoved into her hands by a stranger. "Why, David?"

"Why what?"

"Why do you want to take me to a quiet place to eat?"

He thought about it. "I'm interested in you as a person, I lust after you as a woman, and I don't like to drink alone on Thursdays."

"Today's only Wednesday."

"It must be the first two then."

"Oh, Jesus." She dismissed the cab with a wave of her hand. "There's a place not too far from here. We can walk."

7

BELKNAP GAUGED THE WALK at forty minutes, and by the
time they'd left behind the detritus of urban decay north of
the Capitol and headed southeast toward Stanton Square,
he'd guessed their destination. On a quiet street of corniced,
post–Civil War row houses with brightly painted fronts and
gingerbread window boxes, she pointed out an adjoining
pair converted to apartments in the fifties. Hers was one of
three on the combined second floor; the living room had a
beige rug, pale yellow walls, a number of pole lamps, a
comfortable scattering of Danish furniture, and an absurd
gimcrack alabaster Venus on the mantel over the gas-log
fireplace. The small dining area was an extension of the
living room, and he caught a glimpse, over potted plants on
a homemade brick-and-plank divider, of a kitchen remod-
eled in stainless steel.

"Like it?"

"Of course."

"I was five months on a waiting list to get it. The stuff for
drinks is in the cupboards over the sink. I'm going to
change."

He would have liked to change, himself. His shirt was
soggy from the walk, his face grimy. He fixed the drinks,
listened to sounds made by a shower, and sat on the couch,
long-legged, not quite fitting, his body an obstacle course
placed in his way by God, his thoughts still traveling in
circles around the events of the day, like lost alpinists
looking for a St. Bernard.

It was unsettling to be working with Malkin again, to be back in a world where nothing was ever what it seemed, to be facing questions he'd long ago decided it was wiser never to ask. He thought again of that January evening in Moscow when Malkin had told him about Philby and then sent him on his way with the throwaway line about the Russian girl he'd met at a party at Moscow State University. He'd told Malkin about her a few days after the party, because if he hadn't, Malkin would have found out sooner rather than later. And Malkin, being Malkin, was delighted the KGB was aiming a girl at young David Belknap and advised young David Belknap to let himself be compromised at the first opportunity. It would be a dangerous game—Malkin had at least been truthful about that—but the benefits from a successful deception exercise would be enormous. Still, nobody in the embassy or in Washington was going to force him to do it; it had to be his own choice. Belknap lamely suggested the girl might not be under KGB control. Malkin managed not to laugh.

It became a more dangerous and complex exercise than Belknap had anticipated. With the wisdom of hindsight, he could even acknowledge that his abrupt assignment to Beirut and the Philby operation had removed him from a situation he was psychologically incapable of handling, and perhaps Malkin, recognizing this, had come to his rescue. That was the only bright side to Beirut. Everthing else had gone badly.

He arrived in Beirut early on the morning of January 23rd, driving from Damascus in a rented car and crossing the border with a passport identifying him as Sam Pappas, Canadian journalist. He made the necessary phone call to signal his arrival, struggled with the hilly streets of a city that seemed to spread in every direction without plan, and eventually found the breathtaking corniche to Byblos. On his right was a landscape of orange groves and banana palms and cypress; seaward, there were hollowed cliffs and reddish sands. When he came to the ambush point marked in the photographs he'd studied in Paris, he turned the car around. By noon, he was in the bar of the Hotel Normandy.

Philby, as predicted, came in soon thereafter. His face was puffed and he looked tired, but he seemed to brighten when the bartender brought him a martini and his airmailed London *Times*. After the regulars who'd greeted him had moved on, Belknap joined him at the bar. Feeling transparent and foolish, he introduced himself as Pappas of the Toronto *Star*. Belknap experienced then some of the legendary Philby charm. Philby, taking him to be a young correspondent on his first foreign assignment and probably in need of guidance, launched into a remarkable analysis of Middle East power politics. He talked nostalgically of the special relationship his Arabist father had had with Ibn Saud during the thirties and forties. Belknap, who knew from his Paris briefing that old St. John Philby had died last September here in Beirut when he'd stopped off for a visit on his way back to Riyadh after a trip to Russia and England, decided he'd been accepted. He ordered a new round of drinks. When they came, he brought out Malkin's Spanish ring.

"An old friend of yours asked me to give you this." Belknap felt like a bad actor in a worse play, but there was plainly recognition in Philby's face and a keener interest in Sam Pappas. Philby stammered his thanks and put the ring in his pocket.

"Your friend wants to see you immediately on a matter of greatest urgency, but it'd be too dangerous for both of you if he came to Beirut. He's waiting in Byblos. I'm supposed to drive you there."

Philby's smile was very gentle. "What's your real name, Pappas?"

"Pappas," Belknap said, trying to summon indignation while mentally cursing the anonymous desk officer responsible for the entire charade.

"And I suppose you're with U.S. Intelligence?"

"God forbid," Belknap said. "I suspect your friend in

Byblos is, however, though he's never admitted it to me. I'm merely repaying a favor and was led to believe he wanted to repay you an even greater one."

"Your friend's name is George Malkin?"

"It's not the name I know him by, but I wouldn't dispute the fact his real name might be different from the one I know."

"All right, Pappas," Philby said wearily, "we'll go to Byblos."

"Fine." Belknap called for the check. Philby put a hand on his arm. "Tomorrow."

Belknap knew better than to protest. "I was told to emphasize the urgency."

Philby nodded. "This is the Middle East. Urgency doesn't mean the same thing it does in Toronto. And it would be unwise to meet you here again." He laughed a little too loudly. "Spies everywhere." He looked around the almost empty bar and scrawled an address on a napkin. "It's a small Turkish restaurant on the Rue Hussein Talhouk. Ten tomorrow morning." Then Philby, clutching his *Times*, was gone.

Belknap walked to another hotel on the seafront and phoned the number he'd used that morning. He reported the unavoidable change of plans and received permission to spend the rest of the day as a tourist. "You might want to visit the Grottes des Pigeons," the soft Texas voice at the other end said. "It's a famous local landmark. If you care for belly dancers, I'd recommend the Chanticleer. And try not to get run over before ten tomorrow by the bastards who drive cabs around here."

At nine-thirty the next morning Belknap was waiting in the Turkish restaurant on the Rue Hussein Talhouk. At eleven-thirty, with no Philby, he knew something had gone wrong. But not until he returned to Paris did he learn that Philby, the evening of their meeting in the Normandy Bar, had made an excuse to leave the cab in which he was riding with his wife to a party at the home of a British diplomat and hadn't been seen in Beirut again. Nor anywhere else, until he broke for air in Moscow.

Belknap bit down on an ice cube. His glass was otherwise empty, justification enough to build a new drink. The sounds of the shower had stopped. In mind's eye he saw Vanessa toweling herself, one slim foot on the tub, the other on the bathroom tile, steam touching her like morning mist. Her skin would be glowing and her breasts, as she bent to dry her toes, delightfully pendulous. Belknap wondered what kind of hell she'd give him and what kind of sparks would fly if he barged in and innocently handed her a drink. He'd done stupider things with women.

He caught a flash of legs and terrycloth robe as she crossed the little hallway to her bedroom. He peered into his new drink for insight and thought with detached melancholy of women who'd once been in his life. Sometimes he felt as if he were a third-rate Ulysses, blindly following his erections as they led him like an erratic compass needle into strange bedrooms scented with promises and surrounded by trouble. With happiness ever after always just beyond the next coupling.

He became aware the Bellboy unit in the inner pocket of his jacket, now draped over the back of one of those free-flowing Danish chairs, was emitting a steady beep. He pushed himself away from the comfortable oblivion of the couch, flipped the Bellboy to *Off*, and scanned the room for a telephone. Hathaway must have something to pass on about San Diego or Cleveland.

He went to the closed bedroom door and knocked. "Are you decent?"

"Oh," she said. Long pause. "Come in."

She was wearing a white blouse and tailored red slacks and was seated in front of a vanity, frowning into its mirror as she applied lipstick. He saw the telephone on a stand beside her bed, but walked instead—Ulysses the Wanderer on the prowl—to her vanity bench and stood behind her. They looked at each other in the mirror. Then Belknap said, "Vanessa?"

He put his hands on her shoulders and bent to kiss the nape of her neck. She turned her head and protesting, said, "Hey!" But then she came into his arms as rivers flow into the sea, and they kissed. Her cascading hair lay on his upturned hands like an offering to heaven. "I'm afraid you're going to have to get undressed again."

"I'm afraid I am."

"I think I'm obligated to help," he said, and found the buttons at the back of her blouse.

He explored the strawberry birthmark on her left breast, the dark inviting aureoles, the curves and hollows and swells that led to the downy triangle where she was forked, and then there was the good feel of her hand fondling his erection and guiding him into her. For a time he lay there quietly, stroking her damp hair and tasting her parted lips, not wanting the beginning to end or the ending to begin but moving slowly within her until her pelvis began a tantalizing rhythm of its own, and for him it was like skating in the sky until the world fell away below. Her legs clamped behind him and together they began the last powerful ride. Mouths locked, bodies slippery with sweat, they traveled as one until, with a little cry she thrust upward hard and then his own exquisite spasms consumed him.

At last he buried his head in the hollow of her throat. "I don't want to move away. I want to be inside you when I die."

She laughed. "Who brings us our food?"

"To hell with food." Bracing himself on his elbows, he gazed into her dark eyes. "I'll eat you when I get hungry. You probably won't believe this, but all I came in here to make was a telephone call." He went down to say hello to her nipples.

"Ah, that's nice."

"I wouldn't want them to think we're forgetting them."

"I've a confession, David. You're getting heavy."

"I knew it was too good to last." He rolled onto his back. It was almost dark, but he'd lost all sense of time. "Somewhere in the living room, a couple of drinks are wondering where we are."

"I'll get them."

Not sure how long she'd been gone, still drifting in postcoital seas, he suddenly saw her in the doorway, clutching an indistinct mass. Four additional pillows landed on the bed. "Antony and Cleopatra on a barge down the Nile. *Prepare!*"

By the time she reappeared with the drinks, he'd arranged the barge. Three pillows for each of them, propped against the white leatherette headboard. He was already reclining against his three, and when she fitted herself next to him, he gave the barge captain an indolent signal to cast off.

"Did you know," he said, "that streaking didn't start in the nineteen-seventies? They used to do it in Antony's Rome."

"David, you're a historian too!"

"Indeed," he said gravely. They'd somehow reached a pleasant position in which his hand was casually around her shoulders, holding a breast hostage, and hers was casually on his limp member. It was a delightful way to discuss Shakespeare.

"Some place in *Julius Caesar* there's a reference to the Feast of the Lupercal. All the hotspurs in Rome that day ran naked through the streets, waving an olive branch or some damn thing. Antony led the pack."

It seemed a good thing to toast, so they touched glasses and drank.

"What about the phone call, David?"

"Yes," he said, brushing her hair with a kiss. "Hathaway's out there somewhere in the real world, and all he wants is to louse up our sex life. Do you want that?"

"No."

They toasted that decision, too.

"Tell me about yourself," she said, touching the scar on his right cheek.

He sighed. "Well, I was an only child and—"

She kicked his ankle. "Not that particular kind of crap. Tell me, well, how you got into this business.

"One of life's small but irreversible accidents. Near the end of my last year in law school at Berkeley, a professor called me into his office. In an oblique way, he discussed the opportunities and challenges in intelligence. I was dumbfounded, because as an undergraduate I'd been a student activist. This was a couple of college generations before Mario Savio and the Free Speech Movement, but the ferment was fermenting. And in law school I'd gotten involved with the National Lawyers Guild, which'd been on the A.G.'s list since the Year One, and I was dating a girl who was an organizer for the Socialist Labor Party.

"But I was young and gullible, and the tweedy professor made intelligence sound exciting. When I expressed guarded interest, he said I'd be hearing from someone. A few weeks later I met a spook with the improbable name of Jones in a motel near the campus. Later I was invited to Washington for closer inspection. They ran their checks, gave me their tests, and eventually put me into the pipeline. They must've known me better than I knew myself, because I discovered I belonged not to the militant left but to the amorphous center, with perhaps a slight leftward tilt. Intellectually, at least. In short, I'd emerged from the cocoon as—can the word be used these days without drawing mocking laughter?—a liberal. I'd watched students topple governments in various parts of the world—South Korea and Syngman Rhee came to mind at the time—but somehow Utopia never evolved. Revolutions, I began to think, weren't much different from changings of the guard at Buckingham Palace. Different officers, different faces in the ranks, but outside of a reallocation of privileges, the same old shell game.

"And once I was in the pipeline, I discovered I wasn't all that unique. Most of my fellow trainees professed to be liberals, albeit passive ones. I could count the right-wingers on one hand. The rest of us knew the United States wasn't God and Russia wasn't the Devil, but we saw, or thought we did, that Armageddon might be just around the corner unless we knew the Soviets' secrets and intentions. So it wasn't simply a business of saving our country, it was a business of saving the world. Looking back, I find it hard to believe I was ever that naïve.

"Well, when the training was over, I was selected to stay on as a junior instructor—the blind leading the blind. Eventually I got overseas. I made a bad beginning in Moscow and Beirut, loused up things I wasn't experienced enough to handle, but then I had some breaks and got a reputation of sorts as a salvage man."

"Salvage man?"

"The guy who goes through the wreckage when there's been a bad accident. Like Beowulf."

"And that's why Malkin brought you down from New York?"

"Only the Almighty can read Malkin's mind, and even of that I'm not sure. I don't know why I'm here. I don't want to be here, I'm uneasy here, but in a dubious way I perhaps owe George for something that happened long ago when we were passing out bribes to Middle East rulers like cotton candy. So here I am." He kissed the tip of her nose. "Can dinner wait a little longer?"

"Oh, I think so," she said solemnly. Her fingertips had been tracing a design in the hairs of his chest, but now she gradually eased herself from his encircling arm. Then her hair was spilling around his loins and her tongue and mouth were ministering to him. He sighed with the splendor of it.

"I think we're getting results."

"I'm a young forty."

"Not the way I heard at the office."

"Times change."

When at last she mounted him and was sweetly in the saddle, he held her breasts like doves.

She removed two small steaks from the refrigerator's freezer. "Always on hand for emergencies. But I'm afraid this establishment doesn't have a salad bar."

"Then I'm leaving." He slid off the kitchen stool. "Hate to fuck and run, but I can't enjoy a steak anymore unless it comes with a salad bar."

"All right." She broke open a package of frozen French fries. "But you'll miss the late show."

"Late show?"

"Forget I said it. A man your age probably wouldn't be up to it. It's absolutely wild."

Belknap laughed and looked at her affectionately. "Vanessa, why's the chemistry so good?"

She smiled. "Mysteries, David, mysteries." She took his hand. "Let's go into the living room."

"Well, the true professional," he said, "almost never gets caught because he's careless. He gets caught because his luck runs out, and the commonest way his luck runs out is through a defection. A man defects, and to buy his passage he brings with him everything he can. Sometimes it's the actual names of agents, more often it's information that, through patient investigative work and backtracking, eventaully leads to names. That's the way it happened with Kim Philby, with Rudolf Abel, with George Blake, with Heinz Felfe, with Erich Fehler."

She looked at him over the rim of her glass. "Tell me about Erich Fehler, David."

The unexpectedness of the question threw him off balance. He stared at her uncertainly, measuring the possibilities yet not wanting to make her a part of his own confused suspicions. Since she'd said in his office today she'd been in West Berlin in '68 herself, it could be merely idle curiosity about events too hurriedly swept under the rug by the men in the corridors of power in Bonn. But could anyone really be interested in Fehler all these years later out of idle curiosity?

"How'd you know I was involved in the Fehler fiasco?"

"When we met this morning, I knew I'd heard your name before. When you mentioned Fehler, I remembered I'd heard it in connection with him."

"But who told you about the connection?"

She didn't answer immediately. She had to adjust an ashtray. She had to adjust the collar of her blouse. "My father . . . after I came back from Berlin. Of course, he had no business telling me things that hadn't appeared in the German press, he was breaking all the rules, but even in the Agency fathers sometimes do that with daughters—particularly if the daughter's husband was murdered in that same country two months later."

He thought a moment, testing the story for logical consistency, balancing choices. And then, for better or worse, decided to trust her. Up to a point.

"It began a few months after Dubček came to power in sixty-eight. What they called the Prague Spring. A high STB officer who apparently could already hear the rumble of Russian tanks in Wenceslaus Square decided he wanted to buy insurance, so he put out lines and they landed in a tangle on Malkin's desk. The STB man was cagey; he indicated he might want to come over at an unspecified date, but any talking about quid pro quos had to be on his turf. Even though it smelled like a typical agent-provocateur scenario—blind dating always does—Malkin wanted a peek at his wares. So he decided to send a Czech expert in our shop to do the peeking. The day the Czech expert was to leave, he went to the hospital, supposedly with an attack of kidney stones. Since it was too late to call off the meeting, I was picked to go in his place. All the way to the airport Malkin kept assuring me that if it was a setup and they caught me in flagrante, he had a rescue operation geared up, ready to go.'' Belknap laughed mirthlessly. "My security blanket.''

He rattled the ice in his empty glass. "It was very exciting in Prague that spring. Dubček really was trying to give them back their freedom. The joy in the air was tangible. I checked in at the Alcron with a cover that wouldn't have stood up two hours under good interrogation and started on the elaborate ritual the STB man had worked out for establishing contact. I had to march up to the Hradčany and take the castle tour. If there wasn't contact there, I'd a fallback to a bridge on the Vltava, and so on and so on. Nothing happened the first day. I began to think I was weaving a pretty good web around myself if they'd been tailing me, because I was sure as hell one restless tourist, and I hoped Malkin hadn't been lying about the rescue operation.''

He went to the kitchen to fix another drink. "Do I turn the steak?''

"And put a low flame under the French fries. There's a choice of green beans or sliced tomatoes.''

"Sliced tomatoes. It'll remind me of a salad bar.'' He put an extra slug of whiskey in his glass. "The next day I was supposed to go to the Stromovoka. A lovely wooded park, tapestried with history. Two hours there, and nothing happened. My fallback was a restaurant off Wenceslaus Square. I ate lunch there, and as I came out a nervous blond gentleman approached. We went through recognition mumbo-jumbo, then he whisked me into a car.''

Belknap returned to the living room. "I was beginning to sweat, because we were heading toward the Knights of the Cross Monastery—STB headquarters—but he took a turn and went south into the countryside. He got to the point quickly. He wanted a Swiss bank account, and safe passage and a new identity if the Russians came in. He wouldn't give us anything on Czech networks—it turned out he was a patriot after all—but he'd give us a potful on the Russians, the Poles, and the East Germans. It was hard to tell which he hated most. I told him it sounded interestitng, but I'd have to get back to my principals before cutting a deal. And of course I was thinking it was a beautiful way to lead us through hoops if he was a plant. They could have us chasing our tails all over Europe. So I pressed for a sample of his wares as a gesture of good faith. We haggled like Arabs in a bazaar . . . finally I got my sample."

"And the sample was Fehler?"

"It wasn't that simple." Belknap walked to the window. "Do any of your neighbors drive an unmarked black delivery van and leave it on the street all night?"

She joined him at the window. "I've never really noticed."

"Draw the drapes."

"Aren't you overreacting?"

"Probably. The antenna looks normal enough, but I don't know beans about recent advances."

"Who'd want to eavesdrop on us?"

The naïveté of the question irritated him. The possibility it was deliberate irritated him more. "Anybody ever swept this place?"

"Of course not."

"The Malkin I knew used to make sweeps compulsory. Once a month."

"This is Washington."

"Sure. Where was I?"

"The STB man gave you a sample."

"Yes." He sat on the couch. "He said he was going to give me a West German who was a Russian agent. The Russians were so pleased with his work they'd made him a citizen and a major in the KGB. He was a free-lance photographer with political and journalistic contacts in

Bonn. And evidently running a formidable network. It supposedly included an admiral, a Bundeswehr colonel, a senior civil servant, and two prominent politicians. The catch was, my cautious canary couldn't—or wouldn't—give me any names or narrow the identification of the photographer. But he did have one intriguing fact we could try to check out: the Bundeswehr colonel, as a young man, had fought in Russia and been captured during the siege of Stalingrad. I kept pumping for more detail, such as whether the photographer actually lived in Bonn, but soon realized I'd everything he was willing to part with at the moment. So I said I'd be back in two weeks with a proposition. He said no, a second trip by me would attract attention; it had to be someone else. A very nervous character."

Belknap stared off. "I reported to Malkin and he became excited. He had me hustle over to General Fehler to repeat the story. Fehler, as head of Section Seven, was our liaison with the *Militärischer Abschirm-Dienst*. A tough old monocled Prussian right out of an Erich von Stroheim movie. The moment he heard my story, he fired aides off in every direction to arrange for background printouts on current Bundeswehr colonels who'd served in Russia during World War Two. Then, as a kind of repayment gesture, he impulsively gave me a copy of the Burgdorf Report."

"Something's burning!" Vanessa cried.

"Oh, hell, I forgot to turn the steak." He followed her to the kitchen, mumbling apologies. She opened the door of the broiler. Hot grease sputtered and jumped. Smoke poured out. She put the broiler tray on top of the stove and gave the skillet containing the French fries a vigorous, unfriendly shake. "The steak's salvageable, barely. What's the Burgdorf Report?"

"The story can keep."

"No, I'll warm the steak at the last minute." She wasn't happy. She activated the fan over the stove. "Get thee to the living room, Ace. I don't trust you out here."

* * *

"I have to take you on a detour," he said. "In the early sixties, the Germans discovered that a former junior SS officer named Heinz Felfe was a spy who'd roamed the counterespionage departments of the *Bundesnachrichtendienst* at Pullach for ten years. The news sent shock waves through the Adenauer government and shattered General Gehlen's reputation—the myth surrounding him somewhat resembled Hoover's here, but you know all that. Yet he somehow hung on, which was good for us, since in happier times Dulles had given him a golden handshake of two hundred and fifty thousand marks. Then Adenauer was deposed by Erhard, who demonstrated his opinion of Gehlen by kicking Gehlen's BND liaison cadre out of its chancellery offices. In sixty-six Erhard was in turn deposed by the Grand Coalition, with Brandt as foreign minister, and it must've been a bitter, bitter day for Reinhard Gehlen. Brandt, while mayor of West Berlin in sixty-one, had been given a BND appreciation that no East German initiative was likely in the immediate future. The Berlin Wall went up that weekend, and I don't suppose Brandt had ever forgotten. After a year or so in the Grand Coalition he persuaded Kiesinger to create a select commission headed by Helmut Burgdorf to investigate the BND. The commission wrote a secret report supposedly detailing nepotism, corruption, maladministration, and a penchant for hiring ex-Nazis. But the report was so tightly held that not even Gehlen had been allowed to see a copy. Malkin had been using every source we had, including Fehler, to obtain one, because it was assumed U.S. Intelligence appeared in the report in a bad light and Washington wanted to be able to prepare ammunition to discredit it. Malkin had come up against a stone wall.

"Okay, end of detour. I'm in General Fehler's office—the Bundeswehr's center for military counterintelligence—and he casually passes me a copy of the Burgdorf Report, our inside name for the select commission's investigation. I was staggered. What I was holding in my hot little hands would make me a hero when I got back to Malkin, and it certainly wouldn't do me any harm in Washington." Belknap gave Vanessa a wry smile. "I was more ambitious in those days."

She smiled back. "What happened next?"

"The good general passed me this bundle of dynamite and said we could keep it overnight. And added with a broad *Gemütlichkeit* we were on our honor not to make copies. I hustled back to Malkin, who reacted like a cat with a saucer of fresh cream. He made a copy for Washington and told me to keep the one I'd received from Fehler in my safe overnight."

"What about current Bundeswehr colonels who'd fought in Russia?"

"There were a number, Fehler's staff discovered. He invited Malkin and me to his office after receiving the printouts. But few of them had been captured, and none at Stalingrad. Fehler also tried to check out free-lance photographers in the Bonn area. Hopeless task, of course. Every third West German's a free-lance photographer.

"Malkin was discouraged. He felt the STB man had been aimed our way to get us to waste manpower chasing a nonexistent network. I was inclined to agree. On the other hand, if he *had* been aimed at us, his masters must have known we'd check out the colonels. So why give us information that'd give the game away when we did? By negative inference, I decided the STB man had been telling the truth. At least as he understood it."

"Which puts you at odds with Malkin?"

"Oh, yes. I asked him to send our Czech expert, now that his problem with kidney stones was under control, to Prague to keep the rendezvous. That's when Malkin's patience ran out. He wasn't going to risk his Czech expert on a dangerous, damn-fool mission like that, not when the sample we'd been offered was worthless."

Belknap moved his shoulders in a gesture of tired resentment. "The discussion was academic. A few days before rendezvous time, word filtered back the STB man was dead."

"Dead!" Vanessa seemed shocked to hear of the death of a man she'd never known. "But how?"

"Maybe he caught a very bad cold," Belknap said, drawing on residues of that same tired resentment. "People have been known to catch very bad colds under interrogation. Also measles and chicken pox, always fatal. The obit in *Rude Pravo* noted his demise but not the circumstances."

He decided to get another drink. He might not have earned it, but he certainly needed it. From the kitchen he said, "I'd a gut feeling there'd been a leak. Difficult to be sure. He'd been very nervous when I saw him in Prague. Might've given himself away. Nervous people often do. Should I warm the steak?"

"Please. How are the French fries?"

"You won't like them, either." He rejoined her in the living room. "I tried out my gut feeling on Malkin, but by then he was fed up with the whole business. Anyhow, there wasn't a shred of evidence to indicate the STB man had died of anything except natural causes. So I was the good soldier and did nothing. Only, the gut feeling kept gnawing at me . . . and I decided to go looking for the photographer. On tiptoe. Because if I called on extra bodies, it'd get back to Malkin fast, and he'd cut off my arms and legs and maybe my head."

He smiled thinly. "God looks after children and fools with the first name of David. In early August of sixty-eight, there were rumblings the Russians might be planning a move in Czechoslovakia. The Warsaw Pact troops were holding maneuvers on their parts of the Czech border. The West Germans were holding maneuvers on their part. There were tirades against Dubček from East Berlin. Everybody was trying to sniff out a clue as to Russian intentions. And what was David Belknap doing? He was down at Oberürsel trying to get a reading on Russian intentions from a freshly minted Czech defector who'd been a first deputy in the counterespionage section of the Ministry of the Interior."

"Oberürsel?"

"You don't know it? Near Frankfurt. The Germans used it during the war as an interrogation center for captured Allied airmen. Even the urinals were bugged. Especially the urinals. In sixty-eight we were using it as a debriefing farm for defectors. If you were very cooperative and your wares didn't have obvious cracks, you might get a ticket to someplace safe, and then again, you might just be sent back to the place you'd left in such a hurry. Mine wanted his ticket badly. He'd been singing for ten days. I read all the transcripts."

Belknap took a long pull on his drink. "It's a grand and glorious business, milking men as if they were udders on a cow. Squeezing here, squeezing there. At the time I never thought about it twice. I had that old-time religion.

"So I felt a few voyeuristic shivers when I came across an item about a West German photographer who'd visited Prague in the early sixties to cover a trade fair and been arrested for allegedly taking photographs of power stations. West Germany made a diplomatic protest; the Czechs ignored it. Then the Russians made a sub rosa request for his release, and he was sprung. I asked to talk to the canary. He couldn't remember the photographer's name, but he was terribly anxious to please. He went through his mental file cabinets with a vacuum cleaner. The photographer, he was almost certain, had a finger missing from one hand. Even if that was incorrect, he was definitely bald and had buck teeth. The canary had been one of his interrogators."

Belknap's inner ear told him his speech was getting slurred. "Counterespionage," he added with tipsy profundity, "is the art of finding, then fitting together, missing pieces. I found the photographer. It took about ten days. He'd a fine head of handsome gray hair, but wigs are easy to come by. What enchanted me were his buck teeth and a missing left pinky. I'm related to Sherlock Holmes on my mother's side. Vanessa, food's called for. I'm about to fall on my face.''

"The sliced tomatoes are superb.''

"Don't be nasty, David. You were the one who forgot to turn the steaks. I'll take partial responsibility for the French fries.''

They were eating in the flickering shadows cast by weeping red candles. An old Beatles record was playing on the stereo. Belknap added a massive dose of ketchup to his plate to kill the taste of burnt meat. "The photographer's name was Willi Speer. A rather celebrated Bonn free-lancer. Anything from the go-go girls of the jet set to earthquakes in Peru.''

"And trade fairs in Prague.''

"Right on.'' Belknap gave up on the steak and tried the French fries, then wished he hadn't. "The problem was, to get a reading. I considered a bag job on his apartment off the lovely Poppelsdorfer Allee, but if things went wrong, I'd spend the next five years in a German jail and Malkin wouldn't even send me cards at Christmas. Then along came August twenty-first. The Russians punched into Czechoslovakia, and I got so busy I had to forget Speer. In September, I was able to get back to him. I took some leave I had coming, put a beeper on his Mercedes, and spent a few days bird-dogging him. Didn't pick up any indications of network activity and started wondering if I'd the wrong man. Finally I decided to risk trying to get, outside of channels, whatever dossier there might be on him. I'd a longtime drinking companion in the BfV, we'd gleefully broken a few rules together, so I buzzed down to Cologne one night to make my pitch. The next day I had a summary of Speer's BfV dossier. He looked reasonably clean, but one item caught my eye. He'd a sister who worked as a secretary in the *Militärischer Abschirm-Dienst*, though not in Fehler's section. Still, it started me thinking. I decided to go after the sister.''

In the retelling, he was reliving it, and the details stood out in his mind as if it had been yesterday. "She was a stunning redhead, and on Tuesday and Thursday evenings she almost always had the same gentleman caller. One Erich Fehler. On Wednesdays and Fridays she had lunch with her brother. It was such a professionally beautiful cover—for all of them. Goaty old Fehler got laid on Tuesdays and Thursdays, and who could fault him for that? Sister and Brother, if that's what they really were, got together on Wednesdays and Fridays, and who could fault them for that? Of course, Sister probably passed to Brother whatever Fehler had brought her the night before, but such are the wicked ways of the world. The next step was to check Bundeswehr archives . . . that's when it all fell into place. Fehler had been promoted from colonel eighteen months ago and in World War Two had been captured at Stalingrad. The STB man had been right all along. It was just that his information was slightly dated; he didn't know about the promotion.''

Vanessa restively adjusted one of the candles. There was muted excitement in her voice. "So now you were ready to go to Malkin?''

"And he was stunned. Of course, he'd a social as well as professional relationship with Fehler. He was also furious at me for having mounted my little private operation. But I had the goods, there was no getting around it, and he agreed, subject to Washington's approval, to brief the Germans. Though the Germans, he told me, weren't going to be happy. It might even force the chancellor to resign. If, that is, Fehler was actually involved. Malkin still couldn't accept the idea. Fehler was a bit of a womanizer, he allowed, but still a marvelous host and raconteur, with one of the best wine cellars in Bonn. Why, he said to me, six months ago Erich handed us a sergeant at Wiesbaden who'd been playing naughty games with the East Germans. Maybe the Russians handed him the sergeant to hand to us, I replied. Malkin gave me a look, and I thought I'd be on my way back to the States, special delivery, before the day was over."

"And the Germans? Did they cooperate?"

He studied her thoughtfully. "Sure. The trouble was—as Malkin pointed out—there were too many cooks. The BfV security people, realizing they had a political hot potato, felt they had to brief the minister, and the minister, to keep his skirts clean, briefed his counterpart in Defense. Then the chancellor's office was brought into it. Fehler and Speer and his sister were put under surveillance, because if the STB man was right, there were also an admiral, a high civil servant, and two prominent politicians in the network. The Germans wanted a handle on the network before they started any interrogations. By October, it was obvious they weren't going to get that handle . . . neither Fehler nor the Speers made a single wrong move. Nobody's inner radar is that good, and Malkin was convinced there'd been a leak on the German side."

"What about you, David?"

"What about me, what?" he parried.

"Did you think there'd been a leak on the German side?"

He pushed away his plate. It had all, he saw now, been leading to this. She must have seen the Fehler file, she was pressing too hard. But who would have given it to her, and why? It certainly wouldn't have been Malkin. And what was her role in the complex game set in motion when she'd peeked over the rim of her glass, an uncharacteristic hint of archness in the stylized pose, and asked him to tell her about Erich Fehler?

Strange bedrooms, he thought. Scented with promises and surrounded by trouble. Was that why Malkin had brought him down from New York? Belknap could have wept.

"What're you after, Vanessa?"

She was startled. "What do you mean?"

"You've damn near put me through a third degree. I haven't talked this much about Fehler since the damage assessors worked me over. What do you really want to know?"

"Nothing." He saw the irritation flash in her eyes. "Why is an expression of interest in a historical event suddenly suspect? Forget Fehler. Fuck him!"

He tried to regroup. Maybe he was wrong. Maybe it was as straightforward as she claimed. Paranoia, he thought. It was still the prevailing life-style in the world to which Malkin had brought him back.

"Let's not do that to him," he said propitiatingly. "The fact is, Vanessa, I'd become a bit player by October. The Germans were calling the shots, and some genius on their side decided to interview Fehler. A soft interrogation, they call it. The main idea's to give the suspect a case of the jitters, then watch to see what he does next." Belknap managed a passable imitation, appropriately stilted, of a self-conscious BfV security man politely stalking a Bundeswehr general. "Herr General, my apologies for the intrusion. But it has been brought to our attention that Herr Belknap once informed you a Czech source had stated that a West German photographer, name unknown, was a Russian agent. Purely for informational purposes, not at all to interfere in your private life, we are interested in knowing why you never mentioned to Herr Belknap that a young lady you have been seeing was the sister of just such a photographer."

Vanessa smiled slightly. Reprieved?

Belknap wondered, and talked quickly to get them past the question he still hadn't answered for her. "But it never got to the stage of soft interrogation. Somebody tipped Fehler. Maybe, Malkin speculated later, one of Fehler's old comrades in arms in the Defense Ministry. Too many cooks, et cetera. Anyhow, Fehler panicked and, instead of going to ground, blew his brains out. And there was no way to put the lid on it. Christ, it was on TV, the blood and the gore, before Malkin or I knew it'd happened. By the time the Germans swooped on the Speers, they'd flown.''

"Was it really suicide?"

"The Germans said it was. Despondency over poor health.''

"What did Malkin think?''

"Malkin? Malkin thought the Germans wanted to sweep it under the rug and was happy to oblige. The Germans, he said in his jolly unflappable way, were our hosts and had to be allowed to clean their own stables. Which, he assured me, they were quietly doing. Extremely quietly. Because the Palais Schaumburg had issued an edict: no more spy-scare headlines. Fehler was bad enough. But a few days later, General Wendland, Gehlen's old Number Two at Pullach, disposed of himself with a pistol. About the same hour that day Admiral Lüdke used a shotgun on himself in a hunting lodge in the Eifel. The next week, Schenk, a high official of the Ministry of Economics, hanged himself in his Cologne home.''

"I remember. The German press called it the 'October of the Suicides.' What about you, David? Did you think Fehler's death was suicide?''

The moment of truth, he thought. Or untruth, depending on your needs. "I thought the Germans"—he paused—"or somebody, had given him early retirement. It might've been suicide, though. The Roman kind, where they put a Luger on your desk and tell you they'll step outside while you think about alternatives. The kind they permitted old General Beck in the Bendlerstrasse July twentieth of forty-four, when Goebbels and Major Remer reversed the coup d'état.''

Belknap got up from the table. He'd had enough. He went to the living room and parted the drapes. The unmarked black van was still there. Paranoia, he thought, national pastime of the damned.

8

"How's the headache?" Myrt asked.

"Not too bad," Brdnowski said, managing to sound saintly and miserable at the same time. "What kept you? Besides fallen arches."

Myrt tossed her purse onto the overstuffed. "The Greek made me stay late to make up for time I missed on the top of the shift. The tips are better when the drunks come in around nine anyhow. When we got off, Olga wanted to tell me about this dirty movie her boyfriend took her to last night. We had a couple of drinks in the back booth and a lot of laughs, because the movie wasn't just dirty, it was funny too. We should see it, Brdnowski. It's about a mad scientist who invents a drug gives you an erection you can't get rid of for seven days."

"I'd like to meet him," Brdnowski said glumly.

"I wish you could." She chortled knowingly.

"It's very discouraging," he said, trying not to sound as victimized by the course of human events as he felt. "All I had from you this afternoon was a phone call after you left the hospital. I didn't know the Greek was going to keep you late. So while you're gabbing in the back booth with that dumb Swede, I'm pacing the floor, climbing walls, and about to jump off a high cliff. Just because I was worried about *you*, Myrt."

"You were worried about *me*?" She let out a long slow whistle. "That's the best news I've had since I slid on the squashed tomato in Safeway last month and got two bags of free groceries to cover my pain and suffering." She gave him a juicy kiss to prove she meant it. "Forget about the furs and diamonds, just worry about me more often. It's the little things go to a woman's heart."

Brdnowski wasn't going to be distracted from the main issue that easily. "What I've been waiting to tell you is, something happened here after you left for the hospital."

"Okay, gimme a sec to get out of my first line of defense." She started toward the bedroom, hoisting her skirt and flashing the satiny pink of her girdle. Brdnowski couldn't help admiring her plump white thighs and the jiggle they carried like a government seal of approval. Myrt was something, on her good days anyhow, and the way she'd handled Miss Hatchet Face at the hospital was one for the books. In spite of his troubles, he laughed at full throttle as he replayed Myrt's telephoned account of their meeting.

He was still laughing when Myrt came out of the bedroom as if she'd been fired from a cannon. "What the hell happened in there, Brdnowski?"

Brdnowski bottled his laughter and shoved in the cork. "That's part of what I've been waiting to tell you."

"The mattress is on the goddamn floor. My clothes, your clothes, are all over the place. My hope chest's upside down. The—"

"I cleaned up most of it," Brdnowski said. "The kitchen's back together, there's not a sign of anything out there. And the bathroom and living room are okay now. I just didn't do a perfect job in the bedroom."

"So what the hell's going on?"

"I had a visitor." Brdnowski took a breath and waited for the explosion. "A detective."

There was no explosion. The air escaped from her with the steady squish of a punctured tire. "Detective?" She went into a bit of panic. "My perfume. My girdles. My nightgowns."

"He wasn't looking for those." Brdnowski pressed his slight advantage. "But supposing he had been? I mean, you want perfume, girdles, nightgowns, I'll buy them. You don't have to boost them. Honest to God, you don't."

"Brdnowski!" She had her hands on her hips and her legs solidly planted a mile apart, and she looked a little like a detective herself. Or a tough matron with eleven brothers who were all tough detectives. "You're stalling again, Brdnowski. What've you done this time?"

He pulled at his ear, not sure of the best way to go. "The fact is, Myrt, I screwed up last night. The locksmith got my license number, gave it to this detective. He came here looking for the briefcase."

"Isn't that wonderful! Brdnowski, what is this fatal attraction you have for trouble? If the last banana peel in the world was on a highway between Washington and Miami, I could blindfold you, start you up the road to New York, and within five minutes you'd manage to slip on it."

"Things didn't go too badly, Myrt," he said docilely.

"Didn't go too badly! That bedroom looks like a hurricane hit it."

"You should've seen the kitchen before I cleaned it up."

"When's he coming back to arrest us? I want to be sure to have my girdle on."

"I don't think he's coming back." Brdnowski brightened. "It's like murder. To get you for murder, they've got to have a body. To get you for taking a briefcase, they've got to have a briefcase."

"Why'd you keep it from me you were also a lawyer? What about the silver dollars?"

"It's no crime to have silver dollars. What could he do? Sit down, I'll fix you a drink, massage your feet. You've had a hard day."

"I can tell you have, too. Your beard looks as if mice have been sleeping in it. You've also been slaving over a hot stove. What have you fixed for dinner, Mr. Cold Stove?"

"Frozen pizza." Brdnowski smiled modestly. "Made a special trip to the store to get it."

"Open my purse. There's a classy medal in there for

people who walk two blocks for a frozen pizza. There's another for people who stick a frozen pizza in the oven. You get to wear them both."

"All you need is a little drink."

"All I need is a big drink, plus somebody to tell me how I got in a household like this. Brdnowski, the guy in the hospital isn't dead, and whoever he is, the only way we get out from under is if he dies. Or stays unconscious until Nixon's on Mount Rushmore. What are we going to do, check on him every four hours the rest of our lives?"

"Maybe you could phone the hospital. Get the latest report."

"Maybe you could take a flying leap out the window and land on your head in the street."

Brdnowski made a strategic retreat to the kitchen. When he returned with drinks and trepidation, she was lying on the sofa with a cushion behind her head and a *No Trespassing* sign posted on her face. He gingerly handed her a drink and sat so she could put her feet on his lap. "I'm pretty proud of you, Myrt."

"It shows, too."

"I mean it." He rubbed her feet. She always liked that. "The way you handled things at the hospital. The way you figured things out last night."

"I'm telling you something, Brdnowski. I can feel it. Our troubles are just beginning." She flopped onto her stomach. "My feet are okay. It's my back is killing me."

He massaged her back and shoulders. She always liked that, too. But this time she began to laugh.

"What's wrong?"

She turned her head sideways, one glassy green eye staring up at him as if it belonged to a fish on a platter. "I was thinking of the movie. The part before the mad scientist puts his drug in the city water supply."

If she was thinking about the movie instead of about Brdnowski the village idiot, he figured it was safe to steal a quick squeeze from one of her beautiful melons. "What happened?"

"The mad scientist got called to Washington to show his invention to the military. In case the drug could be used as a secret weapon. The general in charge asked for volunteers from all the services. When he got them together, the mad scientist passed out these little pills, and pretty soon it looked like the volunteers from the ranks had tent poles holding up their trousers. It was the general's job to prove they couldn't stay that way seven days. He brought on some sexy nurses who'd also volunteered, and they worked and worked on these guys, and got nowhere. So the general has another idea. He calls his men out of the barracks at five in the morning for a roll call. They're kind of shivering in the dark, because most of them are naked, but they fall in at attention and the general walks along the first row, asking each volunteer his name. Finally he comes to a guy with a tent pole Olga says you'd never believe, gives it a fast chop, and says, 'Did that hurt, soldier?' The general's naturally expecting the tent pole to drop like a dead rocket."

Brdnowski said stoically, "I can see how he might expect that."

Myrt got control of her laughter. "The guy answers, 'No, sir!'"

Brdnowski stole another quick feel. "He must've been a Marine."

"The general, he can hardly believe it, says, 'But why not, soldier?' And the guy says"—Myrt gave him a poke—"'Because it belongs to the man two rows behind me, sir!'"

Brdnowski broke up.

Wakened in the night by a siren, unable to get back to sleep, Brdnowski made his way to the living room. The neon sign advertising the hamburger joint across the street bathed the walls with a yellow haze.

He thought about the man in the hospital and, after pouring a glass of milk, phoned St. Albans and asked to be connected with the nursing station for Room 510. He told the nurse he was Joseph Smith's brother, just off the plane from Idaho. Had Joe regained consciousness? Not yet, she said, but if he'd leave a number where he could be reached, they'd let him know the moment there was more information.

"I'll call back tomorrow. Haven't got a room yet."

He lit a cigarette. If the man regained consciousness and was a government agent, he'd tell the other agents his briefcase had been in a cab driven by a guy named Brdnowski. When the agents found him, he could swear the briefcase must've been taken by one of his fares. But if the agents brought the police into it, he might as well cut his throat before Detective Joey Rosenbaum happily did it for him.

Things would be even more slippery if the man in the hospital was a spy. He or his friends would want Brdnowski as much as they wanted the briefcase, and the way they would want him was dead, because a dead cabdriver wasn't a very useful witness when it came to describing a fare who was actually a big-time spy in disguise.

Maybe the answer was, he and Myrt should get out of town.

But if they did, and the man was a government agent after all, running away would be the same as a confession. Besides, they had to be in Washington to nurse the chain letter; they couldn't let a once-in-a-lifetime chance go down the drain because of some crummy briefcase.

The chain letter was another of Myrt's brainstorms, hatched as they were tossing down boilermakers with Olga and her boyfriend in the back booth at the Greek's. Olga's boyfriend showed around a flyer describing a foolproof investment that cost only $5 and could return over $1,000. Myrt told him not to waste his money, it was another version of the old chain-letter scam. "Only the names at the top of the list make money."

Two boilermakers after Olga and her boyfriend had left, she'd had the brainstorm. The two of them would start chain letters to help worthy causes in which their own names, or rather names they'd temporarily borrow, would always be near the top. Since they were both lapsed Catholics and at times felt guilty about it, they decided to help Catholic religious orders.

After they'd sobered up, the idea still seemed solid. Since they wanted to send the letters to people likely to be Catholics, they decided to go through phone books looking for Polish or Italian names. They picked Chicago and Poles for their first mailing. Brdnowski had once heard there were more Poles in Chicago than in Warsaw.

Myrt spent her next day off at the Public Library going through the Chicago phone book for names and addresses. When she had two hundred prospects, she put together a friendly letter explaining how the lucky person receiving it could give to a worthy cause and make money at the same time. The lucky person was told to send $5 to the name at the top of a list of five names, make up a new list by removing the top name and adding his own to the bottom, then give the new list to five dependable friends who'd be asked to do the same thing.

The first name on Myrt's list was the Convent of the Little Sisters of the Poor near Pittsburgh. The second was sometimes Dora Dollson and sometimes Dave Dollson, Post Office Box 612, Ellis Substation, Washington, D.C., since Myrt had rented the box in both names. The third was a Trappist monastery outside St. Louis, while the fourth and fifth, taken from the Chicago phone book, were twenty-four-carat Polish.

They'd mailed the letters last week. Myrt had figured out that even if only ten of the two hundred prospects took advantage of the chance to help the Little Sisters of the Poor and then brought in five friends each, so as to move the

Trappists to second place on the list, the two of them could still pick up a bundle. And more than a bundle if those Chicago Poles really cared about the Little Sisters of the Poor. But it meant they had to be on the scene to clean out Box 612 in case there was more mail than the box could handle.

Brdnowski lit another cigarette. Even if they couldn't afford to get out of town, they at least ought to get out of the apartment. Except this might also look suspicious if the man in the hospital was actually government. What they needed was a reason for getting out of the apartment that was pure gold. Gold so pure it would stand up whatever happened at the hospital. And suddenly he had the answer to everything.

Standing in the darkened bedroom, Brdnowski could see her body sprawled over most of the bed—her side, his side, and all the open space between, like a homesteader staking a claim to everything west of the Mississippi. The red satin nightgown she'd lifted from somewhere the weekend he'd gone to New York without her to watch the Yankees was hiked almost to her waist, and one of her snores was starting. It started deep with the low rumble of a bowling ball returning from the end of the alley and then, gathering momentum, charged Brdnowski's eardrums like a team of snorting firehorses. Brdnowski almost had a change of heart.

But he went to the bed and began shaking her. "Hey, Myrt, wake up!"

She came groggily into present time. At first she thought he was her Uncle Max—Brdnowski remembered he was the uncle who'd been double-jointed and made a mint with the carnival as the India Rubber Man—and then she thought the apartment was on fire. It took a lot of work to convince her the smoke she was smelling came from his cigarette.

After he put it out, he popped the question: "Myrt, let's get married."

"I'm not sure I'm awake. I'm still dreaming. Say it again, Dream."

"Let's get married."

"You're not a dream?"

"I'm Brdnowski."

"You're not sick, you're not running a fever?"

He shook his head.

Letting out a triumphant whoop, she pulled him down between her breasts. "What I'd really go for is a wedding in some quiet country church. Romantic, know what I mean?"

"Right." His nose was having a little trouble getting air.

"Today wouldn't be good. I have to get my hair done first, and Elsie's off on Thursdays." She giggled. "I could skip the hair."

"No, don't skip it," he said too hastily.

She lifted his head by seizing two good fistfuls of top thatch. "Brdnowski, do I smell a rat? There's not some catch in this proposal?"

"Honest, Myrt."

"So what's the timetable?"

Brdnowski cleared his throat. It probably wouldn't be very romantic, not like a country church anyhow, to tell her the timetable depended on when the man in the hospital regained consciousness, and that roughly speaking, he'd like to tie the knot about ten seconds later. And then leave the apartment in a cloud of honeymoon dust for any out-of-the-way motel in the area.

"Well, Friday or Saturday probably."

"You got places in mind for a honeymoon?"

The Arctic, he thought. The middle of darkest Africa. The jungles of the Amazon. Basically any place on the earth's surface where government agents and Detective Joey Rosenbaum and unhappy spies couldn't reach them via long-distance telephone or local assistants.

"Paris?" she said hopefully. "We could boost a credit card."

"I was thinking of closer to home."

"Oh, I'm feeling good. I'd a hunch this was going to happen."

"Woman's intuition. Wish I could put it to work at the track."

"After the honeymoon's over, you know what we'll do?"

"Move into separate beds, probably. That's what happened with most of the guys I know. Takes about a year."

She grabbed him down below. "Not us, Brdnowski! We'll go to some little town in the Midwest and find a cheap location for a burger joint. We'll start The Home Run, you in the kitchen, me out front, fan-dancing with ostrich feathers for our best customers. We don't have to start big, but word about our burgers, every one a home run, will get around fast. In five years we'll have a chain."

Brdnowski began to get excited. "The biggest ones, we'll call them Home Runs. Plenty of dills and onions. But we'll have Three-Baggers and Two-Baggers to build volume. And One-Baggers for the kiddie trade."

"Hey, Brdnowski, you're about to bat a home run down there yourself. Twice in one night—you're headed for the Baseball Hall of Fame!" She wrapped herself around him exuberantly, but Brdnowski had already begun to wilt. Myrt let out a sigh. "Me and my big mouth. When we start the honeymoon, do me a favor. Tape it shut when the lights go out."

9

THE RINGING OF THE PHONE wakened Igor Demichev. The early morning light was as painful on his eyes as needles. His wife stirred uneasily beside him. Groaning, he reached for the damnable instrument.

The apologetic voice of Lieutenant Nikitin greeted him: "I am sorry, Comrade General, to be calling at such an hour, but it was felt here you should know. The anticipated message from New York arrived during the night."

Demichev tried to orient himself. Moments ago, in a dream he was already having difficulty recalling, he'd been parachuting behind German lines in the last months of the Great Patriotic War. The reception committee was composed of twenty female partisans, all of them nude. They ran toward his descending parachute with shrieks of joy. But thanks to Vasali Nikitin, who'd not even started serving his time on Earth in those glorious days, he'd never know the denouement.

"New York?" he said hoarsely and covered his other ear to muffle his wife's irregular gaspings.

"New York," Nikitin said, "also discovers Edgar is missing."

Demichev got out of bed. "All right, we move according to plan. I'll be there in an hour." He shook Natalia's shoulder. "Wake up, Natasha, some hooligan's placed a bomb in our building. We've only minutes in which to escape."

106

"No," she mumbled, "this time, Gosha, you must make your own breakfast."

In an apartment above them, a toilet flushed. "Moscow awakens," she said, one hand groping along the floor for her crumpled Parisian nightgown. "What ministry is responsible, Igor Fedorovich, for plumbing noises that travel even through buildings on the exclusive Kutuzovsky Prospekt like messages sent over a jungle telegraph?"

"The Ministry of African Affairs."

She laughed. "You're in a surprisingly good mood for having been awakened at this inexcusable hour."

"Protective coloration. The day will get worse before it gets better."

"What is it this time?" She slipped into her gown. "Have you discovered the United States is secretly building a road to Hell? No matter. Our heroic Soviet engineers will build a better one. The unspeakable plumbing in Moscow apartments can wait."

Demichev sighed. It was what came of being married to a concert pianist. Irreverence one moment, artistic temperament the next. It made life interesting, but it was sometimes trying.

"What's really the trouble?"

"Chessplayer. Through events no one could have predicted, through events we don't fully understand yet, our irreplaceable North American asset is in a situation of extreme peril."

Her eyes widened in astonishment, as they did when she received bouquet after bouquet of flowers on the final night of a long-running performance, most ordered by her current personal manager. "Should you be telling me this? Secrets of state."

They laughed together. It was an old joke between them, this mock concern, though sometimes Demichev suspected it might also be a signal she was beginning to be as bored by his stories of office problems as he already was by her stories of intriguing rivals in the world of the concert stage. But he affably followed the script:

"Of course I shouldn't. On the other hand, what's the value of privilege if one doesn't occasionally abuse it?"

She smiled. "The life of a general is hard."

"As is the life of a concert pianist. Now, can we be serious a moment before I shave and you make for your general a Spartan breakfast of eggs and Danish bacon? We've prepared over many years for the day when Chessplayer might find himself in jeopardy. Now we're required to act. If we should fail, your general's career could also be in jeopardy, so failure's officially prohibited. And in all of this we depend ultimately on one Ivan Glukhov."

"Your man in New York?"

"Well, one of them." He walked to the closet to select a suit appropriate to the day's momentous business. "On reflection, perhaps the eggs and bacon should be preceded by strawberries with Devonshire cream. It's absurd, maybe even criminally so, to be overly Spartan when lives and careers are at stake."

10

IVAN GLUKHOV SLEPT fitfully Wednesday night. Perhaps, after all, he should've phoned Irina, the seemingly willing switchboard girl at the mission. Carefree sex might have made the hours until dawn less difficult for both of them.

It was hard sometimes to order priorities, to separate what ought to be done from what had to be done. An old Russian proverb said, "Put on the first shoe before putting on the second." It was what made old Russian proverbs so enchanting and worthless. But Glukhov knew he had to put on one shoe or the other, it was just a question of which to put on first. Which was probably the whole point of the proverb.

In the small kitchen of his small apartment near the Soviet U.N. Mission, Glukhov cut an orange in half and started to boil an egg. Whatever was to happen to him today shouldn't happen on an empty stomach.

It was strange. Everything about his future had seemed so uncomplicated on that unforgettable morning in early 1968 when he'd reported to the North American Department of the First Chief Directorate, and an unknown major, after declaring him the exemplary Soviet Man, took him into the deputy director's office for special instructions.

Colonel Igor Demichev was a burly, handsome, gray-haired Ukrainian, radiating geniality and confidence. He signaled the major to leave and told his secretary they weren't to be distrubed unless somebody started World War III.

"Certain things I'm about to tell you, Glukhov, must never be mentioned outside this room."

"Yes, Comrade Colonel."

"You've been selected from many other fine young men to manage an agent—not only today and tomorrow but possibly for years—who in time may accomplish more than any other agent in history. This is not said lightly."

"I understand, Comrade Colonel."

"He's young—about your age in fact. Perhaps you'll grow old together. Gracefully, I hope."

Glukhov smiled in the way one does for colonels who make humorous remarks.

"His code name is Chessplayer, and that's the only name by which you'll refer to him outside this room. He's with U.S. Intelligence and once served in Moscow, where he was compromised by a young lady. You and I know how these things happen, it's one of the unpleasant sides of our work. In this case, it happily developed the young man was already predisposed in our direction. He's now stationed in Bonn, operating under diplomatic cover. You'll also be sent to Bonn under diplomatic cover. However, he's far too valuable an asset to be put to the risk inherent in face-to-face meetings with you. On this point I want no misunderstanding. There's never to be personal contact—whatever the emergency that might arise."

"I understand, Comrade Colonel."

"You'll deal with him only through *duboks* and cutouts. Ordinarily in a matter this sensitive, you'd not be told his true identity. For both your protection and his. In this case, an exception has been made. Since you'll be members of the same diplomatic community, you might meet by chance at a diplomatic function. Such a chance encounter could well be fatal to him—if we assume, as we must, U.S. Intelligence by then had learned you're a KGB officer. Innocent as that chance encounter might be, it could put him under suspicion."

"I understand, Comrade Colonel."

"I'm therefore going to give you his true name. And show you his picture." Demichev passed a photograph across the desk. "Study it as we talk. With his picture and his name engraved in your memory, you'll be able to take appropriate action to avoid accidental encounters. Would you like a Turkish cigarette, Glukhov?"

"Thank you, Comrade Colonel."

"His name is David Belknap."

"David Belknap," Glukhov repeated.

"Yes, and now forget you ever heard it. Except in that small compartment of your mind where you keep your survival kit." Demichev tapped his cigarette on his wrist. "To give you the necessary awareness of Chessplayer's value, I tell you in utmost confidence he transmitted information enabling our great English agent Kim Philby to get out of Lebanon in time to thwart a last-minute U.S. plot to kidnap him. It's something to think about, Glukhov."

"It is indeed, Comrade Colonel."

"And as Chessplayer advances in his own service, he becomes even more valuable."

Glukhov decided to risk a little levity. "What they'd perhaps call in Hollywood a 'hot property.'"

"You've the idiom nicely, Glukhov. We picked the right man when we picked you. And as Chessplayer advances"—Demichev winked—"so do you. That's something to think about, too."

"It is indeed, Comrade Colonel."

"To put it bluntly, Glukhov, you're his guardian angel. Totally responsible for his safety, except for"—Demichev thought a moment—"events beyond your control. You must learn to think like him, feel like him, and above all, never to ask too much of him. We can afford to wait. Ripe grapes are best. The older man in Bonn you're replacing did ask too much. Pushed too hard. Older men are more concerned with time. Mortality. Younger men such as yourself"—Demichev smiled companionably—"know they're immortal. It's why I find it hard to forgive anyone who's half my age. Even you, Comrade Glukhov. How's your sex life?"

Glukhov blushed. "Adequate, Comrade Colonel."

"Well, be careful. It isn't what you do in bed they hang you for, it's what you say." Demichev stood up, brimming with hospitality he was apparently too pressed to share. "You'll be arriving in Bonn at an interesting time. From the standpoint of challenge. Chessplayer has fortuitously received garbled information about one of the Fourth Department's West German networks from an STB opportunist looking for greener pastures into which to piss. In the very near future he'll find his greener pastures, greener than he expected, but the information, garbled as it is, could eventually lead to the network. So it's been decided that if more information about the network comes into Chessplayer's hands, fortuitously or otherwise, he must pursue that information in normal investigative fashion, wherever it leads. Not only to build his cover and improve his chances of advancement—we can always sacrifice a few minnows to fatten a shark—but also to guard against the possibility his own service is testing him. It's the worst part of our business, Glukhov. You never know whom not to trust. However, I digress from my point. There's no predicting the direction in which Chessplayer may be forced to move during the next few months. Both of you may have to make quick decisions. It'll keep you on your toes, I expect. Well, the major's waiting outside. He'll show you pertinent sections of Chessplayer's file and brief you on your duties in Bonn."

Glukhov, posted to Bonn as an economic adviser, arrived at a time when the Gehlen Organization—or what had been the Gehlen Organization before it was removed from direct CIA control in 1956 and incorporated into the Federal Republic's security apparatus as the *Bundesnachrichten-dienst*—had fallen on bad times. Too many spies, beginning with Heinz Felfe and Hans Clemens, had been found hiding in the cupboards. Everyone knew Gehlen had to go, and although the bitter power struggle over his successor as Germany's spymaster had been settled, the politicians still had to arrange a graceful exit for this extraordinary professional survivor who'd waltzed from wartime service as a Hitler general into a postwar love affair with the CIA and then into the not entirely receptive arms of *Der Alte* without missing a step . . . until recent years.

How the mighty, Glukhov thought from the safe sidelines of history, had fallen.

To add to Gehlen's misfortune, the present chancellor had created a commission chaired by the respected elder statesman Helmut Burgdorf to poke into every cranny of the Federal Intelligence Service. The result of its labors was a politically explosive secret document with the inside name, at KGB headquarters, of the Burgdorf Report. The disinformation specialists in Department A of the First Chief Directorate, always happy to exploit governmental discord, wanted to obtain and then leak a copy to the German press. Unless, of course, it was critical of Soviet activities in West Germany, in which case it would have to be discredited. Glukhov was ordered to give the matter the highest priority.

Glukhov never even had to put the problem to Chessplayer. The Burgdorf Report was the first thing his beautiful new agent delivered, several days after his arrival, through a double cutout and dead-letter box. Glukhov ran an ad in the personal columns of the *Bonner Rundschau* to signal the material had been received and, in his exuberance over such an auspicious beginning, tacked on the code words for *Well Done!*

Everything went well for Glukhov those first months in Bonn. At a summer reception given by the Economics Ministry for members of a Polish purchasing commission, he even caught a thrilling glimpse of Chessplayer going after Baltic herring at the buffet table. But mindful of

Demichev's sage warning in Moscow, he immediately made his way to the far end of the marbled ministry hallway.

It bothered Glukhov, however, that his covert work seemed almost entirely limited to Chessplayer. Of course, he performed the standard vacuum-cleaner chores of any KGB officer on station, such as passing back to the *rezident* interesting rumors picked up in contacts with Bonn officialdom or, if he met a German national who seemed a prospect for recruitment, funneling the information into the KGB's great central *Zapiski* files. But because of the importance the Center placed on his relationship with Chessplayer, it had prohibited extracurricular activities that, if exposed, could lead to his expulsion for abusing diplomatic privileges.

The prohibition was frustrating not only to Glukhov but also to the *rezident,* a humorless, suspicious survivor of the last hard days under Beria, who took his revenge on the Center for its intrusion on his right to full command over those under his jurisdiction by assigning Glukhov the most trivial nonhazardous extra duties his seasoned conspiratorial mind could devise.

In August Glukhov temporarily escaped from the *rezident's* methodical small humiliations by taking a long weekend at Bad Godesberg with a typist from the cultural attaché's office. When she archly told him while they were sunbathing beneath the peaks of the Siebengeberge she was sure his job as an economic adviser was only a cover and he was really a KGB officer, he had to wish the Center would stop wasting taxpayers' rubles paying KGB swallows disguised as typists to get KGB officers disguised as economic advisers to admit they were in the KGB. Why was Colonel Demichev still testing him? Why? It complicated so many things, particularly sex. And it was depressing to realize he was such a poor judge of character. Of all the girls he'd lusted after in the embassy, she was the last he'd have expected to be a swallow.

When he insisted he was only an economic adviser, she

pouted briefly, then told him not to worry, she liked his eyes and smile anyhow. An hour later in their room, when he was courteously helping her out of her bikini, it dawned on him she wasn't a swallow after all, she was simply a wholesome village girl who had the crazy idea there was something glamorous about being in the KGB and getting to read secret dispatches to a constipated *rezident* through a half-open bathroom door. Life in the KGB, he thought as he undid her last string, was making him too suspicious. As the old Russian proverb said, it was better to trust a woman and be disappointed than to eat your borsch alone.

Returning from the sexually exhausting weekend at Bad Godesberg, Glukhov found the KGB colony within the embassy in a state of tension. Word had come from Moscow something was about to happen in Czechoslovakia, and among junior personnel the betting was, there'd be an invasion. Nobody knew how Bonn would react, but it had moved troops to the Czech border, and surveillance of embassy personnel had become so intense the *rezident* ordered the temporary suspension of all contacts with agents. Not until three weeks after the invasion did Glukhov receive clearance to reopen communication with Chessplayer.

Chessplayer's first return message was shocking. Through information given by a defector at Oberürsel, he'd identified the free-lance photographer operating the network his Prague STB source had described in the spring, as well as one of its members, a general in the *Militärischer Abschirm-Dienst*. Chessplayer was furious. Why hadn't the Center given him the names of Willi Speer and General Erich Fehler months ago and warned him away? Then he could have steered the investigation in a dead-end direction. Now there was no turning back, because German as well as U.S. Intelligence was involved.

Glukhov not only understood Chessplayer's anger, he felt similar anger, because Moscow Center hadn't given him the names either. Another of the bureaucratic stupidities perpetrated in the sacred name of "need to know." Somehow he had to convince Chessplayer that Ivan Glukhov, his loyal friend, his guardian angel, wasn't responsible for the chickenshit on the carpet. He also had to alert the Center, so network members could be warned and the network itself put to sleep until the extent of the threat was known.

At the end of September there was more bad news. Chessplayer's report indicated General Fehler was beginning to crack under the pressure of knowing German security was investigating him as a possible spy. This, too, Glukhov could understand. The general had run with the hounds too long not to know what happened to the fox at the end of the chase. Chessplayer's reports expressed concern that Fehler, in a desperate effort to avoid spending what remained of his life in prison, might go to the authorities before they came to him. Chessplayer's concern took on added significance when it became clear Fehler had no interest in the escape plan organized to get him out of West Germany. He was too old, he'd resignedly informed his controller through a still secure channel, to spend his remaining years as an expatriate in Moscow or a fugitive living under an alias in some neutral country.

There was pathos here, and Glukhov the novice in espionage was touched by it. Spies, like other men, grew old, weary, and afraid to wander from their backyards. Spies disposed to giving state's evidence, however, weren't like other men. Even Glukhov the novice in espionage knew that. When he learned, not many days later, Fehler had shot himself, he felt compassion for the aging general who'd tried to live in two worlds and been at home in neither. But he wasn't going to try to find out whether it had really been suicide. Colonel Demichev would never tell him anyhow. Even if it had been the Germans.

In January of 1969 Glukhov received orders to return to Moscow for debriefing. Yuri Subotin, his best friend in the embassy, brought him the news. Yuri, an irrepressible adventuresome spirit, also wanted him to take in a transistor radio for one of his girlfriends and a hand-held hair dryer for another. Glukhov, who'd been thinking of taking in a few things himself on his first trip home, didn't like the idea of adding to his risk by acting as quartermaster for Yuri's harem. Yuri swore the risk was zero. He'd an uncle in Moscow Customs who'd once told him over vodka they never checked the luggage of returning diplomats.

Glukhov nodded unhappily. He kept forgetting he was supposed to be a diplomat. But Yuri was right: on arriving in Moscow, he'd had no trouble with his luggage. It entered his mind that if a person were recalled to Moscow two or three times a year, he could bring in enough contraband to go into business for himself. Swiss watches, German cameras, French champagne, Scotch whiskey. Glukhov laughed; he was dreaming, and knew it.

The following day he was welcomed cordially by Colonel Demichev. Spread out on the colonel's desk were architectural sketches. "Our new headquarters building, Glukhov. Scheduled for completion late next year. Add thirty-six months to that, and you might be almost on target. What do you think of the architecture?"

Glukhov studied the sketches. It would be undiplomatic for a diplomat to say the architects' conception of the future headquarters building bore an embarrassing resemblance to photographs he'd seen of the CIA's headquarters at Langley, Virginia. "It has a rather commanding style," he ventured at last. "Part Bauhaus, part Greek Classical. Of course, I'm not an architect."

Demichev seemed mildly surprised to learn this. But he couldn't be, of course. It wasn't always easy to tell what the colonel was really thinking, or when he was making a small joke.

"How are you getting along with Chessplayer?"

Glukhov felt encouraged to make a small joke himself.

"To tell the truth, Comrade Colonel, we don't see each other too often."

Demichev laughed with such gusto he had to wipe tears from his eyes. "Ah, Glukhov, it's wags like you who make life worthwhile. But now, regrettably, we must turn to business. Business so sensitive it must never be discussed outside this room."

The business was also complicated, and Glukhov didn't entirely understand it. On his way back to Bonn he was to stop in Geneva and, using identification forged by the Center, open a numbered bank account as Gottfried Forst, Bonn importer. From time to time, Center laundrymen would make payments to it through a Liechtenstein corporation called Ottawa Factors, Ltd., which payments Glukhov would transfer to a numbered account Chessplayer apparently had in another Geneva bank. On occasion, however, it seemed Chessplayer would make certain payments to Gottfried Forst's account, which Glukhov would then transfer to a third numbered account in Bern, whose owner Demichev didn't identify. Before Glukhov could press for a fuller explanation of these puzzling transactions, Demichev jovially adjourned the interview and sent him to the major for his debriefing.

On his return to Bonn after his side trip to Geneva, Glukhov discovered the *rezident* had moved him to a smaller office. Life kept getting harder to understand. In Moscow Colonel Demichev treated him like a hero, in Bonn the *rezident* treated him like a cross he had to bear, in Geneva his new banker treated him like a shady but prosperous—and therefore tentatively respectable—importer named Gottfried Forst. Glukhov wondered morosely if he was having an identity crisis.

Matters weren't helped when Yuri Subotin popped into his matchbox office and exuberantly announced he'd had a vasectomy while Glukhov was living it up in Moscow. The *svoloch* wasn't even considerate enough to ask if the radio and hair dryer had been delivered safely.

Indifferent to Glukhov's pained expression, Yuri blithely recounted the advantages of his operation. Why didn't Glukhov see the embassy doctor about one for himself? It was an office procedure, with no discomfort. Yuri would guarantee that. And it'd make him a new man.

Glukhov shook his head. He didn't want to be a new man. He just wanted to be himself, and the older he got, the more diffficult it became.

In 1971 Chessplayer was transferred to London, and Glukhov, sadly no longer a novice in espionage but still discreetly on the prowl for a less complicated way of life, was recalled to Moscow while the Center arranged his own transfer to London. One evening in the lobby of the Metropole, where he was staying, he encountered Yuri Subotin.

Yuri was no longer with the KGB. Notwithstanding his miraculous vasectomy, he'd failed his last annual physical and been retired. But he'd landed on his feet, something Yuri always did well, with a job in the cultural-exchange program, where he specialized in matters connected with the film and publishing industries. This evening, as engagingly flamboyant as ever, he was escorting two ladies he introduced as aspiring actresses, though to Glukhov's skeptical eye they looked slightly tarty. Glukhov he introduced as one of Mother Russia's brightest young diplomats, certain to be foreign minister before the decade was over.

As Glukhov made modest noises of disavowal, one of the ladies staked a claim to his arm and Yuri insisted they all have dinner at the Aragvi, because he was in the mood for chicken *tabaka*, a noble bottle of Kinzmarauli, and other Georgian ambience. And reservations wouldn't present a problem; Yuri had a connection. Yuri always had a connection.

They sailed out to Karl Marx Prospekt and walked, arms

linked, to Gorky Street and the Aragvi, where Yuri, as promised, quickly solved the reservations problem while at least fifty people continued to wait for tables. It turned into a splendidly festive evening destined to end amorously, although when Glukhov at some point confided to Yuri he'd soon be going to London, Yuri became thoughtful and suggested they meet privately the next night. He'd an idea he wanted to discuss.

They discussed it over fine export vodka in Yuri's small apartment on Piatnitskaya Street. There was a *samizdat* author who'd written a hilarious novel about Kremlin backroom politics during the last years of the Khrushchev regime. There was an Italian publisher who was anxious to publish it. It was simply a matter of getting the manuscript into his hands. What would Glukhov think about taking it to London and mailing it to him anonymously? There'd be a handsome commission for his services, paid before he left Moscow.

Glukhov resisted. Bringing in perfume or hair dryers was one thing. Taking out manuscripts was something else. Yuri was sympathetic. He poured vodka. He reminisced about a night of small-hours conviviality in Bonn, when Glukhov had boasted about bringing in lingerie, dishwashers, and microwave ovens for KGB generals. It was a night Glukhov remembered. The air between them had been filled with brandy fumes and braggadocio, and Glukhov had unfortunately promoted the KGB majors for whom he'd run shopping errands in Paris and Stockholm to generals and added dishwashers and microwave ovens to their shopping lists.

Yuri wanted to know what had happened to the Ivan Glukhov of the good old days. The manuscript was not only hilarious, it was a minor classic. It deserved to be published, and it would be. It was just a pity the handsome commission would now go to someone less worthy than Glukhov. But more than anything, Yuri regretted that the

Ivan Glukhov he'd always admired for his dash and spirit no longer seemed to exist.

When Glukhov reported to London, he took along the manuscript and handsome commission, and over the next two years performed other remunerative chores for Yuri, who seemed to have an endless list of authors and film personalities who wanted something quietly taken out or brought in and would pay generously. Their commissions he deposited in the secret Swiss bank account, conveniently under his sole control, of Gottfried Forst, importer, and then wasted hours developing unworkable schemes for buying a Volvo without arousing suspicion. Or suspicion's handmaiden . . . envy.

In the other secret part of his life, Glukhov studiously developed his understanding of Chessplayer's psychology and, as occasion required, deposited in dead-letter boxes friendly notes that encouraged him, cajoled him, or expertly fielded complaints about bureaucratic ineptitude in the Center. Yet much as he enjoyed the pace and style of London, Glukhov couldn't say he really found his life satisfying. In moments of extreme Slavic melancholy, he reflected on one of the many inspiring observations on life Colonel Demichev had shared over the years of their close association. "What every Slav needs in order to be truly happy, Glukhov," Demichev had said with a profound Slavic sigh, "is a truly tragic love affair."

In 1973 Chessplayer abruptly returned to the United States, so abruptly the news came to Glukhov not through Chessplayer but through Colonel, now General, Demichev, as clearly shaken by the inexplicable turn of events as Glukhov.

In time Chessplayer was apparently able to advise Demichev through a special channel of the cause of his abrupt departure. He'd been assigned to transmit a million-dollar payment U.S. Intelligence annually gave King Hussein for granting it extra latitude in its operations in Jordan. The payment was customarily made in diamonds, since they were easily moved from country to country and didn't require laundering. Chessplayer flew from London to Amsterdam to pick up the cut, polished stones and, after their carats had been noted, signed a receipt. Carrying the diamonds in a chamois pouch taped to his thigh, he flew to Cairo to complete the transfer to Hussein's royal bagman, who left for Amman that same evening with the booty.

Barely back in London, Chessplayer learned he was in serious trouble. The carats for which he'd receipted in Amsterdam had been found short in Amman; about three hundred thousand dollars' worth of diamonds were missing. Hussein, professing total confidence in the rectitude of his bagman, was in effect accusing U.S. Intelligence of trying to chivy him. *Face* was even more important in the Middle East than *baksheesh*. To be shortchanged in a transaction involving both was the ultimate indignity; Hussein wanted a head, other than his bagman's on a platter.

In London Chessplayer protested his innocence. He had believers and he had disbelievers. In the alarmed confusion reaching all the way to Washington, he was summarily recalled for more intensive interrogation about the missing diamonds. A blue-ribbon commission offered him the choice of submitting to a formal investigation of his entire intelligence career or else resigning with the Scotch verdict of Not Proven. Chessplayer, afraid such an investigation might develop leads to his KGB connections and also believing such leads might already be in the hands of his overly polite inquisitors, chose the Scotch verdict. He resigned and established in New York City a company to investigate industrial espionage.

Glukhov, listening to General Demichev's detached account of this impetuous unilateral abdication of duties by an irreplaceable agent, had to marvel that his mentor accepted the situation with such stoicism. If nothing else, it demonstrated his general was a man not wanting in compassion. Since 1963 Chessplayer had been engaged in the most dangerous game in espionage, but there are limits to the stresses any man can endure in the secret world. Though Demichev had invested heavily in Chessplayer, he was wise enough to recognize men aren't machines and decent enough not to threaten Chessplayer with exposure merely because he'd reached the limit of his endurance. In the last analysis, the KGB did look after its own.

Chessplayer, Demichev continued philosophically, simply needed time for his nerves to heal. In due course he'd again be providing valuable information, gathered not only from his new friends in upper echelons of U.S. industry, but also from his old friends in the intelligence community.

"Then it's your opinion, Comrade General," Glukhov said, "that Chessplayer's still viable?"

Demichev delightedly slapped the desk. "Glukhov, you're everything I promised myself you were. This mastery of idiom. I've never forgotten the day you coined the expression *hot property* to describe Chessplayer. And now *viable*. Without doubt, you're the man best qualified to be sent to New York when Chessplayer's again"—he paused bemusedly—"viable."

"And in the meantime, Comrade General?"

"In the meantime, Glukhov, patience. Ripe grapes are best."

Glukhov never understood how he survived the next fifteen months in the Center's Library for Foreign Publications, where he spent much of his time dispiritedly translating three weekly U.S. tabloids called the *National Enquirer*, the *Star*, and the *Globe*, simply because a renowned academician admired within higher echelons of the KGB for innovative approaches to applied psychology had written a classified paper postulating that this somewhat incestuous triumvirate of periodicals best mirrored the reality of the American psyche. Each of the tabloids, Glukhov discovered, sold millions of copies at supermarkets and seemed to thrive on an endlessly recycled mélange of UFO landings, acupuncture cures for cancer, dietless diets that took off ten pounds a week, confessions by former movie actresses of love affairs with an eccentric billionaire named Howard Hughes, scientific proof of reincarnation, breezy reports on unhappy love affairs of TV celebrities, and predictions by famous psychics of earthquakes, stock-market crashes, political assassinations, and the winner of next year's Kentucky Derby. If the renowned academician's theory was even half correct, the gullibility quotient of the U.S. public must exceed that of the nomads of the northern Siberian tundra, who still believed women became pregnant by drinking reindeer milk spiced with powdered horns from the stag.

It wasn't only the dullness of his work that tried Glukhov so sorely, it was also the loss of a style of living he'd come to consider normal during his salad years in the West. In Moscow he no longer received a foreign-duty allowance, nor was he able to execute Yuri Subotin's lucrative assignments. He hadn't realized the extent to which he'd come to depend on that extra money, and the readjustment was painful. It was almost as if all the years with Chessplayer had been a waste. Not for the Center, of course, which had garnered a bountiful harvest from the soil tilled by this remarkable agent. But a waste for Ivan Glukhov, bit player in the Center's mysterious grand designs.

Then a knock on his apartment door one evening during this season of his deepest discontent brought Yuri Subotin back into his life. Yuri, wearing a suede jacket over a turtleneck sweater, skintight blue jeans, and hand-tooled cowboy boots, brandished a bottle of export vodka and presented a Beatles album still in its store wrapper before he'd even crossed the threshold. From a pocket of his jacket he produced a jar of Caspian Beluga, which had cost him his old Timex with the broken minute hand. The album, he said, was a gift for the sake of auld lang syne; he'd acquired it earlier today in return for a small favor, simply a pair of tickets to the Bolshoi, and he'd thought immediately of Glukhov, the Beatles' former Number One fan in Bonn.

Glukhov laughed. The same old irrepressible Yuri, the man with a thousand irons in the fire, always living *po blatu*, and a tonic better than any doctor could prescribe. When the caviar was gone and the bottle half finished, Yuri began describing the once-in-a-lifetime opportunity he'd stumbled on last week in Leningrad. There were two nearly priceless seventeenth-century Stroganov icons available from an absolutely trustworthy source, but it would take thousands of rubles to cement the deal. On the other hand there was a French museum curator, here on a cultural-exchange program, who without blinking would come up with three times the seller's price and take on the headache of smuggling them out of the country. Yuri himself was temporarily a little strapped—he'd invested heavily in a Fabergé enamel-and-gold Easter egg with a miniature of the Gatchina palace inside, the one presented to the czarina by Alexander on the second Easter after his coronation. Glukhov, however, must surely have most of the money he'd put aside during those palmy days in London. Was it still in that Swiss bank?

Glukhov, pleasantly numbed by the vodka, tried to remember when he'd told Yuri about the Swiss bank. And though feeling pleasantly omnipotent, he knew it would be slightly less dangerous to cut his throat than to enter the stolen-icon business. Trafficking in blue jeans and Beatles albums with the *farshirovshchiki* was one thing, but trafficking in icons, those sacred relics from the storehouse of Russia's heritage, was almost on a par with trafficking in state secrets.

Yuri waved his protests aside. For Glukhov it'd be risk-free; he'd merely be the banker and the funds would be untraceable. Yuri and the seller and the curator would be taking the risks.

Glukhov countered that, because of currency restrictions, he'd no way, at least from Moscow, of getting at his Swiss bank account.

Yuri nodded resignedly and poured more vodka. He dumped the rest of the bottle on a helpless cockroach working its way along a crack in the flooring toward the toilet closet. Glukhov reprimanded him. Yuri apologized profusely. It was just that his mind was on other things. Never before had he done such a thing to a helpless cockroach. Suddenly he clapped his hands. He had the solution! It'd cost them a slice of pie, but what deal was ever put together without *vzyatka*? He knew an Italian filmmaker from Cinecittà, a sleezy little pansy actually, yet reliable when the money was right, here on another cultural exchange, who could stop in Switzerland on the way to Rome and arrange a withdrawal of the necessary funds from Glukhov's account. All Glukhov needed to do was supply written authorization.

Glukhov the pragmatist sighed. For better or worse, he was in the icon business.

The first transaction in icons led to a second and a third, and as Yuri had promised, everything went like clockwork. Still, it was madness to get further entangled in this dangerous sideline. Glukhov was therefore doubly relieved when, in May of 1974, General Demichev finally gave him the promised New York assignment.

Chessplayer, the general told him over a multicourse lunch at the KGB Club, had been reactivated. He'd not of course returned to government service, but he was willing to supply industrial secrets on a limited basis. More important, a young U.S. soldier with whom he'd had an extremely special relationship in Germany—Demichev gave Glukhov a man-to-man wink—but who was having financial and personal difficulties, had recently been assigned to guard duty at an intelligence facility in Washington. It was better that Glukhov not know the names of the soldier and the facility, but Demichev could tell him, again in utmost confidence, the soldier was willing, for substantial payments, to make available some of the classified information to which he might occasionally obtain access.

Glukhov would go to New York as an economic expert attached to the Soviet U.N. Mission and be responsible, among other things, for getting the payments to Chessplayer, who would get them to the soldier, since the soldier was at this stage unwilling to deal with Soviet personnel directly, on the not unreasonable ground, Demichev added tolerantly, such exposure would increase his own risk. Later, when the soldier gained confidence and learned that selling state secrets was generally as easy as selling a used car, Chessplayer would introduce him to an intermediary. Russian, of course, but posing as American for the fine young soldier's continued peace of mind. Thereafter the intermediary would handle most of the contacts, and though his introduction to the skittish soldier couldn't be pushed unduly, the sooner it took place the better, because Demichev didn't want Chessplayer to be at risk one moment longer than necessary. And neither would an intelligent fellow like Ivan Glukhov—Demichev winked again—since he'd have the high honor of being solely accountable for Chessplayer's safety.

"And the intermediary, Comrade General? He's presently in the United States?"

"And has been the past eight years. He operates a secondhand bookstore in Greenwich Village. His code name is Edgar."

"Ah," Glukhov said, "an illegal."

Demichev gave him a pleased, fatherly look. "Your characteristic perceptiveness, Glukhov, hasn't been dimmed by the months of regrettable exile in the Library for Foreign Publications. Perhaps, since the two of you will soon be silent partners in this operation, you'd like to know his background?"

Glukhov lit the fine, fat Cuban cigar his host had been good enough to offer. "A pleasure, Comrade General."

Demichev pushed away his dessert plate and called for a liter bottle of Courvoisier. Edgar, he said, had been born in the United States to Russian parents and lived there until he was fourteen, when the family went back to Leningrad to visit relatives in late summer of 1939. Trapped there by the outbreak of war in Europe, later caught up in the Great Patriotic War, they'd never returned.

The parents died during the terrible winter of the Leningrad siege, when starving cats and dogs were slaughtered by the millions in futile efforts to save a starving population, but the boy survived and at war's end was fighting with the Red Army. He was even decorated for valor. Given his background and war record, the MGB naturally had its eyes on him early. After extensive testing of his political reliability over a period of years, and after the MGB had gone out of business in 1954 and the KGB had gone into business, the necessary long years of training Edgar for service as an illegal in the U.S. began.

Demichev waved a hand. He didn't want to bore Glukhov with details of the training, and anyhow Glukhov would be generally familiar from survey courses during his own training with the procedures followed for preparing an illegal. Massive daily doses of contemporary U.S. politics, life-styles, regional differences, movies, TV shows, slang, food habits, breast and automobile fetishes, et cetera. Advanced instruction in photography, microdot technology, cryptography, invisible inks, clandestine radio, and allied specialties. Then a trial run, in which Edgar spent a year in Western Europe as an ostensible U.S. tourist to test his ability to carry the role. And a second trial run, in which Edgar was turned loose in Moscow as an ostensible U.S. professor researching Alexander the Second's Edict of

Emancipation and given the mission of spying on military installations without detection.

Demichev sighed. It was a pity the ridiculous rules imposed by the security people would keep Glukhov and Edgar from ever meeting face to face, because Edgar was a charming, cultivated man. Demichev also knew, and he wasn't going to accept denials, there was a secret and talented intellectual hiding behind the clown's face Ivan Glukhov sometimes put on for the world. He only wished two such kindred spirits could become the friends they deserved to be.

But it was as futile to protest this kind of injustice as it was to protest the hour the sun rose. The important thing was, Glukhov would now know his new associate was a brilliant, experienced, dedicated agent, and every bit the equal of the legendary Colonel Abel. It was always dangerous to offer one's personal opinions as historical truths, but Demichev was willing to take the gamble: men like Edgar and Abel didn't make mistakes. Abel was eventually caught by the FBI only because his assistant, a frightened alcoholic opportunist named Reino Hayhanen, had run like a headless chicken into the arms of U.S. Intelligence in Paris while en route to Russia for harmless discussion about some of his imprudent personal activities in the United States. But Glukhov wasn't a Reino Hayhanen, and who knew what miracles two such exceptional men as he and Edgar would achieve together?

Just then Glukhov heard the bomb explode. *"Comrade General!"* he cried, and buried his head and arms against the table for protection from the blast.

The acrid smell of sulfur was overpowering. Glukhov, discovering he was still alive, summoned courage to lift his head from the table. As he looked around, he felt ashamed, embarrassed, and wretchedly foolish.

The water in the egg pan on the kitchen stove of his New

York apartment had boiled away. The egg had exploded, splattering the grimy ceiling with whitish-yellow debris. With his fingers, Glukhov combed eggshell fragments from his hair. He grimmaced, offended not so much by the stench as by his inexcusably ludicrous behavior. And to have sat daydreaming like some moony schoolgirl recreating the scenes of her first romance, when his house of cards was collapsing on every side, was almost a crime. A crime called suicide.

He wet a mop and took vengeful swipes at the filthy ceiling. Swearing under his breath, he put a slice of bread in the toaster. He bit savagely into the pulpy sweetness of the remaining orange half—when had he eaten the first half?— and tried to collect his thoughts.

Late yesterday evening, Moscow time, the Center would have received his message that Edgar was missing, and the shock waves must be rattling Lenin in his tomb. Men like Edgar—how could he ever forget General Demichev's lecture on historical truths?—didn't make mistakes. But somebody had, and the unpleasant notion making a knot the size of a fist in Glukhov's stomach was whether some careless action of his own had led to Edgar's secret arrest by the FBI. Yet whether it had or not, General Demichev might assume it had, and that was only part of the problem. He might also assume Ivan Glukhov had assisted the FBI. Glukhov swallowed hard.

The toast popped up. He spread it liberally with margarine and grape jelly, then washed it down with a cloudy mixture of hot tap water and instant coffee. He turned on the little radio by the sink and listened apprehensively to the morning news. Of course, even if the FBI had arrested a Soviet illegal, it wouldn't be on the news until it suited the FBI's convenience.

Trouble was endless. If Edgar had been arrested, then Chessplayer himself might be in immediate danger. Not because Edgar would talk—men like Edgar and Abel never talked—but because the mistake that had led to Edgar, whatever it was, might also lead to the soldier who was Chessplayer's homosexual friend, and the soldier was the weak link, Demichev had made that clear enough. The soldier would talk and keep on talking until his interrogators in desperation finally cut out his tongue to make him stop. Glukhov wiped his forehead. Chessplayer in danger was Ivan Glukhov in worse danger, because only Ivan Glukhov, bumbling guardian angel, had to answer to General Guardian of Guardian Angels Igor Demichev.

Then Glukhov had the most unnerving thought of all: Chessplayer himself might now be missing.

11

BELKNAP WAS ON HANDS AND KNEES trying to discover how the shredder worked when Malkin appeared in the doorway, immaculate in a rust-colored jacket, white silk shirt, regimental tie, and light gray flannels. Peeking from below the flannels was a pair of tasseled Gucci loafers. Maybe he was on his charitable way to a charity lawn party to referee a charity croquet tournament.

"You have to plug it in first, David. Then it works beautifully." He inspected the wall map of Washington. "Hotel room satisfactory?"

"Fine."

"You look far better than yesterday morning. You must've slept well. I always find my first night in a strange town difficult." He settled in one of the chairs on the far side of the desk. "David, I know you and rules invariably have an adversary relationship. It's part of your charm. But there's one rule around here that has to be obeyed. When your Bellboy transmits a signal, you must check in with ComOpsCenter."

ComOpsCenter. It was another of those quaint jargon phrases stolen from the Navy or possibly picked up at a rummage sale of old CIA slang. And Belknap could guess that at night the Communications Operations Center consisted of a bored functionary more or less monitoring the switchboard while his transistor was tuned to a talk show.

"ComOpsCenter sent you several signals yesterday evening. None were answered."

"Must've turned my Bellboy off accidentally."

Malkin smiled, and an eyebrow flew up, like a bird flushed from cover. "They've improved everything, David. Shredders, scramblers, even Bellboys . . . the sending unit gets a positive indication if the signal's been received. ComOps got a positive after the first signal."

"That's fascinating. The things they do with electronics. The hotel maid must've tinkered with mine while I was showering. I noticed the bed was turned down when I came out of the bathroom."

Malkin nodded tolerantly, as he would if a panhandler claimed ownership of the Brooklyn Bridge and offered it as collateral on a short-term loan of a fiver. Malkin enjoyed watching people lie poorly. "It isn't that I've turned old-maidish in my dotage, David. But the volatile situation we already face because of the theft of the Beowulf papers could become more so any moment . . . depending particularly on what country obtained them and its motive in returning them. Two of those Bellboy calls were from me and were urgent."

"Sorry."

"Hathaway was also trying to reach you. He had to settle for me. Your Hungarian, Hustvar, was located in San Diego quite easily. He was parked in the county jail, had been parked there the past three weeks."

"And the woman in Cleveland? Myrtle Bessmeyer."

"Left her last known address there over a year ago."

"Can we trace her through Social Security? If she's working, there's be FICA deductions."

Malkin rubbed the bridge of his nose. "Cumbersome, and basically unsatisfactory. The master computer at Baltimore Social Security isn't programmed with current addresses for the millions of account numbers. Baltimore would have to work back to regional offices. Takes forever, and by then your information's out of date anyhow. Hathaway's going to try to trace her through a relative. Father's dead, mother's whereabouts unknown, but there's an uncle who travels with carnivals, which of course isn't too encouraging either."

"What's McElroy like?"

Malkin frowned. "Which McElroy do you mean?"

"My liaison with Metropolitan Police."

"He's a cagey old Scotsman on the chief's staff. Excels at protecting his rear, and more importantly, the chief's. Bit of a politician too—a man has to be in that job. He's the poor fellow congressmen call when they get caught in awkward circumstances in YMCA lavatories. You'll like his burr, though. It'll make you think of the Highlands and heather."

Belknap pushed the phone button controlling his direct line to McElroy. They were interested, he told McElroy, in a woman named Myrtle Bessmeyer, age thirty. He read off her aliases.

"She's been arrested for shoplifting in department stores, but the rap sheet doesn't show Washington. Still, there's an outside chance she was picked up here and not charged. What I'd like is a canvass of the heads of security of department stores in the District to see if she's in anyone's files."

"Would you be wanting this information yesterday, Mr. Belknap?"

Belknap laughed. He was going to like McElroy. "Would you be able to get suburban police departments to make similar inquiries?"

"Oh, they're friendly lads. Long as you don't stroke them against the fur."

"Captain McElroy, two more things. The FBI should be delivering photographs of Bessmeyer to your office about now. Could you get them to the precincts and suburban police by special messengers?"

"They'll be delivered an hour after we get them. What else is it, then?"

"There's a chance she was involved in the mailing of a package wrapped in paper cut from Safeway shopping bags. There's a chance she lives near the Ellis post office. And if she's in Washington at all, there's a chance she's a waitress. Could you assign detectives to work Safeways in that area to see whether the checkers can remember anyone resembling her? And another team to work restaurants, diners, fast-food outlets, and bars. Plus somebody to interview counter clerks at Ellis. Maybe she's been there to mail certified letters, whatever."

"Ah, that asks for a lot of manpower, Mr. Belknap. We'll do our best. How large is the area you want us to cover, then?"

Belknap swiveled in his chair and looked at the black lines he'd drawn to enclose the area around Ellis. He read off street coordinates and, after hanging up, said to Malkin, "I see what you mean about Highlands and heather."

"He left when he was twelve, I'm told. He must have worked hard to retain the burr all these years."

Belknap opened his safe. No little mice had come visiting. "Those two urgent calls . . . were they about Bessmeyer or something else?"

Malkin brought out a Montecristo and lingered over the ritual of preparing it with a gold cutter. "The vault guard assigned to the NSC reading room last night never showed up."

Belknap's jaw dropped. "You've located him since?"

"No, he's disappeared. It's one of the reasons I wanted to reach you. When I couldn't, I put Tiffany on it. He had two of his men go into the guard's apartment. He'd left in a hurry. Clothes still on hangers. Opened can of tomato juice on the kitchen counter."

"Anything incriminating?"

"In a laundry hamper. A Hallicrafter shortwave receiver."

"You'd a search warrant?"

Malkin was astonished. "Really, David! Of course not."

"When you find him and it gets into court, you may have a lost case. The poisoned fruit of the poisonous tree."

"Court? How would it get into court?" Malkin struck a

match and carefully cured the cigar's tip. "Besides, he probably cleared Mexico City yesterday, on his way to Russia via Cuba. Oddly enough, he's a friend of yours from Germany. That's the other reason I wanted to get in touch. I thought you ought to be the first to hear."

Belknap steadied himself. "Germany?"

Malkin nodded benignly. "Frank Willis. Your MP friend at Oberürsel."

Belknap gazed out the window. Frank Willis must have arrived at Oberürsel about a month after the Fehler operation had gone sour. He was a nineteen-year-old MP assigned to guard duty in the defector debriefing area. He was polite, eager to succeed in the Army, and not very bright. Starting back to Bonn one afternoon, Belknap had seen Willis standing outside the main gate trying to hitch a ride and offered him a lift. Willis had a three-day leave, and Bonn was his destination. He was a compulsive talker, and Belknap heard a great deal more than he cared to hear about growing up in West Virginia as an orphan under the care of a maiden aunt who put away a pint of moonshine a day and refused to believe the South had lost the war.

Willis didn't know exactly what Belknap did when he visited Oberürsel, but was bright enough to realize the visits had some connection with Intelligence. He asked if you had to be a college graduate to get into the work Mr. Belknap was doing. Belknap laughed, somewhat charmed by this rare encounter with an innocent abroad. He let Willis out of his car at a public phone booth in Bonn. One of Willis's buddies had given him the home number of a German girl. Willis spoke no German and the girl evidently spoke little English, but Willis marched to the phone booth as if the Marines had landed.

If life were predictable, that should've been the end of his relationship with young Willis. But the next time he was at Oberürsel, Willis found an opportunity to take him aside. In

Bonn on his three-day leave, he confided, his whole life had changed. He and Ingrid had fallen in love. Belknap, wanting to escape the clutch of this apprentice Ancient Mariner, muttered a congratulatory banality and tried to move off. Willis detained him, his manner suddenly conspiratorial. On their last evening, he said, they had gone to a beer cellar where they ran into her cousin's fiancé. Toward the end of the evening when Ingrid had gone to the lavatory, the fiancé offered to sell Willis some drugs. Willis made clear to Belknap he wasn't interested in drugs, but he decided to lead the German on. The German quoted prices, then added mysteriously that information could also purchase drugs.

Willis was convinced, he earnestly told Belknap, the German was after military secrets and probably a spy. What did Mr. Belknap think?

Belknap was torn between amusement and irritation. He'd underrated Willis. Willis wasn't bright, but at nineteen he was quite apparently an operator. Belknap supposed the incomparable Ingrid probably did exist, but the cousin's fiancé had to be a figment of Willis's fertile imagination. For if the cousin's fiancé did exist, Willis knew enough about Army procedures to know he should have gone to his superior officer or else Army CIC. The fact he'd instead come to Belknap suggested an elaborate ploy to get into whatever work it was he thought Mr. Belknap did.

Belknap made a noncommittal reply and put the incident out of his mind until, a week or so later, he was playing chess with Malkin. Their occasional games were bloody, no quarter asked or given, but conversation was permitted. In anecdotal vein, he told the story of young Willis and should have anticipated what would happen. Malkin, with his passion for deception games, insisted that Belknap instruct Willis to learn what the cousin's fiancé, whose existence Malkin accepted as an article of faith, was actually after. Mellowed by the good bourbon the loser from their last session was always obligated to supply the next time they played, he delivered a homily on contemporary espionage.

The Russians and their Eastern bloc friends, he said, were clever. He'd never deny that. But sometimes they were damnably sloppy about recruitments, and it was entirely believable to him that one of their hired hands could have made exactly the kind of stupid, head-on approach that'd been made to Willis. So it was worth looking into. If drugs were the only thing the fiancé was dealing in, Belknap would simply cut loose from Willis. But if drugs were the cover for an effort to penetrate Oberürsel, Belknap and Willis could play the fiancé like a yo-yo, feeding him doctored information until the next Ice Age.

Malkin was right about one thing. The fiancé did exist. But the information he wanted, it developed over weeks of comic-opera negotiations, wasn't military secrets. He wanted to know whom to bribe at Army installations in the Frankfurt-Bonn area so his financée's father, a freedom-loving, anti-Communist beer distributor, could be privately informed of the bids unscrupulous competitors were making when existing contracts to supply NCO clubs with local product came up for renewal.

Absurd as the negotiations were, Willis carried them off with considerable panache, and Belknap began to think he had possibilities. The trouble was, working with Willis was like working with an overgrown puppy that, though full of affection, was as foolishly apt to try to tree a bear as a cat. Belknap tried to teach him to leave the bears to the bear hunters, but liked him enough in the end to write an extravagant letter of recommendation for the Advanced MP Training School near Wiesbaden.

"Willis was never actually a friend of mine, George. You know that. More an innocent I was trying to steer in the right direction."

"Poetic license on my part, then. But he did rather look

up to you. I still remember the worshipping way his eyes followed you the time you introduced us. Ever hear from him after Germany?"

"Never." Belknap stared hard at Malkin. "Yesterday you told me the balloon was up, and the world on fire. We talked about potential Beowulf suspects. VIPs with vault access. Guards who might, under the right conditions, gain unauthorized access. Why didn't you tell me Willis was one of those guards?"

"A fair question with a simple answer. You were going to learn about Willis as soon as you saw the duty roster." Malkin looked at him with a smile behind his eyes. "A little earlier, a little later . . . same outcome in the end."

"Same outcome in the end? My Swahili's rusty, but the translation I get is, you thought even yesterday Willis was the hole in the dike."

Malkin examined the ashy tip of his Montecristo as though conducting a silent dialogue with a trusted spiritual adviser. "You oversimplify, David."

"The hell I do. It wasn't my reputed headhunter's instincts you were after when you brought me down from New York, it was my remote connection with a dumb West Virginia hillbilly. You thought I could break him better and quicker than anybody else."

Malkin's drawn-out sigh forgave the irrationality of all mankind since the beginning of time. "I know you're upset . . . I should've been more forthcoming. But I asked you to come because I really do need your superlative abilities."

"You didn't ask me to come. I was shanghaied."

Malkin sighed again. "Beowulf's so important, so important. Can we dispense, at least for now, with semantic quibbles? Willis is missing. Let's concentrate on that."

Belknap rummaged through a desk drawer for cigarettes he thought he'd left there yesterday. Inability to find them increased his frustration. "All right. What happened to Willis after Germany?"

"Thank you, David, for reasonableness. What happened was, Willis chose not to reenlist when his tour was over. It seems an eccentric aunt in West Virginia left him a comfortable inheritance. Wrapped in a gunnysack in a potato bin. He used it to buy into a fried-chicken franchise. He and his partners got into financial difficulties, but the partners were fleeter of foot. He was the only one forced to take bankruptcy. It apparently left him bitter and vulnerable—I'm speaking now from the wonderful pulpit of hindsight. The girl he'd married, not the Divine Ingrid of course, divorced him. Fuel to the flame, perhaps. Who knows? He reenlisted here in Washington about a year ago. Well, you know how the computers work. His background, clean record. He was eventually detached to NSC guard duty with the rank of sergeant."

"Did you ever run into him over there?"

"My, yes. He introduced himself. We talked about Germany, this and that."

Belknap shook his head. "Willis wasn't cut out to be a spy. Wasn't smart enough."

Malkin smiled indulgently. "I know. Like that sergeant in the Armed Forces Courier Center at Orly you mentioned yesterday. They said the same thing about him after his arrest. He and Willis had something else in common. They were both extremely suggestible. It'd just be a matter of knowing the right handle."

"But if he did turn his coat, what made him run at some unknown time in the last twenty-four hours?"

"Why does the gazelle flee the stalking tiger? Spoors and danger borne by the friendly wind. He must've been told Beowulf had been returned. NSC vault guards were going to have to answer a lot of questions. Even Willis would've realized that. Of course we need to bear in mind that the good Samaritan who told him had a powerful incentive to persuade him to run."

"Who was the good Samaritan?"

"If I knew that, David, I wouldn't be calling on you,

would I? For the moment, though, I'd put my money on the man who mailed the package from Ellis."

Belknap again swiveled in his chair to study the street map of Washington. "No, he's not your good Samaritan."

"Oh?"

"He's an innocent bystander. Maybe not so innocent, but still a bystander. The briefcase didn't belong to him. I suspected that yesterday. Today I'm sure. Vanessa recognized the claim stub on it as one used by the Library of Congress. If the man who mailed the package owned the briefcase, why would he let us have a stub that'd provide a starting point for picking up his trail? Why would he include a dopp kit containing his razor and toothbrush and some kind of pills? Same with the shirts and underwear. Besides, the half-assed medical report says the man who owned the razor was middle-aged. The man who mailed the package, the mail-truck driver says, wasn't."

"You've a lot of confidence in these tea leaves you're reading, David."

Belknap came around slowly in his chair. Malkin was making friendly sign-language overtures to a pigeon on the window ledge. "It can't see you," Belknap said. "Pigeons are farsighted."

"LaRue knew a lot about pigeons too," Malkin said absently. "He used to claim the pigeons in Lafayette Square were the transmigrated souls of our early political heroes. God had sentenced them, as a form of divine punishment, to never leaving Washington. All they could do in retaliation was defecate on government buildings. LaRue would leave bread crumbs for them on that ledge—he was a strong believer in lost causes—and in time became convinced he'd identified Aaron Burr and Daniel Webster. He used to have conversations with them. He was our in-house Dr. Dolittle. An interesting man, LaRue. Inclined at times to go off half-cocked, but interesting."

Reluctantly, he brought his attention back to Belknap.

"So since the man who mailed the package isn't the owner of the briefcase, what is he?"

"A link, nature unknown, to the owner. My long-shot guess is, the two weren't connected operationally. So if we find the man who mailed the package, we may have a witness able to tell us something about the man we're actually after . . . the man who probably picked up the stolen copy of Beowulf in the Library of Congress from Willis or a person unknown. I still have trouble with the idea of Willis as the thief; nevertheless, when he was on night duty, would the door to the reading-room vault be open or locked?"

"Normally it'd be locked. Unless someone had made special arrangements to work in the reading room after hours."

"Was Willis assigned to night duty through normal rotation on the roster, or had he requested the assignment?"

"Ah, you're thinking of Orly again. The sergeant who volunteered to work the unpopular shift for the extra perks. And easier access. Yes, that's an interesting speculation. We'll have to look into it."

"You've checked hospitals? The morgue? In case he was hit by a car, had a heart attack . . ."

"Tiffany's section would've done that routinely. Now everything's been turned over to the FBI's Washington field office. Tiffany's men discovered a key to what appears to be a safe-deposit box, but it'll be a devil of a job to locate the bank." Malkin stood up, beaming. "Vanessa, you're looking radiant. That's what her beauty sleep does for an attractive woman."

"I should meet you this early every day, George. Am I interrupting?"

"I was leaving," Malkin said with just the right touch of regret. "Please remember about the Bellboy, David."

* * *

"Not necessarily radiant," Belknap said, admiring the way her clinging yellow dress went with her hair, "but you do look as if you've had a good thumping, which is even better." He smiled at her. "Yesterday I didn't notice you had dimples."

"Yesterday you didn't notice a lot of things. What'd George have on his mind?"

"He knows I was at your apartment last night."

"Oh, come on."

"I'm an expert, world class, when it comes to reading between lines elliptically delivered by George Malkin. He knows. Probably because of that unmarked black van."

"Your incipient paranoia's beginning to bother me."

"It's not so incipient."

"What's it matter if he knows you were at my apartment?"

"It doesn't. What matters is, he wanted to deliver an oblique message that he knows. If the van had a parabolic mike or similar equipment, he also knows everything I told you about Fehler, and that makes me highly uncomfortable."

"What's so special about what you told me?"

"Use your imagination."

"David, please don't be that way." She touched his arm. "We've been lovers, let's try to be friends. Something's eating away at you. What is it?"

He drummed his fingers on the desktop. "I think I'm being set up."

"For what?"

"I don't know. But give me one good reason why I was plucked out of nowhere to be point man on Beowulf? I don't like the exposure I'm getting. I'm too old to want to be another of the Cold War's walking wounded."

"Tell Malkin you're getting out."

"I've thought about it. But once upon a time—did I unload this last night too?—I got the assignment of carrying some diamonds to Cairo. The annual bribe for King

Hussein. I delivered them to His Majesty's emissary, an Oxbridge clone in a *kaffiyeh* who insisted on tea and crumpets at four in the afternoon while we sat in his Hilton suite making the transfer. It developed later some diamonds were missing. Hussein raised holy hell, and I became the sacrificial lamb. I had to face a secret commission of inquiry in Washington. It was a glowing testimonial from Malkin that in part persuaded the commission to give me the option of resigning, with my record officially clean. I was an embarrassment, and this was the easiest way to bring Hussein back into the fold. The alternative, if I wanted to put on the gloves, was one of those really brutal inquests, where hanging judges would look under every rock on which I'd ever walked. I'd done dubious things, plenty of them; nobody shovels manure all day and comes home at night smelling like a rose. I bought the first option. Yesterday Malkin called in his marker."

"Maybe he owes you more than you owe him."

"Maybe. And maybe I don't like the way history seems to be repeating itself. This time maybe I'm going to put on the gloves." Belknap managed a deprecatory smile. "And he huffed and he puffed, he even blew the house down. Okay, enough! When's Sybil Pruett going to get me a new combination for this safe?"

"She refuses, David. Says nobody's ever had sole possession of a combination."

"That's cooperation I truly appreciate. Particularly when security's so ironclad there's already been a leak about the return of Beowulf. An NSC vault guard's missing."

"I know. I saw Tiffany in the hall." She hesitated. "I knew Willis slightly."

"Really? Did you go to the reading room often at night?"

"No, I met him when he was working days. Malkin would send me there for odds and ends. Willis was extraordinarily agreeable. And talkative, Lord. I heard his whole family history."

"That's the Willis I knew, too. In Germany. Late sixty-eight." He waited for her reaction. There wasn't one, which itself was surprising. "I'm getting the feeling it's a very small world. Maybe too small. Come in, Cal. You've the noble bearing of a man who's made sacrifices above and beyond the call of duty. Sorry I couldn't be reached last night. Switched off my Bellboy by mistake. You get any sleep at all?"

"Just enough to whet my appetite for more." Tiffany wasn't as jaunty as yesterday—loss of a good night's sleep could do that to a man, even a professorial type—and he'd more of a middle-aged paunch than Belknap remembered. The knot in his flared tie was loosely cinched an inch below his collar button, but the senatorial thatch of white hair was in mint condition. The bowl of the calabash floated in front of his chin like an extra appendage.

Shading his eyes against a dusty splash of sunbeams, he squinted dubiously at the street map of Washington behind Belknap. "Those are interesting squiggles, old boy. What do they tell us?"

"Not much, probably. They're intended to narrow the search for the man who mailed the package to the area around the Ellis post office."

"Then you need a new entry. Willis's apartment is in that same neck of the woods."

Belknap, taken by surprise, knew he had to ask Tiffany for the address, which he then marked on the map.

"You'll be interested in this." Tiffany handed across a Xeroxed sheet. "It's the take-off from the reading-room's vault log of Beowulf access you asked for yesterday. Covers last Friday through this Tuesday. By date and time of day."

Belknap scanned the sheet and looked at Tiffany questioningly. "Two entries, and the same person each time."

"Precisely."

Belknap examined the entries again. An Allen Lundhoven had checked Beowulf out of the NSC vault at four-fifty Friday afternoon, returning it at five-twenty. And Saturday morning he'd checked it out at eight-ten, returning it at eight-forty. It fit so neatly the theory of surreptitious access to Beowulf he'd laid out yesterday for Malkin that Belknap was suspicious. "What time did Willis come on duty in the evenings?"

"Six o'clock." Tiffany produced another paper from his shapeless jacket. "All the guard schedules are here."

"So Lundhoven would've been logged in and out on both days by a guard other than Willis?"

"Looks that way."

Belknap felt better. Willis was still a suspect, and there was nothing he could do for poor Willis about that, but at least there was now another candidate. He pulled Lundhoven's file from the stacked FBI summaries in his safe and started giving Tiffany and Vanessa the highlights. "Age forty-three . . . consultant for the Horizon Institute . . ."

"High-powered Washington think tank," Tiffany interjected. "The honchos over there don't speak to anyone in government lower than generals and undersecretaries."

"What do these honchos do? When they're not speaking to anyone lower than generals and undersecretaries?"

"They decide when the world will end, and the best way to do it. While they're waiting, they decide when we'll run out of oil, copper, manganese, platinum, potable water, breathable air, and maybe even TV commercials. And for hefty fees they collaborate with Pentagon brass on strategic planning papers, and the generals have to bow three times and salute twice before they're even allowed to read the first page. Since Lundhoven's on that damned exclusive Beowulf access list, he's probably one of its authors, with a continuing assignment to keep his contributions to it current. What's your summary say about his professional background?"

"It says he's got a Ph.D. in Economics, another in Petroleum Geology."

"Well, there you have it, old boy."

Belknap caught his breath. "Jesus, he was an exchange

student at Moscow State University—I somehow missed this yesterday—in academic sixty-two, sixty-three."

"Makes the cheese more binding," Tiffany said cheerfully.

"Did you ever meet him while you were there, David?"

He gave her an even look, searching again for nuances. "Not that I know of."

"Might be worth jockeying this chap a bit," Tiffany said.

"Might be," Belknap agreed. "How long would it take to put taps on Lundhoven's home and office phones?"

"Depends on who's available and who's ahead of us." Tiffany sucked on the calabash; Belknap heard coffee percolating in the bowl. "As hard to get hold of a good wireman these days as a good plumber. Maybe by tomorrow morning if we're lucky."

Belknap couldn't believe it. "Goddamn it, Cal, we're supposed to be rescuing the hotshot wise men over there"— he jabbed furiously in the direction of the White House— "from their own mind-boggling folly, and those conniving movers and shakers are so rotten scared about this genie they've let out of the bottle, they've temporarily given Malkin just about total authority over the whole fucking intelligence establishment. Yet you're telling me we have to stand in line for a wireman? Ain't gonna wash, Cal. Pass the word to whoever handles these jobs, he'd better get cracking in the next ten minutes or he'll be on the beach by noon."

Tiffany moved like a shot toward the door.

"Hold it!" Belknap said. "There's more. Can you double-team Lundhoven when he's in his car? Twenty-four-hour coverage."

"No problem there," Tiffany said instantly.

"All right, lay it on. I've the germ of an idea."

"Big oak trees from little acorns grow." Tiffany laughed modestly.

"This'll be just a sapling, but maybe worth the planting.

I'd like you to make a botched initial contact with Lundhoven."

"Oh, one of those. Bumbling investigator with phony I.D. interviews subject about, say, a deceased neighbor or business acquaintance. In course of interview, bumbling investigator is exposed as fraud and hurriedly splits."

"You've got it, Cal. Use a car with dead-end plates; it'll add to Lundhoven's problems. How soon can you get on it?"

"Right away," Tiffany said smartly. He cinched his tie. "I'll pop off. Much to do, and no time like the present to do it."

Belknap waited until Taffany was well down the hall. "All right, how'd you know I was in Moscow in sixty-two?"

She bristled. "That's supposed to be a secret, too?"

"It's not a secret, but I'd appreciate an answer. You seem to know one hell of a lot about my curriculum vitae."

"Malkin mentioned it, I believe."

"You believe?"

"God, you're impossible!"

"Not always," he said wearily. "Just sometimes." He moved to the window. The pigeon that had served as the prop for Malkin's little fable about LaRue looked up, fluttered its wings, and set off in search of Aaron Burr and Daniel Webster. It probably had a miniaturized parabolic mike implanted in its breastbone, too. Washington was that kind of town, and the Soviet Embassy on 16th Street wasn't far away.

12

ALLEN LUNDHOVEN, wearing faded Bermuda shorts and beach sandals, was pushing a rotary mower across his front lawn when the green Ford came down the Georgetown street and stopped in front of his house. The man with prematurely white hair who got out stared with considerable interest at Lundhoven's beard and ran his eyes over the auburn pelt that ran from his throat to his hips like seaweed on a deserted shore.

"Dr. Lundhoven?"

Lundhoven throttled down the rotary's motor. "What is it? Life insurance or storm windows?"

"I'm from the FBI. Special Agent Edwards." He produced an alligator wallet and showed credentials.

"I thought you fellows always traveled in twos. Like star-crossed lovers."

Edwards laughed dutifully. "Could I talk to you a minute, sir?"

Lundhoven used a T-shirt hanging from a scraggly poplar to wipe his face and armpits, then put it on. North of the navel it had a hole the size of a grapefruit. "Come inside. It's cooler."

There were a grand piano and xylophone in the living room. There were Indian blankets on the wall. There were wooden carvings and Mexican pottery. Tinkling mobiles dangled from the ceiling. A capuchin monkey sat on the arm of a rattan rocker. A skunk was sleeping on the center cushion of the couch. "Don't mind Bismarck," Lundhoven said, "he's been to Denmark and had the operation. I bought him to get even with Carlotta when she got the capuchin. What do you want, Edwards?''

"Your office said you were leaving for Chicago at noon, so I thought I'd stop by on the chance of catching you. Your neighbor across the street's being considered for a high federal appointment. I wondered if I could talk to you about him.''

Lundhoven chased the capuchin from the rocker and sat down. He got up quickly. "The little son of a bitch must've just taken a pee." He sat next to Bismarck and glanced at his watch impatiently. "Which neighbor?"

"Silas Kerwin."

Lundhoven digested the information perhaps five seconds. He took Bismarck onto his lap and stroked him absently. "There're a lot of misconceptions about skunks, Edwards. People think if you don't get behind them you can't get sprayed."

Edwards nodded, but was apparently having difficulty deciphering the message. He said cautiously, "Well, about Silas Kerwin . . ."

"Our conversation's off the record?"

"Totally."

Lundhoven dipped into a bowl of pretzels on the coffee table and pushed the bowl toward Edwards. "Silas is a dear friend. The fact he's a secret homosexual's never affected the relationship Carlotta and I have had with him. We've argued about politics, but I've never taken his tilt to the extreme left too seriously. I think he's well qualified for almost any federal appointment."

Edwards looked pained. "Dr. Lundhoven, I don't want you to misunderstand me. But you yourself are employed by an organization that handles top-secret government projects, and you know background checks are necessary. I'm wondering why you're giving such a facetious answer."

"Pancho! Pancho!" A woman had come into the room. She was lean and muscular, and her blue smock was liberally garnished with palette smears. "Where's Pancho, Light of My Life?"

"I took him back to his toilet-training books, Heavenly Flower, but if it happens once more, we're going to be dining on roast capuchin. Carlotta, this is Mr. Edwards from the FBI, he says, and he wants to know why I married you."

She laughed hoarsely. "Better Carlotta than to burn." She perched on a stool and crossed her legs. "What are you really here about, Mr. Edwards?"

"He wants to know about Silas," Lundhoven interjected. "Silas is in line for an important federal appointment. I told him Silas was a very decent homosexual with extreme leftist leanings."

Carlotta frowned. "That's unfair, Allen. He's not that far left. Lots of non-Communists subscribe to the *Daily Worker*."

"He voted Socialist Labor last election. He told me."

"Mrs. Lundhoven," Edwards said, his voice a study in careful neutrality, "are you conceding Silas Kerwin *is* a homosexual?"

A thunderous discordance came from the grand piano. The capuchin was running up and down the keyboard. Carlotta cocked her head. "Pancho's getting better, Light of My Life."

"The son of a bitch has no place to go except up. When's he booked for Kennedy Center?" He turned to Edwards. "On Palm Sunday Pancho plays the *Messiah*. He was raised in the Congo by Belgian nuns, so he's a tendency to go in for the heavy stuff. What was your last question?"

"I was asking your wife whether Silas Kerwin's a homosexual."

"That's right, you were." Lundhoven stood up. He was a big man and he was angry. "I don't know who the shit you are, but I'm going to find out. One thing's sure, you're not from the FBI. What'd you do, go through the city directory's street index and pick the name of somebody across from us so you could come in and snoop around? Silas Kerwin died five months ago. So who are you and what do you want?"

Edwards rose from his chair, his expression distressed, his manner placating. "There's evidently been a mistake. We get thousands of requests for background checks. I don't know when the one on Kerwin came in, apparently months ago. I'm sorry to hear he's dead and I won't trouble you further."

"It doesn't end that easily. I'm phoning the FBI's Washington field office."

Edwards moved leisurely toward the front door. "That's your privilege, Dr. Lundhoven."

"I'm taking your license number, too."

"That's also your privilege. I'm sorry we've had this misunderstanding."

Lundhoven tracked his visitor down the walk like a hunter with a shotgun about to go off. His wife was at the doorway when he returned.

"Do you think it was wise to challenge him like that? He could've been a robber, a psychopath. What if he'd started waving a knife?"

"He was no robber, no psychopath either, Heavenly Flower." He strode to the hall telephone, looked up the number for the Department of Motor Vehicles, and told the woman who answered he'd just been in an accident. A man in a green Ford was a possible witness, and he had its license number. He'd like the man's name and address. The woman told him he could mail in two dollars for a records check or bring the two dollars down in person.

Lundhoven hung up. "Fucking bureaucrats." He scribbled the memorized license number. "I'll take a taxi to Dulles. That way you've got the car. Toot down to Motor Vehicles and give them two bucks for this schmuck's name and address. Phone the FBI, too. But you won't get anywhere either place. I know the way the bastards work."

"What bastards, Dear Heart?"

"The counterintelligence gumshoes. There's been panic in the streets since yesterday. I'll call you soon as I get to Chicago."

13

IVAN GLUKHOV DIDN'T UNDERSTAND what was happening or, more exactly, what wasn't happening. There should have been an answer by now to the message he'd sent the Center yesterday about Edgar, but in the Referentura code room they kept insisting they had nothing for him.

What would General Demichev expect him to be doing pending the arrival of his instructions? The answer was obvious: use *initiative*. And *analyze*.

Glukhov analyzed.

Edgar was missing, but not necessarily because he'd been arrested. Illegals were as mortal as other men: they could get in accidents, be taken to hospitals, or drop dead in the middle of the street. There was, in fact, a standard procedure to follow when an illegal failed, as Edgar had, to make a *treff* an unreasonable number of times. How had he overlooked it? The illegal's case officer immediately arranged for the KGB recovery specialists to check discreetly the places he worked and lived, and, if results were negative, hospitals and the morgue.

All this was fine, but Glukhov wasn't Edgar's case officer, merely his associate in one operation put together by Chessplayer, and he didn't know whether Edgar was controlled by another KGB officer in New York or directly by the Center. Of Edgar's legend, Glukhov knew only that he operated a secondhand bookstore in the Village. Of his appearance, he knew only that he was about fifty. And since the other details of his legend had been withheld on sound security principles, Glukhov could really do nothing until the Center supplied them. When it did, there might be another problem. An illegal making a high-risk espionage contact was supposed to go to the *treff* without any identification on his person. Because no matter how legitimate the conventional I.D. he'd acquired in the course of embroidering the identity established by his legend, an identity often based on an actual person who had died in infancy but who would otherwise have been about the illegal's age, it couldn't always withstand the intensive investigations certain to occur if he were arrested as an espionage suspect. Which meant that if Edgar had followed proper procedures and was in a hospital or morgue, he was there without a name. How could even the recovery specialists find a person in circumstances like that?

Glukhov walked restively to the window of his third-floor Soviet Mission office and looked down on 67th Street. The tamale vendor on the opposite sidewalk was having a busy morning. A man nearby selling luminescent ties and matching handkerchiefs out of a cardboard box wasn't doing badly either. The cottage industries of New York's streets fascinated Glukhov. It was the kind of initiative that would also truly delight such a connoisseur of initiative as General Demichev.

What actions would Demichev expect him to take?

Suddenly inspired, he knew. Edgar's secondhand bookstore in the Village was probably a one-man operation. Elementary principles of security would make it inadvisable to have employees. So it was simply a matter of garnering from telephone yellow pages the addresses of secondhand bookstores in the Village. It should take only a few hours to give each a quick inspection, and if he found one that was closed, he could inquire at adjoining shops and learn the owner's home address. At the home address he'd acquire more information from helpful neighbors. Tilling the same rich soil as a recovery specialist, he would personally solve the mystery of Edgar's disappearance. And in the process become a Hero of the Soviet Union. Glukhov laughed hollowly.

Still, it was his only alternative, and anything was better than this endless pacing of the cage his office had become.

Outside the mission he dutifully looked east and west to identify potential surveillance. The tamale vendor across from him, as much a part of the neighborhood as the Queensboro Bridge, indifferently watched this inane exercise from beneath the red-and-white awning of his pedal-propelled cart. Since it was the conventional wisdom in the mission that the vendor was an undercover FBI agent, Glukhov gave him his usual affable wave. You could be enemies yet still be friends. It was part of the wonderful camaraderie of espionage.

While waiting for the crosstown bus, a routine first step in flushing surveillance from the duck blinds in the underbrush bordering 67th Street, Glukhov had his second inspiration. On his downtown trip by subway to Greenwich Village, which by regulations required a diversionary uptown trip to the Bronx, he'd use a pay phone in the Bronx to determine whether Chessplayer too was missing.

For a KGB officer, conducting business by telephone was complex. The Center assumed, perhaps even correctly, that all phone calls from the mission were monitored and that pay phones in the vicinity were tapped. Since the Center also assumed that the FBI conducted sporadic and possibly continuous surveillance of suspected KGB officers, KGB personnel in the mission wanting to make a business call were required to do so from a pay phone at least a mile away and, the call completed, to report the booth's location to the *rezident* so it could be placed on the "contaminated" list for six months. Of course, the manpower the FBI would need to carry out such blanket monitoring and surveillance boggled the imagination. At least it boggled Glukhov's, though he wasn't about to advertise the fact.

When he left the subway in the Bronx and had found a suitable pay phone, he nervously placed his call to Chessplayer's office on Madison Avenue. Although he intended to break the connection immediately if the receptionist at Belknap Associates said, in response to his question, that yes, Mr. Belknap was in his office, he knew he was violating General Demichev's long-standing directive against contact with Chessplayer at any time. On the other hand, General Demichev was thousands of miles from the scene of trouble, and what he didn't know couldn't hurt Ivan Glukhov, frightened pragmatist. And technically he wasn't contacting Chessplayer anyhow, he was only contacting his receptionist.

"Belknap Associates," a voice said.

Glukhov put his question.

Mr. Belknap wasn't in town, the receptionist replied. Then where could he be reached? She said she'd check. Two minutes went by. When she came back on the line, she said he was out of the city for an indefinite period and there was no way to reach him. But she could take a message. Glukhov, almost certain she'd been told to keep him on the line so the FBI could trace the call, abruptly hung up.

Shaken, he returned to the subway and boarded a downtown train. Out of the city? he thought. For an indefinite period? Exactly what the FBI could be expected to have the receptionist say if it had taken her employer away for interrogation.

So Chessplayer, like Edgar, was missing. Glukhov closed his eyes and rocked like a mourner to the remorseless metronome clacking of train wheels.

In Greenwich Village he used a taxi to check the secondhand bookstores on his list. None were closed. The search for Edgar was as much a dead end as the search for Chessplayer.

It was almost noon when he returned to the mission. Not

far from the tamale vendor under his red-and-white awning, a young lady, a member of Jehovah's Witnesses, was handing out leaflets. Ivan Glukhov, passing within kissing distance of her enticing outstretched arm, declined the opportunity to be saved. Glukhov wanted to be saved, but only—for the foreseeable future—from the wrath of General Igor Demichev.

14

GENERAL IGOR DEMICHEV, seated on the west side of the long conference table, gazed out the windows at the lovely woods surrounding the First Chief Directorate's sprawling new headquarters off the Ring Road outside Moscow. Almost noon in New York and Washington, and evening here, but in the northern latitudes in midsummer the sun had a long way to travel to reach the horizon. Demichev sighed. It was useless to quarrel with events. But Edgar wouldn't be missing and Chessplayer wouldn't be in danger if, months ago, a Politburo directive hadn't instructed the KGB to determine U.S. intentions in the event of another oil embargo in the Middle East, and if Demichev hadn't been instructed to enlist Chessplayer's aid in determining them.

An asset as irreplaceable as Chessplayer should be used sparingly, should ideally be held in reserve for use only in great international crises, but orders were orders, and Demichev, as jealous about sharing his irreplaceable asset as another man might be about sharing his woman, had offered his objections in vain.

Somebody at the table coughed discreetly. Demichev brought his attention back to the men in the room. Were it not for this meeting, he'd be attending a performance by a concert pianist at Tchaikovsk Conservatoire, but since the concert pianist was also his wife, there was at least something to be said for sitting here with enough troubles to outfit a winter army.

"This much we know," he said, resuming his presentation. "The backup team was properly on station outside the Library of Congress Tuesday morning, ready to provide emergency assistance if trouble developed. Trouble didn't develop, or so it seemed. Edgar entered a taxi. Presumably he told the driver to take him to the airport so he could make the rendezvous in New York. The backup, maintaining the prescribed distance, followed the taxi in its van. Suddenly the taxi made an insane hundred-and-eighty-degree turn into oncoming traffic. Traffic so heavy the van couldn't duplicate the maneuver."

"Evidently the driver of the taxi had spotted the back-up," the helpful expert from the Department of Hindsight interrupted. "The maneuver has the earmarks of a typical kidnapping operation by U.S. Intelligence."

"No, General Pechenko," Demichev said irritbly, "U.S. Intelligence wasn't involved. On this we have the assurance of Chessplayer, who because of the extraordinary circumstances utilized an emergency channel."

"Israelis then?" Across the table Pechenko's moist eyes were like peeled grapes.

"Out of the question. Edgar didn't fish in their waters."

"You've ruled out a defection by your Edgar?"

"Briefly, let me point out he's not *my* Edgar, any more than he's *your* Edgar. He's the *Center's* Edgar. As to defection, perhaps the psychiatric expert has something to say."

Professor Tudin, an unkempt septuagenarian rumored to have once cured the great but altogether fearsome Marshal Pushkov himself of bivouac enuresis, sipped thoughtfully from a glass of goat's milk. He had tangled, straw-colored hair, teeth about the same shade of yellow, and a tic below his one good eye. Demichev doubted that psychiatrists ever felt embarrassment, but if they did, a nervous tic must result in embarrassment of a high order.

"In my opinion, impossible. Entire Edgar psychiatric profile eliminates the hypothesis. The so-called Beowulf papers, plus all the curious items in Chessplayer's inventory of the briefcase, must have been returned without Edgar's cooperation. Exactly how is, for the moment, a mystery."

"Thank you, Professor," Demichev said. "With your kind permission, General Pechenko, I now continue with known facts. First, U.S authorities are conducting an unprecedented manhunt, not only for Edgar but also for the person who supplied him with Beowulf. It's both fortunate and unfortunate Chessplayer sits at the center of this storm, but candor compels me to add he's as close to exposure as he's ever been. This isn't to say we don't have a contingency plan to save him. We do. It's been under development for years, and with each passing year has become more operationally reliable.

"Second, the plan's been irreversibly set in motion. As a result, it was regrettably necessary to take out the young soldier mentioned before our break, since he was Chessplayer's link to Beowulf. However, if the Washington representatives of Department Eight of Directorate S have done their job properly"—Demichev bowed politely to Colonel Zalenin—"his body won't be found for weeks.

"Third, the backup team, though it lost the taxi after the insane turn into oncoming traffic, did obtain its license number. Steps will soon be taken to exploit this information in whatever manner considerations of security require."

Pechenko's jowls quivered with anticipation as he pounced on the prey almost in his grasp. "But why were steps not taken Tuesday when Edgar disappeared? Today, if I'm not mistaken, is Thursday."

"Because, my dear colleague, the information I'm so succinctly presenting was gathered over many many hours by many different people. It then had to be transmitted in a variety of time-consuming ways. And please remember, it wasn't until late yesterday, Moscow time, we even knew Beowulf had been returned and Edgar was missing."

"Yet if we are here," General Pechenko replied, snapping his fingers at an aide who instantly passed him a thick folder, "for the purpose of review and evaluation, as I was given to understand, then perhaps you could kindly tell us something about this remarkable contingency plan."

"Nothing would give me greater pleasure," Demichev lied enthusiastically. "But if you'd be so kind as to study more carefully the regulations, admittedly complex, in the folder supplied by your efficient assistant, I believe you'll find that my lips, whether I wish it or not, are sealed until certain additional events have occurred."

Pechenko snorted like an asthmatic horse. "So it's your position there's nothing to review and evaluate, and that this meeting, which required me to miss the wedding party for my only niece, is a farce?"

"Not at all. Certain matters I can elaborate on informally, and I welcome your valued guidance. Professor Tudin, could you perhaps share with General Pechenko your conclusions about Chessplayer's behavior in this affair? Has he conformed to your profile?"

"More than conformed." Professor Tudin hastily used a dying cigarette to light another. "In the psychic trauma created by the unexpected return of Beowulf, most men in his position would be incapable of action—the same response we observe clinically in soldiers exposed to a sustained artillery barrage. And some men would immediately assume the Center had betrayed them. It took the insight of genius to realize the papers had been returned for reasons beyond our control. It's all the more remarkable, given the crisis atmosphere we know existed in Washington, that he had the skill and the nerve to activate the plan. Of course, I regret the activation. I regret wet stuff under any conditions."

"So do I, Professor," Demichev said, moving his thick shoulders elegiacally. "Particularly when those required to die can claim a degree of innocence. You and I, we're not in the best of all possible professions. But then, this isn't the best of all possible worlds."

"It is not that I care for *mokrie dela* either," Colonel Zalenin, a self-effacing former Guards officer known for his compassionate nature, broke in. "But it is necessary to add that such deaths, when they must occur, are as painless as we can make them. In the case of the young soldier, our representative would have fired a crushed ampule of prussic acid from the nozzle of an apparatus sometimes carried by certain sanitary workers in the United States. The inhaled vapor contracts the blood vessels, and a gentle death follows almost immediately. Later the blood vessels relax, giving the impression of heart failure. So it is clean, and also safe, as long as one takes the special antidotes before and after the firing. Please excuse the interruption."

Demichev waved a hand graciously. Zalenin was such a conscientious fellow. "Professor Tudin, for the further benefit of General Pechenko, could you summarize your professional opinion of Captain Glukhov, upon whom so much now depends."

"Will not fail." Professor Tudin overcame a coughing spell with the aid of the goat's milk, "Ivan Glukhov is not only a buffoon, he's a corrupt buffoon. It is the ideal combination in matters of this nature. On this I can categorically stake my reputation."

"It is not just your *reputation* that's at stake, Professor," General Pechenko said pleasantly.

Demichev winced at such incivility. "How I wish that as colleagues and collaborators, we could dispense with veiled threats."

"Unveiled," Pechenko corrected pleasantly.

"What a curious business we are in," Demichev said as he groped for a suitable nonescalating reply. "Often I wonder about the road I traveled to arrive at this moment in my life. In my youth—this is probably boring to hear—my highest ambition was to be a student of Latin and Greek. Shakespeare, too, influenced me profoundly. I read *Hamlet* in English at the age of seventeen. 'This above all: to thine own self be true, And it must follow, as the night the day, Thou canst not then be false to any man.' Nikitin?"

His young aide came respectfully to attention. "Comrade General!"

Demichev fished through the papers on the table. "You'd better do something about this message of yesterday from Glukhov. Something to keep him harmlessly confused until we arrest him."

15

MALKIN, seated behind the Directoire table he used as a desk, was idly tracing designs on a folded copy of *The Wall Street Journal* with the tip of a jade paper cutter. He seemed on the point of dozing, for which Belknap couldn't fault him. Tiffany was staring with no discernible interest at a scroll-top grandfather clock, so aged its wood was nearly black. Belknap, hoping there'd be an opportunity to take Vanessa to a secluded nearby spot for lunch in order to pursue, in relaxed rather than confrontational style, the intent of her occasionally Delphic utterances since yesterday, tuned in and then out on Tony Armstrong's report of his staff's morning work.

Armstrong, a yellow pad balanced on his knees, was bravely trying to add sex appeal to a wrap-up leading nowhere. The manufacturer of the briefcase could cast no light on the city to which it'd been shipped. The unlabeled pills in the dopp kit, the lab reported, were for insomnia, but could be bought over the counter. Spies weren't the only people sentenced to sleepless nights. The stolen copy of Beowulf, other experts reported, had been reproduced on one of the new Japanese portables; they didn't know the brand name yet. Nor had checkroom attendants at the Library of Congress been able to provide descriptions of specific individuals who'd checked briefcases the first part of the week.

"There's one promising item, though. They compared serial numbers on claim stubs in use today with the one on our stub. By interpolating from their records of daily checkroom activity, they estimated our briefcase was checked between nine and twelve Tuesday morning."

"All right," Belknap said, "we know Lundhoven checked the NSC Beowulf out late Friday and again early Saturday. We know Willis worked the evening shift over there. So let's assume for the moment one of them ran off a Beowulf copy and on Tuesday between nine and twelve delivered it to a postman at the Library of Congress. Let's find out where each of them was during those hours. Lundhoven we can ask directly, then verify with whomever he claims as corroborating witnesses. For Willis you'll have to get a photo and see if checkroom attendants can identify him."

The phone rang, pulling Malkin back from his borderline siesta. "Hathaway," he announced a moment later. "They've found Willis."

He set the receiver in an amplifying cradle. Hathaway's voice boomed through the room. Malkin smiled apologetically and turned down the volume. They'd not only found Willis, it developed, they'd also fished him from the Potomac. Hathaway sounded as if he were reading a weather report. From the contusions around his waist, they speculated his body had been weighted with one or more diving belts that had somehow come off.

Belknap closed his eyes. Poor Willis, he thought, one more random victim on the hit list of history.

Cause of death not yet determined, Hathaway continued, but obviously not from drowning. No water in the lungs. Washington field office had already interviewed other tenants on Willis's floor. No one had seen him yesterday. One woman thought she'd seen a couple of men from a pest-exterminating company in the hall, but it could've been the day before.

"How'd she know they were from an exterminating company?" Belknap asked.

"They were wearing jumpsuits, coveralls, whatever,

with the company name across their backs. And one of them was carrying a cylindrical spraying tank. She doesn't remember the name of the company."

Belknap grimaced. "What floor of the building did Willis live on?"

"Second," Hathaway said.

"Getting a corpse to the street from a second-floor apartment ought to attract a little attention."

"Kitty Genovese didn't attract much attention," Hathaway said wearily, "while thirty-eight people were watching her get murdered. Anyhow, there might not've been a corpse at that point. Maybe someone Willis trusted set up a meeting elsewhere. It'll take a while to learn who his Washington friends were and what they might know about his movements yesterday. Out-of-town friends might also be able to help, but Chesapeake and Potomac's computer isn't set up for fast retrieval of very recent toll calls. We've asked them to track Willis's on a priority basis. He didn't withdraw money from his bank yesterday, and the safe-deposit key that happened to turn up here anonymously this morning—thanks so much for thinking of us—doesn't fit the bank's boxes. He had seventeen hundred in checking and no savings account. In his laundry hamper there was a Hallicrafter shortwave receiver, but I know you wouldn't know about that, because you'd no more go into his apartment without a warrant than you'd steal his safe-deposit key."

Malkin, with the aplomb of a petty thief nurtured from the cradle on the saving grace of small diversions, quickly asked if Hathaway knew the time of death.

"With what the river did to him, we may never know."

Malkin, after returning the telephone to its customary cradle, steepled his fingers in front of his chin. For one ludicrous awful moment, Belknap thought he was going to lead them in prayer.

"Theories?" he inquired benignly.

So it was to be a Socratic dialogue, but Tiffany, like

Barkis, was willin'. "Jolly well seems to me Willis could've been operating solo. Getting marching orders by shortwave, filching crown jewels from the vault, peddling them for hefty additions to a Swiss bank account. Of course this would rule out Lundhoven, a suspect I wouldn't be entirely happy ruling out. I'd like to see that smart-aleck double Ph.D. in trouble so deep they'd have to send down frogmen to find the bottom."

Belknap, in no laughing mood, almost laughed. Cal Tiffany might be human after all. Lundhoven must've put a very hot poker to him in that rinky-dink interview before Lundhoven left for Chicago.

"If Willis was operating solo," Armstrong said, "why would his bankers foreclose on the mortgage?" He waited an extra beat to give his answer a touch more luster. "They must have known he'd be able, once we bagged him, to cough up a name, and they didn't want him to have any extremis coughing spells."

"David, you must have some useful ideas," Malkin said, in a patient, schoolmasterly way.

Belknap, conscious that Armstrong and Tiffany, not just Malkin, were now politely waiting for those useful ideas, had to wonder whether Malkin, his eyes reflecting detached amusement at the odd way things sometimes turned out, might have already told them David Belknap, oddly enough, had once known Frank Willis rather well.

"David?" Malkin repeated shyly.

"Pass."

Sybil Pruett magically appeared in the doorway. "Lunch for everyone, George? Fast Eddy's taking orders."

"Yes, why not? It's been a long morning. A little nourishment might clear the cobwebs. David, we trade with a superb third-generation delicatessen on Seventeenth Street. Alsatian family. Anything French or German, they can do to a turn. Their *tarte aux framboises* is a work of art."

Belknap resigned himself. Lunch with Vanessa, kaput. Other things, too.

16

SHORTLY AFTER NOON, Officer Hoag of the Metropolitan Police Department discovered that the patrol car he and his partner were using had a malfunctioning siren. When they returned to the station for a replacement vehicle, Hoag's partner went to the rear parking lot to pick up the replacement and Hoag went inside to clear the paper work with the sergeant in charge of the shift.

Having nothing better to do while he waited for the shift commander to finish a telephone conversation, Hoag killed time scanning the latest announcements on the bulletin board. His attention was caught by enlarged mug shots of a black-haired woman with a mole on her right cheek. Beneath the physical description was a notice asking anyone who recognized the woman to contact his commanding officer immediately.

As soon as the sergeant was off the phone, Hoag told him he wanted to talk to Captain Vinson about the woman on the bulletin board. The sergeant didn't know anything about any woman on the bulletin board, and he wanted Hoag and his partner back on the street now, not thirty minutes from now. But after Hoag persuaded him to read the flyer, he grudgingly gave permission to see the captain. Hoag, still enough of a rookie to worry about the shine on his shoes and belt buckle at moments like this, ducked into the lavatory to improve himself sartorially before reporting to Captain Vinson's matchbox office next to the Evidence Vault.

Captain Vinson was three months from retirement, and

his desk was littered with Florida real-estate ads. He wasn't interested in the shine on Hoag's shoes and belt buckle, and he wasn't very interested in the woman with the mole either. He was interested in Florida real estate. But he listened sufficiently to learn that when Hoag had taken a wounded black youth to St. Albans yesterday, he'd accidentally knocked a woman's purse out of her hands. Hoag and the woman had had eyeball contact while he helped retrive the items spilled from the purse, and later he'd escorted her to her car. He couldn't remember the car's color, but he definitely remembered a mole on the woman's cheek. He was sure she was the woman in the mug shots on the bulletin board.

They were dutifully sampling—at least Belknap was, maybe Armstrong and Tiffany had had this extraordinary privilege a score of times before—Malkin's unconditionally guaranteed *tarte aux framboises* when word came from Captain McElroy that a probationary MPD officer thought he'd seen Myrtle Bessmeyer in St. Albans Emergency around noon Wednesday. The officer said she was a visitor, not a patient, and was driving a '68 or '69 Chevy with a raccoon's tail on the antenna.

The professional Scotsman on the chief's staff, one eye on laurels for the chief, the other perhaps on the TV cameras he saw in his own future, was anxious to send two detectives to the hospital to check the lead, a notion Malkin excised as cleanly and quickly as great surgeons wield the scalpel. McElroy, not even realizing he'd undergone surgery, settled happily for the opportunity to have the MPD keep an eye out for and report plate numbers of '68 and '69 Chevrolets with a coon-tail pennant flying from the mast.

"Well," Malkin said. He took the last bit of his raspberry tart and seemed astonished to find the plate empty. "Tony, why don't you see what you can do at St. Albans?"

17

ARMSTRONG, armed with credentials identifying him as Special Agent Nolte of the FBI, started with the harried young woman in the reception cubicle in Emergency. She recognized the Bessmeyer mug shots immediately, but couldn't place the occasion.

"Around noon yesterday" he prompted. "When two police officers came in with a black man who'd been shot in a holdup."

"That's it," she cried. "She was here about a patient."

"Man or woman?" Armstrong asked, ready to guess the patient was the man who'd mailed the package at midnight Tuesday.

"Oh, a man."

"And his name?"

"I'm trying to think. This is the first time I've been interviewed by the FBI. I'm sort of rattled."

He tried an encouraging smile. "Well, did he have a beard and possibly a limp?"

"I can't remember whether I saw him. Even ambulatory patients often go straight to an examining room while a relative's giving me the necessary information. Wait a minute . . . the patient came from Amsterdam."

"Amsterdam?"

"A place in Holland. I remember because she said he was in the diamond business. You get all kinds of people in Emergency, but you rarely get somebody who's in the diamond business in Holland. It makes an impression."

"She say anything else? Forget how trivial it might seem."

"God, something does occur to me. It's really crazy. Maybe you don't want to hear it."

"Try me."

"The guy who *brought* him here had a *beard* and a *limp*."

"What 'guy' is this? I thought the woman brought him."

"No, she was just inquiring about the patient."

"The three of them arrived together?"

She closed her eyes. "No, she got here later. I think. I'm all confused. I'm not complaining, but if you knew how many people I handle every day . . . names, faces, Blue Cross numbers, one big blur. Every night I ask myself, what am I doing here? I should've been an airline stewardess. I had the chance, it's a course you take by mail, only the school folded after I'd paid for the third—"

"Let's come back to the man who brought the patient. He had a beard and a limp. What else do you know about him?"

"Plenty," she said with astonishing ferocity. "His name's Harry Murphy and he drives a cab for Yellow."

Armstrong stared at her. "You don't remember the patient's name, yet you remember this cabdriver's." She couldn't be playing games, she wasn't the type, but she was demonstrating a peculiarly selective recall. "Why do you remember *his* name?"

"I guess because he was an obnoxious, cruddy kind of person. Besides, my roommate goes with a guy named Murphy, also cruddy, so it isn't a name I'd easily forget."

"Describe the cabdriver."

"Well, he was big, heavy. Lots of hair. Lots of beard. And cruddy."

Armstrong sighed. "How do you know his name's Harry Murphy and he drives a Yellow cab?"

"He told me."

Armstrong bowed his head, as though in prayer. When

he'd recovered his strength, he said, "Did the woman tell you her name?"

"Probably, but I've forgotten. My memory's not the best on the block."

"Does Myrtle Bessmeyer ring a bell?"

"No."

"Try these. Dora Dollson, Dolly Farmer, Dolly Madison, Myrt Ballinger, Alice—"

"Dolly Madison! I remember. There's a president's wife with that name. I asked her about it. She didn't think she was a direct descendant." The receptionist caught her breath. "Hey, it's coming together. The patient the cabdriver brought here comes from Utah. No, not Utah. Idaho. Pocatello."

"I thought the patient," Armstrong said, awed by this virtuoso inconsistency, "was in the diamond business in Amsterdam."

"No, that was the cousin. Or the son. I'm sorry, I'm all confused again. One thing I'm sure of, though. The patient comes from Idaho."

"How do you know?"

"The cabdriver told me. No, it wasn't the cabdriver. It was Dolly Madison."

Armstrong bowed his head again. Still, the identification of the Bessmeyer woman was solid. Exactly how the patient brought to Emergency on Wednesday fit into the picture he wasn't sure, but at the very least he was connected with Bessmeyer and the self-styled cabdriver. Bessmeyer's print had been on the White House package, and the cabdriver matched the description of the man who'd mailed it.

"Did the cabdriver pick up the patient when he was released?"

She frowned. "I don't remember anyone picking him up. Wait, wait. He wasn't released. He was admitted to the main hospital. You'd better talk to our administrator."

* * *

The hospital administrator was courteous, sympathetic, and fanatically determined to protect the confidentiality of the hospital's medical records. He appreciated the fine work done by the FBI, but if Special Agent Nolte wanted to know names and home addresses of males admitted from Emergency on Wednesday and why they were admitted, he would have to come back with a subpoena. The hospital had been sued in the past for voluntarily releasing such information to law-enforcement agencies, and the trustees weren't going to have it happen again.

Armstrong proposed a compromise. He'd be satisfied with only the names and addresses, which by themselves surely weren't "medical records." The administrator shook his head. Without a subpoena, the hospital would divulge nothing. Armstrong ran up the good-citizen ensign. This, he said somberly, was a national security investigation.

"You told me it was a case of stolen securities, Mr. Nolte," the administrator said reproachfully.

"National security involving stolen securities."

"You'll still need a subpoena."

"Mr. Nolte!" The receptionist in Emergency was semaphoring Armstrong with both arms. "Am I ever glad I caught you! I got my days screwed up."

"What days?"

"It was Tuesday, not Wednesday, Harry Murphy came in with the patient. Just Dolly Madison came in Wednesday. And she said the patient's name was Smith. Listen, I don't know how to begin apologizing. Like I said, my memory isn't the best on the block. Only this time I know I've got it right, because I checked the files. Joseph Smith, Pocatello, Idaho. Lives on a farm. En route to Amsterdam, Harry Murphy said, to do something about diamonds. And taking the Eastern shuttle for a connection with KLM. It's all in the files. I hope this little foul-up doesn't cause bad vibes in my own FBI file."

"Not to worry."

"One more thing, in case it helps. Dolly Madison said she put Mr. Smith into the cab Tuesday morning in front of the Library of Congress."

Bingo!

Armstrong, old enough to know promotions weren't brought by the stork, used one of Emergency's pay phones to let Malkin be the first to know. Then he asked at Admissions for the room number of Joseph Smith. But when he looked into Room 510 from the corridor, it was empty. He sought out the head nurse, displayed credentials, and asked what had happened to Joseph Smith.

She shook her head. It was an unfortunate situation. Mr. Smith had been unconscious from the time of his admission Tuesday until two this morning, when he'd talked briefly with a night nurse and then gone back to sleep until the present shift came on at seven. Dr. Matthews, a resident, had been treating him for a subarachnoid hemorrhage.

A subarachnoid hemorrhage was a bleeding from an abnormal artery on the surface of the brain. Such bleeding was an irritant that could cause spasms of other vessels, thus blocking the general supply of blood. In this case, Mr. Smith didn't have enough blood circulating to maintain consciousness, but did have enough to prevent brain damage. Nevertheless, since the hemorrhaging indicates an underlying abnormality likely to result in new bleeding that could be fatal, Dr. Matthews told Mr. Smith this morning he'd have to stay in the hospital for tests. Upon hearing this, Mr. Smith had become agitated.

At ten o'clock he'd appeared at the nursing station fully dressed, but pale and obviously weak. He announced he was leaving and, waving a ten-dollar bill, asked where he could collect the rest of the approximately five hundred dollars he'd had in his wallet Tuesday, as well as a locked briefcase he claimed to have had before coming to the hospital. She told him money carried by a patient in excess of ten dollars was always sent to the cashier's office for safekeeping and returned when the patient was discharged, but that he hadn't been discharged and couldn't be until Dr. Matthews gave approval. As for the briefcase, there was no record of it on the inventory supplied by Emergency, so he couldn't have arrived with one. She asked him to return to his room and undress, warning him in the strongest terms he could be endangering his life if he left the hospital.

The warning didn't impress him. With a resigned shrug, he told her the hospital could have the money in the cashier's office to cover his bill. Then he made his way, in a manner suggesting great effort, to the elevators. Appalled, she tried to summon Dr. Matthews over the paging system. By the time he answered the page, Mr. Smith, if that was actually his name, was gone.

Armstrong picked up the dropped aside. What made her think Smith might not be the patient's real name? It was hard to explain, she said. Somehow he'd seemed apprehensive when she and Dr. Matthews addressed him in that fashion. And the night nurse reported he appeared baffled the first time she addressed him as Mr. Smith. On the other hand, such a reaction wasn't unusual in someone who'd been unconscious for a prolonged period. Or much less a period, actually. In the recovery room you frequently found that a patient coming out of anesthesia after an operation wouldn't react to his name. But what particularly bothered her about Mr. Smith was that he'd had no I.D. in his wallet, just money.

Armstrong asked for a physical description. The head nurse turned out to be a total-recall observer of mankind. He weighed, she thought, a hundred and ninety pounds. About five ten, probably in his fifties. Balding, with sparse graying brown hair combed so as to hide bald spots. In need of excercise and a less starchy diet.

Armstrong asked if he'd made or received any telephone calls since regaining consciousness. There was no way of knowing, she replied. Since telephone service was part of the basic room charge, the switchboard operators were so busy they'd never remember calls to a specific room. Yesterday, however, a female relative did inquire about him at the nursing station.

With a sense of déjà vu, Armstrong produced the mug shots of Myrtle Bessmeyer. Yes, that was the female relative.

"I decided it'd be useless to order in a fingerprint technician," Armstrong said. "Assorted nurse's aides had already been in the room to change bed linen, leaving behind their own assorted fingerprints."

"Useless," Malkin agreed without looking up. He was seated behind the Directoire table and examining with a magnifying glass a large aerial photograph of what appeared to Belknap to be farm buildings.

"What about Pocatello?" Armstrong asked.

"There are two Joseph Smiths in the Pocatello area telephone book," Belknap said. "Both in Pocatello at this moment. The FBI's checking to see if there are others who aren't in the book, but as of now it looks as if the name Joseph Smith was an invention of the Bessmeyer woman."

Malkin put down the magnifying glass and drew a circle around one of the buildings with a grease pencil. Outside the circle he made an exclamation point, followed by a question mark. "A tantalizing set of contradictions. Mr. Smith, who's not Mr. Smith, had money in his wallet when he arrived at the hospital, so he hadn't been robbed. Therefore his not carrying any I.D. in his wallet must have been intentional. What do you make of it, David?"

Belknap studied hairline cracks in the ceiling. "Smith's probably an illegal."

"Exactly! And with a superlative instinct for survival. Consider how he conducted himself after he regained consciousness at two this morning. He wakes up in what seems to be a hospital. A nurse addresses him as Mr. Smith. As an illegal, how's he to respond? Deny he's Mr. Smith? If he does, he'll be asked for his actual name. But if he fails to deny he's Mr. Smith, he may be walking into a trap set by prospective interrogators only too glad to have him accept a false identity." Malkin smiled appreciatively. "Hobson's choice."

"At two in the morning coming out of unconsciousness, he was probably too disoriented to appreciate his dilemma."

"Yet not too disoriented to be baffled when the night nurse addressed him as she did. And he was alert enough by morning to understand the doctor ws sentencing him to additional time in the hospital. He must have lain there for hours trying to decide whether he was in undeclared custody, the mouse in a cat-and-mouse game, and whether, if he succeeded in leaving the hospital, he'd be followed to whatever place he went for sanctuary.

"And also whether he dare ask about his briefcase, which as far as he knew was in the hospital's possession and still contained the stolen Beowulf papers. Because if he was in undeclared custody, asking about the briefcase would be tantamount to signing a confession. On the other hand, if he was merely a man who'd been brought to a hospital for emergency treatment, what could he lose by asking? The chances were a hundred to one against any hospital employee's having tampered with it. Credit where credit's due. His analysis of his predicament was faultless, and no run-of-the-mill courier could have brought it off. In short, David, a total professional, determined to salvage whatever he could."

"Have you given him a nationality?"

"Russian," Malkin said with relish. "The Czechs and the Poles aren't that good. The Arabs and Iranians haven't been in the business long enough, and the Israelis don't have to operate that way over here."

"A man as sick as he apparently is," Armstrong interjected, "isn't going to travel far. He might have gone to the Soviet Embassy. They've doctors there, an infirmary. If the FBI's still photographing all embassy visitors, we could check on what their cameras picked up today."

"No," Malkin said, "he'd be breaking too many rules by going to ground at the embassy. The answer to Mr. Smith is Myrtle Bessmeyer. Find her and you'll find him."

"What about the cabdriver, Harry Murphy?" Armstrong said.

Belknap, wanting a better look at the aerial photo, stood up. "After George finally managed to get around to telling me about your call to him from the hospital, Tony"—he watched Malkin in vain for a reaction—"I gave Murphy to Tiffany. If the man's engaged in espionage, Murphy's an alias and he probably doesn't drive for Yellow or anybody else. But Tiffany's crew will start with the personnel manager at Yellow anyhow, then touch base with the other companies. Washington first, then the suburbs. They'll be after any driver named Murphy, regardless of first name, and any driver with a beard and a limp, regardless of last name."

Armstrong shook his head. "A third of the drivers probably have beards. That's bad enough. But no personnel manager's going to know who does or doesn't have a game leg without checking personnel records for all his drivers."

Belknap nodded. "Nobody ever claimed finding a needle in a haystack was easy."

18

AFTER HIS RETURN from the futile expedition to Greenwich Village to solve the mystery of Edgar's disappearance by checking secondhand bookstores, Ivan Glukhov forced himself through the motions of eating lunch in the mission's cafeteria, where he learned the Referentura's duty officer wanted to see him.

In the Referentura, the duty officer handed him a priority signal from Moscow. Glukhov deciphered it in the library:

YOUR MESSAGE EDGAR MISSING RECEIVED. IMPERATIVE YOU IMMEDIATELY CHECK HIS BOOKSTORE GREENWICH VILLAGE. ALSO HIS APARTMENT. IF RESULTS NEGATIVE, CHECK HOSPITALS AND CITY MORGUE. TRANSMIT RESULTS EARLIEST. NIKITIN, ACTING FOR GENERAL DEMICHEV.

Glukhov stared at the message, dumbfounded. Then he began swearing. Not only was Lieutenant Nikitin, that oily little bootlicker who ran around Moscow opening doors and flushing toilets for General Demichev, now grandly issuing orders in the general's name, he was bungling them on a criminal scale. Receiving those orders from Demichev, probably too busy with a dozen other pressing matters to handle Edgar's disappearance himself, Nikitin had never stopped to consider the fact Glukhov didn't know the addresses of Edgar's bookstore and apartment, let alone the name he went by in New York. Instead Nikitin had witlessly run like a rabbit in heat to the Cryptographic Section and dispatched his useless, asinine message.

Glukhov furiously lit a cigarette and inhaled so deeply he began coughing. Then, remembering one didn't smoke in the Referentura, he squashed the cigarette against the leg of his chair. Rules, discipline, sacrifice, and other assorted shit; let the fucking Referentura janitor find the fucking ashes on the fucking carpet and report him—the least of his troubles when both Edgar and Chessplayer were missing, and Ivan Glukhov was the man General Demichev would hold accountable. And when it would be tomorrow, New York time, before Nikitin's inexcusable mistake could be rectified and the search for Edgar could begin. And to what purpose if Edgar was already in the hands of the FBI?

Glukhov left the Referentura carrying such a weight of frustration he was surprised he could even lift his feet.

Not made any less resentful by the passage of several hours, Glukhov finished scribbling an angry note to a secretary who'd misspelled four simple English words in a simple letter to an Ohio entrepreneur mistakenly inquiring of the U.N. Mission instead of the Soviet Purchasing Mission about bidding procedures for supplying fertilizer to collective farms. Then he tore up the note. His problem wasn't the secretary, it was Nikitin.

Reacting to a thought scratching like claws at the edge of his mind, he reread Nikitin's message. Nikitin was stupid, a bootlicker to his fingertips, but he wasn't as stupid as the sender of this message had to be. And it was almost beyond belief General Demichev, pressed though he might have been by other matters, would have sent Nikitin to the Cryptographic Section without first advising him that Glukhov knew none of the details of Edgar's legend.

It was then Glukhov saw the truth, and it was chilling: the omission of those details from Nikitin's message had to be deliberate, and neither tomorrow nor any other time was he going to be involved in the search for Edgar. Under the guise of Nikitin's carelessness, General Demichev was methodically quarantining him, as Glukhov had seen other men quarantined when suspected of security offenses and the counterintelligence team wasn't quite ready to close in.

To know he was under suspicion was frightening; not to know why, nor what to expect next, was unbearable. Could General Demichev truly believe he'd betrayed Edgar or Chessplayer to the FBI? If so, the punishment would be swift and terrible. Or was Demichev intending only to charge him with gross criminal negligence? Glukhov heard the echo of his own strangled laugh as he pressed his hands to his eyes.

Not knowing how long he'd been sitting trancelike in the prison of his thoughts, Glukhov realized he had a visitor. Major Shiskin, the representative of Special Service II and head of security for the mission, was standing in front of his desk. Shiskin, tall and spectral, with a nose sharp enough to slice salami, was a man Glukhov relished not encountering any time. To encounter him now was terrifying.

"With regret, Captain, I've orders to put you under immediate arrest."

"Arrest?" Glukhov whispered. "This is some terrible mistake."

"There is no mistake."

Glukhov forced himself to ask the question whose answer he never wanted to hear. "What have I done? I'm a loyal citizen."

"There are many charges." Major Shiskin wearily removed papers from a jacket pocket. "I am permitted to summarize those in this warrant." His glance fell on a buff-colored sheet of paper on the desk. "What is that, Captain?"

"That?" Glukhov reached to retrieve Nikitin's message. "It's nothing."

"It is not nothing. Buff is the color of paper used in the

Referentura. So you've also removed classified material from the Referentura without authorization. Give it to me, please." Shiskin held out a hand and smiled thinly when Glukhov yielded. "This is the decipherment of a top-secret message, Captain. Your newest offense will be added to the charges."

"I brought the message to my office only to study it further."

"Your excuses you'll have to present to others. Now, as to the warrant . . . the criminal hooligan Yuri Subotin was arrested a month ago for black-market activities and has made a full confession, as have the other conspirators."

"Yuri!" Glukhov gasped.

Major Shiskin smiled again. "You are charged with illegally smuggling lingerie, dishwashers, and microwave ovens into the Soviet Union so as to advance your own career by currying favor with high-ranking officers."

"No," Glukhov protested, "I know nothing about dishwashers and microwave ovens."

"You are charged with illegally smuggling out of the Soviet Union *samizdat* manuscripts, bootleg film scripts, Zionist propaganda, and tracts by treasonous dissidents, solely to enable corrupt West European publishers bought by the CIA to libel the Soviet Union. You are charged with violating currency restrictions in order to finance the smuggling of icons out of the Soviet Union, and with illegally buying and selling such icons. You are charged with embezzling KGB funds to further these various corrupt activities from a Swiss bank account standing in the name of one Gottfried Forst, importer." Major Shiskin wearily returned the papers to his pocket. "Of course, this is only the summary."

"There's been a terrible mistake."

"You're repeating yourself, Captain. Now, when the criminal hooligan Subotin implicated you in his confession, the Center directed that you be placed under surveillance. I admit we've lost you a few times, but you'll undoubtedly clarify the gaps under professional interrogation. And willingly explain, I'm sure, such incidents as this morning, when you made an unauthorized phone call from a pay station in the Bronx. One assumes for the moment you were merely phoning your stockbroker."

"I have no stockbroker." Glukhov, realizing too late the absurdity of the answer, added lamely, "I was trying to call my landlord."

"Then you made an unauthorized trip to Greenwich Village, hired a taxi at government expense, and drove aimlessly around on business whose mysterious purpose I haven't yet determined. This too will be added to the charges. I am sorry, Captain. I once sincerely considered you a possible candidate for my friendship, but this is my mistake, not yours."

"But I'm innocent," Glukhov said abjectly.

"Everyone is innocent," Major Shiskin said. "Except the guilty."

"I need time to think."

"I'm afraid you don't have such time. An Aeroflot Ilyushin is standing by at Kennedy for the Moscow flight, waiting to take you on board."

"But this is"—Glukhov groped for words— "preposterous. I've urgent matters on my desk. I have my apartment, the rent's due tomorrow. My belongings. A social engagement this evening I'm unable to cancel." Glukhov could hardly believe it was his own frail voice delivering this ridiculous speech. "At the very least, I need time to make arrangements."

Major Shiskin looked impatiently at his watch. "The plane's already been delayed ninety minutes on your account. With regret, I must take you directly to Kennedy."

"I demand, then, to speak to the ambassador."

This time Major Shiskin didn't smile. He laughed. Uproariously. "What I offer you, Captain, is this. Outside there is one of our limousines. If you give your parole as an officer you'll not try to escape, I won't have to take you out of the mission in handcuffs. In kindness, I'll spare you that humiliation. But keep in mind, I carry a sidearm. I hope not to be required to use it."

"You are seriously telling me we're going immediately to Kennedy, where an Aeroflot plane is waiting?"

"I am seriously telling you that, Captain. Do you want handcuffs, or no handcuffs?"

"No handcuffs."

"I have your parole?"

"You have my parole."

Glukhov, a watchful Major Shiskin at his side, stumbled into the sooty afternoon haze of 67th Street. The limousine, with the overweight mission handyman Vilkov behind the wheel, was at the curb. Westbound traffic was heavy. The tamale vendor on the opposite sidewalk was trying to attract business to his little stand by playing lively south-of-the-border medleys on an ocarina. Glukhov didn't give him his usual affable wave.

"A moment, Captain," Shiskin said. "I must tie this damnable shoelace."

When the major bent over, Glukhov didn't have to think twice. Those mandatory training courses so many years ago in self-defense, useless at the time, useless since, were still vaguely imprinted in memory. His right hand, fingers stiffly aligned with the plane of his palm to duplicate the striking edge of a board, sliced into Shiskin's neck. The major fell forward into the sidewalk.

Glukhov dashed across the street to the tamale vendor. "*Save me, FBI man!* I defect. Am immediately placing myself under your protection."

Dropping the ocarina, the tamale vendor stared at Glukhov with a mixture of bewilderment and panic. Glukhov swore. The *svolock* wasn't an FBI man after all. He abruptly changed course and, like a salmon fighting its way upstream to die, slogged westward against the pedestrian current past Engine Company 39's two open doors, past the 19th Precinct House's stone archway, to Lexington Avenue, then northward to the subway entrance for a train to the downtown Federal Plaza offices of the FBI. His only pursuer, the wheezing handyman Vilkov, ran out of wind and choice Russian obscenities at the end of the first fifteen yards.

19

DETECTIVE JOEY ROSENBAUM swallowed a Tums. Another big day in the annals of crime.

The Woolworth's down the street served the worst pizza in the world—as a detective he ought to know this by now—and the pizza he'd eaten for lunch was no exception. It was as heavy in his stomach as buckshot. He popped another Tums. An insurance bet.

Once a month Nick DePaolo, fifty years out of the Abruzzi, gave Joey a free haircut. The business day had started with a call from Nick. Somebody had stolen the red-and-white barber pole bolted to the front of his shop. Nick, in English nobody would call perfect, named two suspects. Specifically, the bearded hotshots who ran the porno movie arcade three doors down. Nick and other nearby merchants had signed a petition of protest to the landlord when the lease on the arcade was up for renewal several weeks ago. Since then, Argenzio the tailor had received a brick through his plate-glass window and Gerhardt the butcher had unlocked his front door one morning to find about twenty mice, probably introduced through the mail-slot, in charge of the store.

Nick paid taxes and gave free haircuts to Joey Rosenbaum. Now, in his time of trouble, he wanted action. Joey Rosenbaum went to work. In the alley behind the movie arcade, he found the stolen barber pole buried in a dumpster. Nick, informed of the recovery, embraced him and offered a haircut, even though the month wasn't up. Joey took a raincheck.

What else had been big in the world of crime today? Joey Rosenbaum had it all at his fingertips. The hooker who'd lost eighty dollars because she foolishly left her purse and her trick alone in the bedroom of a fleabag hotel while she went to the bathroom. The pensioner who, as he was putting groceries in his car outside a supermarket, was asked by a kindly stranger whether he owned the paper bag the stranger had just found almost under the front wheel of his car. When the bag was opened, it miraculously contained several thousand dollars. Thirty minutes later the pensioner, a thousand dollars poorer after a trip to his bank with the kindly stranger, went down in the annals of crime as another victim of the pigeon drop. Joey Rosenbaum, the lucky stiff who got the anguished plea for help, sometimes felt he'd spent his life working pigeon drops.

Joey Rosenbaum pushed back his chair. In the dog hours before the shift ended, business was often slow in the detectives' bullpen. At the desk next to his, Mahoney, behind on alimony, was half-heartedly trying to coax a confession from a bare-chested teen-ager in hip huggers and hiking boots who'd been picked up because his Suzuki, routinely booted for a parking violoation, had filed-off serial numbers. Down the aisle, Pasternak, the dropout from a Jesuit seminary, was listening to a female wino who wanted to file a complaint against her brother-in-law for pawning her stereo. Melhausen, up on departmental charges for claiming sick leave to go to the track, where he'd been spotted by an undercover agent, was cleaning his fingernails with an icepick. Melhausen was supposed to be suicidal, and everybody tried to watch carefully when he brought out the icepick.

Joey Rosenbaum, marking time while he waited for the bread-and-butter day to end, wandered to the bulletin board to take another look at the mug shots of the woman with a mole on her cheek. The photos had been bothering him since he'd first noticed them around lunchtime. Somewhere he'd seen the woman before, and recently. He played the last week back in slow motion, looking for her face among suspects, victims, and witnesses.

Mahoney shouted across the room, "Joey, you got a call on One. Law and Order himself."

"I'm not here."

"Too late, good buddy."

Joey reached for the nearest phone and punched the button. "Yes, Herbie?"

"So what is it with Harry Murphy of IBM and the stolen briefcase?" Herbie Finemann said. "Or is it impertinent for a citizen to ask?"

"He's clean, Herbie. Checked him out yesterday. But his name isn't Murphy." What the hell was his name? Joey groped for it. "Brdnowski. That's his name."

"Using a fake name, it makes him clean? And this you learned yesterday? Joey, accept my thanks for keeping me informed. From now on, I don't get my news from television. I get it from Joey Rosenbaum, because that way I get it first. The exclusive."

Joey Rosenbaum didn't answer. His smile was beatific. Brdnowski, he thought. He'd seen the woman when he was searching Brdnowski's apartment. No, not the woman, her photograph. In a picture frame on a bedroom dresser. He'd paused to look at it, caught by a kind of dark, shopworn voluptuousness.

He replaced the phone and went back to the bulletin board. Anyone recognizing the woman was asked to contact his commanding officer. That meant the flyer must have come from the chief's office, and whatever the woman was wanted for, it was probably bigger than anything that had ever come his way before. Joey caught the distant scent of a promotion. The trouble was, he wasn't a hundred percent sure of his make, and he'd no irresistible urge to make a fool of himself with headquarters brass. The mole was on the right cheek in the mug shots; he'd an uneasy feeling it might've been on the left in the photograph on the dresser.

"Hey, Joey," Mahoney called. "Finemann's back. Says you were disconnected."

"I'm not here," Joey said, and this time he meant it. He removed the thumbtacks from the flyer and put it in his jacket pocket. Walking fast, he could get to Brdnowski's apartment in twenty minutes.

Joey Rosenbaum was thirty-three, overweight, too short to be a movie star, and too tired to want to be a hero. He liked baseball, TV crime shows, and beer with both. He loved his wife, he was happy she was happy she was pregnant, and he wanted their child to be a boy who'd never become a police detective. Joey believed in a merciful god.

Out of breath from climbing four flights of stairs, he knocked without too much muscle on Brdnowski's door. Getting no answer, he rattled the knob. When a plastic credit card failed to slip the latch, he swore and returned to the ground floor. At the far end of the dark, stinking hallway, he found the manager's apartment. He punched the buzzer.

The door opened a few inches, the chain still on. Joey shoved his wallet through the crack so the woman could see his gold shield. "Official business. Open up."

She was a washed-out forty chasing sixty, her hair was in pink curlers, and the ash on her cigarette was halfway to China. The TV behind her was tuned to a soap.

"Is this a raid or just a courtesy call?"

Joey knew a dozen ways to cut self-appointed comedians down to size, but his feet were sore, his crotch itched, and his stomach was swollen with gas and other bad news. He produced the famous Joey Rosenbaum smile, good in the center, weak at the corners. "Look, we need a key to the Brdnowski apartment. I'll have it back in five minutes."

"What's he done, besides not pay the rent on time?"

An ally. Joey recognized the signs. "Can you keep a secret?"

"Depends," she said coyly.

"We've a tip he's operating a handbook. It'd be nice if we could shut it down quietly. Nice for us, nice for you, nice for the building's owners. Five minutes is all we need. That's a cross my heart, hope to die."

"I'll get the key."

There was an empty Coke carton and a *Racing Form* on Brdnowski's sofa. The door to the bedroom was closed. Joey Rosenbaum checked the kitchen and bathroom, then put his ear against the bedroom door. He waited thirty seconds before opening it cautiously. The bed was unmade. He looked under it and checked the closet. Then he went to the dresser.

He studied the framed photograph of Brdnowski's woman. The mole was on the right cheek. He took out the flyer and compared the mug shots with the photo. Brdnowski's woman was heavier, and the styling of her hair was different, but the mug shots had probably been taken a number of years ago. Anyhow, the nose and the eyes were the same. And the mole, of course, Joey hitched his belt. He'd a good make, and God only knew to what promotions it could lead. The chief didn't waste his time with nickels and dimes and fucking missing barber poles.

Joey, juices flowing, returned to the living room. Luck could be pushed only so far. It was time to locate a pay phone, report what he'd found, and pull instructions on whether he should pick up the woman when she came back. He gave the living room an unfond last take and opened the door to the landing hallway.

Facing him was a man in brown twill coveralls. The man, about to knock, had a startled look, but no more startled than Joey's own. Behind him, another man in brown twill coveralls, a cylindrical tank slung over his shoulder, had reached the last stair.

The first man recovered before Joey. "Mr. Brdnowski?" he said.

"Who are you?" Joey countered.

"Acme Termite Control. The tenant next door reported finding this morning cockroaches in the bathroom." The man's voice was slightly accented. "The manager orders that we inspect your apartment."

"The manager?" Joey said, tensing.

"Yes." The man smiled apologetically. "We may have to"—he tapped the pressure-tank his partner had unslung and was now cradling like a baby—"spray the entire floor. You are Mr. Brdnowski, not so?"

Joey's heart was pumping fast. "You spoke with him before you came up?"

"Just now, yes. Boss's orders. Always we check in first." The man was no longer smiling. He'd very good antennae for a termite controller. "Something is wrong?"

Joey Rosenbaum edged backward in case he had to draw his gun. He thought of his wife, of his unborn son. His right hand drifted to his holster. "I'm a police detective. Step inside. I want to see your I.D."

20

BELKNAP DIDN'T LIKE the vibrations. Too much orchestration of events, an orchestration exuding the familiar odor of rottenness in Denmark. Frank Willis on his slab in the morgue wasn't the only one who'd reached a point of no return.

Belknap was sure now the unmarked black van outside Vanessa's apartment last night had been no accident. It was also passing strange that the man who called himself Harry Murphy had brought up diamonds and Amsterdam when he'd delivered his patient to St. Albans. More of those familiar odors. He not only needed to talk to Mr. Murphy, he needed to talk to him before anyone else.

"Anybody home?" Vanessa said from his office doorway. "The FBI now thinks the two Joseph Smiths in the Pocatello phone book are the only ones in the area."

"Good. I'd hate to have Bessmeyer turn out to have been telling the truth when she dropped that name at St. Albans. Would've spoiled her perfect record. Where're we going for dinner tonight?"

"David, I can't. I'm meeting my father."

"Lucky man," he said sourly.

She laughed and tossed her head. "Phone me later."

"Yeah, sure." But he was remembering last night when she'd said her father had been the source for what she knew about the Fehler business, and of course now her father was retired. Still . . .

"Your father, does he know about the Beowulf business?"

She shrugged. "If you're interested, I'll ask him."

"No, I don't think that's in my brief." He reached for the phone. "Tiffany in the building?"

"Was. About twenty minutes ago."

"See if you can find him. I've got to make a long-distance call." As soon as she'd left, he dialed New York.

"Belknap Associates," the receptionist said.

"Janice, just checking in."

"Oh, hi. You a phone number yet where people can reach you?"

"Still not allowed to give it out."

"Oh, wow. Must really be super secret. We don't even know what city you're in. It's kind of hard to explain when people call and ask to speak to you personally."

"I know. But I'll call each day for messages. What do you have now?"

"Most of the people who called, your secretary could handle the problem. Or else they didn't leave messages. Let's see, from yesterday afternoon about one, there's a man who, frankly, sounded hysterical. He said he *had* to talk to you and left a Washington, D.C., number where you could reach him during the next hour. After that, he said, it'd be too late. He made it seem, I don't know, like the end of the world."

"What's his name? What was he calling about?"

"He said you'd know what it was about. His name's Frank Willis. I'll give you the Washington number if you've got a pencil."

Belknap stared in dazed fascination at the phone. He heard Janice reciting the number and like an automaton, wrote it down. He opened the telephone book and flipped to the W's. But he knew the number was going to match Willis's listing. And that Chesapeake and Potomac toll tickets ordered up by Hathaway were going to show a call from Willis's apartment to Belknap Associates yesterday afternoon.

Willis must have been more than hysterical. He must have been stark raving mad.

"If he calls back, what should I say?"

Belknap worked on his turmoil. "He's not going to call back. He's dead."

"Oh, wow! No wonder he sounded hysterical."

"*Janice*, for Christ's sake!"

There was a little gasp from New York. Janice was twenty, anxious to please, and subject to hives under stress. Belknap mumbled an apology and, still numbed by the Willis phone call, made distracted notes as Janice ran through his other messages.

"The last one came early this afternoon, and I couldn't tell if it was local or long distance. The man wouldn't give his last name. He simply wanted me to tell you he'd recovered from his, now this is the word he used, his 'indisposition,' and everything was all right at his end. The name he gave was Edgar. No phone number, no anything. Just Edgar."

"Edgar?" Belknap repeated incredulously. He looked up and saw Tiffany shambling toward a chair. Trying not to wonder how long Taffany had been soaking up his end of the conversation, he said as much for his benefit as Janice's, "Damn it, I don't know anyone named Edgar. This is crazy."

Putting down the phone, he was overly conscious of the telephone directory opened to the Willis listing. Of course, Tiffany would have to read the page upside down, but that was no trick.

Belknap grimaced; there were a dozen legitimate reasons why it should be open to that page, none of which a man not freaked out on paranoia would feel required to offer. The wicked flee when no man pursueth.

"What was that all about, old boy?"

"Personal business." Never apologize, never explain. At least to Cal Tiffany, who was tamping his pipe and about to make a profound remark.

"No intent to pry," he said equably. "Everybody entitled to daily bowl of rice and daily quota of personal business. What would you say if I told you the gods are smiling on us?"

"I'd say the gods have us confused with someone more worthy."

Tiffany chuckled. "Even the gods make mistakes." He took a pad from his pocket. "I bring news about Harry Murphy."

"Good or bad? No, the gods are smiling. Lay it on."

"To begin with, we've found a couple of Murphys driving cabs, but they don't match the physical description of *our* Harry Murphy. They aren't big men, don't have beards, don't have a limp. At Silver Suburban Metro, though, we got what seems a match. Driver named Brdnowski. I'll spell it. B-r-d-n-o-w-s-k-i. Two things about Brdnowski. One, Tuesday was the last day he reported to work."

"Did he quit, leave town, or what?"

"Called in sick with a headache. He's a history of claiming time off for headaches, the personnel manager says. Two, we're not the only ones looking for him."

The gods weren't so smiling after all. "Meaning?" Belknap said cautiously.

"Some chap called earlier today and wanted to know if Suburban Metro had a photo album he'd left in a cab of theirs on Tuesday. Since Metro didn't have the album in its Lost and Found, this chap asked to talk to the driver. You see"—Tiffany borrowed a smile from the Cheshire cat—"he realized he didn't have his album as the cab was driving away, so he jotted down the license number."

Belknap saw. The passenger just happened to jot down a license number on Tuesday and just happened to wait until Thursday to do anything about it. More of those familiar odors. "And Suburban Metro obligingly checked its records and discovered the cab had been assigned to Brdnowski on Tuesday?"

"Yes, and when the album lover learned Brdnowski wasn't working and then asked if he could have his home address, the person who took his call oblingingly supplied it."

Belknap swore. "How long ago did this passenger contact the company?"

"We couldn't get a fix."

"You've got Brdnowski's vital statistics?"

"The personnal manager was obliging too. Date and place of birth, social security number. Native of Hoboken, now thirty-one, briefly played baseball in the bush leagues." Tiffany tore the top sheet from his pad and slid it across the desk.

Glancing at Tiffany's notes, Belknap marked Brdnowski's address on the wall map. It was several miles from the Ellis post office, well outside the closed figure he'd sagely predicted would define the area where the man who'd mailed the package lived. So much for crystal balls.

"What next, old boy?"

Diversions, Belknap thought. Diversions were next. He wished he were as good at the art as Malkin.

"Cal, I want an FBI check run on Brdnowski and"—he hesitated—"when does Lundhoven get back from Chicago?"

"According to his office, tomorrow at three."

"Too damn late. I want you on the next plane to Chicago. Roust him from whatever meeting he's in—get his schedule from his office—and have him account for his movements between nine and twelve Tuesday."

"Dear fellow, after the way I waltzed with him this morning, that smart-aleck egghead will laugh me out of Windy City."

"No, he won't, because that was the whole point of the exercise. To spook him. By now he'll know the plates on your car are untraceable. He's been around long enough to know how counterintelligence operates. He'll be sweating. And you'll be out of the closet this trip; you'll tell him flat out you're investigating the theft of Beowulf. Nobody but nobody could know that sacred name unless he had the right kind of clearance, and that's your ticket to credibility. If he talks back—but he won't, he'll be as soft as butter in the sun—lean on him. Drop bombs on him. Tell him the NSC vault log shows he checked Beowulf out at four-fifty Friday afternoon and in again at five-twenty, and out at eight-ten Saturday morning and in again at eight-forty. He'll get the message. Find out what he was doing Tuesday morning, get the names of coroborating witnesses, then call in with what you have."

Belknap entered Vanessa's office and closed the door. She gave him a smile he could live on for a week. He looked at the roses in a vase on her desk. Next time he'd bring roses. Now all he could offer was trouble. "I need some special help and advice."

"This little oracle shop always open for business, especially for handsome strangers with a look in their eye. I work from goat entrails, Tarot cards, or zodiacal signs, handsome stranger's choice. Do you have a goat?"

"I did a few minutes ago, but he's on his way to Chicago. If my luck holds, that is. What are the chances Tiffany'll check with Malkin to see if it's okay for me to ship him west to interview Lundhoven?"

"Why do you want him out of the way?"

He smiled faintly. "I love people who answer a question with a question. And when they're as lovely as you are lovely, I love them more."

"Compliment or complaint?"

"See, there's another question."

"Now you're not answering *my* question."

"You really have to meet your father for dinner?"

"Honestly."

"Three would be a crowd?"

"I'm afraid."

"So am I." He wondered if she'd any idea how truly that was true. "Vanessa, I need a full set of all-purpose skeleton master keys and lock picks immediately. How do I get them?"

"For what?"

"Damn it, don't ask questions. Just tell me."

"Sybil Pruett. She handles things like that."

"And I need credentials that'll give me a little weight if I venture into the real world. How do I get them?"

"Sybil Pruett. She handles things like that."

"Last item. I need a gun. A thirty-eight with a shoulder holster."

"David!" She appeared distraught.

"Just tell me. My time's running out."

"Sybil Pruett. She handles things like that. If you pass muster with her, she refers you to the armorer."

"What a jolly life for Sybil."

"David, why do you want a gun?"

"Why do you want to have dinner with your father when you can have it with me? I like guns. Doesn't that make me more exciting?"

"You scare me."

"I scare myself sometimes. But I know who Harry Murphy is, and how to find him, and he's my exclusive property. That's why Tiffany's on his way to Chicago. But somebody else with a very rotten Denmark smell also knows who Harry Murphy is. That's why I need a gun. *D'accord?*"

"D'accord," she finally responded. But she looked absolutely terrified.

21

BRDNOWSKI SLID onto the corner stool. The Greek was behind the bar, pouring evil coffee for an unsuspecting customer. He waddled toward Brdnowski, reached for a mug, and started to pour again.

Brdnowski hurriedly declined. "What's with Myrt, Stav?"

"Powdering her nose like ladies do." The ends of the Greek's thick black moustache curved wickedly upward like scimitars, and his head was as bald as alabaster. "I'm giving her three days off. A wedding present. Leaves me short-handed, but a girl doesn't get married every day."

"Make it a week. It'll take me the full seven to train her."

"You can do it in less. She tell you about the detective?"

Brdnowski's heart skipped a beat. "Detective?"

"MPD dick. Had mug shots of her, or else her twin sister. Wanted to know if somebody like her worked here." The Greek began polishing the top of the bar with a disgraceful wet rag. "Don't see too well without my glasses. Didn't have them just then."

Brdnowski rejoined the human race. "Always knew you'd a heart big as Man o' War's, Stav. Anyhow, you were on the button, it had to be somebody looked like her. Pure case of mistaken identity."

"Well, you've passed along a few long shots turned out nice. More to come, I'd guess. Besides, who wants trouble?"

"Right." Brdnowski studied the plastic mustard dispenser. The salt and pepper shakers were interesting too. "This detective, he say why he was asking about the woman?"

"You ever heard a clam talk?"

From somewhere in back, Myrt entered the traffic pattern and made an almost perfect three-point landing on the stool next to Brdnowski. The Greek produced shot glasses, reached for a bottle of Old Granddad, thought better of it, and went for an unlabeled bottle of bar whiskey. "On the house," he said recklessly. "A girl doesn't get married every day."

"Not to Brdnowski anyhow." Myrt's hoarse laugh carried to the far end of the bar.

The three of them clinked shot glasses and tossed them off. The whiskey was terrible, but the Greek wasn't enough carried away by the occasion to offer a second round to kill the taste. Brdnowski, not too disappointed, hustled Myrt into the Chevy, illegally parked beside a fire hydrant. "What's this about a detective?"

"Beats me, Brdnowski."

"You been boosting things someplace?"

"This is all you got to say to your bride? I could get more uplift phoning Dial-A-Prayer. Where're we headed?"

"We got to pack a few things for the honeymoon. Then we head for an out-of-the-way motel on the Maryland side of the line. Silver Spring."

"God's country," Myrt said, screwing up her face as if she was taking castor oil. "Go by the Ellis post office first. By now we ought to have a few replies to the chain letter, or else those Chicago Polacks got ice cubes for hearts. Brdnowski, you sure you know what you're doing on this wedding?"

"No," he confessed, "but it's like I told you on the phone. I got to the VA Hospital about eleven. I undressed and they gave me a bathrobe with holes under the armpits and no pockets. I spent the next couple of hours, except when I was being examined, in dime-sized waiting rooms with guys so fruity you wouldn't believe."

"Did you pass?" Myrt was trying to peel a package of gum with one hand and apply lipstick with the other.

"What do you mean, did I pass? Sure I passed. They found the same things wrong with me they always find, plus a few more I hadn't thought of last time. Having a headache these past few days didn't hurt, either. The disability's solid another two years. But I didn't have my clothes and couldn't get to a phone where I could talk privately. It wasn't until thirty minutes ago I got a chance to call St. Albans. That's when I learned the guy who owns the briefcase wasn't there anymore. And phoned you."

"And swept me off my feet with that classy proposal. I had the idea, little dumb me, that since Elsie couldn't do my hair today, we weren't taking the plunge until Friday or Saturday."

"I don't need you all gussied up, Myrt."

"Hey, Big Spender. Now level with me, you fork-tongued Polack, are we getting married today just to have a good reason for disappearing from the apartment?"

"Well, if the guy's government, we don't want to look like we're running away, do we? At the same time, we've got to be near enough to take care of the post-office box."

"What I'm going through for a honeymoon in scenic Silver Spring. Where's the wedding? Not in any country church, I'll lay ten to one on that."

"I got us an appointment with a retired preacher who usually handles only celebrities. Supposed to give his customers free champagne too."

"Hey, Big Spender."

"Also, on the back seat's a wedding present."

Twisting around, Myrt plucked a flimsy shopping bag from a pile of dirty shirts.

"Didn't have time for ribbons and fancy wrapping. Had to stop at the bank and raise cash."

"With a woman, Brdnowski, it's the sentiment counts." She peeked into the bag, went victoriously after what she saw. "A white satin nightgown! Lace and bows and everything. Brdnowski, you've got class after all."

"Brides wear white, you're a bride, so you get white."

"You just won a wedding-night fashion show you'll never forget. Plus a few other performances to blow your mind. Where's the ring?"

"Ring?" Brdnowski suddenly felt small enough to crawl under the seat.

"Never mind, Big Spender." Myrt sighed. "I've been carrying one in my purse last six months."

"I'll pay for it, Myrt. Wouldn't be right not to." He coasted to the curb and docked beside a fire hydrant in front of the post office. "Least a groom can do is pop for the ring."

"One thing about you, Brdnowski. In a city where nobody except congressmen can find a place to park, you always manage. If I'm not back in ten, phone Perry Mason."

She was back in three, waving a few letters as if they were winning tickets on a fifty-to-one shot. "I take back everything bad I ever said about Polacks—even you, Brdnowski. Seven replies, and this is our first pickup." She began opening the letters. Each of the first six contained a five-dollar bill. The seventh contained a mimeographed announcement the end of the world was at hand.

"Okay, there's always some crapehanger in every crowd, but I guess it's a free country. Brdnowski, you got any idea what this means? We'll have three hundred bucks, maybe more, before we finish Chicago. And that's just Polacks. We're going to be in business with The Home Run before we get west of the Mississippi."

"I knew it was a lucky day for a wedding," Brdnowski said, trying not to claim too much of the credit.

Myrt fished in her purse for a key. Brdnowski was close behind when she opened the door to the apartment. They both saw the body at the same moment. As Myrt started to scream, Brdnowski clamped a hand over her mouth. "It's the detective," he whispered. "The one who was here about the briefcase."

There were no wounds and no blood, but Brdnowski was sure the detective lying on the rug was dead. He closed the door, then got on his knees and tried to find a pulse. Finally he stood up. His stomach was churning. He was afraid he was going to vomit. "Better sit down, Myrt."

"Brdnowski, I'm soft and feminime on the outside, always the perfect lady, but on the inside I'm built of cast iron. That's what happens to girls who grow up in Gary with a steelworker with bad lungs for a daddy. Forget the scream I didn't quite get out. The man's dead, right?"

"Not for long, either. No marks on him. Maybe it was a heart attack."

"Not likely. Why'd he come back? Why's he dead?"

Brdnowski forced himself to look at the dead man's face. Even in the pallor of death, it registered surprise. "I guess he came back because of the briefcase. And walked in on somebody waiting for us. Or else, somebody after the briefcase and us walked in on him."

"You realize now the guy you took to the hospital was no government agent. And whoever he is, he must've stolen what was in the briefcase."

"Right. And now he's after me. Maybe because he thinks I still have it, maybe because I can identify him. Myrt, we've got to cut out of here."

"Let me ask you something. You know how to use a gun?"

"Learned in the Army."

"Then you'd better grab whatever that poor cop was carrying. We may need it. What're we going to do about him?"

"Beats. No way to get him out of here without somebody seeing us."

"If we don't get him out, they'll think we did it. That's

bad enough. Nothing, though, to having the cops think we killed one of their own."

"But you've been at the Greek's. And I was at the VA Hospital until about an hour ago."

"That's the hour's going to give us trouble."

Brdnowski swallowed. Perspiration was trickling from his armpits. "We could come back about three this morning. Carry him downstairs, load him in the car, dump him in some alley where it'd seem like a mugging."

Myrt looked away. "That was a lie about insides built of cast iron. I'm not sure I got the stomach for dumping a corpse at three in the morning."

"I know I don't, Myrt. But we got to do something."

"For starters, grab his gun. I'm packing a couple of suitcases."

Brdnowski forced himself to remove the holster from the dead man's belt and snapped it around his own. His legs were shaking. He went to the kitchen and poured a drink. He poured one for Myrt, gulped his and a third of hers, and stared at the door to the dumbwaiter shaft next to the refrigerator. He opened the door, looked up and down the shaft, and pulled on the rope until he'd brought the dumbwaiter up from a lower floor. Then he took Myrt's drink to the bedroom.

She was throwing clothes into two big suitcases on the bed as if she were building dams to save the whole city from flooding. She belted the drink without breaking stride. She noticed the holster attached to his belt. "That things sticks out like a sore thumb. You'd better wear a sweater to cover it."

"In this heat? No way." He pulled out the tails of his flowered Hawaiian sports shirt and let them hang over his chinos to hide the gun. "Myrt, I got some news."

"You just won the Irish Sweepstakes? You told me yourself it was a lucky day for a wedding."

"The dumbwaiter," he said. "That's how we take him down. Now. By three in the morning, he'll be stiff as a board."

She suspended operations. "It's large enough?"

"I checked. The apartments below us, the people won't be home yet. We send him to the basement. You stay with him down there while I take the suitcases to the car. I'll bring it around back, park by the basement door. We lug him up the steps, put him in the trunk, and split."

"The poor guy," Myrt said. "You think he's got a wife?"

"I know he's got a wife. She's the granddaughter of that screwball locksmith. I don't know what to say, Myrt. I never wanted him to die."

"I believe you, Big Spender." She turned and clung to him. "Brdnowski, you're all I've got. Don't let me down."

"Myrt"—Brdnowski had difficulty with the words—"you're all I've got, too."

"Oh, damn," she said, "I'm going to cry. Hold me, honey."

Brdnowski, each hand weighted with a bulging suitcase slowly pulling him toward the center of the Earth, started across the street to the hamburger joint's parking lot, where he'd left the Chevy. Twenty feet from the Chevy, he did a double take. A man about forty, a gangling six-footer wearing custom threads, was stealing the good-luck coon's tail Brdnowski flew from the Chevy's antenna. He'd already cut it off and was about to stash it under his jacket.

Brdnowski, unaccustomed to being in the right, forgot his troubles and marched on the enemy to the strains of martial music. Five feet from the Chevy, he came to a resounding parade-ground halt. He dropped the suitcases and placed hands on hips, drill-sergeant fashion. "Friend," he said, "maybe you'd care to explain what you're doing with that coon's tail. You know who I am?"

The man casually adjusted his tie. He had a scar on his right cheek. His eyes were incredibly blue, and steelier than anything Brdnowski had bargained for. "I imagine I do, friend." He indicated the apartment building across the street. "You're the klutz who lives on the fourth floor and has a dead detective named Rosenbaum on his living-room rug."

Brdnowski heard the swoosh of air leaving his lungs for safer places. But for Brdnowski himself, the klutz who'd walked into this buzz saw disguised as a human being, there was nowhere to go except to his knees. And that only so his head could be more cleanly sliced from his neck.

The man looked at the suitcases. "Where're you going on your trip, Mr. Brdnowski?"

For one wild moment Brdnowski considered foisting ownership of the suitcases onto an elderly widow he'd promised to take to the bus station. "Wedding," he mumbled. "I'm getting married."

"To Myrtle Bessmeyer, perhaps? Or is she using another name this week?"

Brdnowski gulped for breath. It was painful. "Who are you?" he croaked. Any frog in the pond could have done better.

"For the time being, your guardian angel. I think. Depends on you. Who instructed you to tell the receptionist in St. Albans Emergency the patient you brought in Tuesday was involved with diamonds and Amsterdam?"

Dumbfounded, Brdnowski wiped clammy hands on his chinos. The man seemed to have the form sheet on all his past performances since time began. What was happening, Brdnowski didn't know, but he did know telling the truth was going to be a hundred times less dangerous than not telling it. "She was giving me a hard time. A guy I'd never seen before almost died in my cab. She wanted his life story. I threw in the business about diamonds for the hell of it. Same with telling her I was Harry Murphy."

"Where'd you pick up this passenger?"

"The Library of Congress, sir, around ten or eleven." Brdnowski was amazed at the extent of his surrender. Since getting out of the Army, he'd made it a point of honor not to call anyone *sir* unless the tip at least equaled the price of the ride.

"Mr. Brdnowski"—the man gestured at pedestrians glancing their way—"let's continue our talk in your car. There'll be more privacy, and I'm sure you'd want that."

Brdnowski suddenly remembered Myrt, waiting in the basement with the dead detective. She must be about to go out of her skull. "I sort of have an appointment."

"In Samarra?"

"I don't know the town."

"In your present circumstances, you should. In an old story, a servant went to the marketplace in Baghdad and was jostled by Death. The servant returned to his master's house in fear and reported Death had made a threatening gesture in the marketplace. He took his master's horse and fled to Samarra so Death couldn't find him. The master then went to the marketplace, saw Death in the crowd, and asked why a threatening gesture had been made to his servant. It wasn't a threatening gesture, Death replied, only a reflex of surprise at seeing him in Baghdad, since the two of them had an appointment that night in Samarra. There are people who want to kill you, Mr. Brdnowski, and you don't want to help them by fleeing to any place like Samarra. Please sit on the driver's side and keep the engine running. The people who want to kill you might return without waiting for an invitation."

"Yes, sir." Brdnowski quickly loaded the suitcases and slid behind the wheel. "Trouble is, Myrt's alone with that detective. I don't know what she'll do if I don't show up pretty soon."

"Your shirttail, when you're sitting as you are, doesn't conceal that gun at all well. Is it the detective's?"

"Yes, sir," Brdnowski had lost count of the crimes to which he was confessing.

"I had to leave your apartment rather hurriedly by the outside fire escape as you were arriving, but I was there long enough to learn his gun wasn't of any use. It won't be of any use in your situation, either. Before you're tempted to do something foolish with it, get rid of the holster—under the seat'll be fine—and give me the gun."

"Yes, sir." Brdnowski passed across the gun. The man cracked it open and, satisfied with his inspection, slipped it into a jacket pocket.

"The gun wasn't of any use to Detective Rosenbaum, because he probably died from inhaling prussic acid sprayed in his face by some kind of Stashinsky device. Bodgan Stashinsky, Mr. Brdnowski, was a Russian assassin operating in Germany in the late fifties. The device has been improved since then."

Brdnowski, though confused by what he was hearing, saw rays of hope. The man wasn't at least accusing him or Myrt of killing the detective.

"In his jacket pocket, Detective Rosenbaum was carrying mug shots of your good friend Myrt circulated by the Metropolitan Police, which I claimed in my temporary capacity as your guardian angel. Why don't you tell me exactly how he knew enough to come to your apartment to find her?"

"I don't know."

The man's expression was bleak. "I thought we'd reached a point where you realized anything less than total frankness would drastically shorten your life expectancy."

"What I meant was," he said hastily, "I don't know how he knew about Myrt. He knew about me because he came to the apartment yesterday." Brdnowski had to jump a very high hurdle to get to the next sentence. "There was a problem with a briefcase."

"The briefcase you and Myrt mailed to the White House?"

Brdnowski, discovering he'd lost the power of speech, could only nod.

"What was the problem?"

"Well, after I left the hospital I noticed the briefcase belonging to the guy I'd taken there was still in the cab. I got to the garage too late to turn it in at Lost and Found, so I took it home. Then Myrt and I got to worrying maybe the briefcase contained important papers needed at a meeting or something, because the guy had been in such a hurry to get to National. Only now he was in the hospital and not able to get to the meeting. So we decided to open it, get any papers to whoever was supposed to have them."

Brdnowski filled his lungs. Myrt would've been proud of him. "Since we didn't have a key, I took the briefcase to a locksmith, who unlocked it. Of course, I wouldn't let him see what was inside, it wasn't his business, but he thought it was and got pretty mad. Then, when Myrt and I finally opened it, we saw how right we'd been. There were not only important papers, there were important government papers. We didn't look at them, it wasn't our business, but we could tell by the first page it was secret information and figured maybe the man in the hospital had stolen it. We decided to mail everything to the president. We didn't want a medal, we didn't want a reward, we just wanted to help the president. Along with the papers, I gave him my lucky horseshoe and Myrt gave him a nice ship in a bottle she'd won in Atlantic City."

"Where does the detective fit into this patriotic saga?"

"He's related to the locksmith. The locksmith was so mad at not getting to look inside the briefcase he took my license number and gave it to the detective, and he came around to ask about the briefcase."

"Whereupon you told him you'd mailed it to the president?"

"No, sir, I'd never do that. Those papers were secret; it wasn't his business. If the president wanted to tell him later on, that was up to the president. I told him my handicapping books were in it, only I couldn't find my key, that's why I'd gone to the locksmith. When he asked to see the briefcase, I told him some guy made off with it while my girlfriend and I were having an argument in a bar."

The man, silent too long for Brdnowski's comfort, finally

said, "As one horseplayer to another, Mr. Brdnowski, my advice is, stick with that story through thick and thin. If you live, there's a fifty-fifty chance you can put it over, and if you don't live, it'll still be a classic." He put the coon's tail in the glove compartment. "Every police car in the city's looking for a Chevrolet the age of yours with a tail like that on the antenna. That's why I cut it off."

Brdnowski was bewildered. "But I thought *you* were the Law."

The man smiled ambiguously. "I'm your guardian angel."

Brdnowski sniffed the faint odors of bargaining power. If the man was working against the police, something wasn't kosher. "Is there a name I can call you by?"

"I think we can find one. How about Fred? Do you like Fred?"

"Sure," Brdnowski said, nonplussed. "I've got nothing against Fred."

"Good. Now let's tuck your car in a more out-of-the-way place and go up to your apartment for a little talk with Myrt."

Brdnowski coughed. "There's something I forgot to mention. She's in the basement. What happened is, we took the dective down on the dumbwaiter. We were talking about maybe putting him in the car."

"You do have interesting talks, you and Myrt. But you happen to be right, it's not a time for you to be sought for questioning about the death of a police detective. It could lead, among other things, to your having to explain the briefcase you mailed to the White House, and people far more important than either of us don't want to hear about that briefcase on the evening news."

"Right," Brdnowski said, catching another whiff of future bargaining power.

"How were you planning to get the body into your car without being seen?"

"Back of the building. The trunk of the car can be put smack against the door to the basement steps."

"All right, drive around back. There's a small additional matter to take care of. I removed a key stamped with the number of your apartment from one of Detective Rosenbaum's pockets. He undoubtedly obtained it from your building manager. It needs to be returned. Inconspicuously and promptly."

"We can forget the key, Fred. The manager's a zombie, watches TV all day."

"A zombie still knows how to complain to the police about a key borrowed by a policeman and not returned. While we're putting the body in the trunk, your resourceful Myrt can get an envelope from your apartment. She'll put the key in the envelope and slip it under the manager's door when we're ready to leave."

"Right. But what do we do about your car?"

"I came by taxi. Plus two buses and a department-store escalator. You've stumbled into the big leagues, Mr. Brdnowski. Sudden death is the name of the game."

"Hi, Myrt, I'm back," Brdnowski called as he started down the basement steps.

"Where the hell you been, Brdnowski?" she hissed from the dankness below. "This place's worse than a graveyard at midnight."

"Listen, Myrt, I don't want you to panic." He felt his way carefully in the windowless gloom. "I brought a friend."

"You brought a *what*?"

He could tell she'd throw something at him, if only she had something to throw. "She's a little upset," he whispered over his shoulder to Fred. As his eyes adjusted to the gloom, he was able to locate her. She was planted in the doorway to the furnace room, teeth bared and lips curled back like a starving dog in a serious dispute over a bone.

"Myrt," he said quickly, "this is Fred. Fred knows

everything about St. Albans and the briefcase. Fred knows everything about the detective, and so much more it'd take the rest of the week to tell you." Brdnowski, thinking she was going to faint, moved forward to catch her.

"We're under arrest?" She hugged herself pathetically.

"You're not under arrest, Miss Bessmeyer, but you're in extreme danger."

"Myrt, it's going to be okay. Fred's going to help us with the detective."

"Help us," she said tonelessly. "I don't get it." But the sap was beginning to flow again. Brdnowski could tell. She stepped out of the doorway for a closer look at Fred. "You're not a cop?"

"He says he's our guardian angel. I'm beginning to believe it."

22

HATHAWAY WAS UNCOMFORTABLE. "We've received some curious information. Does Belknap happen to be with you?"

"I'm alone," Malkin said.

Hathaway proceeded cautiously. "Did you know Belknap and Frank Willis were friends?"

"Oh, yes. In Germany, though. David took quite an interest in Willis's career. Recommended him for advanced MP training, in fact."

"I'm not talking about Germany, although that's something I wish you'd shared earlier. I'm talking about here. Chesapeake and Potomac long-distance records show Willis phoned Belknap's New York office yesterday afternoon."

From the silence at the other end of the phone, Hathaway judged the man to be in shock. He realized he was wrong when Malkin said, "How odd. Just this morning he was telling me he hadn't seen Willis since Germany."

That was also information the Bureau should have been given earlier. Hathaway's resentment of the high-handed secrecy over there was increasing. They always wanted help, and in return they offered not even crumbs from their table. "We're going to have to interview the receptionist in his office who took that call."

"No! That's absolutely the wrong way to proceed. First, there's undoubtedly a reasonable explanation, which David'll be able to provide. Second, if by some remote chance there was no reasonable explanation, you'd accom-

plish nothing by such heavy-handed tactics. Except frightening the receptionist, who'd pass on to him every detail of the interview. Besides, the whole thing's absurd. Willis probably phoned lots of people yesterday. We can surmise he was in a state of complete panic."

"This is the only long-distance call he made."

"Immaterial. We know nothing about his local calls. In view of what's at stake and my own responsibilities, I'm instructing you officially not to make that interview."

"It's too late. New York was contacted thirty minutes ago, priority basis." Hathaway couldn't fault Malkin for trying to protect one of his own; it was how you maintained morale. It was also why he'd let those thirty minutes pass before phoning the man. Whatever else happened, nobody was going to be able to fault the Bureau for foot-dragging or favoritism.

23

A MILE FROM THE APARTMENT, they found an alley deserted enough for safe disposal of the body. Myrt insisted on saying a prayer. Her eyes were moist when she returned to the car.

Brdnowski, easing into late-afternoon traffic, half-turned toward the man wedged in with the suitcases and dirty shirts in the back seat. "What happens next, Fred?"

"You rent a car, get rid of this one. After Miss Bessmeyer drove to the hospital to ask about Joseph Smith of Pocatello, your Chevrolet's—"

"See what I mean, Myrt?" Brdnowski broke in proudly. "He knows everything about everything."

"I'm not arguing the point, Brdnowski. Just curious why you're patting yourself on the back because of what *he* knows."

The sap was flowing again, all right. For once Brdnowski was pleased to see her back in her ornery, faultfinding ways.

"Fred," Myrt said, "or whoever in hell you are, I wish you'd stop calling me Miss Bessmeyer. Makes me nervous. Call me Myrt."

"And just call me Brdnowski," Brdnowski said, not to be outdone.

"Your Chevrolet's only reliable identifying feature," Fred continued, "was its raccoon's tail. But now that it's known Brdnowski and Murphy are the same person, the police, and others even more anxious to find you, will have access to its plate numbers. That's why you want it off the streets, immediately if not sooner."

"Right," Brdnowski said with alacrity. He drove to the nearest car rental, signed for a flashy red Datsun station wagon, and turned the Chevy out to pasture in a parking garage off Connecticut Avenue.

"What happens next, Fred?" Brdnowski asked as he headed northwest on Connecticut. The Datsun was handling like a dream.

"Park on a side street somewhere. I need your undivided attention."

Brdnowski didn't like at all the promise of trouble those words carried. Beside him, Myrt was stealing glances at her wristwatch, probably wondering when the marriage-license bureau and the preacher in Maryland rolled down the shutters. He shot her a don't-rock-the-boat look, trying to signal that the wedding wasn't too high on Fred's list of things needing to be wrapped up today.

"Why are you making faces at me, Brdnowski?"

"Me?" He kicked her foot. "I'm not making faces. I'm looking for parking." He played a long shot, turned right on Belmont, and found a space. A legal space. No fire hydrants, no signs prohibiting parking by anyone less than heads of state. "My lucky day," he said to passing traffic. No one else was interested, that was for sure.

"The detective," Fred began, "isn't the only person who's been murdered since you mailed that briefcase. I tell you this because I want you to realize you're in over your heads in an espionage operation gone haywire. One side wants you dead. The other has no great wish to have you live, because you've seen top-secret material that's not supposed to exist. The fact you claim not to have read it is immaterial. In this business nobody believes such claims. And sworn promises of future silence are unbankable; the best guarantee of silence is an obituary. Do I have your attention?"

Brdnowski nodded numbly.

"Why do you think the people who killed the detective are so interested in killing you, Brdnowski?"

"I guess because I can identify the guy I took to the hospital."

"True. But nurses there could do the same thing. So perhaps you, and possibly Myrt, know something you don't realize you know. Something that could expose one or more members of an espionage ring. They want you dead before you discover, or someone else discovers, what it is you know."

"I don't exactly follow."

"Brdnowski, he's saying you might have seen or heard something when you picked up the fare at the Library of Congress or on the way to the hospital that you don't remember seeing or hearing. Right, Fred?"

"That's part of it, Myrt. Did you have a conversation with him?"

"Well, he said he wanted to go to National. And he looked at my TD permit, asked if my name was Brdnowski."

"Was anybody else standing near him when you picked him up?"

"Come to think of it, there was a guy in front of me working on his van. He had the hood up, I guess he was stalled."

"Describe him."

"Didn't pay any attention. Anyhow, all I saw was his back. He was wearing, yeah, a brown jumpsuit."

Brdnowski, watching Fred in the rearview mirror, could tell his answer had aroused a lot of interest. Fred leaned forward like a jockey turning into the homestretch. "Two men dressed that way were supposedly seen in the building where the other murder victim lived. Was there a company name on the back of the jumpsuit?"

Brdnowski concentrated. "Might've been . . . couldn't tell you for sure."

"What about the van? Color, make, company name on the side?"

"Didn't pay any attention. One thing, though. After we started along First, the fare looked like he was waving to some guy down the block."

"Can you describe him? Tall, short, young, old?"

"An older guy. Sort of medium height."

The next question from the back seat seemed casual, but Brdnowski knew it wasn't. Fred's eyes in the rearview mirror were even steelier than they had been in the hamburger joint's parking lot. "Did everything that was in the briefcase when you opened it get sent to the White House?"

Brdnowski fixed his gaze on the scenic wonders of the weather-beaten pickup in front of them. He grunted in surprise as a hard kick landed on his shin. "Tell him, you jerk. The life you save might be your own."

He rubbed his leg. She must carry lead weights in the tips of her shoes. "I guess what Myrt means is, there were a few silver dollars we decided not to send."

"It wasn't a *few*," Myrt said to Fred. "It was exactly a *hundred*, each one protected by clear plastic and sitting in an unsealed small blue envelope. On each envelope it said *Eisenhower Uncirculated Silver Dollar*, and gave the year, seventy-three. On the back was a kind of mailing label you can peel off that said *Brinkermans, Coin Dealers*. The envelopes were in four packs, each pack held together by a rubber band."

"Where are they now?"

"I tossed them in one of the suitcases."

"Brinkermans? Do you know if that's a Washington coin dealer?"

"Looked it up yesterday," Myrt said triumphantly. "Lower Connecticut Avenue. From the street number, it must be close to the Mayflower."

Always the big mouth, Brdnowski thought, understanding better the feelings of those early Christians tossed without their personal okay into a free-for-all with a lion.

* * *

It was a small, tastefully disorganized shop in which coin collections shared overhead with board games, lithographs, and toy soldiers refighting set-piece battles. A frail, white-haired woman was dusting one of the hilly battlefields. Belknap guessed the scene was Waterloo. Napoleon's colors flew from the standard of a retreating fallen horseman. A frail, white-haired man sat on the top of a frailer stepladder, watering a hanging plant. They were husband and wife as surely as the Gemini were twins.

The woman stopped dusting and smiled. The man descended cautiously from the ladder. Feeling he was interrupting almost sacred rites, Belknap presented the credentials identifying him as Fred Ryan from the Treasury's Office of Special Investigations. "Mr. and Mrs. Brinkerman?"

"Mr. and Mrs. Adams," the man replied tolerantly. "Brinkerman is the former owner, very respected among numismatists in the area in spite of now residing in a locked ward at St. Elizabeths, so we kept the name."

"I'll take only a minute of your time. We're interested in a gentleman who bought a hundred uncirculated Eisenhower silver dollars from you on Monday or Tuesday."

"Why, that was dear Mr. Moore," Mrs. Adams said delightedly. "You weren't here that morning, Jeremiah."

"Then it'd be Tuesday. That's when I had the appointment with my starving dentist. We wholesale a bit to the trade. Mr. Moore drops in occasionally when he's in Washington."

"Thinning grayish brown hair, about a hundred and ninety, fiftyish?"

"Yes, that's Mr. Moore," Mrs. Adams said. "A charming man, very bookish. Seems to know so many of the English poets and recites from them beautifully. 'Heaven from all creatures hides the book of Fate . . . All but the page prescrib'd, their present state.' His specialty's really stamps, not coins; that's probably why he's turned to us from time to time over the past few years."

"Not just for coins, either. He once bought a full set of Grenadier Guards and a partial set of Hussars for his young nephew, who'd apparently just lost his tonsils to a starving surgeon. We hope he isn't in any trouble."

"Not at all. But he might have information related to a matter under investigation. Our informant claimed not to know his real name, but did you say your Mr. Moore had indulged in harmless bragging about having bought a hundred Eisenhower dollars from you earlier in the week at a good price. That's why I'm here. I suppose he wrote a check?"

Mrs. Adams laughed. "Not Mr. Moore. Old-fashioned that way, dosen't trust banks. Always pays cash. Four hundred dollars for the forty-percent silver San Francisco gem uncirculated Eisenhowers of seventy-three, which *is* a good price in the present market."

"Where does he have his place of business?"

"New York City," Mr. Adams said. "West Forty-second or Forty-third. He's asked us to drop in if we're ever up there, but with my arthritis we stay pretty close to home."

"It's Forty-second, Jeremiah. I can't for the moment think of its name, though I remember his saying once he'd a view of the Public Library. It's not on the street either, probably second or third floor. Nothing pretentious, I'm sure. Mr. Ryan, wouldn't you like a cup of tea and a scone? You look as if you could use a little nourishment, if you don't mind my saying so. Of course, anybody looking at Jeremiah would think I kept him on a ration of hardtack and water."

"Tea and a scone are just what I need, but I'm already late for a meeting with my supervisor. Do you recall Mr. Moore's first name?"

"Never volunteered it," Mr. Adams said, "and we never force ourselves, you know. We aren't starving dentists, starving surgeons."

Belknap, his mind prowling the north side of 42nd Street,

nodded absently. Maybe there was a lovely pot of gold at the end of the rainbow after all. Except this lovely pot was of silver.

Brdnowski started the engine and played drag-racing tunes on the accelerator. "Learn anything, Fred?"

"Blind alley," Belknap replied, prospecting for leg room in the rear of the Datsun. "Nobody remembers a recent sale of a hundred Eisenhower silver dollars."

As he restively lit a cigarette, Belknap wondered whether the bookish Mr. Moore, alias Joseph Smith, would have had the physical stamina to get back to New York after he left St. Albans. Mr. Moore, or rather those telltale silver dollars leading to his door, explained why someone badly wanted to dispose of Brdnowski and Bessmeyer before they could pass on what they unknowing knew. But some missing element in that chain of events, some element Belknap couldn't quite identify, kept tapping for recognition at the back door of his consciousness.

Brdnowski suddenly punched into the motorized cavalry of early rush-hour traffic as if in command of a halftrack. Belknap, hearing clarion blasts from the horn of the car behind, braced himself for a crash. Brdnowski unconcernedly leaned out his window and told the driver where to shove his horn. Lamblike, he returned to the fold. "What happens next, Fred?"

"Where's the wedding taking place?"

"Just over the D.C. line. Silver Spring."

"And the honeymoon?"

"We figured on a motel in the area, so it'd be easy to get back to the city if the mood hit us."

"The mood isn't going to hit you. Until I give the word, you don't leave your motel. No phone calls, either, unless you want to share his-and-her slabs at the morgue. You have your wedding, find your motel. Then we adjourn to the honeymoon suite and go over everything that's happened from the time you got to the Library of Congress."

"Sure sounds cozy," Myrt said. "You spending the night with us too, Guardian Angel?" She emitted a forlorn laugh. "Don't mind me, Fred. I never saw a corpse until today . . . outside of my daddy. My mom, she left us early, so I don't know what happened to her. My kid brother died when a motorcycle he stole hit a garbage truck just before he was supposed to ship out to 'Nam. Brdnowski and me, I guess we got to trust you. We sure got nobody else."

"Well, there's your uncle with the carnival," Brdnowski said. "And I got a half-sister in California, at least she was last I heard, but I'm not going to split hairs with the bride." He swung off Dupont Circle and headed northeast on New Hampshire. "If it's okay with you, Fred, I'll pick up Sixteenth to Alaska Avenue and cut over to Georgia. This preacher I've lined up is a couple of blocks from the Silver Spring Holiday Inn. You don't think we got a tail, do you?"

"Fred's too smart for that, Brdnowski."

Belknap bemusedly adjusted his tie. Under the aegis of what whimsical patron saint did these two not-quite-noble savages run wild in the urban woods? But if he could manage to keep them on ice the next twenty-four hours— and if wishes were horses, beggars would ride—he might for a change be the one orchestrating events. With grateful acknowledgments, of course, to his collaborator, Mr. Moore, for artistic and other valuable insights.

Brdnowski jabbed a button on the stereo. Strident rock, light years from the orchestral score for which Belknap was writing program notes, burst from the speakers. He stayed with his own score and, staying with it, recognized the element missing from the chain of events leading to the death of Detective Rosenbaum. It wasn't a shocking discovery—he'd played ostrich with its head in the sand too long to claim that—but it was still a shock to see everything laid out so unequivocally just as he was starting to believe he'd bought time in which to maneuver. The deck—why should he be surprised?—had been stacked from the beginning.

All the more reason, though, to take possession of those four packs of Eisenhower silver dollars before he said au revoir to the honeymooners. They were going to be his insurance policy of last resort.

"Brdnowski," he shouted above the frenzy of amplified guitars, "pull up by the first pay phone."

24

AT OPPOSITE ENDS of a bench in Lafayette Square, southwest of the bronze, verdigris equestrian statue of Andrew Jackson, two men stared into the dusk falling on the north portico of the White House.

At one end there was Malkin, slim, elegant, politely distant in a style perfected over generations by those blooded young Englishmen destined from birth not only for Eton and Cambridge but also, barring revolution or abolition of the Honors List, for a splendid obituary in *The Times*. That his own rites of passage had taken him instead, thanks to a teacher's encouragement, from a rural Illinois schoolhouse during the Depression to four impoverished years as a scholarship student at Northwestern, then to eventual baptism in intelligence via the OSS, had long ago become irrelevant. Malkin, living so many years in a menagerie of mirrors, had himself become a figure in a mirror, reflecting traits, selectively winnowed from experience, that seemed best suited at any particular moment to the persona required by his calling. This evening his features in profile suggested seasoned wiseness and careless superiority, like the bas-relief effigy of a distinguished civil servant on a commemorative coin.

At the other end there was Hathaway, who had begun his FBI career as a clerk at the end of World War II. He had spent the recent part of his thirty years in the Bureau living on his knees, driven there by the unpredictable tyrant he still called Mr. Hoover. During the director's very last years, when the Seat of Government had become a snake pit and nobody knew which inspector or SAC would next be on the bricks, Hathaway had also lavished the old man with flattery, gossip about his favorite enemies, and instant accomodation to his prejudices. It was no way to live, but at SOG it had been the only way to survive. Hathaway had put up with it not only because he'd given the customary hostages to fortune, but also because he loved the Bureau, and because Mr. Hoover wouldn't be around forever, though at times he'd been less than sure about that. Those had been bad days for the Bureau; these were bad days still. But Hathaway was a loyalist, determined to see it restored to greatness.

Of course, some habits could never be broken. He still observed the punishing weight norms set out in the old Metropolitan Life tables for a six-foot man of large frame, kept his black hair cut medium-short, and unfailingly wore the uniform: white shirt, subdued tie, conservative suit, and black shoes with a high shine. He was fifty-one and not averse to becoming the next director if the cards fell that way.

"I know you're wondering," he said to Malkin, "why I insisted on meeting here. But what I have is too sensitive even for the scrambler, and it would have attracted the wrong kind of attention if I'd come to your offices." It ought to be unnecessary to mention the additional advantages of meeting on neutral ground. "Does anyone know you're seeing me?"

"I followed your instructions."

Hathaway chose to ignore the linked nuances of boredom and impatience. What he had on the burner was going to be so unpalatable for Malkin, it was impossible to guess which way the man would jump. Hathaway very much wanted him to jump in the direction of cooperation. It was why he was even willing to forgo the pleasure of pointing out, as he went along, just how wrong Malkin had been in their earlier clash over the Willis toll tickets.

"About an hour ago, I learned that an extremely frightened KGB officer attached to their U.N. Mission as an economic adviser threw himself into our arms this afternoon. He claims he was under arrest and being forcibly returned to Moscow by Shiskin, chief of mission security, when he saw a chance to escape by disabling Shiskin with a karate chop. Our videotape coverage of the mission's entrance confirms the incident. What ultimately gives the story credibility is, he left a very dead chief of security on the sidewalk."

Hathaway paused until a handholding couple, sharing, as they walked by, a cigarette wafting the unmistakable smell of marijuana, disappeared into the dusk. He tracked the firefly glow of the cigarette as it erratically danced westward along Pennsylvania Avenue. "The Russkis are already raising hell with State. Not only has one Russki murdered another, but the murder, according to them, occurred on premises subject to their sovereignty under the Vienna Convention. They want their national surrendered, and surrendered now. The New York police aren't any happier. They view it as a crime committed on the sidewalks of New York, and the suspect as thier exclusive property. Hell, it happened almost across from the Nineteenth Precinct. The FBI's denied knowledge of his whereabouts, and probably no one believes that. For the moment he's in safe harbor at Twenty-five Federal Plaza."

"Jurisdictional warfare," Malkin mused, "always enhances the predisposition of governments and their bureaucracies to fight to the death over the wrong molehill. Does your man know he's wanted for murder?"

Hathaway nodded. "New York decided, since he was attached to mission technical staff, not diplomatic staff, that letting him know the Manhattan D.A. could prosecute him for murder was the kind of healthy jolt needed to discourage protracted dickering over quid pro quos."

"I suppose that's one way to teach him the alphabet. But if he knows anything at all about his rights, he knows

Article Thirty-seven of that same Vienna Convention extends immunity from criminal prosecution to members of a mission's technical staff as well.''

"Since he was under arrest by his own government," Hathaway replied blandly, "there's a question as to whether he was still a member of the technical staff. Be that as it may, he was so anxious to stay in safe harbor, he was more than ready to talk first, dicker later.''

"And what's this noble fellow's motive for defecting? Aside from making the world safe for democracy.''

"The usual grab bag. He'd always put duty and country first, but had become increasingly disillusioned by this and that. It predictably soon boiled down to survival. Specifically, he'd once been into black-market and smuggling activities, occasionally even financing them from a Swiss bank account set up to get funds to an agent named Chessplayer. One of his partners recently got nailed for other illegal activity and began naming names. That's why he was on his way back to Moscow.''

"Well, we can hardly expect any of them will be another St. Francis of Assisi. This one, I presume, is supposed to hold special interest for me?''

Thirty years in the Bureau had taught Hathaway the virtues of diplomacy in this kind of sensitive encounter. The man beside him occupied a far higher position than he in the intelligence hierarchy, and such men had countless ways to strike back at heralds who brought bad news. Still, the man beside him had just provided the opening; the tape would prove it if matters got to that sticky stage where a transcript had to be produced, so why pussyfoot around? Businesslike directness, impersonal recital of the facts . . . those were the qualities to get onto the tape.

"His name's Ivan Glukhov, and to deal with the heart of the matter, he claims he's the case officer for Belknap, code name, Chessplayer. A Soviet agent, he claims, since at least sixty-three.''

A panhandling squirrel, coming down from a yellowwood tree to investigate the silence, raised its paws to plead for a bread crumb. Malkin sighed.

"Glukhov's trying to sell you the Brooklyn Bridge."

"Perhaps, but he hasn't stumbled yet. What he's selling comes in two categories. Information we can check immediately, information we can't. The immediate's ringing true. On the other, we need your help, because you know names, dates, and events that aren't in our files." Hathaway mustered an ingenuous expression. "That in fact probably aren't in anybody's files. I assume you know of Demichev, First Chief Directorate?"

"Yes, I know of Demichev. As he undoubtedly knows of you and me. Their *Zapiski* files begin where the Book of Genesis leaves off."

"Demichev once told Glukhov that Belknap was responsible for Philby's getting out of Beirut just as your people were about to cart him away. Any truth in that? Was Belknap even in Lebanon in sixty-three?"

"I've no authority to discuss the Beirut operation"— Malkin broke off—"you're not taping this conversation, are you, Hathaway?"

"No," he lied in good conscience, since he was sure Malkin was also breaking the unwritten ground rules. A man would have to be a fool, which Malkin wasn't, to accept a summons to an urgent secret meeting on a bench in Lafayette Square, agenda undefined, without arranging insurance.

"All right, I'll go this far. There was no way to get at Philby in Beirut without creating unmanageable political problems. David and I were in Moscow. I'd a friendship with Philby dating back to the Spanish Civil War . . . he saved my life under circumstances we won't waste time on now. I'd also a ring, a keepsake from those days, with which Philby was familiar. Washington, knowing all this ancient history, decided to have the ring delivered to Philby to persuade him to leave Beirut for an ostensible meeting with me. Obviously I couldn't be the messenger, so David was chosen.

"So yes, David was in Beirut, but his being there means nothing, because if in fact he was under Soviet control, he didn't have to get to Beirut to warn Philby. He could have done it from Moscow."

"If in fact he was under Soviet control, maybe he did do it from Moscow. Glukhov says the KGB engineered a compromising sexual liaison to recruit Belknap, then discovered he was already ideologically disposed to cooperate."

"Your defector does seem to have a superficial familiarity with David's brief time in Moscow and Beirut. But the business with the girl at Moscow State University, if that's the girl he's talking about, was a deception exercise designed to turn a tidy profit for us."

"I don't know what girl he's talking about, and I doubt he does either, since his early material on Chessplayer comes from hearsay he's picked up over the years."

"Yes, that's one of the problems with hearsay, and I've yet to hear any hard facts to justify taking the man seriously."

"Those I'm coming to," Hathaway said stolidly. He still didn't want Malkin as an enemy, and the man would be eating rancid raw crow soon enough. "Glukhov took over management of Chessplayer in the spring of sixty-eight. He was told Chessplayer had just supplied Moscow the name of an STB agent peddling information that could expose a Soviet network in West Germany. The peddler, as a result, was going to be put out of business. My question is, did Belknap in fact have dealings then with such an STB agent?"

Malkin's expression continued to reflect mannered skepticism, but he was plainly no longer bored. "Perhaps it'd be useful," he said laconically, "to take a turn around the square."

Hathaway smiled. Everything comes to he who waits, unless he waits for an uptown bus on the downtown side of the street.

* * *

"I can't get into specifics, but David did meet that spring with an STB man who died soon afterwards. Of natural causes, as far as we could tell." Malkin absently kicked an abandoned skateboard on the curving, cobbled walk. "What else did your drop-in have to say about that period?"

"As soon as Glukhov arrived in Bonn, Chessplayer supplied him with a copy of something called the Burgdorf Report." Hathaway watched two pigeons squabbling in the stubble of a barren flower plot adjoining the esplanade to Pennsylvania Avenue. "Was there any such report?"

"Hathaway"—Malkin's voice was uncharacteristically petulant—"this is extremely awkward for me. I've really no business discussing the events of sixty-eight, but—"

"The equation is changing," Hathaway suggested cautiously.

Malkin shrugged noncommittally. "If memory serves, David did obtain the Burgdorf Report from our MAD liaison and briefly had it in his safe. It's difficult, so many years later, to remember the exact sequence. We had the Russian invasion in August. There was also a messy problem with our German friends. We got onto—I should say David got onto; it goes back in a curious way to the STB contact—a Soviet network involving military and political figures. The Germans didn't want to face the realities."

As Malkin, Hathaway thought, didn't want to face present realities. "That would be the network," he pressed, "involving a free-lance photographer named Speer and a Bundeswehr general named Fehler?"

Malkin this time made no effort to conceal his distress. "Your information from Glukhov is again correct. But if David had been under Soviet control, he wouldn't have been in the business of exposing a Soviet network."

"He had no choice. Both he and Moscow suspected the information he was getting about the photographer from his source at Oberürsel had been put on his plate by Counterintelligence. He had to expose the photographer's network to avoid the risk of exposing himself."

"More of the Gospel according to Glukhov, of course."

"Persuasive, however." Hathaway could almost feel sorry for Malkin. One of the realities the man couldn't face was the possibility of betrayal by a trusted associate, and perhaps out of loyalty to the associate, or simply out of a consuming need to preserve a posture of infallibility with respect to his judgment of men, he was waging this futile rear-guard action.

"And has Glukhov"—Malkin steered Hathaway onto the salmon-pink brick pathway leading to the Lafayette statue in the square's southeast corner—"been able to pick David out of a photo lineup?"

"There's been no lineup. New York field office had no immediate access to a photo of Belknap. I was hoping you could supply one. Perhaps you've an old album from Germany?"

"Perhaps."

"He did describe Belknap, however. Tall, lean, hair beginning to gray, scar on right cheek. How's that sound?"

A guttural staccato throbbing filled the sky. Malkin glanced at the lights of the helicopter circling the White House landing pad. "This is not only extremely awkward for me, Hathaway, it's extremely distasteful. No matter. Let's get on with it."

"Glukhov followed Belknap to London in seventy-one. A year or so later Belknap got in trouble when certain diamonds he was supposed to deliver to Cairo turned out to have a short count. Correct?"

"Correct," Malkin said curtly.

"It's Glukhov's theory Chessplayer stole the diamonds so as to be forced to the sidelines. Man couldn't cope any longer with the strain of a double role. Whether the theory's right or wrong doesn't really matter, because by seventy-four he was again working for the Russkis. That's why Glukhov was assigned to their U.N. Mission."

"And the nature of his alleged relationship with David from that point on?"

"The same as in Bonn and London. With a significant added element. Chessplayer, Glukhov learned before leaving Moscow, had had a homosexual relationship in Germany with a U.S. soldier—name unknown to Glukhov—who in seventy-four had been assigned to guard duty at a Washington intelligence facility. The soldier was having financial problems and willing to supply Chessplayer with classified information . . . for a price." Hathaway, sure he'd delivered the coup de grâce to any lingering illusions Malkin might have about Belknap, felt it was time to be charitable. "I'm afraid the soldier in question has to be Frank Willis. Do you know whether he was having financial problems in seventy-four?"

"He'd been through a bankruptcy and divorce. It's probably why he reenlisted." Malkin looked away and watched traffic on Pennsylvania Avenue. "It's true he did seem to worship the ground David walked on. In Germany, you understand. But I can't believe David's homosexual. He's been married, had many relationships with women."

Hathaway, still practicing charity, nodded. "Bisexuality isn't that uncommon. Apparently Belknap introduced Willis to a Soviet illegal posing as the owner of a secondhand bookstore in Greenwich Village. About fifty, according to Glukhov. Code name, Edgar. He became Willis's postman. Edgar was supposed to make a delivery in New York Tuesday afternoon. He didn't show up. Didn't show up Wednesday, either."

They had come to the heroic bronze of the Marquis de Lafayette, attended by those four less celebrated French noblemen who had also cast their lot with General Washington and the thirteen colonies. Across Madison Place, a few lights shone from the Grecian, anciently gray Treasury Annex and the reddish-brick Court of Claims building.

Malkin turned north toward St. John's Parish House. "Edgar may be a man we've been looking for. A hospital patient here until mid-morning. We missed him by a few hours."

"It happens." Hathaway, wanting another charitable writeoff, added, "In fairness, I have to tell you that when New York interviewed the receptionist at Belknap Associates, she stated someone identifying himself as Edgar phoned earlier today and said he'd recovered from his indisposition. I'm sorry."

"Why be sorry?" Bitterness crept into Malkin's voice for the first time. "Facts are facts. You told me this afternoon Willis, who had a shortwave receiver in his apartment, had phoned David's New York office yesterday, and I dismissed the implications. I learned a few hours ago David sent a member of my senior staff to Chicago on what now seems a deliberate wild-goose chase, and I dismissed the implications. He also requisitioned a gun from the armorer and skeleton keys from our housemother, and I dismissed the implications. Why he wanted the gun and skeleton keys I don't yet know, but the staff officer sent to Chicago had information about a cabdriver for whom we were looking, and now the cabdriver's missing. And this morning David apparently lied to me about his relationship with Willis. Hathaway, we don't know each other well, we don't know each other at all, but I'm not going to dissemble. I'm—how shall I put it without too much self-indulgent bathos?—I'm in a state of shock."

"Understandable."

Malkin responded with a wintry smile. "To say I feel betrayed is an understatement. But our only job, yours and mine, is to select the best immediate course of action. You people, once you've the necessary evidence, generally favor arrest and prosecution in cases of this kind."

"Not necessarily."

"Not necessarily, but generally. We, on the other hand, like to convert a loss entry to a profit entry, either by making the agent an unsuspecting channel for disinformation or by turning him, in which case the possibilities are endless. But David's too experienced to be fooled for long by spoon-fed pablum, so I rule out the first alternative." Malkin broke his stride. "Before we take any other steps—this is vital—I need to confront him privately. I know this man. I can turn him. In fact, everything could come to a head before the evening's over. He phoned from somewhere at the end of the afternoon and left a message asking to meet in my office at ten tonight."

"Interesting." Hathaway had the uncomfortable feeling Malkin was outflanking him. "Where's Belknap staying in Washington?"

"The Hay-Adams."

"All right, I'll have Washington field office put him under surveillance once he shows at the Hay-Adams or your offices."

"It wouldn't work. He'd quickly discover it, and that would send him to his bolt-hole. We don't want a repetition of Burgess-Maclean. I'll see he doesn't get away."

"We're also planning to check out Greenwich Village secondhand bookstores in the morning."

"Glukhov doesn't know the name of the bookstore?"

"That's what he claims. It may be a bargaining counter. He claims Edgar isn't under his control and that he picked up information about the bookstore in Moscow."

"If that's true, it's possible Edgar's now in some other business, but by all means check out the Village. What are your immediate plans for Glukhov?"

"To try to avoid friction with NYPD, we're about to take him out of Federal Plaza on a stretcher to a waiting ambulance, then bring him here by plane for further interrogation."

"Good. I'd like to talk to him myself."

"One other matter. It'd be helpful if we knew Belknap was in Washington rather than New York on Tuesday."

"He was a witness here before a congressional committee. I happened to catch it on the evening news." Malkin resumed his leisurely pace. "But if Willis, as you say, was passing information to Edgar, David could've been in San Francisco and it wouldn't have mattered. The ultimate irony is, and believe me, Hathaway, it's a humbling irony, I brought David into the investigation of the package mailed to the White House—which, off the record, contained stolen NSC material—not only becaue he's superb in such operations, or so it had seemed in the past, but also because I knew he'd once had a special relationship with Willis. Although I didn't know then what I've since learned from you about the probable essence of that relationship, Willis, as an NSC guard, came to mind as a suspect. I thought, though I couldn't openly admit it to David, that if Willis was involved, David could get him to talk."

"I'm beginning to have a better grasp of cause and effect. As soon as you told Belknap about the package, he'd realize an interrogation of Willis was inevitable, and a confession likely. That was when Willis's death also became inevitable."

"A death for which I bear heavy responsibility."

Hathaway, not inclined to dispense absolution, gazed beyond the small magnolia on their left, where spume from the two east fountains formed translucent parasols.

"One element in your scenario bothers me," Malkin said tentatively. "If Glukhov was David's case officer, and if David decided, as you suggest, that Willis had to be disposed of, he presumably would have requested KGB assistance through Glukhov. You haven't mentioned anything about Glukhov's role in Willis's death."

"Because he seems to have had no role. As I said earlier, he didn't even know Willis's name. Nor the name of the intelligence facility."

"Or so he prudently claims. Whatever else a defector might admit, he's not going to admit complicity in the death of a U.S. soldier. Anyhow, his claims of ignorance are irrelevant. David could've supplied him with the necessary information for finding Willis."

"Apparently they communicated through cutouts and dead-letter boxes. Too time-consuming in this emergency. My guess is, Belknap used a channel that went directly to a KGB hit team."

"Yes, possibly. At the same time, no defector ever tells the whole truth. Glukhov might shield David in certain areas simply to shield himself."

It occurred to Hathaway that Malkin too might shield Belknap in certain areas simply to shield himself. Instead of trying to turn Belknap, he might offer him, or frighten him into taking, a backdoor route to Canada or Cuba. Belknap would win safe passage to Moscow, but he'd carry with him all his dirty laundry. Malkin, and no doubt others taken in by Belknap over the years, might prefer a solution like this to having Belknap around to hang out that laundry when the damage assessors began apportioning blame. Hathaway decided after all to have Washington field office pick up Belknap's trail at the Hay-Adams or Malkin's offices. If Malkin chose to open the door of the cage, the bird wouldn't fly far.

"Chessplayer," Malkin said musingly. "I wonder if David chose that designation himself. We all indulge our fantasies, you know, when it comes to code names."

Ahead of them, illuminated by an overhead light on H Street, a bearded young entrepreneur wearing sawtooth cutoffs and a buttonless denim vest sat on a campstool strumming a guitar. A red kerchief covered part of his bare chest. In front of him on the grass for the offertory was an upturned cowboy hat. Several couples, arms linked, bodies swaying, listened as he sang of doomed lovers. The incense of marijuana again announced itself to Hathaway. He suddenly realized he no longer remembered how it had felt to be young.

"The odd thing is, David isn't that good at chess. When

we used to play, I'd beat him handily most of the time. Yet I'm not that much of a chess player myself."

"I hope you're on your game tonight."

"Yes," Malkin said, dropping a dollar bill in the cowboy hat, "we'd better hope that, hadn't we?"

25

A RECTANGULAR GROUPING of couches and club chairs softly upholstered in brown leather dominated the small lobby to the right of the Hay-Adams entrance. Chandeliers highlighted the dark patina of paneled mahogany columns that flowed into marbel arches. In one of the chairs, a man about thirty-five was reading the *Star*. Belknap studied him carefully before turning left to the registration desk.

When he asked for messages, the desk clerk produced a sealed envelope. No return address. It could be a note from Vanessa, except she was supposed to be spending the evening with her father.

In his room he poured a drink from his suitcase flask, took it neat, and opened the envelope. Stapled to the upper right corner of a single sheet of paper was a man's ring with an inscription in Spanish. Belknap stared at it, stunned yet fascinated. It had to be the ring, or a nearly perfect imitation, he'd given Philby over a decade ago in Beirut.

He put a hand to the bed's headboard. His eyes moved at last to the unsigned message scrawled in green ink:

> *Per contingency plan, this ring will establish bona fides of sender. Information just received from New York friends that G this afternoon found new employment and is undoubtedly offering rare chess item for immediate delivery to prove sincerity. Situation requires removal of rare chess item from local market without delay. Per*

238

contingency plan, travel itinerary and related documents needed for safe transfer of item available nine tomorrow morning at New York emergency location. Ring to be used to establish your own bona fides.

Belknap poured another drink. His hand didn't shake, and he was pleased about that, because it meant his anger was stronger than his fear, and his fear was very strong indeed. For one savage moment he almost wanted revenge more than he wanted his own survival.

He pocketed the ring, entered the bathroom, and sent the shredded note into the Washington sewer system. He washed his grimy face and hands. It was a quarter to ten by his watch, time to fish or cut bait.

He tossed onto the bed the Detective Special he'd confiscated from Brdnowski, and a penlight and glass cutter and two rubber suction cups he'd bought after leaving Brdnowski and Company at their Silver Spring motel. The gun issued by the armorer stayed in the holster strapped over his left shoulder. From a closet hanger he removed a lightweight jacket bought when he was twenty pounds heavier. Did they make pockets larger when the jacket was larger? Belknap didn't know, but the bulge created by Brdnowski's gun in the discarded jacket was unacceptable. It couldn't hurt to try more accommodating tailoring.

He donned the replacement jacket, placed Brdnowski's gun in the right-hand pocket, the other items on the bed in the inside breast pocket, then picked up the phone.

"House detective," he told the Hay-Adams operator. "It's urgent."

Seconds later, a hoarse male voice said, "Security."

"My name's Belknap, and I'm using my room phone so I can talk privately without further upsetting the lady I intended to take into your fine restaurant. A man in the lobby who's pretending to be reading a newspaper exposed his genitals as we walked by. Though we won't be eating here now, the lady's too upset, we'll wait in the restaurant foyer in case you need us as witnesses.''

"All right, Mr. Belknap, I'll check him out, but you realize we can't detain the man unless we catch him in the act.''

"Well, if that's the way these things work, we might as well leave immediately. But can you at least keep him in the lobby with some kind of, uh, well, casual conversation until I get back to the lady and we're safely on our way? I don't want any scenes, I don't want any lawsuits against the hotel either, but I can't guarantee what might happen if he showed up in the restaurant foyer before we'd left. If we go down those stairs to the basement public phones, can we still get out the H Street doors at this hour?''

"Sounds to me the sensible way to handle it, Mr. Belknap.''

"Appreciate that immensely. My granddad used to keep a suite here year-round. I'll be starting for the lobby the moment I hang up.''

Turning smartly right as he stepped from the elevator, Belknap kept his eyes on the carpeting, but his peripheral vision caught both the newspaper reader's abrupt loss of interest in his paper and the house detective moving in on him with the dispassionate purposefulness of an experienced ex-cop.

Once in the restaurant foyer Belknap took the basement stairs three at a time. Then a short passageway, and up twelve steps to double doors opening to the sidewalk. He sprinted past the U.S. Chamber of Commerce building, cut northwest at the corner, and stopped to catch his breath on the other side of Farragut Square.

He placed the call to Malkin from an outside pay phone. A superannuated voice at ComOpsCenter put him through a recognition drill. When Malkin came on the line, Belknap tested the waters with bumbling vagueness.

"George, I know I set up our meeting for ten, but the damn car had a flat. I'm lucky to have found anyone to fix it this hour of the night."

"What car? I didn't know you had a car. Where are you?"

"At a gas station in Arlington. I rented the car this afternoon. The attendant's working on it now. I'll be about thirty minutes late."

"What're you doing in Arlington?"

"That's one of the things I want to explain when I see you. There's something else you should know. Frank Willis phoned my New York office yesterday. I learned this afternoon. How he knew I was in business in New York is beyond me."

"Well, right now I'm concerned about the cabdriver, Brdnowski. Tiffany called from Chicago to report on his Lundhoven interview. Lundhoven was in meetings all morning last Tuesday. He supplied names of the people he was with; they can be contacted tomorrow. But the cabdriver Tiffany says he told you about before you sent him to Chicago is missing. Not in his apartment, hasn't been reporting to work. Where is he, David? Arlington?"

Belknap took a moment to decide whether Brdnowski should be in Arlington, or simply missing. "I did go by his apartment, George, but he wasn't there then, either."

"Too bad, too bad. However, there have been other developments. You might find them interesting."

Belknap found himself unable to resist the bait. "Such as?"

"Do you remember the name Glukhov? Ivan Glukhov?"

"Glukhov?" As he wiped the perspiration on his forehead, he could feel the throbbing of his pulse. He was too out of training to be running footraces through the streets of Washington. And to be trying to defuse loaded questions. "There was an Ivan Glukhov on the Soviet diplomatic roster in Bonn. In London, too. Early on, I think somebody tagged him KGB."

"That marvelous almost total recall of yours, David, I've always envied it. More recently Glukhov's been attached to their U.N. Mission, but naturally you wouldn't know about that."

"No," he said uneasily, and waited. Why was Malkin gratuitously serving up sensitive information on an insecure line?

"This afternoon he put away their head of security. On the sidewalk in front of the mission. Desperate man, obviously. Contacted the FBI immediately afterward. Hathaway's had him brought down here . . . there have been tantalizing hints he might have information of interest to us."

Belknap waited painful seconds. "What kind of information?"

"Ah, well, you know the FBI. Hathaway's playing it close to his chest. But I'm hoping you and I can get a crack at Mr. Glukhov first thing in the morning."

"It's difficult to talk from this phone, George. The traffic . . . you can probably hear it."

"Always a busy place, Arlington. Don't rush to get here. I've things to keep me occupied . . ."

Belknap walked briskly up Connecticut to the May-flower, then sauntered through its block-long arcade to 17th Street. Satisfied he was clean, he flagged a cab and asked to be taken to Georgetown. As they crossed the M Street bridge, he told the driver to turn on 28th and park the other side of Dumbarton. He gave the driver ten dollars, plus half of a twenty, and promised to be back in fifteen minutes with its other half.

The address that he had picked up en route to Silver Spring for the Brdnowski nuptials by phoning—after he had called the institute and left a message for Malkin—the one CIA man still in town who owed him favors, was a Federal-style townhouse on O Street. Gary must have thought it odd that his old creditor Belknap was asking him, rather than Malkin himself, for Malkin's address, but oddness is relative. He must have encountered things far odder since his day had begun. As for the old creditor, he had no suitable alternative. Malkin hadn't been listed in the phone book.

Manicured shrubbery and ironwork railings adjoined each side of the brick entranceway steps. Malkin probably still followed the rules he'd laid down over the years, which meant he wouldn't keep classified material in his home. Which meant there would be nothing too special about locks and other security devices. A silent burglar alarm perhaps, but Belknap intended to be finished within five minutes. The photo he needed shouldn't be difficult to find. And should it happen the master keys and picks wouldn't open the door, he was reluctantly prepared to use the glass cutter and suction cups on a windowpane.

There was a cloud over the moon, a gift from gods unknown. Belknap climbed the four steps to the front door. The third key opened it. He slipped inside and listened in the darkness. The thin beam from the penlight revealed a vestibule and marble refectory table. On the floor in the living room to his right was the same Bokhara that Malkin had had in Bonn. There were two fragile Queen Anne chairs, a love seat and long sofa upholstered in gold brocade, a teak chest inlaid with ivory and supporting two jade lamps, and, over the mantel, a large Gainsborough landscape he remembered that Malkin had bought at Sotheby's that first year in London.

Belknap shone the penlight on the stairs to the second floor. Somewhere there had to be a study, and in the study there should be photos and albums. The first vestibule door he tried led to a bathroom, the second to Malkin's study. A pair of nubby, tweedy armchairs faced an uncluttered mahogany desk. The rug was Persian, rich and worn. Two walls were lined with books. In the center of the third wall, beneath a dainty, mullioned window, was pedestal with a bust of Mozart. Antique muskets were mounted in display cases to the right and left. A curtained glass door in the corner led perhaps to a garden in back. A small rosewood table, its inlaid top a chessboard, stood near the curtained door. The beautifully crafted Staunton chessmen, the work of a Tirolean woodcarver, had been a birthday gift from General Fehler soon after Malkin set up shop in Bonn. Belknap wondered what Malkin thought each time he moved a pawn.

A floor creaked in the deserted house. Belknap held his breath, listening. He went to the bookshelves and ran the penlight up and down. On one shelf he found a small framed photograph of Malkin, posed in stylized tourist fashion in Red Square, an astrakhan on his head, the spires of the Kremlin in the background, as if he were reporting from Moscow for the evening news. It was too dated, of course, to be of use now. On an adjoining shelf he found another small framed photograph, equally stylized but recent enough in time to serve: Malkin in a blue blazer and white flannels (had he just come from a cricket match at Lord's?) standing next to a costumed, impassive beefeater at the Tower of London.

As he slipped the framed photograph into a jacket pocket and turned to leave, the overhead light went on. In the doorway was a barrel-chested man in his fifties with wiry sandy hair, buttonhole eyes, and the flat, squashed nose of a former boxer. He was wearing a soiled T-shirt, khaki slacks, and plimsolls. Belknap absorbed the bad news in a split second, as well as the tattoos of mermaids on his stocky arms and the Smith and Wesson in ready position.

"Excuse me, sir, if I startled you." He flashed a keyboard of white teeth in a friendly smile. "I'm Eddy Mathers. Since it was thought you might be dropping by, I was asked to keep an eye on the place. I've also been instructed to ask you to surrender the weapon you were issued by the armorer, so we can avoid any unfortunate incidents. Gently does it now, sir."

Belknap slowly removed his jacket and draped it over his extended left arm. With the first finger and thumb of his right hand he delicately plucked the gun from his shoulder holster and offered it, butt first, to Eddy Mathers.

"Kindly set it on that chair behind you, sir. Gently does it."

Belknap placed the gun on the tweedy chair. "You a Navy man, Eddy?"

"Marines, sir. Twenty-five years. Inchon in fifty, Lebanon in fifty-eight, Guantánamo in sixty-one and sixty-two, Saigon in sixty-three when the generals went after the Ngo brothers, Tel Aviv during the Six-Day War, Khesanh in sixty-eight."

"You've been a few places."

"It was an education, sir, I'll grant you that. I miss the Corps, but this job's an education, too. Could I ask you to move two feet forward, sir?"

Belknap moved two feet forward. He kept his left arm, draped by the jacket, casually extended. The weight of the snubnosed Detective Special in the jacket's right-hand pocket was comforting. "I think Vanessa Holden was telling me about you on my first day. Fast Eddy?"

"A lovely lady, Miss Holden, and I'm sorry we're making each other's acquaintance under these circumstances."

"Am I under arrest, Eddy?"

"Well, sir, we don't use that term in the unit, but I've been instructed to ask you to join me in my car, which means I'll have to use cuffs and put you in the trunk until we get to our destination. You'll have no trouble breathing, however. I was also instructed to delay your apprehension until you'd found whatever it was you came here looking for. If you'd kindly hand it over."

Belknap reached in a pocket and brought out the framed photograph of Malkin at the Tower of London. He tossed it at Eddy's feet. Eddy, gun aimed at Belknap's heart, bent to retrieve it. "Nothing fancy now, sir. We don't want any incidents." He frowned as he studied the photograph. "This is a picture of Mr. Malkin."

"It's what I came for, Eddy."

"I'm sure it is, sir. But it is puzzling, you have to admit. Do you mind if I use Mr. Malkin's phone for further instructions? I'd appreciate your sitting in the other chair with your hands on top of the desk. My goal is to have no incidents."

Belknap sat down, bunching his jacket on the desk. He folded his hands on top of the jacket. Eddy sat behind the desk and began dialing with his gun hand. Belknap scratched his nose and slowly lowered his hand to the jacket's right pocket. "Eddy?" he said softly.

"Yes, sir."

"Put down the phone. I have the drop."

Eddy looked up from his dialing. He smiled. "Now, none of that, sir. You behave yourself, or we'll be having an incident."

"Eddy, we've already had the incident." Belknap produced the Detective Special. "Put down the phone."

Eddy, still smiling, got to his feet. But he had enough sense not to try to bring his own gun into the play. "I'm afraid, sir, I'm going to have to remove that weapon from your control."

Belknap squeezed the trigger. There was a firecracker pop. Eddy's gun flew from his hand. Eddy looked at his empty hand, amazed. Belknap hoped he also had enough sense not to get himself killed.

"That's excellent shooting, sir. For the time being, you seem to be in charge."

'Thank you, Eddy. Please assume the position."

"What position is that, sir?"

"Against the bookshelves. Arms and legs spread-eagled. Stand three feet from the wall and lean into it. You've had training in martial arts?"

"Judo basically, sir. I also did some instructing at Quantico during a stateside tour in sixty-nine."

"Nothing fancy, then. We don't want any incidents." Belknap approached warily from Eddy's rear. He guessed the ex-Marine, notwithstanding the gun aimed at his spine, would make his move when the space between them had narrowed to inches, but since Eddy was expecting to be searched, Eddy's expectation gave Belknap the edge. A foot away, he brought the butt of the gun down on the base of Eddy's skull. Eddy fell with a weary grunt.

It was a paralyzing blow that would have put most men out of action for hours. With luck, it might hold Fast Eddy for thirty minutes. Belknap returned his other gun to its holster and put on his jacket. In the vestibule bathroom he found a roll of adhesive tape from which he tore enough strips to lock Eddy's mouth in neutral. He borrowed Eddy's belt, donated his own tie, and trussed the limp arms and legs as best he could.

He unlocked and opened the curtained glass door. He hauled Eddy to the threshold and rolled him like a coal sack down the steps leading to a lovely sunken garden. He locked the door, retrieved the spent shell, a few bullet fragments, the ruined Smith and Wesson, and the framed photograph of Malkin.

Outside the house, the trembling started. He nodded politely to a woman walking a Great Dane. He got rid of Eddy's gun, the other debris from the study, and the glass cutter and suction cups in a storm sewer. He was surprised, as he walked down 28th to Dumbarton, to find the cab still there. Twenty dollars wasn't what it used to be, but it still bought something.

"Long fifteen minutes," the driver said without rancor. His radio was tuned to a baseball game. He was munching potato chips and washing them down with a can of beer.

"Lafayette Square," Belknap said. He separated the photograph from its frame. The frame went out the window. The photograph he folded in his wallet. He wondered whether Malkin had posted Eddy Mathers to the house because of intuitive brilliance, or because a snitch named

Gary had passed along news of a late-afternoon phone call from an old creditor. He looked at his watch. It was ten-forty and paranoia was alive and well in Washington.

It was time to talk about Eisenhower silver dollars and an old Spanish ring. Belknap pushed the doorbell of the Lafayette Research institute and adopted a pose of nonchalance for the benefit of the inside guard, presumably walking from his desk's monitoring consoles to the one-way viewer. The door swung open. The functionary who'd been on duty last night bowed slightly as he bolted the door. Belknap bent over the desk to sign the register.

"I've been asked, sir, to collect and receipt for the gun you drew from the armorer this afternoon."

Ignoring his sense of absurd déjà vu, Belknap opened the left side of his jacket, untied the shoulder sling, and laid the holstered gun on the desk. As he started toward the stairway, a man built much like Eddy Mathers moved out of the shadows. "Excuse me, sir, not that way."

"Oh, yes. I've an appointment with Mr. Malkin."

"Mr. Malkin had to go out suddenly, sir. He wants you to use the guest room downstairs. Very comfortable, sir. TV, magazines, a wet bar. He should be back before long."

Belknap knew about Malkin's guest rooms. The ones in Bonn and London had been in basements, too. They had doors without inside knobs and no windows and an armed guard in the hall outside at all hours. He couldn't believe Fast Eddy had regained consciousness, then freed himself and contacted Malkin, but something had happened to change the equation. Perhaps the newspaper reader in the Hay-Adams lobby had been laid on by Malkin as insurance, in which case the unclever lie about the breakdown of a car in Arlington would've been blown as soon as the newspaper reader shook free of the house detective. The unclever lie about Arlington must have triggered the kind offer of the guest room.

"I won't be needing to use it, thanks. I'll get with Mr. Malkin in the morning."

"He was most definite, sir, about talking with you tonight. I'll show you down."

"Have to decline. Sorry." He backed toward the front door.

"You're making it awkward for me, sir, since I've orders to escort you there, willingly or unwillingly." He took a few more steps into the light. The fingers of his right hand played a casual tattoo on the stock of his sidearm.

Belknap was remembering the front door had to be unbolted. A half-second delay at most, but a half-second too long against a man ready to draw. "You don't leave me much choice. Lead the way."

"After you, sir. The downstairs door is straight ahead to your left."

The door was of heavy oak and reinforced with steel plates. It opened under protest as Belknap pulled on the oversized brass knob. In the dim light, the fifteen or so rough-hewn steps looked as if they'd been sawed from bridge timbers. Testing the first step, he said to the man behind him, "Is ComOpsCenter down there?"

"That'd be the building next door, sir. When Mr. Malkin returns, you might want to ask for a tour."

Belknap descended slowly. "My guess is, these steps date to when the house was built. Well over a hundred years ago. Nothing to walk on in bare feet."

"A lot of history in these old houses, sir."

"Maybe even buried treasure, plus a skeleton or two. Been in this job long, Sergeant?"

"That's a very nice guess, sir. How'd you know?"

"You reminded me of the top I had in my first outfit."

"What outfit was that, sir?"

"It wasn't really an outfit with a name." Belknap spun right in a half-crouch and lunged with both hands for the man's gun arm. He pulled forward and down, and the body behind him neatly somersaulted over his shoulder. "Just a place where you more or less learned to look after your own best interests."

In midair, the ex-sergeant instinctively curled into fetal position to protect his head, but when his body crashed brutally on the steps, momentum sent it bouncing downward like windblown tumbleweed. Belknap, hoping damage to the man was less than it appeared and that the noise had been absorbed by the thickness of the oak door, had his Detective Special out before he reached the landing. He turned the knob and shoved. The guard at the desk, opting immediately for noncombatant status, raised his hands.

Belknap, far more frightened than the white-faced guard, wondered what would be waiting for him on the street. "*Over here! Move!*"

The guard moved. Belknap pointed to the basement. "Down there."

"I'm not allowed to leave my post, sir, until I have a relief."

Belknap heard an edge of hysteria in his own abrupt laugh. Sedentary functionaries would still be at their posts when the world ended. "I'm your relief. Face the wall." He brought the gun down on the guard's head with minimum force, caught the slumping body, and desposited it on the basement landing.

He was working the bolt on the front door when he heard the nervous command to raise his hands. He swore as he whirled and dropped to one knee to make himself a smaller target. He'd forgotten the wicked, roving eye of the reception-area TV camera, monitored from the second floor by the guard opposite the tiny elevator. Now the guard was standing in the gloom at the top of the marble staircase, taking aim with both hands, Police Academy fashion. But he was another sedentary functionary, not an Eddy Mathers, and the distance was too great for accuracy unless he'd been spending his weekends on the firing range. Belknap, not knowing the characteristics of the Detective Special, got off an educational shot to teach the guard heroism was a risky business. As the man obligingly scuttled for cover, Belknap freed the bolt and slipped out the front door with his weapon once more in a jacket pocket.

The street seemed deserted, but he no longer believed in Santa Claus. His altogether modest ambition was to get to Pennsylvania Avenue without receiving a bullet in his back.

26

HIGHER AUTHORITY had intervened. General Igor Demichev didn't know the details, but late last night General Pechenko, now sitting across from him with the smug look of a toad breakfasting on fat marsh flies, had evidently called in a favor owed by a Politburo friend. The friend had then contacted a fellow member of the Politburo, KGB Chairman Andropov, who a few minutes ago in his office had politely but firmly suggested that Demichev be more forthright with Pechenko about the Chessplayer contingency plan.

So here they sat at the long conference table, eight in the morning Moscow time, the kibitzers and second-guessers and viewers-with-alarm, all waiting for Demichev's revelations so they could nitpick the contingency plan to death. It was nitpicking with which he could live, however, since by this hour all the critiques in the world by the armchair experts on Pechenko's side of the table couldn't change the outcome of the Chessplayer rescue operation.

"It is now midnight Thursday in Washington," he began, because he knew Pechenko found recitals of the obvious irritating. Except for himself, Pechenko never suffered fools gladly.

"Our latest information from there naturally lags some hours behind actual events." Demichev watched with dismay as old Professor Tudin dipped a thick crust of pumpernickel into a bowl of gruel. Beside the bowl was a wedge of cheese that looked as if it had been sliced from the muddy boot of a Lapp border guard. Of course, eight in the morning was early for a meeting by Professor Tudin's septuagenarian clock. The renowned psychiatrist performed best at the end of the day when lesser men in their sixties and fifties would agree to almost anything he proposed in order to escape his monologues on the unrecognized philosophical brotherhood between Freud and Lysenko. Tudin was a survivor. Even Beria had been one of his patients—psychosomatic psoriasis, it was bruited at the time; it was stressful in the inner circle during the Generalissimo's last years.

Next to Professor Tudin, Colonel Zalenin, representing Department 8, stared somberly at his folded hands. With cause, for the shy former Guards officer wore a black mourning armband in honor of the fallen martyr Major Shiskin. Demichev hoped, and knew the generous Zalenin shared the sentiment, something could be done about Shiskin. A posthumous medal, perhaps. Life was harsh, life in the service of one's country harsher, especially in a place as barbarous as New York, but if they could get him a medal, there would be an automatic increase in the widow's pension.

"The lag in information is understood," General Pechenko said, hammering each word as if it were an obstinate nail. "Our interest"—he waved a pudgy hand to include the officers and specialists on his side of the table—"is in the remarkable foolproof contingency plan about which we have heard so much and learned so little."

"If that has been so," Demichev replied, "I apologize."

"You know it has been so."

The man, Demichev thought, had all the charming delicacy of a defecating elephant. "Let me then try to remedy any such unintentional oversight. You already know the plan was conceived a number of years ago for Chessplayer's protection in a time of emergency. Professor Tudin will explain Captain Ivan Glukhov's role in its execution."

The professor pushed aside his bowl of gruel and fixed

his one good eye on Pechenko. "Glukhov provides a classic case of applied Pavlovian conditioning. He was recruited because he was thought to be an impressionable bourgeois opportunist, and we've never had cause to regret the diagnosis. In the course of his training he was exposed to various safe adventures in minor corruption—bringing in contraband for superiors, trading in the black market for his own account—and he never disappointed us. Later he was led step by step into more serious criminal activity."

"For what worthy purpose?" one of Pechenko's officers asked sardonically.

Tudin lit one of his vile cigarettes and contemptuously fixed his twitching eye on the interloper. "To create the required conditioned reflex. Stimulus-response psychology, Comrade. It was necessary to know that when the right stimulus was someday applied, the right response would occur."

"And this relates to Chessplayer's present situation in what fashion?"

"Perhaps a review of the historical background will clarify the relationship," Demichev interjected amiably. "When Chessplayer was stationed in Moscow in late sixty-two, he had on his staff an inexperienced young man named Belknap. Chessplayer had sufficient seniority to keep with him over the years a personally selected junior aide. In his judgment, Belknap was ideal for the role, which of course at some unknown future time might require the junior aide"—he shook his head sadly—"to be sacrificed for the greater good of mankind.

"With our cooperation, Chessplayer began the slow process of involving Belknap in matters that might in retrospect seem incriminating should his past activities ever be investigated. As a first step, he was encouraged to have an affair with a student at Moscow State University. Quite fortuitously, Chessplayer himself was ordered about this time to assist in an attempt to take Philby out of Lebanon. The details don't matter, but the attempt hinged on the delivery to Philby of a certain keepsake ring. Chessplayer chose Belknap to deliver it, so that when Philby disappeared immediately afterward, there might perhaps be one more curious item in Belknap's personnel file. The next contribution was ours. Professor?"

Professor Tudin exhaled a streamer of smoke nearly as yellow as his teeth. "We needed an asset we didn't have in inventory, a safely expendable, self-indulgent buffoon, so we had to start from scratch with the best raw material available. Ivan Glukhov was chosen. But to make him convincing in his future role, which might someday involve hostile interrogation, he had to undergo the training given a handler of agents." Tudin sighed with the weight of his memories. "Occasionally overzealous instructors wanted to fail him for various academic or character defects. We were forced to intervene more directly than we wished. Very trying."

"Sometimes the difficulties even tempted us to abandon the project," Demichev conceded. "The value of Chessplayer, the duty to protect him should unpredictable events put him at risk, made us persevere. After Glukhov graduated, we sent him to London to see if, once abroad, he'd behave as irresponsibly as his profile promised. When he'd passed these tests, we brought him back to Moscow where, in accordance with Professor Tudin's expert prescription, he was exposed to maximum boredom combined with maximum temptation."

Professor Tudin's self-deprecating smile was as thin and brittle as museum papyrus. "My contribution, Comrade General, was merely in suggesting the prescription for corruption. Yours was in the vital execution."

Flattery of any kind from this unkempt survivor of so many disgraced regimes was so uncharacteristic that Demichev briefly questioned his own hearing. "A bird," he countered, "cannot fly until it is hatched."

"When did this particular bird finally hatch?" Pechenko inquired.

Demichev ignored the gibe. "In early sixty-eight we felt the time ripe to bring Glukhov to my office for his Chessplayer indoctrination."

"You proceeded with admirable caution."

Innocence shone from Pechenko's plump face. But the remark was surely another gibe, not a compliment, not when it came from Pechenko, who carried in his genes the sly meaness of a Siberian timber wolf. "By this time Chessplayer and Belknap were stationed in Bonn. Chessplayer had sent Belknap to Prague to hold hands with an STB turncoat soon destined, according to his horoscope, to meet an untimely end. One more step in the slow process of putting interesting uncertainties in Belknap's file. But in Prague he acquired information that could endanger Fourth Department assets in West Germany, and though Chessplayer was discreetly trying to discourage follow-up, his position was awkward. We needed Glukhov on the scene not because he would have been of use in an immediate emergency, but because he wouldn't be credible in a future emergency unless he could demonstrate personal familiarity with the problems developing in Bonn.

"In my office I told him he'd be Chessplayer's new case officer. I gave him Chessplayer's background. He'd been sexually compromised in Moscow. He'd provided the Philby warning. And so on, and so on. And of course I told him Chessplayer's actual name was Belknap and showed him a photo so he could avoid accidental encounters at diplomatic functions."

Demichev turned to Lieutenant Nikitin, seated behind him, and said sotto voce, "Bring in our major." He swung back to face the stolid Pechenko coterie. "Some of you will remember the Burgdorf Report, which did nothing to help General Gehlen's reputation. Our late dear friend General Fehler had supplied us a copy before Glukhov left for Bonn. It was fed back to Glukhov on his arrival, ostensibly a housewarming present from Chessplayer. General Fehler also loaned Belknap a sub rosa copy for transmission to Washington. To close the circle. Washington's records, if consulted at a future time, had to reflect Belknap had had access to the Burgdorf Report. With such sticks and straw, we began to build Glukhov's perception of his agent."

Pechenko's grizzled eyebrows lifted skeptically. "You were confident by then that if the right button was pushed, Glukhov would defect?"

"Of course not. He hadn't yet been involved in enough serious criminal activity to guarantee that essential result." Demichev heard the door behind him open and stood up, beaming. "Yuri, how good to see you!"

Major Yuri Subotin, Nikitin a deferential step behind, clicked his heels. He was in KGB dress uniform, his medals and ribbons—a few so secret they could only be worn here—marching like scarabs across his chest. His pomaded black hair glistened in the sunlight pouring through the windows. His bloodshot eyes and dark-complexioned, sensual face showed the ravages of a night's carousing, yet who, everything considered, could find fault? Demichev embraced him and led him toward the conference table.

"For those who don't already know this gallant officer, I present Major Subotin." Swept along by his occasional penchant for hyperbole, he added, "If this affair has a hero, it is Yuri Sergeevich. In Bonn he operated the carillon that played the music Ivan Glukhov heard. The messages, the information, that came through *duboks* and cutouts to Glukhov from Chessplayer came only from Yuri Subotin. The Swiss banks Glukhov later dealt with on Chessplayer's behalf were responsible only to Yuri Subotin. Glukhov wasn't running Belknap, he was running Yuri Sergeevich."

Lieutenant Nikitin, acting on Demichev's prior instructions, began to clap softly. Applause gradually rose in the vast room like a fluttering of wings. In response, Subotin bowed. "One only does one's duty, Comrade General."

His breath carried the stale fumes of his hangover, and, notwithstanding the immaculate uniform, his armpits stank, but Demichev didn't think anyone except Nikitin would notice as long as they kept him standing. Demichev walked to the windows with the measured pace of an honorary pallbearer at a state funeral, knowing every eye would be on him. You couldn't be married to a tempestuous, vase-throwing concert pianist and not learn how to capture the attention of an audience.

"In effect"—he looked out at the woods and followed the course of a stream as it tumbled and frothed down a hillside of pines and birch—"what we created for Ivan Glukhov was a Potemkin village. Chessplayer was real, but he was unreal. Chessplayer existed, but he didn't exist. Our sticks, our straw, our cottages along the river banks." In his mind's eye he saw the frothing stream as a great river. He saw the festooned ship churning up wake, and at its rail the Empress, twirling a parasol while her debauched, one-eyed lover, a hand gently on her elbow, pointed out the sights. Demichev wondered if he was mad, whether everyone had become mad in this world where only mirages could be believed. "The sticks. The straw. The cottages along the river banks. All of them illusory, of course. Empty. Except as inhabited by Glukhov's imagination."

Waiters from the officers' mess brought in fruit, pastries, and bitter Turkish coffee. Professor Tudin cut into his discolored cheese with a boned jackknife he claimed was a gift from Stalin. Tudin had once cured of stuttering the son who had been captured and killed by the Germans. General Pechenko cupped an apple and, as if wringing the neck of a chicken, cracked it in half. Colonel Zalenin sipped coffee with his same abstracted look. Even though his duties in Department 8 on occasion required him to order assassinations, never an easy burden to bear, Zalenin was in such cases at least dealing with strangers. The burden was so different when you lost, as in the case of Major Shiskin, one of your own. Demichev resolved to invite the troubled man to his dacha in Zhukovka for some hunting after the present difficulties were settled. Not the best season for a good hunt, but it was the decent thing to do. Then he recalled that Zalenin, with his distaste for unnecessary violence, hunted only mushrooms.

"Once Chessplayer and Belknap had been transferred to London," he continued, "it might have seemed peculiar to Glukhov if, when he got there himself, he found his good friend Yuri Subotin on hand. So another officer was assigned to operate the London carillon, and Yuri Sergeevich made his invaluable contributions from Moscow. He became a civilian, a man with a bit of a hand in everything, eh, Major?"

"One only does one's duty, Comrade General."

Demichev took a bunch of Albanian grapes from a fruit plate and pondered the absurd ironies. Subotin wasn't a hero; his armpits stank, and he looked like a cheap incarnation of Joseph Goebbels circa 1936. But he'd been the right man for the job; casual treachery fit him like a second skin. "There was an 'accidental' meeting with Glukhov in the Metropole. One thing led to another, and the major persuaded him to smuggle out a *samizdat* manuscript that viciously libeled almost the entire leadership."

"It wasn't too difficult."

"No, you're too modest. Glukhov was a slippery fish to land." Demichev's gaze moved to the room's north wall and the hagiographic portraits of Chairman Andropov flanked by his two immediate KGB predecessors, Vladimir Semichastny and Aleksandr Shelepin. Above this unlikely troika, that ruthless old Chekist and spiritual father of them all, Feliks Dzerzhinsky, looked down benevolently. "As time went by, Glukhov accepted other remunerative commissions from his old Bonn companion."

"I merely tried to carry out your instructions, Comrade General."

"In which you were eminently successful. But curiously enough, in London an odd event occurred. Not in London, exactly. Somewhere between Amsterdam and Cairo. Belknap lost some diamonds."

"Diamonds?" General Pechenko said. He put down a pastry he'd been about to sample. "I've never heard about any diamonds."

"That's precisely why, my dear colleague, I'm now telling you about them. According to Chessplayer, they were intended for Hussein. Some of them were stolen. By Belknap or an unknown person. The mystery was never solved."

"Unsolved mysteries bother me."

"They bother all of us, but sometimes we have to live with them."

"Why would Belknap steal diamonds?"

"Why would anyone steal diamonds?"

"What happened to him? Was there an inquiry?"

"Of sorts. Belknap was given an option to resign, and did. He went into private business in New York."

"Perhaps someone, on a clear sunny day, discovered your Potemkin village and decided to put an ocean between Belknap and Chessplayer."

"It wouldn't be necessary to arrange a theft of diamonds to do that."

"Nevertheless . . . your operation may have been compromised."

"Impossible." Demichev was beginning to be alarmed by Pechenko's persistence. What he didn't need at this delicate time was Pechenko's undisciplined army of second-guessers rooting through operational records for evidence of carelessness, or something worse, in security procedures. "Only Chairman Andropov, Professor Tudin, Colonel Zalenin, Lieutenant Nikitin, and myself knew key details. On the outside and knowing less, only Major Subotin and Captain Smikov, who operated the carillon in London."

"You've overlooked one name. Ivan Glukhov. He might have discovered his dead-letter boxes were being serviced by Subotin or Smikov. It would give him the unpleasant feeling he was expendable and quickly send him in search of a sympathetic ear on the other side."

Professor Tudin's irreverent cackle could only have been duplicated in a hencoop at daybreak. "It is my paper on the true believer I'd like you to read sometime. It's a pity I wrote it before I became professionally involved with Ivan Glukhov, the truest of the believers. Over there"—he took aim with the tip of his knife at a general compass heading for the United States—"they could use lie detectors and Pentothal, even thumbscrews and enemas fifty percent sulfuric acid, and he'd still tell them Belknap was Chessplayer." He impatiently speared the last of his cheese. "And vice versa."

"Moreover, we've Chessplayer's assurance this is exactly what happened"—Demichev favored Pechenko with a reasonable facsimile of a smile—"when Glukhov went calling on the FBI yesterday."

Professor Tudin abruptly stood up and, with his crotchety, sublime indifference to any business interfering with his own, declared, "I must exercise my bowels."

Demichev announced a ten-minute recess.

"Nikitin?"

"Comrade General!"

"Over here." Demichev guided his aide to a corner of the room where they could confer privately. "The expert from the Department of Hindsight may for once not be on the wrong track."

"What do you have in mind, General?"

"Subotin. We may not have kept him on a short enough leash when, to make the right impression on Glukhov, we put him in business as a swashbuckling freebooter operating out of the cultural-exchange program. The actresses, the orgies, the cars, the expense accounts, they may have gone to his head."

"You speculate someone turned Subotin, General?"

"There would certainly have been the opportunity. Consider the number of foreign film directors, playwrights, and publishers he dealt with."

"Not to mention the hockey players and swishy couturiers."

"When you successfully smuggle out an icon, there's an insidious temptation to try again. Look how it affected Glukhov. If Subotin took the plunge on his own, and the foreigner he was selling to set him up with a Swiss bank account, he was ripe for blackmail."

"Have you a course of action in mind, General?"

"Belknap got into trouble with those diamonds in seventy-three. I think the period to target is the previous six months. Go over the surveillance reports on Subotin in that period with a toothcomb. What we're primarily after are his contacts with cultural-exchange groups from the United States." Demichev clenched his jaw as a new thought struck him. "If somebody's running Subotin, he'll be reporting everything we're discussing in this meeting at the first opportunity."

"I could escort him to my office before we resume."

"No, Pechenko would immediately get suspicous. The man's paranoid."

"Afterward?"

"Afterward have two men escort Subotin to the safe house on Granovskovo Street. Give him plenty of liquor and all the women he wants. Otherwise, keep him incommunicado."

"And tell him?"

"Tell him that during our recess Pechenko expressed suspicion about him and we're trying to keep him beyond the general's reach until the success of the Washington operation proves just how mistaken Pechenko was."

"Professor Tudin's returning, General. Also Major Subotin."

Demichev turned. Subotin didn't appear as queasy. The trip to the bathroom must have helped. "Did you notice his armpits?"

"Well, I don't think he'd an opportunity to bathe this morning."

"Five days minimum, Nikitin. He reminds me a little of Goebbels."

The lieutenant considered. "There is a resemblance."

"I've a small secret to share, Nikitin. I'm recommending you for promotion. The pistons that drive a great ship's engines must travel down as well as up. So must loyalty between its captain and his crew."

"With the return of Belknap to the United States," Demichev resumed, "the mechanism created for Chessplayer's emergency protection was temporarily useless . . . he was accordingly put to sleep until we could evaluate the changed circumstances. This wasn't the sacrifice it might seem, since we all know an agent so highly placed must be used only in matters of greatest importance to the state. But when Chessplayer was recalled to Washington to head a new intelligence apparatus, the carillon could again operate credibly. It became feasible to post Glukhov to New York, where Belknap still resided."

"Who was to operate the carillon this time?" Pechenko asked testily.

"Glukhov."

"*Glukhov!*"

Demichev smiled. As he often told his wife, it wasn't always necessary to throw a vase to capture someone's attention. Occasionally she responded by throwing a second vase, but he still believed in the dictum. "In my briefing of Glukhov before his departure, I told him Belknap was again active. And I told him about the young soldier."

"What young soldier?" Pechenko didn't handle frustration well. This was well known. He looked as if he were going to hyperventilate. In a few minutes he'd be calling for a paper bag into which to breathe. It had happened before.

Demichev inclined his head to Colonel Zalenin, who was eating a peach. "The young soldier Department Eight had to neutralize on Wednesday."

"Ah, yes." Pechenko's lupine grin exposed his three rotting steel crowns. In the next five-year plan, at least in Demichev's opinion, cosmetic dentistry should receive higher priority. "This is the soldier whose body, according to the foolproof contingency plan, wasn't to be found for weeks, yet somehow washed up on the shores of the Potomac in less than twenty-four hours."

Zalenin put down his peach and dabbed his lips. In his retiring fashion, he said, "There was an unfortunate problem with the weights. A member of the disposal team miscalculated the pull of the tide. The diving belts came off. The field manual on disposals will be revised . . ."

"We're getting ahead of the story," Demichev interrupted, knowing what would happen if Pechenko and Zalenin got into a discussion about the physics of tidal forces and the buoyancy of dead bodies. "In his briefing, Glukhov gained an impression the soldier and Belknap had been romantically involved in Germany." He wasn't happy with his euphemism, which he employed only out of courtesy to Professor Tudin who, notwithstanding his many decades as a pioneering psychiatrist, always became visibly upset when he heard explicit references to homosexuality. Another of Tudin's harmless quirks probably, like his compulsion to wash his hands before urinating instead of after, but sometimes Demichev felt the professor ought to consult a psychiatrist. The trouble was, if you told a psychiatrist he ought to see a psychiatrist, he'd tell you you were crazy.

"Glukhov also gained the impression the soldier, by then at an intelligence facility in Washington, would be passing Belknap classified information, and that later the soldier would be introduced to an illegal who would take Belknap's place in the transmission chain."

"Was Glukhov told the illegal was Edgar?" Pechenko asked.

"Of course. Glukhov had to know something about his future associate."

"Of course. And by now he's undoubtedly told the FBI everything he knows about his associate."

Demichev sighed. "Yes, he's told them Edgar operates a secondhand bookstore in Greenwich Village and a lot of similar nonsense about Edgar's having been born in the United States of Russian parents, who took him to Leningrad to visit relatives shortly before the Great Patriotic War. Ah, Pechenko, we're not complete amateurs. Glukhov doesn't even have a physical description for Edgar, since they communicated through cutouts, and so forth. Edgar dealt only with *our* Chessplayer. Glukhov thought Edgar dealt with *his* Chessplayer. It's that simple: Glukhov was operating his own carillon. One more important point. Our Chessplayer used the Edgar channel only for information to which the soldier could have had access. This didn't occur often, though often enough to keep Glukhov a true believer. All other Chessplayer information moved through another channel."

Pechenko's tongue flicked his upper lip. "But you'll have to admit, Igor Fedorovich, a KGB officer with Glukhov's length of service would have other secrets to offer when he arrived on the FBI's doorstep like a foundling."

"Only one secret, Anatoli Petrovich. The identify of Chessplayer."

"So you say. But he knows KGB training methods. He knows the many matters with which he must have been involved in Bonn, Moscow, London, and New York."

"KGB training methods? They've been public knowledge—purely between us and our competitors, you understand—for years. Consider just a few on the roll call of defectors before and after Glukhov started his training in sixty-three. Khokhlov, Tuomi, Stashinsky, Goleniewski, Golitsin, Sakharov, Nosenko. Consider Nosenko, who travels west after the Kennedy assassination with information about Lee Harvey Oswald and becomes privileged to spend three years in solitary in a cell around which U.S.

Intelligence builds an entire house to keep its existence secret. Do you think such a man holds back from his interrogators the slightest details of training methods?

"As to the many matters with which Glukhov must have been involved after his training was over, perhaps you'll be good enough to tell me what they were. In Moscow between foreign assignments, he was kept busy translating stories appearing in the U.S. press and then writing reports no one read. On his foreign assignments, he was as isolasted from real events as packaged kasha on a grocery shelf. We knew of the mission he might someday be called upon to perform."

"It seems you've thought of everything, so excuse the few questions I ask only in my ignorance. Yesterday, I've been informed, two of Colonel Zalenin's men killed a Washington detective. In New York Glukhov himself killed one of our men. Were the deaths of the detective and Major Shiskin also part of this foolproof plan?"

"The wet stuff desolates me. Yet even a foolproof plan can have minor flaws. As long as it accomplishes its purpose, the flaws are merely the price of success. Our friends on the other side have a phrase for it: there is no free lunch."

"And we need to remember," Colonel Zalenin added with the punctilious objectivity Demichev so admired, "Major Shiskin's death wasn't our fault. It occurred because Glukhov deceived us. His personnel records showed he almost failed the self-defense course he took years ago. There was thus no reason to expect he could use karate to such devastating effect. Shiskin, after arresting him, was supposed to bend down to tie a shoelace when they reached the street, so the prisoner could simply push him over and escape on foot. It was extremely unfair of the prisoner to behave as he actually did."

"Major Shiskin was a brave man," Demichev said. "For a brave man there is always a posthumous medal. It will improve the widow's pension."

"There is no widow. His wife fell off a ferry while on a holiday cruise in the Crimea eleven years ago."

"I am desolated. Children?"

"One child, who died in infancy. Major Shiskin was not a happy man."

"In view of this background," Professor Tudin said thoughtfully, "it's possible the man had a death wish."

"Even so," Zalenin said, "I agree he ought to receive his medal. There's an aunt in Tiflis, almost blind, who'd probably enjoy looking at it."

Demichev nodded approvingly. "Take care of it, Konstantin Dmitrevich. If there are difficulties with the bureaucrats, tell them the aunt doesn't have long to live. If there are still difficulties, tell them I too shall sign the papers. Now"—he brought his attention back to Pechenko the Troublemaker—"this detective you mentioned, he is another story."

"I am sure."

"Events moved so rapidly in Washington yesterday we couldn't always provide appropriate guidance. For example, when Chessplayer informed his control that Edgar had been admitted to a Washington hospital on Tuesday under the name of Joseph Smith, the mystery of his disappearance after he left the Library of Congress was explained.

"But by the time Chessplayer learned all this, Edgar was no longer a patient. He'd walked out of the hospital earlier with only ten dollars. After making emergency contact with the embassy, he was met by an experienced officer. The officer supplied him with funds to return to New York, but questioned whether he was physically in condition to make the trip. Edgar insisted he was, and since there seemed to be no satisfactory alternative and it was desirable to get him out of the Washington area as quickly as possible, the officer agreed on the understanding Edgar would seek out a doctor. It turned out to be the proper decision, because subsequently Edgar, through telephone contact with our U.N. Mission, signaled his safe arrival in New York.

"Before he left Washington there was also an informal debriefing. Edgar remembered entering a cab in front of the Library of Congress, and the name of the driver, but little else. He did supply a detailed inventory, however, of all the items then in his briefcase. Since the officer wasn't otherwise familiar with events since Tuesday, he didn't realize there was something very wrong with that inventory."

Pechenko theatrically registered astonishment. "What could be wrong?"

"Edgar's inventory included a hundred silver dollars he'd bought from a Washington coin shop."

"Bought for what purpose?"

"Support of his legend. In New York he's a dealer in coins and stamps. But those silver dollars didn't appear on Chessplayer's inventory of the items in the briefcase at the time it was opened."

Pechenko shrugged. "So the cabdriver stole the silver dollars before mailing the briefcase. Where is the problem?"

Demichev reluctantly made the unavoidable admission. "The silver dollars were in packets that identified the Washington coin shop, where Edgar is known to the proprietors as Mr. Moore, a New York coin dealer."

"I see." Pechenko touched a boil in embryo on the tip of his nose as if it were a talisman. "To protect Edgar, you had to recover the silver dollars before U.S. Intelligence could interrogate the cabdriver?"

"Recovering the silver dollars wouldn't, I'm afraid, eliminate the name of the coin shop from the cabdriver's memory. It became necessary in additon to prevent any such disclosure. Unfortunately, this complex problem, along with the news Edgar had been a patient in a hospital, didn't come to my attention until after the adjournment of our meeting yesterday evening. Because the urgency of the situation required immediate action, I was deprived"—Demichev smiled ruefully—"of your valued counsel."

"And thus deprived"—Pechenko's darting tongue made another sweep across his upper lip—"you gave your approval for *mokrie dela*?"

Demichev moved his shoulders. "A simple matter of security. But I gave no approval for any adventures with a detective."

"This being so, how did the detective happen to become a corpse?"

"He tried to arrest two of Colonel Zalenin's men when they came to the cabdriver's apartment."

"One is required to point out," Colonel Zalenin interjected, "the detective had no warrant at all. This my men will swear to. One regrets what happened, naturally, but the detective was clearly acting unlawfully. Please excuse the interruption."

Always impressed by this reticent officer's fierce loyalty to his men, Demichev said, "No one, Konstantin Dmitrevich, can fault a soldier for defending himself."

"My gratitude, Comrade General, for your understanding. One is also required to point out that my brave men attempted to leave peacefully. But the detective insisted on trying to draw his gun."

"Detectives are the same world over," Demichev said resignedly.

"What I am interested in," Pechenko said, "is why the detective was present at the cabdriver's apartment."

"So am I," Demichev said, "but I don't happen to be a confidant of the chief of Washington detectives. Maybe the cabdriver was being investigated for supplying prostitutes to customers."

"Yet if he was being investigated because of matters connected with Edgar's disappearance, your whole operation's already been compromised."

"It hasn't been compromised."

"So we hope." Pechenko tilted back and folded his

hands on the comfortable beachside frontage of his paunch. "In any event, you've at least recovered the silver dollars. Perhaps the death of the detective was a small price to pay for Edgar's continued security."

Pechenko delivered this speech, which he had to realize was garbage, with a smile as innocent as the bite of an asp. Demichev used the weak excuse of lighting a cigarette to organize a counterattack. "With the death of the detective, it became too dangerous for Colonel Zalenin's men to conduct a search for the silver dollars. Perhaps the detective had a partner waiting on the street, or already on his way in. More to the point, recovery of the silver dollars—this I've already explained—wouldn't resolve the problem of the cabdriver's memory."

"Even more to the point, Edgar is blown. Or will be as soon as U.S. Intelligence visits the coin shop. You'd better get him out of the country."

"Not necessary. The coin-shop proprietors, according to Edgar, are husband and wife. No employees. It pains me to say this, but it doesn't truly matter whether the trail leading to Edgar stops with the cabdriver or stops with the proprietors."

"You are littering Washington with corpses. This is madness."

"In a war, there will be casualties."

"Are we at war?"

"I think you yourself, Anatoli Petrovich," Demichev said patiently, for Pechenko again looked as if he was going to hyperventilate, "have told me this many times."

"And you, Igor Fedorovich, have told me many times you had a foolproof plan for protecting Chessplayer. Yet all I hear of are dead bodies. It seems to me, but then I'm a simple, unsophisticated man, this isn't exactly evidence of your remarkable plans' foolproof nature. What assurance have we that your tame defector will still be believed even twenty-four hours from now?"

Professor Tudin leaned across the conference table and,

shaking an arthritic, nicotine-stained finger almost in Pechenko's startled face, shouted, "You've the assurance of my professional ethics! Would I lie in delivering my prognosis that this idiot Glukhov will successfully perform exactly as he's been programmed? What kind of a society do we live in where a doctor is treated with such disrespect?"

"Furthermore," Demichev said, sincerely determined to prevent any hyperventilating, and not just Pechenko's, "we've provided modest supporting touches to complete Glukhov's case against Belknap. For example, a shortwave receiver was left in the young soldier's apartment. And a long-distance call was made from there to Belknap's New York office urgently asking the receptionist to have her employer contact the soldier. After Edgar's reappearance, another message was left, this one purportedly from him."

"More recently, the Washington *rezident* dispatched from the embassy an officer, believed to be known to the FBI as KGB, with instructions to take extraordinary measures to lose his predictable FBI surveillance before proceeding to his actual destination, so long as he made sure he didn't succeed. In due course, faithful bloodhounds padding behind, he left an anonymous note for Belknap at his hotel. The note, which obliquely described Glukhov's defection and set out meaningless escape procedures, would naturally be gibberish to Belknap. But attached to the note, in order to give a signal the gibberish had to be something other than it seemed, was the ring he'd given Philby, delivered to Washington by diplomatic bag earlier in the day. If, because of this signal, he kept the note and it was eventually found on his person, well"—Demichev good-humoredly pretended to slash his throat—"its contents would be as fascinating to the FBI as their knowledge of its place of origin. If he got rid of the note, reasonable FBI men might reasonably conclude he'd done so because it was too incriminating to retain."

He bowed apologetically to Pechenko. "I've taken too much of your valuable time. I felt it my duty, however, to demonstrate why Glukhov will be believed not only twenty-four hours from now, but also twenty-four years from now. I'm most grateful for your patience."

"I am thinking," Pechenko grunted.

In an effort to plant before the thinking season was over, Demichev dipped into inventory for more olive branches. "Your questions, Comrade General, have been extraordinarily perceptive. All of us on this side of the table now move forward with greater confidence because of the way you've made us rethink fundamentals."

"I am thinking we don't care at all about twenty-four years from now. What we care about is three, six, nine months from now, because after this Belknap is arrested, U.S. Intelligence will conduct exhaustive investigations of the conflicts between the story he'll tell and the one your defector tells. And Belknap will hire lawyers who'll conduct their own investigations. I am thinking Glukhov's version of events cannot withstand the scrutiny it will receive over the months Belknap is awaiting trial. Someone will find flaws, discrepancies. So I've only one last small question." Pechenko's smile was as artless as the rouge on a whore. "Can you guarantee your defector's story won't unravel under such circumstances?"

"I cannot," Demichev conceded graciously, "and I again express appreciation for the astuteness with which you've gone to the heart of the matter. Glukhov's story will unravel like a thread pulled from the sleeve of a cheap Romanian suit." He met Pechenko's bewilderment with a reassuring wave of his hand. He sometimes felt he should have devoted his life to teaching. He enjoyed educating people, even people like Pechenko. "But it will never come to this, because Belknap isn't going to be brought to trial. He'll be shot while resisting arrest. Or while exercising an opportunity, deliberately provided after his arrest, to escape. The details are in Chessplayer's capable hands."

"Another corpse," Pechenko grumbled.

"Granted," Demichev said obligingly, "but from the

plan's inception it was agreed, and for the very reason you mentioned, the affiar had to end cleanly. I try to be philosophical; it's not easy. It's far less easy for Chessplayer, since Belknap is in a sense a friend. Yet duty always demands sacrifice, and it's a measure of Chessplayer's idealism that he makes this sacrifice without complaint. I, too, constantly school myself to avoid self-pity."

"You are an example to us all, Comrade General," Zalenin said.

"My gratitude, Comrade Colonel, for your understanding."

"When can we expect the announcement of Belknap's death?" Pechenko asked impatiently.

Demichev sighed as he glanced at his watch. One moment the KGB's in-house Rasputin was complaining about corpses, the next he was complaining about their absence. "Since it's already past midnight in Washington, we may have to wait until morning, their time. Or slightly longer if Chessplayer encounters complications. In which case Colonel Zalenin's men can provide assistance."

"Complications!" Pechenko's clenched fist became a sledgehammer ready to splinter the conference table into a hundred fragments.

Demichev retreated hastily. "There will be no complications. You have, dear Anatoli Petrovich, my unqualified word on that." Instantly regretting the reckless promise, he scrambled to the safer high ground of rotund generalities. "When the whole affair's viewed objectively, it's apparent everyone gains by Belknap's departure from the board. We gain because we accomplish our goal of protecting Chessplayer. Our competitors gain because they've put their house in order without the messiness of a trial or other awkward publicity. Of course, they'll still conduct postmortems into the damage done by Belknap and then compile tedious reports on their finding; they've a fervor rivaling that of the Germans for this kind of liturgical paper work, but it won't change the historical verdict. No one in

Washington—and, in fairness, no one in Moscow—likes to tamper with a tidy solution to an embarrassing problem, which is what Belknap has become."

"To us, Comrade General?" one of Pechenko's aides asked with a worried frown.

Although this penetrating question could only be asked by an Uzbek herdsman, Demichev tried to be charitable. "No, Comrade, not to us. We've nothing against Belknap. Why should we? Anything he's ever done to harm us has been done only as part of his job. In our profession, we try to behave as gentlemen . . . there are codes of conduct. One is, never punish your enemy for doing his duty." Discreetly signaling Lieutenant Nikitin to be ready with supporting applause, he resumed the challenging task of trying to inspire another slow learner. "I've already confessed my youthful infatuation with Shakespeare. In one of his plays, forgive me for not recalling its name, he answers your question far more eloquently than I. 'And do as adversaries do in law, Strive mightily, but eat and drink as friends.'

"This is how I feel, how you should feel"—he held out his arms in that encompassing gesture his wife employed to embrace an entire audience when she took curtain calls after a concert performance—"about Belknap."

Lieutenant Nikitin began to clap softly. Applause once more gradually rose in the vast room like a fluttering of wings. Even Pechenko, his expression dazed, as though he had just arrived without his wallet in another century, was inexplicably on his feet, mechanically slapping his fat hands as if they were wet fishing boots about to be hung on a peg.

27

NOBODY HAD PUT A BULLET in his back after he'd left Malkin's hospitality center, and Belknap was certainly grateful about that, though he should have realized nobody so inclined could expect to travel far if he left a corpse almost at the guardhouse next to the White House gates. Surveillance was another matter. He discovered it soon after he found a cruising cab on Pennsylvania.

It was a well-mannered surveillance, however—nobody tried to shoot him, nobody tried to return him to the hospitality center—so it obviously wasn't another of Malkin's thoughtful courtesies, like the offer of a basement guest room. It was also, he discovered when he induced his driver to run a few red lights, an extremely determined surveillance, and it played tag well. Until he ducked into an all-night massage parlor in the heart of 14th Street's combat zone and traded an emaciated brunette fighting acne and boredom three twenties for access to the alley via the grimy window of her cubicle. When he stumbled against a garbage can in the darkness, he heard her cheering him on like a pompom girl.

He invested another thirty minutes in textbook evasion to convince himself he'd shaken free. It was past midnight when he walked down the quiet street of painted brick façades and louvered ornamental shutters.

The lock on the front door yielded easily. The stair

carpeting muffled his cautious ascent to Vanessa's apartment. He aimed the penlight at the lock on her door and tried the more likely master keys on his ring. Then, experimenting with the picks, he tripped the tumbler. He swore silently when he discovered the inside night chain was engaged.

He studied the auxiliary tools on the key ring, none longer than his forefinger. One was a delicate miniature hacksaw, probably superb for slicing celery. Another resembled a jeweler's wire cutter, probably superb for snipping hairsprings. Some genius assigned to technical backup had forgotten that the links in night chains were usually tempered steel.

He removed the laces from his cordovans and, knotting them together, produced a five-foot length of homemade string. He tied one end around the metal button that rode in the slotted plate attached to the inside surface of the door. He fed the other end up the inside surface and over the door's top until it dangled in front of him. After closing the door, he took up slack and gently slid his end of the string toward the hinged side of the jamb. It wasn't, he knew from experience, a difficult operation as long as there was a sufficient gap between the lintel and the top of the door. The metal button responded to the diagonal tension by sliding along its slotted track until it reached the circular aperture from which, if the laws of gravity were still in effect, it would sometimes drop. And sometimes not, which was why certain unauthorized entries might qualify as an art form of sorts.

Belknap, not the compleat angler he'd once been, fished for perhaps ten frustrating minutes before he sensed the welcome telltale tug on his line. He slipped inside, kicked off his shoes, and sent the penlight beam around the living room. The alabaster Venus on the fireplace mantel gave him an encouraging wink, or else an admonitory frown. High on adrenaline and low on patience and feeling the hot breath of demons on his back, he couldn't spare the time for precise analysis.

He stood at the open bedroom door, listening to her soft respiration. She was sleeping face down under a sheet. The skirt and blouse she was planning to wear in the morning were draped across a flowered chaise. A faint breeze stirred the curtains. He sat gingerly on the edge of the bed. "Vanessa," he whispered. He touched her back. "Vanessa, wake up."

She stirred. Her body turned slowly until she was staring, eyes wide and frightened, at the ceiling. Then she saw the shape of him in the darkness. She sat up, pulling the sheet to her shoulders. "What the hell are you doing in my bedroom?"

"Easy," he pleaded. He fumbled with the lamp on the night stand. She shielded her eyes against the suddenness of light. Her breathing was agitated. "You've broken into my apartment, which is inexcusable, and you've scared me witless besides. You're either drunk or crazy, and you don't look drunk." She reached impulsively for the phone on the night stand and noticed the clock. "My God, it's almost one in the morning! Who in hell do you think you are?"

As she picked up the receiver, he caught her wrist. "Please. I broke in because I couldn't risk phoning. I also couldn't risk waking the people in the two other apartments on this floor while trying to wake you. I need help, please believe me about that, and a place to spend the rest of the night. Right this moment it's the best way to stay alive."

"Explain," she said tersely.

He released her wrist. "Have you talked with Malkin tonight?"

"That's explaining?"

"Okay. Our friend Harry Murphy is actually a cabdriver named Brdnowski. Somebody wanted to kill him yesterday afternoon, but instead killed a detective who happened to be in his apartment. It looked like a KGB-type operation. Prussic acid, maybe a related cyanide.

"Brdnowski and his girlfriend Myrt are amateur, and in

some ways quaintly disorganized, urban gypsies, not averse to occasional petty theft. She's the one with shoplifting on her rap sheet. He's the one who mailed the briefcase. But whatever else they are, they aren't spies. Our so-called Joseph Smith, owner of the briefcase, is the spy. So why did somebody who's probably KGB want to kill Brdnowski and possibly Myrt?"

"Wonderful! You broke in to ask a riddle."

"No, damn it. You told me to explain why I'm here. To do that, I have to sketch the background. Brdnowski didn't return everything he found in the briefcase. He held back a hundred uncirculated Eisenhower silver dollars. But how could the KGB know this, and why should it care if it did?" He was pacing the floor, giving another lecture. Adrenaline, he thought, and tried to stem the flow. "The fact is, it couldn't know unless Joseph Smith, when he walked away from the hospital, supplied it a description of what had been in the briefcase, and unless—"

"Why aren't you wearing shoes?" Still clutching the sheet, she replaced the phone. "Is that part of the burglar mystique these days?"

"Forget the shoes. I want you to understand the silver dollars. The KGB couldn't know Brdnowski had them unless it also knew they weren't in the briefcase when the Secret Service made its inventory in the early hours of Wednesday. Outside of the Secret Service, how many people knew *every* item in that inventory? Well, Malkin knew, I knew, you knew. Armstrong and Tiffany knew. I don't think you're a Soviet agent. I don't really think I am, so there are only three little Indians left, and I don't have any trouble eliminating two of them."

It was strange, she wouldn't meet his eyes. "What are you saying?"

"Hell, you know what I'm saying. But let's stick with the silver dollars a moment longer. They were in packets that carried the name of a Washington coin shop. Joseph Smith bought them there, because his cover's a coin-and-stamp business in New York. The owners of the coin shop gave me his New York name, New York location. That's why somebody with a slight KGB odor tried to kill Brdnowski. He'd unwittingly stumbled on information certain to end not only Mr. Smith's career as an illegal, but possibly the one little Indian's as an agent in place."

"And Malkin is the . . . one little Indian?"

Such demure hesitation, he thought. Why was she playacting? "Malkin's a Russian mole. Malkin stole Beowulf. Only I've been set up as the scapegoat. The way Willis was set up."

"That's an enormous accusation, David."

The first time she'd used his name. He'd no idea whether it was a good sign or bad sign. He wished he could read her. He couldn't even tell whether she was expressing shock or disbelief or something resembling indulgence for the rantings of a sick mind.

"Are you talking about suspicion or about proof?"

"Not proof that would stand up in court. I might be able to get that kind, though. With your help." He studied his reflection in the vanity mirror. He needed a shave, his jacket was smudged with grease collected on his outbound trip from the alley window at the massage parlor, and the pulse in his temple was throbbing like a wounded sparrow.

"Frank Willis phoned my New York office Wednesday. But I hadn't seen him since Germany. He didn't know where I lived or what I did. So it had to be somebody posing as Willis. All part of setting me up." He fumbled in his pocket for the Spanish ring. "Malkin gave me this in Moscow. I was supposed to deliver it to Philby in Beirut. I did. Tonight it was returned anonymously. Anonymously? It is to laugh. Obviously Philby wasn't the messenger, so that leaves the KGB. With it was an unsigned note telling me in a kind of childish code to collect escape documents in New York. It also told me to use the ring to identify myself when I claimed the documents. All part of setting me up."

He could hear the plaintive weariness in his voice. How

nice it would be, for so many different reasons, to be invited to share that bed. "I've been under surveillance since I picked up the note at the hotel about nine-thirty, by whom I'm not sure. In New York yesterday a KGB officer named Glukhov defected. He'd been in Bonn and London at the times I'd been in those two places. How he fits in I'm not sure either, but since Malkin took pains to let me know about Glukhov even though I was calling from a public phone, and also to hint Glukhov might have information relating to Beowulf, he has to fit in somehow. The clincher was, I remembered as we were talking that the unsigned note had referred by the initial *G* to somebody who'd just found new employment in New York."

"Can I see the note?"

A stirring of interest? "I got rid of it. A mistake probably, but I didn't want to add to my problems by carrying it around. Especially if my luck ran out while I was taking care of the evening's remaining business. Which it almost did. Twice. A little before eleven I kept an appointment with Malkin at the institute. An unconvincing liar wearing a forty-five told me he'd gone out, then insisted on escorting me to the dungeon. I wanted to live, so I took a stupid chance with an ancient martial-arts move. He ended up at the bottom of the basement steps and, I'm afraid, badly damaged. I'm sorry about that—the man was simply following orders—but I've sworn off the Golden Rule for the duration, and I'm a mite sorrier for myself, since what happened provides one more excuse for shooting me on sight. They'll be combing the city for the mad dog."

She shifted restlessly under the sheet. She looked bewildered and sad.

"Vanessa, this isn't a case of paranoia I've contracted in the last two days. I vaguely suspected Malkin in Bonn after the Fehler business went sour. Yet there was nothing concrete and it was terribly easy to play ostrich. After I was forced out of government intelligence work, I had a lot of time to think. I replayed small incidents. London, Bonn,

Moscow. The Philby fiasco. Why should Philby go to ground right after I gave him the ring Malkin gave me? I was clumsy enough with Philby, but could I have been clumsy enough to start him on the road to Moscow? Maybe the ring itself was the signal to start him on that road.

"I could have dined on these speculations the rest of my life, but what was the point? I'd lost any urge to be a crusader, particularly a dead one, and I'd discovered it was easier to travel without a monkey on my back than with one. But when Malkin brought me down here, my monkey came with me. I kept getting signs and portents, not of supernatural origin, that somebody was walking on my grave. When Brdnowski and Myrt told me about the silver dollars, everything came together."

"Where are the silver dollars now?"

This was another kind of stirring of interest. He parried with a polite smile. "In a safe place. Brdnowski and Myrt, also. They'd planned on getting married yesterday afternoon. Trouble was, Brdnowski had forgotten to arrange for a marriage license—I did tell you they were quaintly disorganized—and it seems there's a wait of a day or so before the knot can be tied. Blood tests, too. When Myrt learned this, I thought she was going to deck him with a right to the jaw."

He sat on the vanity bench and studied labels on crystal perfume flacons. "Brdnowski said the man who got into his cab might have waved to someone as they were driving along First. Could that someone have been Malkin? Who knows? But I thought it worth a shot and decided to get a fairly recent photo to show Brdnowski. I phoned Malkin, set up that evening meeting in his office in order to buy a free run at his house. Then I made a bad mistake. I asked a CIA man I thought owed me more than he might owe Malkin for Malkin's address.

"When I broke into Malkin's I walked into the loving arms of Fast Eddy. Not only that, he knew I was coming the way a tree knows sap will flow in the spring. Which means my CIA contact passed my inquiry to Malkin. I don't think Malkin has quite enough ESP to post Fast Eddy to Georgetown simply because I requested an evening meeting in his office."

"What happened to Eddy?"

"Eddy encountered an accident."

"What kind of accident?"

The alarm in her voice puzzled him. "I don't think it was fatal. He's convalescing in a lovely garden at the back of the house."

"My God! He can't be left there." She reached for the phone and began punching buttons.

He depressed the cradle. "*Vanessa!* Don't you understand what I've been saying? Call anyone you want, but not from this phone. It's bugged, I'm positive. I told you yesterday Malkin knew I'd been with you the night before. That's why I couldn't risk phoning you, why I had to break in."

She swore, then threw back the sheet. She was wearing a lovely pink nightgown split at the sides like an *ao dai*. "We've got to get to a phone."

"What's the emergency?"

She emitted a bitter laugh. "You dumb lovable bastard, Malkin didn't post Fast Eddy to Georgetown. The emergency is, we have to get him out of that garden before Malkin discovers him."

He stared at her, numbed. "*You* sent him?"

"No, but I'm afraid I know who did. *Damn!* This may be the endgame." She sprang to her feet. "Would you kindly get out of my bedroom while I dress? Strike that. Get the hell out of my bedroom while I dress!"

Lovable, he repeated to himself, savoring the word as he relaced his shoes. He could forgive a great deal for a word like that, and he realized now there was going to be a great deal to forgive. He thought about the unmarked black van he'd seen from her window Wednesday night. *Who'd want to eavesdrop on us?* she'd said. And, *Tell me about Erich Fehler, David.* She had primed and worked him like the village pump.

In the bedroom she'd reacted to his story with such curiously deliberate reserve. But my, she'd certainly come alive when he mentioned Fast Eddy. The web must be very tangled indeed.

When she came into the living room, she was wearing the lime-green blouse and beige skirt that had been on her chaise. Her blonde hair was brushed severely back and held by a barrette, accentuating the planes of her face. A light raincoat was draped over her arm. He showed his surprise when he noticed the small suitcase she was carrying. "I don't think it's a good idea to come back," she said. "Ready?"

"I was going to boil water for instant coffee. It's been a long night."

"There isn't time."

"When do the explanations start?"

"We'll take my Porsche. I'll try to explain a few things once we're out of here. Thanks for stopping me from using the phone. It could have been disastrous."

"*De nada.* Is it okay to say you look decently stunning?"

She kissed his cheek in sisterly fashion. "I'm sorry about a lot of things, David."

She handled the Porsche with authority. "There's a pay phone a few blocks from here. It's going to be raining by morning. Our half-assed summer rain that's three parts mist and one part used bathtub water."

He glanced at the sulky night sky. He sniffed the humid air. An old salt full of an old salt's weatherman wisdom. "I think you're right. Who are your masters, Vanessa?"

"I *have to* make the phone call first. Can you trust me until then?"

"Do I have a choice?"

"You're right about Malkin, of course."

"Life is funny. I've heard that said."

"But I never knew you'd be in danger of getting killed. Will you at least believe me about that?"

"Yes, I'll at least believe you about that."

She parked in front of a shoppette. "I'll make the call."

She spent twenty minutes talking on that outdoor phone. A long time. Long enough to roust a stand-by assassin from slumber and have him on his way. Long enough to concoct another, newer, better story to unload on the expendable cat's-paw. Belknap prayed he wasn't once more trusting the wrong person. Strange bedrooms, he thought, scented with promises and surrounded by trouble.

She bestowed another sisterly peck as she slid behind the wheel, but she was plainly distressed and maybe angry. "Eddy's situation is under control."

"Well, that just tickles the hell out of me. So whom do you work for? Or do you sort of free-lance?"

The tires gave a little shriek as she executed a tight U-turn and headed west toward the Capitol. "There's a CIA counterintelligence operation run by my father. I work for him."

"It figures. Old CIA soldiers never die, they just fade away to a consulting job. Put *consulting* in quotes, please. So that's why you were having dinner with him and I wasn't welcome."

"He canceled the dinner."

"But now he's given you your instructions on how to handle me?"

She sighed. "You're partly right. And I don't like some of the instructions. He wants to see you. He lives in Alexandria. I'm supposed to take you."

He laughed caustically. "Fast Eddy extended a similar invitation. Only he was going to handcuff me and lock me in the trunk of his car. Your father must be some gracious host. Why does he want to see me?"

"He has a great deal to tell you and wants you to help him. He hopes to persuade you to forget about Malkin . . . he'll tell you why. He hopes to persuade you to surrender Brdnowski and Myrt. He hopes to persuade you to surrender those silver dollars."

"This is an amazing man. By now Malkin'll have some very heavy hitters prowling the city for me. He's also got the FBI and the Metropolitan Police at his beck and call. The airports, the bus and train stations, are probably bottled up. Yet your father wants me to forget about Malkin and surrender my life-insurance policy?"

"He may be able to fix it so you don't need that policy. Which you never should have needed anyhow." She shot past a traffic light as it changed to red. "I'm not taking you anywhere you're not willing to go. And if I take you to Alexandria, I'll bring you back. I swear to that."

"What does your father know about Glukhov's defection?"

"Nothing. He'll be trying to find out while we're on our way. That is, if you decide to go."

"Do you love your father?"

She hesitated. "That's difficult to answer."

"It shouldn't be."

"When I was growing up, he treated my mother badly. When they finally divorced, he cheated her in the financial settlement. Later she found out and won a new settlement, but lawyer friends have told me this isn't uncommon. God knows, when my second marriage went on the rocks, I learned how mean-spirited and unforgiving I could be. My father, surprisingly, was supportive during that mess, paid some of the psychiatrist's fees. Things have been better between us since that time . . . until recently. But I'm not sure I can describe what either of us feels as love. He's one of those relentless cold-war warriors whose one great passion is the war itself."

"Did he ever remarry?"

"Yes. I'm not close to Helen. She's a brooder and a whiner, though she and John seem to understand each other." She turned to him uncertainly. "Your choice, David."

28

THEY DROVE DOWN Washington Street past Christ Church, where Robert E. Lee had owned a pew, and the small cemetery where his soldiers owned graves. When they reached the Mount Vernon side of Old Town Alexandria, Vanessa turned onto a winding road bordered by lovingly restored Colonial homes. Her father's, half-hidden by climbing ivy and wisteria, had carved eavestones and a fanlighted doorway. She composed a precise rat-a-tat-tat with the brass knocker.

"David," she said when the door opened, "John Littlejohn." She touched her lips to her father's forehead. "John, this is David Belknap."

John Littlejohn, whose parents had to have been pranksters or indefatigable optimists to christen him as they had, must have been the runt of the litter. He was about five-four in height and carried a jolly Dickensian plumpness below the waist. His upper body was stocky, his arms overlong, and his face slightly pocked. His eyes were coldly appraising, and his smile wasn't much warmer. The top of his bald head was an archipelago of little freckles. He was wearing a yellow polo shirt, tan slacks, and suede moccasins. And from these loins had sprung the woman beside him. Genes, Belknap thought.

Littlejohn led them into a living room decorated by someone who knew American antiques. There were Martha Washington chairs, two Sheraton sofas, drum tables, a gilt banjo clock, and a few Currier and Ives lithographs and

Audubon bird prints. Fine pewter tankards, mugs, and plates were on display in a pine cupboard.

"Brandy, anyone?"

"I could use some strong black coffee," Belknap said.

Littlejohn walked through the dining room into the kitchen. Belknap noticed a maplewood chessboard on a Pembroke table. The position of the carved pieces indicated a discontinued game.

"Well, Mr. Belknap," Littlejohn said when he returned, "you've created a little problem for us." He sat down opposite him. "The question is, how are we going to solve it?"

"Maybe you could begin by telling me the problem, sir." Already Belknap was disliking the man's magisterial high-handedness.

"Fair enough. It's been known for some time that George Malkin is a Soviet agent. For exactly how long is classified information." Littlejohn moved his shoulders. "I've always liked George. Clubbable. We've been through a lot together, starting with the OSS. Manning the barricades. Keeping the Goths from the gates." He gestured toward the chess set. "Comes over now and then for a game and the kind of pheasant dinner Helen prepares so well. Always opens with Pawn to King Four when he's White. Just like Fischer." He laughed. "Of course, as a chess player, George isn't exactly Fischer."

"I know. I've played with him."

"Well, now. What do *you* use against his Pawn to King Four?"

"Sicilian," Belknap said. This man was unreal. He glanced at Vanessa, sitting stiffly on the edge of a sofa, as if she were balancing teacup and saucer at the vicar's annual garden party. She looked lost.

"Nothing wrong with that. Personally, I prefer a gambit. In counterintelligence too. Often produces surprising success. Which brings us to Operation Trojan Horse."

The names, Belknap thought, my God, the names. Beowulf, ComOpsCenter, Trojan Horse . . .

"Trojan Horse is a vastly intricate deception exercise for the exclusive benefit of George Malkin."

"*John!*" It was a woman's voice calling urgently from upstairs.

He walked to the foyer. "Yes, pussycat?"

"There's smoke coming from the Crawford place. The house must be on fire."

"All right, dear. I'll take care of it." He came back to his chair and addressed Vanessa. "Helen's a little quirky these days. Always imagining mini-disasters. Fires, burglars, squirrels in the attic. It's a menopausal thing." He sat back reflectively. "After Trojan Horse had been authorized at the highest level, I was assigned the job of making it work. I built George a marvelous toy, wound it up, and let it run. The toy was a new intelligence agency, so secret it doesn't even appear in organization charts of our intelligence structure. The Lafayette Research Institute. I keep two hundred people busy around the world generating product for George to gather from his office on Lafayette Square, and the only things he gathers are those we want him to gather. You've heard of a Potemkin village, Mr. Belknap?"

He nodded. He almost felt sick, but it was a sickness of the spirit and heart.

"In effect, what we created for George Malkin was a Potemkin village. The Lafayette Research Institute was real, but it was unreal. It existed, but it didn't exist. Illusion and mirage and emptiness, except as transmuted by George's imagination. His imagination was our philosopher's stone."

Littlejohn crossed his stubby legs. "In the bargain, of course, George acquired impressive new titles and a large staff, and from time to time we had to supply him product that damaged our interests. Couldn't have him losing the confidence of his clients, could we? But these are the tradeoffs you encounter in disinformation operations. Live with them as best you can. The bottom line is, is the program as a whole cost effective? Can you show a profit when the bank examiners arrive? Trojan Horse always met that test."

Littlejohn's eyes had lost their coldness. They were alive with the light of what seemed to Belknap akin to madness.

"We naturally built safeguards into the operation, such as having some of our people on hand in the Potemkin village. To watch the store, so to speak. Vanessa, Eddy Mathers. Sybil Pruett, the housemother over there. A few others you don't need to know about."

Belknap found his voice. "Tony Armstrong, Cal Tiffany. Are they part of your operation?"

Littlejohn laughed good-humoredly. "No, they're just your everyday good and faithful servant. Tending the vines, harvesting the grapes."

There was a wail of sirens. Littlejohn, surprised, went to the window and parted the drapes. "I'll be damned. The Blankenship car's on fire. I knew damn well it couldn't be the Crawfords' house. It's practically solid brick and has a sprinkler system besides."

"*John!*" the upstairs voice called out. "The Crawford place *is* on fire."

Shaking his head, Littlejohn walked to the foyer. "It's all right, pussycat. It's just the Blankenship car. I've taken care of it." He returned to the living room, still shaking his head. "I think it's the hormone treatments. They're making her hyperactive. I'll have to jawbone the doctor."

"Would that coffee be ready by now?" Belknap said.

"So you and Sybil were the nursemaids," he said when Littlejohn had gone to the kitchen, "and Fast Eddy was watchdog."

"Yes," she said in a tired, unhappy voice.

A phone rang once, stopped. "Is there a phone in the kitchen?"

"Yes," she said in the same dispirited voice.

"What about all this stuff about a husband who was killed in a goddamn alley in Germany and a lousy second marriage and a job in an advertising agency? Was any of it ture?"

"It was all true."

"And you'd read a file on me before I met you in Malkin's office. You knew about Philby. You knew about Fehler. You knew about the diamonds. Right?"

"Yes." She looked down at her hands and shook her head. "And I lied when you asked if John knew about Beowulf. But I never knew things were going to happen the way they have happened. I never knew Frank Willis would be killed. I never knew a detective would be killed. I never knew there'd be the slightest danger for you. I never knew John had sent Fast Eddy to pick you up at Malkin's, I didn't even know you were going to be at Malkin's. David, you don't know how sorry I am."

"And you invited me into the sack. That's what I can't understand."

"That wasn't planned."

"What about the unmarked black van parked outside your apartment Wednesday night? Was that unplanned, too?"

"Why don't you ask him?" she said abjectly.

"Do you think—excuse me all to hell for saying it—the brains of that man in the kitchen are slightly scrambled?"

"I don't know. God, I don't know anymore."

When Littlejohn came back fifteen minutes later, he carried earthenware mugs, a coffee carafe, and a brandy bottle on a silver tray. And a bagful of apologies for the delay. "Helpful information, though. Responses to buckshot inquiries I scattered after your phone call, Vanessa. Lot of catfish in the river tonight. Mr. Belknap, the surveillance you told Vanessa you'd encountered in the last few hours was FBI. Not a Malkin team, not a Soviet team." His smile was as thin as a worn-out dime. "Should make you feel better."

"Why's the FBI interested in me?"

"Well, you've a little problem there, too. We'll tackle it down the line." He began pouring coffee. "Brandy sweetener, anyone? No? I'll have a dollop, I think. Well, as I was saying before the damn sirens went off, Trojan Horse consistently showed a profit. Until the return of Beowulf in that damn briefcase. I suppose its return was bought about by—I take this position temporarily—blind chance. It also could have been brought about by our enemies. The Goths are always at the gates."

"You've lost me, Mr. Littlejohn. From what Malkin said, I assumed Beowulf detailed plans for preemptive strikes into the Middle East in the event of an OPEC embargo, like the one during the Yom Kippur War."

"Let's assume you're more or less in the ballpark. Then shouldn't these, uh, preemptive strikes, if indeed they're part of Beowulf, be preceded by a few staged incidents? Terrorist attacks, say, on U.S. embassies, kidnappings of U.S. officials, sabotage in the oil fields?"

"Sure. Bring on the Apocalypse, bring on the dancing girls, and we'll all have a ball. My God, when you funnel details of that kind of gunslinger contingency planning to the Soviets via George Malkin, you not only signal your intention to use force, you also give the Soviets a free ride on Sir Galahad's horse. If they decide to retail the Beowulf product to the Arab states, the whole Middle East becomes a hissing snake pit. And in the process, somebody might tickle the dragon's tail. Where is it written, sir, that any of this would help us win friends and influence people?"

Littlejohn's soft rumbling laugh sounded like artillery faintly heard fifty miles from the front. "Nicely put. The trouble is, Mr. Belknap, you don't understand the metaphysics of espionage."

Metaphysics of espionage, Belknap thought, marveling. But maybe the man was right. Maybe espionage *had* become a religion, and here was one of its high priests, sprinkling holy water, double-think, and obfuscation.

"Espionage, like Gaul, is divided into three parts." Littlejohn sipped thoughtfully from coffee sweetened with more than a dollop of brandy. "To wit: sources, methods, evaluation. Of the three, evaluation is *primus inter pares*. In January of nineteen-forty, a German plane carrying a Luftwaffe staff officer became lost in bad weather and mistakenly landed in Belgium. In the staff officer's briefcase were plans for an invasion of the West, scheduled for one week later through Belgium and Holland. The officer set fire to the plans, but the Belgians prevented their complete destruction. What happened? Well, Hitler postponed the invasion, and British and French intelligence evaluators, to their everlasting regret, decided the material was a plant.

"In January a year later, the U.S. commercial attaché in Berlin learned from German sources Hitler was planning to invade Russia in the spring. Secretary of State Cordell Hull warned the Russians. In April Churchill made another attempt, but Stalin, suspecting a British plot to pull him into the war, decided these and similar warnings were a plant.

"In nineteen-fifty Nehru's *éminence grise* Krishna Menon warned us the Chinese would come into the Korean War if MacArthur went north of the Thirty-eighth Parallel. But Menon was suspected of Communist sympathies, so MacArthur's evaluators decided the warning was a plant. MacArthur crossed the parallel in the fall, announced 'the boys would be home by Christmas.' By November, the Chinese were pouring across the Yalu. Pray learn, Mr. Belknap, from these lessons of history."

"*John!*" The voice upstairs.

Littlejohn went to the foyer. "Yes, pussycat?"

"That Commie son of a bitch is sending secret messages to Moscow again."

"All right, dear, I'll take care of it." He returned to the living room. "New neighbor on our north. Ham radio nut, you might've noticed his roof antenna. Twenty years in the Navy, now he's got two months to go before he retires from Commerce with another honey of a pension. Gives him just enough time, he claims, to nail down a job in the private sector as a lobbyist for the auto industry and qualify for Social Security when he's sixty-five. Anybody with that kind of gutsy dedication to triple dipping has to be your basic hard-shell capitalist. Operates the radio at crazy hours so he can gab with hams in countries where it's already daytime or else earlier in the night. Helen's spouting this Moscow claptrap because his antenna, if it's turned a certain way, blankets her TV set with snow. Whenever she gets a little frustrated, she always thinks the Goths are at the gates.''

Littlejohn, rearranging himself in his chair, rested his moccasined feet on a needlework cricket. "It's one thing to misread the enemy's intentions when your sources haven't been able to provide evidence of them. But these lessons from history show how common it is, on all sides, to misread his intentions even when your sources *have provided* evidence. If I were to tell you, Mr. Belknap''—he studied the iron and brass fireplace tools decorating the hearth—"you might be dead before this new day ends, I probably wouldn't convice you. But if I'd been stealing the mail of a professional assassin and showed you the letter in which he described how he was going to carry out the assignment, and if you know the letter was genuine, I warrant I'd get your attention.

"If we told the Russians we were going to play hardball the next time somebody went in for fun and games in the Middle East, and we weren't going to sit on our butts watching while we and Japan and the Common Market went down the tube, we might or might not convince them. But if they'd been stealing our utmost-top-secret contingency plans, or what they thought were utmost-top-secret contingency plans, and they knew the stolen goods were genuine, I warrant we'd get their attention. The stolen kiss is sweetest and the stolen document is irresistible. That's perhaps what Beowulf's about, Mr. Belknap.

"Now the Russians are pragmatists and the Middle East

is already a hissing snake pit and nobody walks into a buzz saw on purpose. The Russians aren't going to be retailing the Beowulf product to the Arab states, because if they do, word gets back to us, and then we know somebody's stealing utmost top secrets and we go looking for the thief, which isn't the Russians' idea of a genuinely happy ending. But if they *should* try any retailing, why"—he smiled briefly—"maybe it will turn out the Beowulf papers, notwithstanding the seeming NSC logo gracing the title page, are actually a clever forgery, and we in our outrage at this new Russian provocation make available to our Arab friends certain experts in the field of questioned documents who point out the defects, skillfully hidden though not quite skillfully enough, that establish the forgery. And thus one more infamous Russian disinformation campaign is exposed. Perhaps that's what Beowulf's really about, Mr. Belknap."

Littlejohn gestured impatiently. "Well, catfish don't wear dogtags. Whatever Beowulf's purpose, the return of that damn briefcase threatened to destroy the Potemkin village built to make George Malkin a conduit for doctored state secrets. When we learned of its return in the very early hours of Wednesday, the Trojan Horse Oversight Committee met in emergency session in the Old Executive Office Building, and it was decided at the highest level to put George in charge of finding the mole. Opinion was unanimous"—Littlejohn smiled again—"George could at least be counted on not to expose himself as the mole. So he was wakened from the sleep of the just, told he had White House authority to command the resources of all government agencies, et cetera, and asked to get cracking."

Littlejohn offered more coffee. Belknap, who had lost his taste for coffee and almost everything else available in this house, shook his head. Vanessa didn't look up.

"Next thing we knew, he'd issued orders to have you brought to Washington. It was unexpected and unsettling. What was his motive? We didn't know, how could we? We knew *who* you were, of course, but not *how* you fitted into the dicey situation in which George now found himself. So Sybil Pruett suggested that George make Vanessa your assistant, and he was receptive. Sybil would keep an extremely close eye on George the next few days and Vanessa would keep an extremly close eye on you.''

Vanessa was clutching her hands. She was very pale.

"Sybil's a wonderful woman, totally amoral. Did George ever tell you they had a fling in London during the war?'' Littlejohn pursed his lips judiciously. "Well, Vanessa quickly discovered when she was showing you LaRue's old office that you had certain negative feelings about George. That was unsettling too. It became imperative to determine whether your negative feelings were limited to a personality clash based on events in the past or whether they included suspicions of dear old George himself based on events in the past. It wasn't a time to have a loose cannon rattling around the deck.''

"So now we come to the black van," Belknap said bitterly.

"Yes, Vanessa said you'd noticed it. Clumsy of us, the thing stands out like a kangaroo pushing a shopping buggy, but when Vanessa phoned to report you were at her place, it was the best we could do on short notice. The eaves-dropping equipment inside it can be aimed to monitor conversations in any room having windows facing the street.''

"What would you have done if we'd gone to a restaurant instead?''

"I'm sure we'd have found a way to tape your recollections of your time in Bonn, Mr. Belknap.''

"I'm sure, too.'' At least she hadn't let the deranged bastard tape their lovemaking. The bedroom windows faced the back, not the street. "Since Vanessa was reporting everything I said anyhow, why were you taping me?''

"Good question, sir! We had to have a tape to run your recollections through a voice-stress analyzer. Some experts claim it's better than the polygraph. Point is, if you refused to admit to any suspicions about George, we had to know if you were telling the truth. George Malkin at the head of the Lafayette Research Institute is an irreplaceable disinformation asset, and we didn't and don't intend to lose the asset because some catfish like you comes barging in and upsets the grand design."

Belknap looked at Vanessa. She closed her eyes. A tear trickled down her cheek. "What did your remarkable machine deduce about me?"

"It deduced you were lying frequently. It deduced you believed George was indirectly responsible for General Fehler's death and under Soviet control."

"It's a clever machine, all right."

"So that's when we knew you were going to become a problem."

"Tell me, Mr. Littlejohn, since it's all family here, because I've fucked your daughter, I don't know whether she's told you about that too, but I have, how did—"

"You're getting emotional, Mr. Belknap, and this isn't the time to get emotional. Pray attend me with respect to that."

"David!" Her voice was anguished. "You were used, and it's vile. But I was used, and also never knew it. I never intended to bring harm . . . to you . . . to anyone."

"Well, I'm not getting emotional, Mr. Littlejohn. I was simply going to ask, how did Frank Willis fit into this wonderful grand design? Was he under your control or Malkin's control? Or was he just a poor dumb soldier who got zapped in the cross fire?"

"Willis was a pawn. Pawns sometimes get sacrificed."

Littlejohn got up and straightened an Audubon print on the fireplace wall. "Helen's been dusting. You can always tell. She forgot this, though." Picking up a discolored corncob pipe on the mantel, he brandished it as a lawyer might a confirming courtroom exhibit. "Since the Beowulf problem began, I've naturally been getting reports from the institute several times a day. So I knew from Sybil you'd signed for a gun and skeleton keys, and you'd left a message arranging a late-evening meeting there with George. All quite puzzling, particularly the meeting with George. Were you going to shoot him? Couldn't have that, could we? Then I learned from a mutual acquaintance you'd asked for George's home address. Things began to make sense. You wanted George out of his house because there was something in it you wanted. Mr. Belknap, you were no longer a loose cannon, you'd become a rogue elephant. I sent Eddy Mathers to George's to protect you from yourself.''

Belknap laughed mirthlessly. "Where's my protector now?"

"Georgetown University Hospital. For observation, to see if he has a concussion." Littlejohn, his back to the fireplace, jabbed the air with his pipe. "What it comes down to, Mr. Belknap, is this. I want you to do certain things for me; in return I'll do certain things for you. I want those Eisenhower silver dollars, I want the cabdriver and his paramour so it can be politely explained why they're going to forget they ever saw any silver dollars or any Washington coin shop's name on the packets, and I want you to forget you ever learned the name and address of the New York coin dealer who bought them, because—"

"I never learned them. I don't know what you're talking about."

Littjohn frowned. "Vanessa said over the phone the owners of the Washington shop gave you that information."

"Well, that's odd, because the owners didn't know anything about the man, except he supposedly came from New York. They weren't even sure about that, because he didn't pay by check. Vanessa must have been mistaken."

"Vanessa?"

"I think," she replied in a frail voice, "I must have been mistaken." Lifting her head, she looked directly at her father. "And you said over the phone you wanted David's help and hoped to persuade him to turn over the silver dollars. But you're not doing any persuading, you're issuing orders, and I'm not going to sit still for it."

Littlejohn gaped. His face reddened. He clamped the empty pipe between his teeth. "I try to give up smoking, and Helen manages to leave my favorite pipe practically under my nose. Pussycat, you'll sit still, and so will Mr. Catfish. I'll make myself clearer. I don't want just a *cold* trail from the cabdriver to the Washington coin shop to the man in New York. I want *no* trail at all. It ought to be apparent that if we know George Malkin's a Soviet agent, we know the identity of his postman. We don't want anybody interfering with George's postal service or George's postman, because any such interference would disturb George and George's employers in ways too terrible to contemplate. And in spite of the assertion Vanessa must have been mistaken, it's an interesting coincidence the postman *is* a New York coin dealer. An illegal. His code name is Edgar."

"Edgar?" Belknap said, caught by surprise.

"Name's familiar?"

The phone call to Janice, he thought. What was it she'd said when he touched base with her. Some gibberish about a man named Edgar who'd recovered from an . . . indisposition.

"And of course I want you to forget about George Malkin. In return, I can offer you your life and your freedom, although the latter may take a while to arrange."

"That's a very generous offer, Mr. Littlejohn."

"Smart-aleck remarks aren't going to take you anywhere. You're a man badly in need of friends. Influential friends. Without them, for openers, you'll probably be dead before this day ends."

Belknap heard Vanessa's gasp. He heard the banshee screeches of two cats fighting in the night. "You've been reading the professional assassin's mail?"

"No, I merely put facts together. Draw appropriate

conclusions. The KGB, responsible, I'll wager, for Willis's death, would be equally interested—I think you'll see why shortly—in ensuring yours. For substantially identical reasons, so would George Malkin. And he had access, as you well know, to the required resources. Do you still have your appendix?"

Confused by the non sequitur, Belknap nodded mechanically.

"Excellent!" Littlejohn regarded his favortie corncob pipe with a certain sadness, then snapped the stem. "*Sic transit gloria mundi.*" He dropped the pieces into a cane kindling basket on the hearth. "We've doctors with the necessary clearances for matters of this kind. In the morning George will be told by Sybil you were taken to a hospital with acute appendicitis shortly after midnight. That'll explain your 'absence' to his satisfaction. Bear in mind he's unaware you broke into his house. The doctors will actually remove your appendix, of course, no use trying to flimflam an old hand like George with a ghost operation, ghost surgeons. We'll see you're well guarded during your convalescence, and when you've recovered, we'll—"

"Mr. Littlejohn, nobody's going to remove my appendix."

"Pray do not pass a death sentence on yourself so hastily. Your predicament is so hopeless only influential friends can save you. The man you assaulted without provocation on the basement stairs at the institute was pronounced DOA when the ambulance got to George Washington University Hospital."

Shaken, Belknap cupped his mug and gulped tepid coffee. "I'm sorry," said weakly.

"No doubt, but it won't help his wife and children. And an unprovoked assault that results in death is murder. Local authorities, I can promise, will prosecute. Unless . . ."

"It wasn't unprovoked." Even using both hands to steady the mug, Belknap couldn't control the incipient trembling.

Littlejohn arched his brows in measured surprise. "The

guard on duty, the hapless fellow you also assaulted, though not as viciously, reports the victim merely asked you to wait in the downstairs guest room until George returned. After all, you'd made the appointment, not George. I'm sure he was anxious not to miss you simply because other business had unexpectedly come up. But you refused to wait. The victim, a federal officer acting in the line of duty, then informed you he'd been ordered to see that you waited. At which point you agreed."

"Have you ever seen one of George's guest rooms?"

"I've seen the one at the institute. It's relaxing, comfortable, far more so than your typical guest room at your typical downtown club. But conviction for murder is only part of your predicament, Mr. Belknap. Glukhov, this defector you mentioned to Vanessa, has told the FBI you've been working for the Soviets since sixty-three and he's your case officer."

The strangled cry that rose from Vanessa's throat was part despair, part fury. The look she gave her father was scorching. Even Belknap could feel its heat. "That's a wicked, wicked lie! It's also a wicked, fucking lie, and you know it, John."

Littlejohn regarded her with the same ambiguous sadness he'd extended to his favorite corncob pipe before he abruptly destroyed it. Belknap tensed; this crazy fanatic was also one mean, unpredictable son of a bitch.

"What is the lie, dear? That Glukhov accused your Mr. Belknap of being a Soviet agent, or that the accusation is true? Not the former, I assure you, and Glukhov's cited, I'm told, convincing chapter and verse to support the latter. People qualified to make judgments in this area find him totally believable. He further impressed the interrogators by his willingness to take a lie-detector test in the morning. Shortly after his arrival in Washington, he even selected a photo of you taken in Bonn, Mr. Belknap, from a photographic lineup of five male Caucasians about your age and build. George, who was present at the lineup, bless his heart—this is why he couldn't keep his appointment with you and so sincerely wanted you to await his return—kindly supplied the photo."

"I deny everything," Belknap said in a parched voice.

Littlejohn smiled indulgently. "Probably your best move." He walked to the chessboard, then around it, studying the chessmen from each player's perspective. He advanced a black pawn. "That's probably the best move, too. There's a possible mate for White in five, but when I'm playing for both sides, I try not to rig the game. Yet there's always the insidious temptation to play more sincerely for the side that seems to have the best position. A double agent—would you agree?—must face the same temptation. Well, we all know and grieve about the bad press the FBI's had since the Old Man passed on, so it's not hard to understand why they're hot to trot with their walk-in from Sixty-seventh Street. Hathaway, who'd dance the hornpipe on hot coals to become the next director, must already be filling scrapbooks with the headlines from an espionage trial featuring you as defendant and a former KGB officer as star witness."

Littlejohn burped and patted his overhung stomach. "What a pretty kettle of fish! Of course, we could arrange to help you disappear, it'd at least keep the KGB from your door. But it'd make a poor impression on the FBI and D.C. Homicide, since both these estimable organizations will want to have long unfriendly chats with you and they tend to draw all sorts of unfortunate conclusions about a suspect who elects instead to disappear. Further compelling reasons, you see, to go into the hospital. Then, after your emergency appendectomy, the doctors will certify that, because of complications, it'll be a week before you can have visitors. This not only keeps the FBI and D.C. Homicide and other unwelcome company from your door, it also avoids the nasty incriminating consequences of flight. More important, it gives your influential friends, providing you show a proper spirit of cooperation, a chance to determine the best countering moves. I must confess, however, that arranging your ultimate freedom is going to be a lengthy process.

"We can't very well discover some morning that Glukhov has, say, hung himself out of despondency . . . that would give future potential defectors mistaken notions about our hospitality. But in time we should at least be able to persuade him to recant this Chessplayer story. If not, if he's your typical *nyet* prima donna, we can always put the prosecution out of business by refusing, for overriding reasons of national security, to make him available to testify. The murder charge is more complicated, the days are long since past when we could call off a local prosecutor by whispering *national security* in his little pink ear. Still, there's more than one way to skin a cat. And dull a prosecutor's ardor."

Belknap roused himself. "And to sacrifice a pawn. So, point one, nobody's removing my appendix. Point two, I'm not giving you the cabdriver, I'm not giving you the silver dollars. Point three, I'm not forgetting about George Malkin."

Littlejohn shook his head ruefully, but his eyes were predatory and his smile was feral. "Then it appears we've reached an impasse and you'll have to deal with your troubles by yourself. For your own safety, I advise surrendering to the authorities immediately, not only because otherwise you'll be hunted as a dangerous fugitive, which entails the risk of getting shot by a nervous hunter, but also because the KGB—you surely realize this by now—will apply all its skill and cunning to finding you first. And they're very good at finding people, and very efficient when they do. Witness Frank Willis, witness the dead detective you reported to Vanessa."

"There isn't any dead detective. You can search the cabdriver's apartment, and you won't find a dead detective. Why would a detective be in the apartment anyhow? I made up the story . . . it was the only way to get her attention in a hurry." He glanced at Vanessa. "Sorry about that."

Littlejohn stared at him suspiciously. He poked his thumbs into the waistband of his slacks and rocked back and forth in time to his indecision. "So there is no detective? What about the silver dollars?"

"What about them?"

"Where are they?"

"I'm glad you asked, because they're my life-insurance policy, and it's a policy with some of the damnedest provisions you could imagine."

Anger mottled Littlejohn's pockmarked face. It wasn't a pretty sight. "Meaning what?"

"Meaning, I gave the silver dollars to an old friend on *The New York Times*. With the usual sealed letter of instructions one sometimes leaves with a trusted friend in case bad things happen to the writer. The policy's coverage isn't limited to death by design or accident, such as getting shot by a nervous hunter or getting knocked off the road by a truck on our way back to the District from historic Alexandria. Even if I die from a violent sneeze, the letter gets opened. There's another interesting feature. If I fail to contact my friend for a period of longer than twenty-four hours, it also gets opened—that's your standard mysterious disappearance clause. And the letter spells out everything I told Vanessa, plus a wee bit more. My friend's a damn fine reporter. If he has to open that letter, I think he'll win a Pulitzer. But then, I owe him."

"I seriously doubt you've had time to make such an arrangement, Mr. Paper Tiger, but play out your string if it amuses you. Play out your string."

"Don't worry, Mr. Littlejohn, I will."

Littlejohn spat onto a hooked rug in front of the hearth. "You're not only a renegade, you're a renegade from the human race. You've not only the unmitigated gall to accuse me of planning to have you killed, you've the odiousness to accuse me of planning to have my beloved daughter killed."

"With respect, sir, what you've already done to your beloved daughter is, in my opinion, almost as demented."

"With respect, sir! What kind of catfish crap is that ? And who gave you your smartass ticket to call me demented?"

"You're getting emotional, Mr. Littlejohn, and this isn't the time to get emotional." Belknap was afraid to look at Vanessa. But he could hear like rolling thunder her painful shallow breathing. He'd either gambled everything and won, or gambled nothing and lost. Time would tell, it always did.

"I've a simple goal, Mr. Littlejohn. To survive. You've demonstrated how stupid I've been and how serious my troubles are, but I'm not stupid enough to come here at about two in the morning without paid-up life insurance, and if you want to seriously doubt that, that's your problem. With respect, sir, I think you're half-mad. I think you and your wonderful influential friends are willing to see the Middle East—hell, civilization itself—go up in flames so you can continue to play this insane game you call Trojan Horse. Ask not for whom the bell tolls, Mr. Littlejohn. I carry insurance, and I'll show you soon enough for whom it tolls."

Littlejohn seemed not to have heard or, if he had, not to care or comprehend. He seemed to have crossed some strange psychological threshold that masked his face with an emotional flatness almost catatonic in its rigidity. "Who gave you your ticket? Name one person. I dare you. No, I double-dare you."

His hand made whisking motions in the air, as though chasing off a harmless but irritating swarm of gnats. "People like you"—the voice was flat too, and slurred— "have presided at the fall of every great civilization. People like you are history's quislings, and when the Goths are at the gates, you give up your bread and circuses to garland them with flowers. But those who serve freedom know the price of freedom is sacrifice and eternal vigilance, because the enemy is everwhere and nowhere. No quisling like you can betray my secrets, because my secrets are secret. I have built an edifice. I have been decorated by the French, I am a chevalier of the Legion of Honor." He vigorously scratched an armpit. "But why should you care, when you'll be dead before this day ends? Belly up . . . one less catfish stinking up the river. Never will you be a chevalier."

Belknap stared into the distance. "I'll collect now on the return ride you promised. If that's okay."

"Yes," Vanessa said faintly, "that's okay."

"You want to take him upstairs before we go?"

"No, Helen will come down as soon as we've left."

"Super. But I see what you mean about not being close."

Vanessa backed the Porsch from the Littlejohn driveway. Belknap surveyed the charred carcass of what must have been the Blankenship car. "How long have you known?"

"David, I just don't know how to answer. When you deal with a family member, it's different from dealing with strangers. You never see as clearly. When you think you see, you never quite believe. It's so much easier to explain aberrant behavior with a catchall label such as eccentricity. At least until now. There's never been a performance like tonight's."

"Well, breaking points. Obsessions. All that jazz. He reminds me of Forrestal. Our first secretary of defense thought the Russians were coming up the Potomac and took himself out a sixteenth-floor window at Bethesda. Your father's different, he'll take the world out instead." He grimaced. "Forget I said that. How do you feel?"

"Gutted." She hesitated. "And perhaps . . . liberated."

"Life." He watched patches of mist swirling in front of the headlights like ectoplasm. "That half-assed rain you predicted is about to start."

"I was right about that, at least." She started the wipers. "If you'll let me, if you'll trust me, I'm going to help any way I can. But you'll have to tell me what to do."

He nodded wearily. "Only first, somebody has to tell me. What do you know about ditching unwanted company?"

"Not much."

"Your father probably ordered up surveillance before we arrived or when he was in the kitchen. In case the offer of the free appendectomy was declined. Maybe, oh, four cars working in tandem. You carry a flashlight? Pliers? Screwdriver?"

"Glove compartment."

"Okay, when we turn onto Washington Street, stop under the first good overhead light. What do you see in your rearview mirrors?"

"Nothing yet."

"Well, they'd be more subtle, I suppose. When we stop, I'm going to lift the hood and fiddle with the engine. You'll still be able to crank the motor, but it won't catch. About once every thirty seconds, though, make the effort. Provides an excuse to sit there. Whenever there's no traffic, which ought to be most of the time at this hour in this weather, I'll do my poking around."

"For what?"

"Who knows?"

It took five minutes to find them. He restored the engine to anti-fiddle status and slammed the hood. He got in the car and held out one palm to display the prizes.

"You're soaked!"

"What do you expect from a half-assed drizzle and no umbrella? The smaller item in my hand is a battery-powered transmitter with a probable range of a mile. The other's a transmitter with a probable range of five miles. I've never seen one like it, the miniaturization, the electronics, are fantastic. Let's take off. It'll bother them if we don't start showing movement."

The engine produced a melodious vibrato and she headed north along the deserted street. "Where were they?"

"The little fellow was magnetically secured to the inside of the rear bumper. It's the one I was supposed to find. The other was on the chassis a distance in from the bumper. Secured with a tension-clip, more dependable than magnetic attachment. It's the one I wasn't supposed to find. Without the flashlight, I'd have missed it. Your father must've put them in place while we assumed he was in the kitchen. Or else a member of the surveillance team. They'll have equipment to home in on the signals, and since they're taking so much trouble to know where we're going, we mustn't disappoint them too quickly. Know of an all-night trucker's stop in the area?"

"I think there's one the other side of Arlington."

"Then that's our first port of call."

It was an asphalt junkyard littered with diesel rigs, twenty or more pumps arranged like a squad of robots on parade, and weatherbeaten cinderblock buildings camouflaged in battleship gray. On the roof of the restaurant, a one-story extension of the service bays, rainswept neon advertised beer and downhome cooking. Next to the restaurant was a store offering Western wear and discount stereo tapes, and next to it a long, low bunkhouse.

Vanessa angled the Porsche between a station wagon and foreign compact parked in front of the restaurant. It was almost four in the morning, yet Belknap could see, through the car's windshield, through the restaurant's sweating windows, truckers and other customers stoically waiting for booths. Most of the country worked in the daytime, but most of its wheels rolled at night. He wondered what would happen if the Teamsters ever decided to shut down the system. "Which one do you like," he asked, "the Dodge wagon or the import?"

"They're both attractive, but the Dodge looks sturdier. Bolder."

"Done," he said. He got out of the car and transplanted

the transmitters to the Dodge. He used the screwdriver to remove its Ohio license plates, then pried off the four hubcaps. He delivered his booty to Vanessa, went into the restaurant, and asked the cashier to page the owner of the Dodge. "It's an emergency, ma'am." He gave her the Ohio license number.

She flicked the switch on a stand mike nestled against the cash register and cut into the loudspeaker's bluegrass guitars and fiddles with the message. A man rose from a rear booth and ambled toward her. He was brawny and bearded and carried the soggy stub of a dead cigar. "I'm the Dodge. What's the rap?"

"Fella here says you got an emergency."

Belknap cleared his throat. "The wife's the one said I'd better let you know. Two punks about seventeen just made off with your hubcaps and plates. They're driving a scummy red pickup, one taillight's out. They turned north on that access road the other side of the bunkhouse."

The man looked stupefied. "Those spokes are custom chrome." Over his shoulder, he bawled, *"Flo, get your ass up here!"*

Flo popped out of the booth. She was brassy and sassy, but knew her master's voice. She trotted toward him like a well-trained puppy. He fished for his wallet. He pushed two ones at the cashier. "That'll take care of the coffee and doughnuts." He hesitated, as if debating proprieties, then pushed another dollar bill at his benefactor. "For your trouble, pal."

Belknap shook his head. "Like the wife told me, I do you a favor, next week you do another guy a favor, week after he does some other guy a favor, and we set up vibes can maybe travel round the world."

Flo arrived. "What's up, Rufe?"

Rufe ground the cigar butt into dust under the heel of his boot. "Two little pricks been stripping Bessie. They got the hubcaps and the plates."

"Jesus, Rufe, that stuff's custom chrome."

"Time's wasting. They're tooling north in a red pickup."
He delivered a mighty thump of gratitude to Belknap's
shoulder. "Pal, you're a sweetheart."

"Talk about pricks," the cashier said to Belknap, "some
prick lifted my battery night before. It's a jungle out there."

Belknap followed Rufe and Flo outside. Rufe gunned the
Dodge's engine and burned rubber backing almost to the
first row of pumps before he braked and shot off, spray
flying in all directions, for the access road beyond the
bunkhouse.

"Well?" Vanessa said as Belknap opened the Porsche's
passenger door.

"Well, in theory our company always stays several miles
behind, it's the advantage of the equipment they carry, the
target can never spot the surveillance. But"—he smiled at
her—"it's a jungle out there, maybe the hyenas aren't
performing the way theory says hyenas perform. Maybe,
because of the rain and weather, they sent somebody in
close for a visual check, in which case they might've seen
me transplanting. In which case they won't be at all
interested in the decoy booming out of that access road. So
let's park behind the restaurant long enough for our
company to pass this place of sorrow and track the Dodge,
if they're so minded."

"Done," she said, and began backing.

"But since they won't be so minded if somebody saw the
business with the Dodge, after a while we'll go into
Arlington and find a nice one-way street. A nice *long* one-
way street."

"Oh?"

"If you're towing a pilot fish in your wake, nothing
forces him to surface as quickly as a trip down a one-way
street at ten miles above the speed limit. As long as it's in
the wrong direction. Either he declares himself by following, or he loses you."

"Dare one ask about the cars"—she pulled in behind the
restaurant and shut off the motor—"traveling in the right
direction?"

"If we happened to meet any at this hour, they'd climb curbs and brick walls to get out of our way."

"And a police cruiser traveling in the right direction? With one of those big red spotlights and a hooting siren that won't accept *Bug off!* as an answer."

"Well, we're not drunk, the Porsche isn't stolen, and I don't think our trackers would consider it in their self-interest, not yet anyhow, to pass a description of your car or the fugitive riding shotgun in the passenger seat to local cops on routine duty. But if we do encounter a police car, you dazzle the officer with your sexiest smile, explain it's you first time in Arlington, apologize profusely, and end up getting a traffic ticket. Which we'll have Malkin fix through his connectins in high places."

She laughed dubiously. "Your nonchalance tends to be unsettling."

"Nonchalance, hell. That's adrenaline bluffing on deuces." He glanced at his watch. "Ten minutes more here. Then Arlington."

"And if there's no pilot fish?"

"Then we can follow the Potomac to the Beltway and take the Beltway to Silver Spring."

"Dare one ask, why Silver Spring?"

"So we can get a few hours of sleep before the world ends." He wound down the window to let the soft wind blow soft rain across his face. "And there's a very nice Holiday Inn in Silver Spring."

Given the predictable unpredictability of Brdnowski and Myrt, he'd belatedly realized on the Beltway it would be folly to take a room where the unwed honeymooners were honeymooning. The *No Vacancy* sign in front of the Holiday Inn made it unnecessary to improvise excuses for seeking safer camping grounds.

At the one-hundred-room Trade Winds, a two-story

complex built around a series of courts, the desk clerk, a fine specimen of weary indifference to anything less than an earthquake underfoot, seemed unconcerned about the disheveled appearance of the male member of the party. He languidly made available a registration card.

Belknap signed as Mr. and Mrs. Rufe Dutton of Cleveland. He identified their auto as a '72 Porsche and gave as its Ohio license the numbers and letters on the plates of Rufe's Dodge wagon. The desk clerk cursorily inspected the completed registration and, after learning the Duttons didn't plan to check out by eleven in the morning, collected two day's charges and supplied a key.

Vanessa parked at a right angle to the door of their ground-floor room. "So we're the Duttons from Cleveland."

Her voice was accusatory. He was fighting exhaustion, she looked as if she might be fighting tears. The shock waves from Alexandria were finally catching up. The only surprise was, it had taken this long.

"Nobody's interested in the Duttons. I'm also going to replace your plates with the plates from the Dodge. Motels require a guest to supply the license number of his car because of state law, but motels this large often have a little man who scoots around in a golf cart making sure only cars belonging to guests are parked on motel property. If he finds a freeloader's, he sometimes does spiteful things, like summoning the police and getting the car ticketed. Once it's ticketed, the motel can legally have it towed away.

"By mid-morning, if not sooner, one or more of the various parties casting nets for me will also be casting nets for a Porsche with your plates. Police in the area won't be told why the Porsche is important, they'll simply be told to report its whereabouts if sighted. They may even be told to check motel and hotel registrations. That's why we don't use your license number on our registration. And because of that little man in the golf cart, whom we don't want summoning the police, we don't use a fictitous license number. Interesting the owner of the Dodge in giving immediate chase to a red pickup wasn't the only reason for stealing his plates."

"Does it occur to you"—the peckish sniff with which she interrupted herself had a touch of the bluestocking triumphant—"that by now he'll have reported his stolen plates to the police?"

"It occurs to me, sure. There's a national stolen-car list that goes out daily by Teletype. Police are always looking for those cars. On highways, city streets, even in parking lots. Then there's a national stolen-plates list with about zero priority. If police see a car with stolen plates, they move in. But they don't go looking for stolen plates, don't go round checking motel and hotel registrations, there isn't the manpower. Once I've changed the plates, we can't use the Porsche on the street. Nothing will happen to it here, however."

"I'd like the room key," she said curtly.

The Ice Maiden cometh. But why had she suddenly become prickly? He carried her suitcase to the door, his wet feet squishing in wet shoes each step of the way. He changed the plates and, like any responsible artisan, returned the screwdriver to the glove compartment. The tinny spattering of rain on the car's rooftop masked all other night sounds. He looked at the eastern sky, hunting beginnings of dawn, but saw only roiling scud. Through the half-opened door, he caught glimpses of Vanessa moving about.

He started toward the room and his right ankle, without warning, turned inward. He stumbled and fell, landing in a sprawled position on the narrow sidewalk in front of the door. The pain shooting from his ankle was intense. There were abrasions on his hands.

She stood in the doorway, watching, "You're human. You're human after all. You can stumble, you can fall."

"I'm human." He slowly got to his feet. "What made you think I wasn't?"

She pressed her fingers to her temples and drew them down the planes of her face. "Ever since we left Alexandria, you've been performing like some goddamn machine."

"I don't know what's wrong about that." He limped into the room.

The décor was late twentieth-century caravansary plastic. The spread on the king-size bed was authentic imitation tiger skin, and the headboard was upholstered in authentic button-tucked black Naugahyde. The bedside step tables supported ovoid lamps resembling cremation urns and, like the nondescript bureau, were finished in that lifeless transparent veneer intended to eliminate forever the liquor stain and the cigarette burn from the nation's inns. The green shag rug looked as if it might need mowing before the week was over, the vinyl armchairs were as shiny as the elbows on a miser's suit. The clothes rack had the standard one hanger and the bathroom alcove's Formica built-in had the standard two drinking glasses encapsulated in milky polyethylene. Belknap knew without looking the toilet seat would have a matching doily.

Vanessa's suitcase was open on a webbed luggage stand. He was glad to see she'd thought to bring the lovely pink nightgown split at the sides like an *ao dai*. He was sorry he couldn't pull from a back pocket pajamas designed by Pierre Cardin. He wondered if a shower, if anything less than reincarnation, could make him whole.

He checked the dead detective's gun for damage done by exposure to water, then deposited it tenderly in a bureau drawer. "I'm human," he said turning to face Vanessa. "And ever since that spooky shootout with your father, I've been quivering like the stag at bay. I want very much to still be alive when this day ends."

He shook his head, because he felt like weeping, and machines must never weep. "I remember once playing poker from six in the evening to six in the morning. I went through seven hundred dollars I couldn't afford to lose, several quarts of whiskey, and probably a hundred packs of cigarettes. My mouth was raw, my eyes were bloodshot, my legs and back were aching, my hands were filthy from handling cards and chips, and all I wanted in the world was sleep. But when I finally went to bed and began to dream, I was still playing poker in one of those tossing, sweating fever dreams worse than a nightmare." He fought off a welling sigh. "I know that when I go to bed, my dreams will be of a man, myself, running, running, running . . . from the FBI, the Metropolitan Police, Russians, Malkin, Littlejohn. I am so tired, so tired . . ."

She moved to him and cradled him in her arms. They wept.

29

HE HALF-WAKENED at some strange hour, vaguely conscious Vanessa was talking on the phone. Enough shallow light filtered through the drapes to convince him it was day, not night. He brought his wristwatch to his eyes, faintly saw it was seven in the morning. He made a weak effort to come more fully out of sleep, then fell back into his dreams.

From dreaming to dozing to dreaming . . . a restive, timeless stupor . . . and unexpectedly he was quite awake, the owner of a marvelous burgeoning erection Vanessa was creating like a work of art with her silken mouth and laving tongue. He threw back the sheet and sighed. "The Goth is at the gate. *Sic transit gloria mundi*."

She momentarily abandoned artistry to look at him, wide-eyed and demure. "You're supposed to be asleep, for heaven's sake."

"How could I have forgotten?"

"But as long as you're awake . . ."

He stroked her hair. "What time is it anyhow?"

"Well, think of a number. We'll see how close you get."

"*Soixante-neuf.*"

She laughed. "Let's ring it and see who answers." She helpfully lifted the skirt of her gown and swiveled her thighs before descending again to her business in hand.

Belknap, responding like a soldier to the trumpet's call to arms, unhesitatingly joined the sweet entangling battle.

This precious intimacy, this sharing and pleasuring, was heart-stopping. He was starving, and he feasted.

Until, afraid the capricious satyr between his legs was about to go its independent, self-indulgent way, he had to cry quarter. He brought Vanessa to a position of supine availability, slid the gown's lace straps from her freckled shoulders, and molded his body to hers. When in a time that arrived too quickly, they reached a gasping, thrusting consummation, and when they had afterward lain together, perhaps for moments, perhaps for days or weeks, she looked up from smoky eyes and said, "Do you think we're compatible?"

They lay on their sides, savoring. Belknap fitted himself, spoon fashion, to the curve of her rump. He encircled her with his arms, deputized his crossed hands to shield her bared breasts from wind, snow, ice, or fire. He nuzzled an ear lobe. "I want you to know I'm not one of those chaps who, after the sadness of *la petite mort*, falls asleep almost before his ravished lady can repair her dishabille. I belong to the school of the après-ski cuddle."

She acknowledged the confession with a lazy bump and grind.

"And I think you're the one about to fall asleep, for heaven's sake."

"Unh-unh," she protested drowsily. She reached around and took solicitous possession of the bashful satyr. She half-turned her head so their lips brushed. "Do you think you could quietly slip into me? No one will notice, no one will mind."

"One can but try," he said, encouraged by the captive's interested stirring.

"One can but help," she replied.

"You're doing fine."

She turned her head again and smiled. "So are you, I feel. Can you find the way or would you like directions?"

Belknap laughed. His turn. And delightedly realized she was possibly right. There might be enough tumescence down there, enough randiness in the old campaigner, to penetrate those moistly waiting lips. And he glided lovingly into her from the rear.

"So nice of you to come, David," she whispered.

"I'm afraid that's a little premature."

"Yes, let's hope so. Regardless of whether neighbors complain."

While his hands cupped her breasts, her hands cupped his hands. When their lips met, their bodies were so fused, their embraces so interwoven, he felt as much a wondrous part of her as the beating of her heart. His lucky penis, blessed with the insouciance of recent sating, traveled up and down and roundabout in the satiny sheath where it was so lucky to be trapped. Belknap felt he could continue fucking this way forever.

"I'm on that magic stairway," Vanessa gasped. Her gyrating hips and pelvis thrust into him, and he thrust back, bewitched by the vaginal contractions so rhythmically clutching and milking him. Forever was going to arrive sooner than he'd expected.

"You're sabotaging me," he whispered into her ear and slowed his movements, luxuriating in closeness. But when, with a sudden ecstatic shudder, she quickened her own, he was lost. He drove into her embracing deepness and clasped her to him as though voyaging with her in wonder to the farthest galaxy. And there were suns and constellations unknown to astronomers, and he exploded in her like a witness to creation.

They held to each other, they clung. At an undefinable time she sighed and said, "So nice of you to have come, David."

"Yes." He sighed. "So nice of you to have invited me. And to answer your question"—he kissed the nape of her neck—"I do think, yes, we're compatible."

* * *

He turned the shower handle from *Hot* to *Cold* and spent daring moments enduring icy spray. He toweled himself and returned to the bedroom. She was lying curled on her side, watching him from cat's eyes. "Your ankle seems better."

"My ankle *is* better. I was attended by a dedicated doctor. Dare one say she looks engagingly wanton."

"Ain't wantin' right now."

He bent to kiss her lips, slightly raised her gown to kiss her pubic thatch. He stood up, threw out his arms. "What a bracing way to start a day!"

Then suddenly remembering, he said, "You were phoning someone early this morning?"

She sat up, her back against the headboard. "ComOps-Center. I thought I'd better tell the duty officer something or other he could pass on to Malkin to explain my absence today. Yours is explained, you're the fugitive. It occurred to me that while the searchers for the fugitive, or some of them, would be told you were last seen leaving Alexandria with me in my Porsche, my father would make certain Malkin himself didn't learn of it. Because in Malkin's mind, Alexandria plus myself would equal John Littlejohn. Malkin would have to wonder why you, why we, were visiting him. Everything would begin to unravel."

"Yes, but why phone the duty officer?"

"I thought, please tell me I'm not wrong, it'd be hellishly in our interest not to have Malkin relating my nonappearance to your nonappearance. In case there are things I can do I wouldn't be able to do if he did make that connection."

He smiled. "So you told the duty officer you had acute appendicitis and were on your way to the hospital?"

"That was my first impulse"—she returned his smile—"but I realized it was a story too easy to check. I told him instead my dearest college friend had been in an auto accident and was near death. Her mother had phoned, begging me to come to the hospital."

"Life's so full of tragedy. Is this hospital in Washington or some other city? And did you name it, name your dear friend?"

"The duty officer didn't think to ask, and"—she shook her head sadly—"I was so upset, I didn't think to tell him."

He laughed. "Ever since you woke up in Silver Spring, you've been performing like some goddamn machine."

"It's probably from being around you so much. Anyhow, they say two machines are better than one. What's next on our calendar, David?"

"Since it's almost noon, let's see if I've made the noonday news. Though I doubt that's the route my trackers will take." He turned on the TV and sat in a chair. "After we quickly get something to eat and I quickly buy a clean, dry set of clothes, we'll pay our respects to Brdnowski and Myrt."

"Where are they?"

He grinned. "We can walk. The Holiday Inn."

"And then?"

"Depends on whether I make the noonday news. If I'm named and a photo of me is shown as a homicide suspect, and if Holiday Inn guest rooms have TV, and the rumor is they do, Brdnowski and Myrt may be a little difficult to handle. On the other hand, they recently had in their possession stolen government secrets, and in their apartment a dead detective whose body they unlawfully removed and dumped in an alley. They should be almost as highly motivated as I am to avoid involvement with the gendarmerie."

"There's the news," Vanessa said as the channel's logo dissolved and the anchorman sincerely looked up from the papers on his desk. Belknap leaned forward.

The lead story celebrated the announcement of a multimillion-dollar redevelopment project along G Street. Washington's beaming mayor and the beaming developers, wearing white hard hats and three-piece suits, admired an architect's scale model of the complex. A great deal was said about planned growth, creation of jobs, revitalization of the inner city, and partnership between public and private sectors.

Belknap relaxed slightly. If his trackers had decided to go public, the story of a man wanted in connection with a homicide occuring almost within hailing distance of the White House would surely have edged out revitalization of the inner city. But when the anchorman reappeared after the commerical and sincerely announced three people had been murdered this morning in a shop on lower Connecticut Avenue, Belknap realized how little he understood about the priorities of TV news directors. When a panning camera showed police forcing back passers-by who were milling around the entrance, he also realized exactly what he was witnessing.

The TV reporter on the scene stood at the edge of the sidewalk, the shop's doorway and display windows framed behind him. "This is Brinkermans, a well-known Washington dealer in rare coins, where early today three people were shot to death. The victims have been identified by police as Mr. and Mrs. Jeremiah Adams, the proprietors, and Mr. Samuel Redstone of Sioux Falls, Iowa, believed by police to have been a customer. Pending the medical examiner's report, it's assumed the shooting took place soon after the shop opened. Police speculate the gunman or gunmen used a weapon or weapons equipped with a silencer, since the crimes went unreported until the bodies were discovered at ten-thirty this morning by—"

Belknap, eyes glued to the screen, said helplessly, "Brinkermans is where the Eisenhower silver dollars were bought."

"With me now is Mr. Charles Elmont, the coin collector from Baltimore who discovered the bodies. Mr. Elmont, what did you first see when you entered the shop?"

Mr. Elmont had the anguished expression of a decent man who had just viewed death by violence, and the confused expression of a decent man beginning to comprehend he had become newsworthy because of it. His responses were rambling and noninformative. Mr. Elmont's anguished face magically disappeared from the screen.

"With me now is Captain Putnam of the Metropolitan Police. Captain, are there any clues as to the identify of the persons involved in these crimes?"

Captain Putnam said curtly any comment on the investigation would have to come from Captain Geeser, who would hold a briefing for the press and "the rest of you fallen angels" at one o'clock. Captain Putnam's mocking face just as magically disappeared.

"Reliable sources have indicated Brinkermans handled on consignment valuable rare coins. Recently the proprietors negotiated the sale of one of the few Brasher doubloons not in a museum. A Brasher doubloon is said to command a price of one hundred and fifty thousand dollars. Accordingly, investigators believe the motive for these murders was robbery, and Mr. Redstone became a victim because he entered Brinkermans while the robbery was in progress."

"Robbery, hell!" Belknap said. "You don't have to shoot someone as harmless as the Adamses in order to rob them." He lowered the TV's volume until he could talk over it and still hear any mention of his name. Hands clenched, he faced Vanessa, who was kneeling on the bed, upper body erect, watching the screen. "My goddamn fault. I should have realized that if John Littlejohn knew Malkin's postman was a New York coin dealer, he'd know the places the postman went in Washington, or anywhere, to replenish inventory. I should have realized he wasn't buying when I told him the owners of the coin shop didn't know the name of the dealer who'd purchased the Eisenhower silver dollars. I should have realized he meant exactly what he said when he told me he wanted no trail at all from the coin shop to Malkin's postman. The Adamses would still be alive if I'd—"

"David! Desist! No more mea culpas! The Adamses were as doomed as Frank Willis, as doomed as the detective in Brdnowski's apartment. But damn it, we're not doomed. Unless we want to be." She sank back on her calves, made an attempt to smile. "We live."

"Yes," he said, touched by her quixotic commitment to hope, "we live."

"If Helen would ever agree, I'd like to have John institutionalized. To see if anything could be done . . ."

He didn't reply, didn't know how to reply. On the TV screen, the anchorman was sincerely describing the carnage created when a car carrying four people plunged over a guard rail on the Beltway during the recent inclement weather. Belknap said abstractedly, "My insurance policy's no longer as credible, of course. I'd counted on Mr. and Mrs. Adams for corroboration of the purchase of the Eisenhower dollars by Malkin's postman. Now everything rides on Brdnowski and the postman. I think it's time for a frank exchange of views with Mr. Moore."

"The New York coin dealer?"

"Alias Joseph Smith, alias Edgar. His shop's on West Forty-second, has a view of the Public Library. The trackers will have staked out Dulles, National, and Baltimore-Washington, including the air charters at each. We'll have to find a nearby small airport and a hungry pilot with no pressing engagements."

"There's Freeway, an airfield at Mitchellville. At a guess, twenty miles from here on the Beltway and Annapolis Highway."

"You'd better carry my gun in your bag until we get to New York. I don't think small charter outfits walk their customers through a metal detector, so we should be okay. We'll take Brdnowski and Myrt with us. If Brdnowski can make a positive identification of Mr. Moore as his Tuesday passenger, the frank exchange of views begins. Mr. Moore has to be persuaded his continued presence among the living depends on his voluntarily confirming and punctiliously substantiating for the little tape recorder we'll purchase en route that Malkin's a Soviet agent. I've a friend with an isolated cabin in the Catskills, south of Monticello. Uses it for hunting and skiing. I can get a key. Mr. Moore will be our guest there. Brdnowski and Myrt will look after his welfare while we return to Washington with out little tape recorder for a frank exchange of views with George."

"I'll get dressed."

"One thing. Brdnowski and Myrt know me as Fred. Yesterday Sybil outfitted me with plastic for a Fred Ryan from something called the Treasury's Office of Special Investigations. Since I don't seem to be making the noonday news, I'd better continue being Fred with them."

"Then I deserve a nom de guerre too." Still kneeling on the bed, she lifted her haunches until her upper body was again erect. Her nightgown was hiked almost to her thighs. "How about . . . Bobbie Jo?" She chastely adjusted a strap on her gown. "Do I look like a Bobbie Jo, David?"

He shook his head. "You look like Venus rising from the sea."

She sat in front of the bathroom alcove's mirror brushing her hair. She was wearing the same beige skirt and a long-sleeved white silk blouse with a wide collar and pearl buttons. "Do we leave my suitcase here?"

"We'll stash it in the car trunk. After I buy new clothes, we'll toss my old ones in it too. And pay for a third day in case we can't get back before eleven tomorrow."

She stood up, put her arms around his neck, and kissed him primly. "Poor baby, you don't care for Bobbie Jo, do you? How about Vee, short for *vive la différence*?"

He placed his hands on her hips. "How about Van, short for Vanessa?"

"There's a nom de guerre I can relate to! Are you as famished as I am?"

"We'll take care of the inner woman immediately."

"Well, that's been taken care of handily, thank you. Just breakfast for the nonce. Or is breakfast too terribly gauche at this hour in Silver Spring?"

He picked up her suitcase. "One can but test the waters."

She opened the door and they stepped into the enveloping sultriness left by the rain. He put the suitcase in the Porsche. "John Littlejohn said he didn't want anyone interfering with Malkin's postman. Let's hope that means Mr. Moore hasn't been shot to death in his shop by another clumsy robber. His untimely demise would play hell with any frank exchange of views."

They started, hand in hand, toward the street. "It'd also be awkward," she said, "if we couldn't get access to that cabin. Maybe you ought to phone your friend to arrange about the key."

"What would I do without you?"

"And you look absolutely miserable in those ruined clothes. Wouldn't you really prefer new ones *before* we eat?"

"I thought you'd never ask."

30

GENERAL IGOR DEMICHEV looked down on the nine asymmetrical domes of St. Basil's Cathedral from their window table in the Rossiya's twenty-first-floor restaurant. Red Square was quiet. The Kremlin beyond was quiet. The only thing not quiet was this window table.

Across from him, Natalia said in a voice of velvet, always a danger signal, "I'm not upset because you missed my recital last evening at Tchaikovsky Conservatoire; I wasn't at my best anyhow. Even if I had been, the KGB has always been your mistress, and the mistress always comes before the wife. You've your irreplaceable Chessplayer to worry about; I've my unscrupulous manager to worry about. All this I understand. I'm upset because you seem afraid, and I've never before seen you afraid. Who are the two thugs at the table nearest us?"

Demichev reluctantly shifted his gaze from the brilliant evening colors and arresting spirals of St. Basil's onion-shaped domes and smaller turrets to the nearest table. "They're not thugs," he said softly, "they're my own men. My paranoid colleague General Pechenko views the temporary difficulties in Washington as a golden opportunity to bring about my transfer to Bratsk—or some other Siberian paradise on the banks of the Angara—as director of security for a hydroelectric plant. The expert from the Department of Hindsight is so paranoid he may even view those difficulties as evidence I'm working for U.S. Intelligence. If I hadn't arranged to have that table reserved for my own men, an informer reporting to Pechenko would now be sitting there trying to overhear and then lie about everything we say."

Natalia spooned Beluga Malossol onto a triangle of bread. "So you are afraid?"

"Of course I am. Some traitor on my staff has to be working for U.S. Intelligence, otherwise we wouldn't be encountering difficulties in Washington. If I don't find him before Pechenko finds him, you may be holding your future salons in Bratsk, where concert pianists aren't precisely as idolized as they are here. Perhaps you should decide to be afraid, too."

"I already have. Do you have a suspect in mind?"

"I always try to have a suspect in mind, how else does a decent man survive in this business?" He laughed heartily. "When making our reservations, I ordered broiled Azov sturgeon. If you'd prefer shaslik or beef Stroganoff . . . ?"

"You know how I love sturgeon, Moscow-style. Accordingly, I forgive you for missing the recital. Now, please notice, I follow your lead and speak as softly as you so your charming thugs won't overhear my indiscretions. Who is your suspect?"

Demichev sampled the other *zakuski* complementing the caviar. "Well, there's a Major Subotin. No, I've never invited him to one of your salons, he's not a type you'd enjoy. But it occurred to me while I was fending off Pechenko today, Subotin has all the defects of character one hopes for in a traitor. He resembles Goebbels, though this isn't the only reason he's probably the traitor. I'm having Nikitin review Subotin's contacts with foreigners, and then I'm having Visko, who can smell out treachery in a cemetery at midnight, discreetly review the way Nikitin handles the investigation, in case Nikitin has somehow been subverted by Subotin. Or by Pechenko. It's painful even to consider the possibility that Nikitin, whom I've treated as a son—today, in fact, I promised to recommend his promotion to captain—would betray me. Yet we learn about life not only from life itself but also from the great writers who tell us about life. Shakespeare, who told us about Julius Caesar and the trusted Brutus, also told us treachery vies with loyalty in the hearts of underlings. Sometimes I almost feel I couldn't be the man I am if I didn't have Shakespeare to counsel me."

Natalia nibbled thoughtfully on a thin strip of smoked salmon. "What exactly are the difficulties in Washington?"

"I wish I knew exactly." He tossed off a jigger of Stolichnaya and took a bite of herring. Natalia, he reflected lugubriously, was putting on weight; the Givenchy dress that matched her flaming red hair was no longer as flattering to her figure as when she'd bought it on her French tour a year ago. Her face, though, was still as lustrous as porcelain, as changeable in its moods as the sea. She'd be lost in Bratsk, but then, so would he.

"A Washington cabdriver stole some silver dollars bought at a local coin shop by one of our illegals, a New York coin dealer. These silver dollars in the hands of the cabdriver, or more accurately, his knowledge of where they'd been bought, not only threatened the security of our illegal, they increased the existing threat to the security of Chessplayer. It became necessary to do something about the cabdriver, but Colonel Zalenin's men, who took on this crucial assignment, were unable to find him. They were additionally obliged to defend themselves from a detective who challenged them in the cabdriver's apartment. Obviously the cabdriver had been warned by someone and gone into hiding. Zalenin's men were thus forced to resolve the problem of the silver dollars by the only other means available."

Natalia bit into a pickled mushroom, then frowned. "Which was?"

"Something wrong with the mushroom, Natalia?" he asked solicitously.

She shrugged. "It has no character. But it's nothing to worry about, and certainly not worth another losing argument with a Moscow waiter. Have you noticed the waiters here are becoming almost as surly as those at the Metropole?"

"It's part of the corruption brought on by grandiosity," he said philosophically. "These three thousand rooms under us supposedly make the Rossiya the largest hotel in Europe, though I suspect the West Germans will try to outdo us soon enough."

"If they do, the hotel will be built by the Japanese."

"And financed by the Saudis. Then blown up in due course by a Baader-Meinhof faction. What a cosmopolitan world progress has created for us! But can anything less than a glass-and-aluminum Hilton built on the moon ever compete with the Rossiya?"

They laughed and toasted each other with Stolichnaya.

"Zalenin's men," Demichev said, "resolved the problem of the silver dollars by arranging for the two owners of the Washington coin shop to be unavailable for interrogation by U.S. Intelligence. Unfortunately, a customer entered the shop while the arrangements were in progress, so Zalenin's men felt required to include him in the transaction."

"And how is this done, Gosha? Do they offer money for silence?"

"Well, Zalenin's men have various methods. How it was done in this case I don't quite know." He looked down again on St. Basil's, admiring the masterpiece created by those two hapless architects selected by Ivan the Terrible to commemorate his conquest of Kazan in 1552. "Zalenin likes to cloak operational methods with mystery, and since he produces results, how can I fault him?"

"But if the difficulties in Washington have been resolved, why are you still troubled about Pechenko?"

"The problem with the silver dollars was only one of the difficulties. Ivan Glukhov, the man you asked me about yesterday, defected the same afternoon. It was a defection we engineered, however . . . he mistakenly thinks he knows the identity of Chessplayer and has nothing except this to offer the FBI in exchange for friendship. The person *he* knows as Chessplayer, as luck would have it, is a longtime associate of *our* Chessplayer, and the FBI has accepted his story." He sighed. "But stories sometimes come apart."

"And this story"—Natalia's instant concern was gratifying—"has begun to come apart?"

"No, not yet." He watched as the maître d' disapprovingly seated a party of inebriated young Africans, probably from Lumumba Friendship University. "As schoolchildren you and I were told, part as myth, part as fact, that Ivan the Terrible put out the eyes of the two architects who designed St. Basil's so they could never again create a work of equal splendor. As a child I was shocked by the story, yet if today there were a hundred St. Basil's in Moscow, would the beauty of even one be appreciated? One might argue, two men experience pain and blindness so all other lives will be enriched."

"No, we have an affinity for madness, we Russians. I see the story as corroboration of the excess that's always been part of our history."

"Not only ours, Natalia. Excess has always been part of the historical imperative. A price must be paid for victory, whether it's the victory of art or the victory of arms. Thus the price of saving Chessplayer is the death of Chessplayer's associate, because only his death can prevent an eventual collapse of Glukhov's story. With this historical truth, even Pechenko the Terrible agrees."

"At least the two of you agree on something."

He glanced at her sharply, suspecting sarcasm, but she was too experienced an actress to show him anything more than an ambiguous smile. Choosing the course of prudence, he treated the remark as innocent and said equably, "And this is the heart of the present difficulties in Washington. Chessplayer took certain steps to ensure that the associate

would be shot while resisting arrest or trying to escape."
Demichev shook his head. "Something went wrong with
his plan . . . precisely what is unclear. Worse, the associate has disappeared, which means he, like the cabdriver, had been warned. Only a blind man could fail to
preceive the warnings must have come from Moscow. I'm
not blind."

"What do you intend to do?"

"About the situation in Washington, nothing, since I'm
here, not there. The Washington KGB, however, will do
everything it can to find the man and then everything
necessary to ensure Chessplayer's safety. It's possible the
man might try to contact Chessplayer personally, which
would solve all our problems, since it's feasible to maintain
a discreet protective surveillance of Chessplayer when he's
away from his Washington office.

"As for the situation in Moscow, I'll have to wait for
Nikitin's report on Subotin, and Visko's report on Nikitin.
And try to keep a paranoid Pechenko from destroying the
grand design."

The inebriated young Africans were becoming noisier,
and he wondered how African students could afford a
restaurant this expensive on Lumumba Univeristy's small
monthly allowance. Unless, of course, they were also on a
KGB allowance. Sometimes the Center's compulsive
squandering of finite resources on farfetched recruitments
and similar dubious adventures appalled him. Each solidly
conceived operation implemented by realists like himself
had to compete for funding and manpower with extrava-
gantly wasteful projects run by dilettantes. Espionage, he
thought morosely, should be restricted by state decree to
those who actually knew what they were doing. And above
all to those who were not paranoid.

"Perhaps," Natalia said, "the person working for U.S.
Intelligence isn't on your staff at all." She opened her gold-
mesh bag, a gift from her Italian impresario the afternoon he
took her shopping on the Via Condotti to celebrate her first

appearance at the Accademia di Santa Cecilia; Demichev still wondered what else that day's gift might have been celebrating. Taking out a tiny note pad and removing the tiny gold pencil clipped to it, she wrote a word. With the same ambiguous smile, she placed the pad in front of him.

Demichev read the single word, then jovially slapped the table. The china danced, as it certainly should. "Why not? Why not? But it would take a braver suicidal fool than me to propose to the chairman an investigation of Pechenko unless I carried proof of his ties with U.S. Intelligence in my pocket. So life now decrees we must give the scoundrel the benefit of the doubt and forget you ever made your wicked suggestion." He raised his glass. *"Za vashe zdorov'e!"*

"A votre santé aussi, mon général!"

Demichev, made pleasantly reckless by vodka, signaled the waiter. "Is our sturgeon ready perhaps?"

"You haven't finished the *zakuski*."

"Even so, is our sturgeon ready?"

"What do you find wrong with the *zakuski*? It is the finest in Moscow."

"I am a cousin of Comrade Brezhnev," Demichev said. "Your insolence will cost you dearly."

"I am a cousin of Comrade Brezhnev's wife," the waiter replied. "I shall report to her your insolence to me. Do you want to create a family quarrel between them or do you want to get your sturgeon?"

"I want to get the sturgeon."

"Then I shall investigate. The chef, the cooks, even the sturgeon. In the meantime, enjoy the *zakuski*."

31

HEARING AN AUTHORITATIVE KNOCK, Brdnowski cautiously opened the door of his Holiday Inn room and found himself facing Fred and a so-so blonde. Underjoyed but putting up a brave front, he cried, *"Hey, Fred!* Welcome back!"

"This is Van," Fred said. "She's with me on the case."

"Right." Brdnowski reluctantly invited them in. The blonde was a trifle thick amidships, but she had a nice upper deck. No competition for Myrt, though. He wondered how he was going to explain her absence to Fred.

"Been watching TV last couple of hours?" Fred asked casually.

"I don't go in too much for the daytime stuff. Myrt likes 'General Hospital,' but we had to miss it on account of taking the blood tests." Seeing Fred was puzzled, he added, "For the Maryland marriage license."

"You went to a doctor's goddamn office!" Fred was upset, Fred was very upset. It came across so clearly Brdnowski couldn't miss it, though he was certainly trying.

"Brdnowski, I told you not to leave this place for anything, damn it."

"The office is just a couple of blocks from here. Except for those couple of blocks, we spent the rest of the time in the doc's office. Except when we picked up the license afterward."

"Jesus!"

"Don't let Fred rattle you, Brdnowski." The blonde named Van handed him an okay smile. "He's a little off his feed. Some bastard stole his license plates last night, so now he can't use his car."

"Right."

Fred was sniffing his way like a bird dog to the louvered doors separating the bedroom from a small dressing area outside the bathroom. "Myrt in there?"

Brdnowski sucked in a lot of oxygen. "Not right this minute."

Fred spun around. "Then where the hell is she right this minute?"

"I think she's gone for our mail."

"Your mail! If she shows up at your apartment, she's dead. Didn't that message get through yesterday?"

"It's not that mail she's after. It's the mail in a box we've got at the Ellis post office."

Fred smiled in pleased surprise, as if he'd bitten into a worm and discovered half an apple. "Isn't that lovely! Particularly since everybody working there was given Myrt's photo yesterday and told to phone the police if she happened to drop by."

"I don't think anybody'd notice her, Fred. The boxes are in a lobby."

"What's so important about this mail?"

"Myrt was afraid the box might get too full. We're running a kind of chain letter." He cleared his throat. "To help the needy."

Fred nodded understandingly. "A few days ago you went out of your way to help the president. Now you're going out of your way to help the needy. Brdnowski, I've this gut feeling that somebody, maybe even me, is going to nominate you as Citizen of the Year."

"The chain letter was Myrt's idea," he replied modestly. "She's the one deserves the credit."

"Make a note of that, Van. When we submit the nominations, be sure Myrt's listed first."

"Is this place blown now?" she asked Fred.

He shrugged. "Perhaps Brdnowski's right, perhaps

nobody'll notice her. If they do, she should be long gone by the time the police arrive. She take the rental Datsun?''

"I wouldn't trust her with it, Fred. Neither would you if you saw the way she drives. Went on the bus.''

"Small favors," Fred said to Van. He removed a photograph from his wallet. "Does the man wearing a blazer and flannels in this picture resemble the person you thought your Library of Congress passenger waved to as you drove along First?''

Brdnowski frowned. "Who's the clown in Aunt Nelly's bloomer suit standing next to him?''

"A guard at the Tower of London who'd chop off your head with a halberd if he caught you saying that. What about the man in the blazer?''

"Don't think he's the"—he broke off—"hey, Fred, almost forgot! After you left me and Myrt yesterday, I got to thinking about the guy messing with the engine of his van when I picked up the fare.''

"And?''

"I remembered the company name on the side of the van. *Acme*. Acme Term Control, something like that. But I checked the phone book and couldn't find it, so—''

"Willis's apartment," the blonde said. "The business about the two pest exterminators maybe seen in the building.''

"Cross your fingers," Fred said. "How does Acme Termite Control sound, Brdnowski?''

"It sounds right on the button.''

Fred and the blonde exchanged glances. Brdnowski, realizing he'd just won brownie points, decided to go for more. "I'll check the phone book.''

"Not necessary. The company won't be listed.''

The blonde had a faraway look. "The van must have been Moore's backup. Which means John was right, the Russians killed Willis.''

Brdnowski listened uneasily. This was heavy stuff. Fred, though, had told him from the beginning it wasn't a game of marbles.

Fred walked to the window and pulled the drapes. "Security," he explained as he turned to Brdnowski. "Everything I've been instructed to tell you is top secret. But if your president can't put his trust in a man who returns stolen documents to him, whom can he trust?"

"Right."

"Your passenger was a Russian spy. We think he operates a coin shop in New York City and calls himself Moore. Through a confidential source we've learned the shop's on Forty-second, near the library. So the three of us are flying to New York to see if you can identify him as your Tuesday passenger. If you can, we're under orders to take him into informal protective custody; if we arrested him officially, he'd have the right to refuse to talk until he'd obtained a lawyer, and the lawyer wouldn't let him give us even the time of day. This isn't how you break up an espionage ring. Moore's small potatoes, you saw that yourself. A middle-aged messenger boy."

"Right."

"We want the ringleaders, and to get them we have to persuade Moore to furnish names. This kind of persuasion isn't exactly done with kid gloves, but it gets results. Of course, it also means Moore will escape prosecution, because he wasn't arrested in a legal manner. Your government considers this a small price to pay to put the ringleaders behind bars for thirty years." Fred took a plastic card from his wallet. "You might want a look at this."

"Fred Ryan," Brdnowski read respectfully. He paused, puzzled. "Treasury Department?"

"Office of Special Investigations. But you're entitled to know the I.D.'s merely part of my cover, the name and department I've been assigned for this case. Van and I actually work out of the White House."

"In the chain-of-command sense," she corrected. "But our offices aren't there. Maybe we should explain why."

Fred nodded. "The methods employed by our unit for

getting results—and the track record's impressive—are a little unorthodox. So the White House understandably builds a few walls between itself and the unit. Sometimes we're Treasury, sometimes Commerce, sometimes Interior, and so on."

"Have we ever been Interior?" Van asked.

"You and I haven't, but Claude told me he was when they rolled up that Czech who was plugged into the Pentagon Situation Room. Another thing about the unit, it operates a safe house in the Catskills—"

"Well, technically it's a safe house, but I don't want Brdnowski expecting something with all the conveniences of home. Basically it's a simple cabin in the woods."

"All right, so sue me." Fred grimaced. The blonde know-it-all was obviously getting under his skin. "Anyhow, this is the way the orders came down. If you can identify Moore, we're to take him to the safe house, where you and Myrt will be in charge. But since Myrt isn't here and we can't wait for her, Van will take over for Myrt."

"That's ridiculous. I don't have to take over. When we get to New York, we can call on Omega Three for safe-house support."

"No, we can't. The way the orders came down, we aren't to touch base with Omega Three under anything less than a Condition Four Alert. Fat chance of that. Worse, we can't go within a hundred miles of the FBI."

"Those scumbags at headquarters! I suppose it was Toby, throwing his weight around as usual?" She looked at Fred suspiciously. "You're sure this is what the orders said?"

"Listen, I didn't believe it myself. And it wasn't Toby, it was the chief. When he told me, I asked him to put it in writing."

Her eyes widened. "You did? That took guts, I admit."

"The chief grumbled, but I ended up with written orders, now in my office safe. So nobody's going to be able to claim later we should have invited Omega Three to the party."

"Sometimes I think this secretive splitting of operations

into compartments has gotten out of hand. And keeping us away from the FBI as well . . . Toby doesn't seem to trust anyone outside the unit." She gave Brdnowski a wonderful smile. "But who cares? I like the idea of the two of us working together in the Catskills."

"Thank you, ma'am," he said, coloring.

"Van, please."

"Right." Brdnowski pulled at his beard. "I guess I missed something," he apologized. "What're we going to be doing there?"

"Just looking after Moore," Fred said vaguely, "until I've reported personally to headquarters on whatever he's shared with us."

Van sat on the edge of the bed. "You'd better leave a note telling Myrt you went to New York with Fred to help crack the case, and you'll be back tomorrow. That way she won't worry."

"And in view of her trip to the post office," Fred said, "you'd better tell her not to spend the night here, otherwise I'll worry. Does she have a friend who could put her up? A friend who can be trusted."

"There's Olga, works tables with her at the Greek's. The two of 'em are tight."

"All right, that leaves only one small matter. After we've located Moore's coin shop, we'll go in together and you'll signal immediately if Moore was your Tuesday passenger. If he was, though, he'll also recognize you. He might panic, and he might have a gun." Fred shook his head. "The last thing we want is you getting shot simply because you tried to serve your country."

"Right," Brdnowski said without any reservations whatsoever.

"The solution is, you'll wear a disguise."

Brdnowski nodded enthusiastically. "I've got a pair of wraparound shades in my suitcase. With the shades and maybe a fake nose we could pick up in a joke shop, I—"

"We're picking up your disguise in a barbershop," Fred

said very offically. "The beard, in short, has to go. Every last hair and whisker."

Horrified, Brdnowski sank into the nearest chair. "Fred, you can't do this to me."

"I know how you feel. But it's the way orders came down."

"Fred, my beard's"—he groped for the words—"a living thing. It's like me. Like my arms, my legs."

"I know," Van said, "it's a rotten piece of luck. But sometimes the pencil pushers at headquarters are smarter than we realize. You have to remember, the people who came to your apartment yesterday intending to kill you *know* you have a beard. Get rid of it, and you keep *them* as well as Moore from recognizing you."

"And unless you get rid of it"—Fred moved his shoulders in a confession of helplessness—"we're not allowed to guarantee your safety."

Brdnowski stood up and sadly admired the fullness of his beard in the mirror over the dresser. "Myrt's going to be very unhappy."

"Oh, that's unfair," Van protested, and he realized he'd somehow disappointed her. "You wouldn't want Myrt styling her hair only one way forever, would you? Women are the same about their men. Personally"—she loaned him another wonderful smile—"I think a clean-shaven Brdnowski will be more Brdnowski than a bearded Brdnowski could ever be. Besides, a beard's a little different from an arm or leg. If you don't like the effect, you can always grow another."

The phone rang. Brdnowski looked uncertainly at Fred, and Fred looked uncertainly at the phone. "Better answer. Might be Myrt."

It was Myrt all right, ready to prove she didn't need a fire chief's bullhorn to be heard as far north as the Pennsylvania line. "Nail a lucky six-pack to the door, Brdnowski, your bashful bride's on her way! With two new blouses, neither of them stolen, and twenty-five more bucks from the good people of Chicago. What's new in Silver Spring?''

When he told her, it was a shock to discover she was as much in favor of barbershop surgery as the pencil pushers at headquarters. Fred, joining him at the phone, suggested she return by taxi, because if she could get to Silver Spring before the barber completed the disguise, she wouldn't have to spend the night with Olga. She could spend it with Brdnowski in the Catskills.

Myrt's gung-ho whoop could have come from the next room. ''Between Olga without a beard and Brdnowski with or without a beard, it's no contest. I'll grab a taxi.''

Leaving the Annapolis Highway at Church Road, Brdnowski drove south on a winding lane through two miles of rolling woods, tobacco fields, and scattered pastureland to a bridge crossing U.S. 50. Dead ahead on the right in a wooded setting was Freeway Airport. He guessed there must be seventy small planes in casual rows on both sides of the single runway.

Fred went into the one-story building next to the hangar to make the arrangements. Myrt asked Van—they'd been jabbering like an old high-school twosome ever since Silver Spring—if women secret agents got the same pay as men. Brdnowski gently massaged his tingling cheeks and jaw. He had the confusing feeling his beard was still part of his face.

Fred returned, looking as if he owned the world. ''We've a six-seat Piper Aztec. Pilot's filing a flight plan for Teterboro, which is seven miles west of the George Washington Bridge. We'll have a cruising speed of a hundred and eighty knots, plus a good tail wind, so we ought to make it in a little over an hour. But the time angle's going to be tight. It'll be almost four o'clock and Moore probably closes his shop at five.''

''Maybe we ought to contact Omega Three in spite of the orders,'' Van said. ''A little insurance to cover our rear.''

"Out of the question. Even if it was the only way to crack the case, the second-guessers at headquarters would send us to Siberia."

"I'd give a month's pay to see those scumbags out in the field just once, harvesting the cash crops. They wouldn't know how to begin."

When the sporty red-and-blue twin engine landed at Teterboro with a bump and frisky hop, a waiting airport van took them to Operations. Fred, moving faster than the competition as a taxi delivering passengers pulled up, signed the driver and promised an extra fifty if he set a new track record to 42nd and Fifth. The reliable old Checker, with Fred beside the driver and Brdnowski between the ladies, took off like a rocket.

"First time," Brdnowski said, marveling, "I've ever been in a taxi. I mean," he added, noticing lifted eyebrows, "in the back seat."

He leaned forward to study the TD permit and tapped the driver on the shoulder. "Is your name Giarrizzo?"

"You want to by it? I'll sell it cheap."

Brdnowski grinned. "I figured it probably was. I have this kind of talent for reading TD permits." He poked Myrt in the ribs to make sure she caught the joke. He'd have liked to give Van a friendly poke too, but she might get the wrong idea.

32

BELKNAP PAID OFF the driver and joined Vanessa and their two pickup commandos in front of the Pubic Library's north entrance. A hirsute trio of stoned West Side cowboys looked them over briefly before resuming negotiations, experience telling them undercover cops didn't arrive by taxi. On the balustraded terrace west of the library steps, derelicts with shipwrecked faces conferred in council, passing judgment punctuated by tobacco juice on life along 42nd Street.

"Drop the gun in my jacket pocket as we're crossing to the other side," Belknap said to Vanessa. "The drivers will be too busy trying to hit us to notice. While I'm buying a cassette recorder, you can use one of those phone booths near Fifth to check yellow pages for places around here selling both coins and stamps."

"Do you need money? You've been throwing it around."

"I'm okay. I put the plane on a credit card the chief issued me. The cover name on it is Belknap. Ryan's Irish, I wonder what Belknap is."

"Lower Slobbovian would be my guess. What's the tab for the plane?"

"Not bad. Hundred and fifty an hour from prop-start to prop-stop, fifteen an hour standby. Brdnowski, you and Myrt can enjoy the street theater while I'm shopping. Pretzel vendors, Hare Krishnas, moonlighting inventors hawking perpetual-motion machines, take your pick."

But when Belknap stepped into the late-afternoon pedes-

342

trian traffic with his new cassette recorder, Brdnowski and
Myrt had disappeared. He swore, realizing too late he
should have taken one of his urban gypsies hostage to keep
the other honest. Then, about ten storefronts to the west, he
saw Brdnowski waving sunglasses to attract his attention.
But where the hell was Myrt?

Since Vanessa was still studying yellow-page listings, he
started walking toward his AWOL commando. And understood, when he at last saw Myrt, why his two fair-weather
soldiers had deserted. The street theater they'd chosen was a
well-attended sidewalk game of three-card monte.

Brdnowski came over, excited. "Remember that uncle of
Myrt's I mentioned yesterday, Fred? The one with the
carnival."

Belknap remembered. Malkin had mentioned the uncle,
too. My God, he thought, Malkin. Exposing Malkin was
the sole reason for this trip. Yet here he was ludicrously
playing nursemaid to two aging street urchins.

"What you're looking at," Brdnowski confided, "is a
scam called three-card monte. The dude behind the upended
cardboard carton is the gunner. He drops the cards, an ace
and two jacks, face-down on the carton. Even a blind man
could keep track of the ace. So the marks pony up to win a
potful by guessing where it is and somehow always lose."

"I know. I invented the game. With a little help from
Methuselah."

"Right. No law says a fed's always got to be a rube. The
broad in the gunnysack outfit and the dude dressed like Mr.
Times Square are the shills. The gunner lets them win to
gull the marks, and good old Myrt blew two fives to gull the
gunner. What he doesn't know is, she practically grew up
on her uncle's knee, at least when the carnival was in town.
He taught her every three-card-monte hustle there is. She's
going to walk off with the marbles."

Myrt counted eight twenties onto the carton. The gunner
matched her and addressed his parishioners. "It's time, my
friends, to crimp this here ace." He bent the card length-

wise with thumb and forefinger. "Because we want to make sure the little lady gets a big hand."

Brdnowski nudged Belknap. "Myrt knows that hustle backwards. The gunner straightens the ace and crimps a jack as he makes the drop. In about two seconds, he's going to lose his lunch."

Vanessa arrived as the cards dropped in a neat row, crimped card in the center. "I've got good news."

Myrt aimed a finger at the card on the right. "That's my baby."

The gunner flipped it. A jack. He flipped the crimped card. An ace. He scooped the money. "Let's have a big hand for the little lady."

The shills led scattered applause. Myrt, looking as if she'd just come off a fifty-mile march, homed on Brdnowski. "The bastard uncrimped the ace during the drop; I know the move and I know I caught it. But then the son of a bitch made some extra move Max never taught me."

"That's the uncle," Brdnowski said. "I hope the mail from Chicago holds up."

"Only one?" Belknap said, elated.

"Only one," Vanessa replied, "dealing in both stamps and coins and near enough to have a view of the Public Library."

He glanced at Brdnowski and Myrt, still watching the sidewalk game from its fringes. "Mrs. Adams thought Moore's shop wasn't on the street."

"Well, the building entrance behind us says Eleven West. Atlantic Stamp and Coin, judging by its listed address, must be in the last building before Avenue of the Americas."

Two unconvincing drunks were approaching from the west. The gunner must have recognized old friends from the Bunco Squad, because suddenly he was sprinting toward Fifth like a gold medalist. One of the detectives, not Olympic class but undoubtedly heartened by Myrt's cheers, gave chase. The other, forced to choose between the two shills, already halfway across 42nd and still not accident victims, and the last player to put down a bet, chose the bird in hand.

"Give thanks, Sister Vanessa," Belknap said. "A few minutes earlier, and Myrt would've been the one about to be taken to Midtown South to give a statement. But how often does luck strike twice in the same place? So somehow keep Her Grace on the straight and narrow while Brdnowski and I are visiting Atlantic. Hijack a taxi, too, and pay up to a million in ransom to keep it anchored at the curb until we come out with Moore. I'll have him well trained by then, and definitely not inclined to make absurd complaints about being abducted to some taxi driver he's never seen before."

"What's our destination?"

"A car rental on Fiftieth. You'll have to handle the rental while I look after Moore. Change his diapers, warm his milk, all the little touches you'd expect from a caring baby-sitter."

As they left the elevator, Belknap put a reassuring hand on Brdnowski's shoulder. "Moore's not going to recognize you without your beard, I barely recognize you myself. But he might recognize your voice. So all you do if you're sure he's your Tuesday passenger, is cough. Then step out to the hall, because I'm going to have to quickly teach him the joys of cooperation, and it isn't something you'd enjoy watching. It might even make you sick."

"You must be one tough son of a bitch, Fred. What're you going to do to him?"

One lucky son of a bitch, Belknap thought, now realizing the Atlantic Stamp and Coin wasn't the only name stenciled on the frosted glass of the door at the south end of the hall. Atlantic shared overhead with a collection agency, watch-repair service, and marriage counselor.

He'd misread Moore. Illegals were supposed to court

anonymity, the counterintelligence mahatmas always said, by operating one-man businesses from premises under their sole control. This was the kind of insulated privacy Belknap had counted on in order to help Moore appreciate the virtues of immediately rearranging allegiances; a lone instructor couldn't simultaneously reeducate his pupil and control frightened witnesses. For the first time he had to wonder if Moore had been lying when he'd told the Adamses he'd a view of the Public Library. But a lie would raise questions about his legitimacy if they visited New York and were unable to find him in this area of 42nd. Moore, he tried to convince himself, would have told the Adamses the truth or told them nothing.

"Change of plans," he said. "I may need you for crowd control . . . you're job's to keep other tenants from making phone calls or trying to leave while I'm gathering up Mr. Moore. I'm empowered by Washington to deputize you a member of the unit for twenty-four hours, so you've now the same authority I have to act for your president on this mission. I hope you're one tough son of a bitch."

Belknap opened the door and saw a dingy reception room with wooden chairs, a cheap pine desk, threadbare carpeting it would have required a leap of faith to believe had seen better days, and filthy windows facing 42nd. The first of two closed doors on the left identified the marriage counselor, the second, Atlantic Stamp and Coin. Through one of the two doorways on the other side of the room, he could see the watch repairer, loupe to eye at a jeweler's bench. The other doorway framed the collection agency, where a balding go-getter, feet crossed on one corner of his desk, was flipping through *Playboy* in search of clients.

The receptionist, a flinty sergeant major who looked as if she could count cadence in her sleep, jabbed a half-smoked cigarette into an ashtray surrounded by decorative coffee-mug stains. "Who ya wanna see?"

"Owner of Atlantic Stamp and Coin."

"Mo ain't in. Ain't been in all week."

Belknap displayed his Treasury I.D. "Ryan, Office of Special Investigations. My partner's Agent Murphy. Out at Kennedy, Customs apprehended a suspect trying to bring a Brasher doubloon into the country. A gold coin worth a hundred grand and change. Markings on this one resemble those on a Brasher stolen from a museum last December. The suspect claims he bought it from Atlantic. We need the owner's version."

"Take my advice, it's free. Save your leather. Mo don't handle goods go for a hundred grand and change. If he did, he wouldn't be renting space and cockroaches in this pisspot. Take my advice, dump twenty years on the flake at Kennedy."

"Murph and I appreciate that kind of citizen input, but Treasury regs require us to get signed statements from all parties. What's the owner's home address, maybe we can wrap the case today, turn it over to the U.S. Attorney tomorrow?"

"Tomorrow's Saturday, Fred," Brdnowski said. "That office will be closed."

"You're new to this jurisdiction, Murph, but assistant attorneys for S.D.N.Y. are fire-eaters. They'll come in tomorrow and be ready to run the flake at Kennedy past the grand jury first thing Monday."

"Here's the address," the receptionist said, scribbling on a pad. "My motto is, dump on the flakes before they dump on you."

"Thanks a mil." Belknap gingerly put the fateful question. "What would be Mo's last name?"

"Moore. Morris Moore. But take my advice, call him Mo."

West 48th. A five-story tenement bleached to a dirty milk chocolate by sun and the seasons. Four rusting fire-escape scaffolds linked by rusting ladders overhung the sidewalk. A shopping-bag lady turned archaeologist was sifting contents of a trash barrel with the tip of a furled umbrella.

Belknap, helping Vanessa out of the taxi, studied fifth-floor windows. Moore's apartment would be up there. Illegals and bats roosted in attics—bats because they were peculiar anyhow, illegals because there was nothing quite like an antenna near the roof to soup up shortwave reception.

"Murph's a member of the unit now," he said as Brdnowski came around from the other side of the taxi. "I deputized him under the twenty-four-hour clause. If Moore's home, we'll bring him out quickly. If he isn't, we'll set up a stakeout . . . you and Myrt can bivouac in the lobby of the Century Paramount on Forty-sixth. I'll page Flo Dutton when he shows up."

"If he isn't home, perhaps I ought to phone hospitals. His troubles aren't necessarily over because he was able to walk out of St. Albans."

The suggestion was offered so casually it took him a moment to realize she was also trying to give him a medicinal dose of reality. It required unpalatable medicines to treat ailments such as optimism. If Moore was in fact a hospital patient, perhaps conscious, perhaps not, there was no way he could quickly be led to light, and then to a waiting taxi. In which case there would be no incriminatory warblings to capture for the little cassette recorder and Malkin's later listening pleasure. He looked at the patchy sky, but the clouds up there had no silver linings either.

"All right, let's go," he said to Brdnowski. The bag lady volunteered a gummy smile as they passed her dig. Belknap assigned Brdnowski to guard duty on the stoop while he went to work on a security door sturdy enough to slow down firemen with axes. But the lock was a burglar's delight. Keeping light pressure on the plug with a tension tool and using a rake pick, he was able to bounce the cylinder pins to the shear line on his second try.

The dominant perfume inside was a blend of rancid cooking oil and stale essence of urine. Graffiti and spray-can sunbursts shared equal billing on flaking walls, even the small elevator at the rear had its own modest collection of graffiti. *I may be schizophrenic*, someone had scrawled, *but at least I have each other*. To which another philosopher, perhaps Morris Moore after a bad day spent eluding real or imagined surveillance, had riposted, *I may be paranoid, but at least I know my enemies*.

The elevator's tired shudder announced their arrival at the fifth floor. In the apartment across from Moore's a woman's nearly hysterical voice said, "Don't tell me you got them from a toilet seat. You think I'm born yesterday?"

"Naw, that ain't what I think, honeylamb," a man drawled. "What I think mos'ly, you don' shut up, you gonna be missin' a mouthful of teeth."

Belknap knocked on Moore's door, listened for movement inside.

"Looks like nobody's home, Fred." Brdnowski poked a thumb over his shoulder. "I'm not claiming the dude's leveling, but back in Hoboken I knew a guy got the crabs just sitting a couple of hours in Ironball Pulaski's Gym watching a Friday-night card."

If Brdnowski's breezy obliviousness to reality could be bottled, Belknap thought as he studied the lock, it could replace anesthesia in major surgery. He started with the rake pick, again trying to bounce all the pins by a single rapid withdrawal, then switched to a feeler pick and began raising them one by one. When he was able to turn the doorknob, he motioned to Brdnowski. They moved inside.

"Hot in here," Brdnowski whispered, looking around the living room.

Belknap nodded. There was also a sickly sweet fustiness that reminded him of moldering hay, but he decided, after glancing at the armchairs, torn in places, the odor came from mildewed upholstery stuffing. Moore was a reader. Books were stacked in disorderly piles against every wall. Sections from last Sunday's *Times* overlapped on a rickety coffee table. The two magazine racks were overflowing.

A scarred oaken table and four unmatching chairs filled the windowless dining alcove at the west end of the room, where a closed door probably led to the kitchen. On the table, lead soldiers in the uniform of Grenadier Guards charged outnumbered Hussars in red busbies. Belknap wondered if guests had ever shared a meal at that table. Could an illegal even risk making friends, let alone bringing them to his shabby hermitage?

Moore, undoubtedly a colonel or general in the KGB and the recipient of medals he might never see and emoluments he might never enjoy, every day must surely experience loneliness to equal any exile's, despair to equal any prisoner's. *A charming man,* Mrs. Adams had said, unaware she'd die because this charming man's life had touched hers, *very bookish.*

The bookishness Belknap could understand. And the lead soldiers bought for a nonexistent nephew recovering from an imagined tonsillectomy. What other companions were there for the night's long reaches? Even rental of a streetwalker's body could be too dangerous. But what produced the inner discipline that enabled an illegal to exchange comfort and privilege at home for hardship and deprivation in a distant land where possible imprisonment or execution was a daily fact of life? What mix of ideological conviction, masochism, and madness disguised as courage produced a Rudolf Abel or Morris Moore?

"You figure we ought to search the rest of this dump, Fred? Might be secret papers could help us nail ringleaders." Brdnowski tucked his sunglasses in his shirt pocket. "I guess you know all there is to know about tearing a place apart, but in case you don't, I picked up a few pointers watching that detective toss our pad on Wednesday."

With Brdnowski for a partner, Belknap thought, who needed Omega Three? He entered the kitchen through the dining-alcove door. Moore was a reader, but he wasn't a housekeeper by a country mile. Dirty pots and dishes filled the sink, ants in ceremonial file patrolled the blistered windowsill. The stove, the walls, were scummed with grease.

He opened the refrigerator. Moore liked diet cola, diet margarine, Danish pastries, strawberry jam, bonbons, red cabbage, rotting lettuce, dill pickles, and glycerin suppositories.

He opened the freezer compartment. Moore, no chef either, liked TV dinners, chicken potpies, burritos, egg rolls, pizza, and French vanilla ice cream. A true cosmopolite, a Renaissance man stoically coping in an absurdly plastic society.

"You're the expert, Fred, but why're we looking for this joker's secret papers in a refrigerator?"

"In the unit, we've a saying. Know your enemy. This being so, is it okay with you if I poke around?" He inspected the cupboards. Moore also liked gin and whiskey. What did the man from Moskova have against vodka?

He stepped into a pullman hallway. The fustiness he'd noticed in the living room was not only stronger, it was rank, and had nothing to do with moldering hay or mildewed upholstery. He started toward the bathroom doorway at the end of the hall. An adjacent door was ajar, and it was from here, not the bathroom, he realized as he approached, that the increasingly fetid odors came. He cautiously nudged the door.

The bed was unmade. On the dresser were a bottle of vodka and empty shot glass. Moore, if it was Moore, and wearing only boxer shorts decorated with cartoon elves, lay on the floor in a dried pool of vomit, vomit whose effluvium was almost lost in the stench released by putrefaction and failed sphincters. Buzzing flies were picnicking on the man's regurgitated last meal.

Brdnowski, gagging, disappeared into the bathroom. Fighting the same nausea, Belknap bent over the corpse. The man must have had some kind of seizure. Perhaps he'd swallowed his tongue, perhaps he'd simply choked on vomit. Gorge rising, he joined Brdnowski.

"Same guy," Brdnowski gasped between retchings while he knelt like a penitent in front of the toilet, "same guy I picked up Tuesday."

Belknap, somehow overcoming his own queasiness, splashed cold water on his face. Reflexes of survival began to surface. He'd have to get rid of any fingerprints he might have donated to doorknobs or kitchen fixtures. He'd have to phone the pilot, on standby in Teterboro, tell him to get ready to return to Washington. And then, with no songbird warblings from Morris Moore to present to Malkin, he'd have to invent a miracle. Before the hunters took him. Before he proved Littlejohn right by joining Frank Willis and Morris Moore before this day ended.

Helping a perspiring Brdnowski to his feet, he tried to fill the shoes of the man supremely sure of next moves. "We're going back to Washington . . . I'll phone headquarters for new orders. My guess is, the chief will want a little more help from you. And he'll probably want to sideline Myrt temporarily, which is better for her anyhow. She can stay with Olga."

A miracle, a miracle . . . but he felt as gutted and helpless as Vanessa must have felt after Alexandria. The death of hope, even hope as fragile as the hope sustaining him since he'd learned of the murder of the Adamses, is a terrible thing . . . he almost believed he could have dominated the endgame if he'd been able to make a terrified Moore spit up a terrified confession.

Exhaust fumes and soot baked by reflected pavement heat generated an acridity for which Belknap, the foulness of Moore's bedroom fresh in memory, could almost be grateful.

He beckoned to Vanessa. "Malkin's postman is dead."

She caught her breath, looked away to watch a jogger wearing a gauze surgical mask to keep his lungs clean and towing two leashed basset hounds to keep the city's walks clean. "I don't understand. John didn't want anything to happen to him."

"Your father isn't responsible. When Moore left St. Albans, he just happened to have an appointment in Samarra. Seizure or stroke, I think."

The jogger passed them, puffing cheerfully but encountering negative feedback from his waddling dogs, who sincerely wanted to make pit stops at fire hydrants. Belknap, concentrating on the miracle he was supposed to invent, said, "This is the way I see it. With Moore and the Adamses dead, the chain leading from the silver dollars to Moore back to Malkin is broken. The tape recording I needed in any confrontation with Malkin is kaput. So events have neutralized my leverage, always dubious anyhow, and my poor purse is empty." And suddenly, gloriously, as he recognized that Malkin wouldn't know about the death of Moore, the miracle revealed itself. But too aware of the ways optimism had cozened him before, he muted the resurgence of hope. "Well, not quite. I still have desperation to spend, and nothing to gain by hoarding it. I'm going to borrow from the Sage of Alexandria, I'm going to convince Malkin he'll be dead before this day ends unless he responds favorably to a certain modest proposal. What kind of gun are you comfortable with?"

"Colt Cobra. Checkered walnut stock, round butt."

"We'll get it. I've a reliable pawnshop connection on Eighth."

"Foch at the second Battle of the Marne." Her lips formed a frail smile. " 'My center is giving way, my right is pushed back—excellent! I'll attack!' "

"Foch had armies to call on. We just have Brdnowski." And desperation, he reminded himself. "Convincing Malkin shouldn't be too difficult, since I'm exceedingly willing to shoot him if he rejects my modest proposal. Preferably in the back. True, I'd get life imprisonment . . . parse *life* as fifteen years in the joint. But what sort of deterrent is that when I'm already wanted for killing the ex-sergeant who was kindly escorting me to Malkin's guest room? And for being a Soviet agent since sixty-three. Besides"—he moved his shoulders—"if the hunters take me before I get to Malkin, prison's academic. I'll be shot while resisting arrest."

She looked at him steadily, solemnly. "Nobody's going to shoot you." She thrust out her jaw. "I won't let them. I'm damn good with a Cobra."

My beautiful Amazon of Forty-eighth Street, he thought. He wanted to take her in his arms, he wanted not to lose her, ever.

"This modest proposal, David. What is it?"

"Tell you on the plane. It requires a little cooperation from the Soviet Embassy." He glanced at Myrt and Brdnowski, twenty feet away. Brdnowski must still be conducting her on a guided tour of Moore's apartment. She looked enthralled.

Vanessa dabbed her face with a tissue. She plucked at the sleeves of her blouse, trying to free clinging silk. She stepped forward and dabbed his forehead. In a little gesture part possessiveness, part tenderness, she straightened his tie. "There. You look almost like David Belknap."

He was conscious of her musk, of a ridiculous constriction in his throat. Some audacious dreamer, a riverboat gambler claiming squatter's rights in his brain, told him to speak now, because later he might never have the chance to speak at all. He concentrated on a window box across the street, transformed it by an act of will into a balcony where perhaps Juliet could have stood. "I never thought," he began, "I'd be doing something like this on Forty-eighth. Or on any other goddamn street."

"Like what?"

Not a good beginning. Take a flyer, the riverboat gambler prompted from the wings, on sentiment. Give her, lovelorn-poet-style, *But, soft! what light through yonder window breaks? It is the east, and—*

"Well, the fact is, I've also an immodest proposal.

Vanessa, if I make it through what lies ahead, would you, could you, be a wife of mine?"

"Oh-ah. David." She smiled through a welling of tears. "How many others would there have to be?"

"Well, it'd depend on performance. We'd have to see."

33

THE RINGING OF THE PHONE wakened Igor Demichev. He switched on a lamp, saw it was one-thirty in the morning. His wife stirred uneasily beside him. Groaning, he reached for the damnable instrument.

The apologetic voice of Lieutenant, soon to be Captain, Nikitin greeted him: "I am sorry, Comrade General, to be calling at such an hour, but it was felt here you should know. Major Subotin is dead."

Demichev tried to orient himself. Moments ago, in a dream undoubtedly brought on by overindulgence at the Rossiya, he'd been wrestling a bear at the Moscow Circus. As he embraced the bear in order to throw it to the floor, he realized he wasn't at the Moscow Circus at all, he was in a cell at the Lubyanka, and the bear he was embracing wasn't a bear at all, the bear was General Pechenko. Both of them were nude and their bodies were covered with axle grease. When Professor Tudin, dressed in the uniform of a guard, entered the cell, Demichev desperately tried to disengage himself, but Pechenko wouldn't release him. Professor Tudin tut-tutted and said prisoners above the rank of colonel weren't permitted to become romantically involved.

"Dead?" Demichev said hoarsely. All that Rossiya vodka, all the undigested sturgeon, were taking their revenge in his bloated stomach. "Where did this happen? And how?"

"To refresh your memory, Comrade General, yesterday

you ordered Major Subotin taken to the safe house on Granovskovo Street, where he would be encouraged to entertain himself in any fashion he wished. He was to be told General Pechenko had become suspicious of him and we were trying to protect him until it could be shown, by the success of the Washington operation, such suspicion was groundless."

"Yes, yes, I remember." Demichev, discovering he had a headache as well as indigestion, carefully eased himself to a sitting position on the edge of the bed. "I suppose he tried to escape and someone had to shoot him."

"No, Comrade General. He spent the evening drinking, dancing, and watching the latest French pornographic movies, confiscated last week at Moscow State University. The officer in charge at the safe house reports Major Subotin consumed a liter and a half of whiskey, five hundred milliliters of brandy, and three bottles of wine between his arrival and the time he retired. Twenty minutes ago, one of the ladies sleeping with him went to the bathroom and found his body on the floor."

Demichev cautiously massaged his stomach. "Was it suicide?"

"That would require an autopsy, Comrade General. The officer in charge reports, however, Major Subotin didn't fall. There are no head injuries."

"Then it's clearly suicide, because a professional debaucher like Subotin could handle twice that amount of alcohol and be ready to crack open a new bottle by the next afternoon."

"More than ready. An autopsy would be a waste of time."

"And of money, Nikitin. If we wasted more money on a traitor like Subotin, Professor Tudin would have to commit the two of us to Kaluga for treatment. Is the person who found the body reliable?"

"In the sense of?"

Demichev regurgitated a sour mouthful of sturgeon and herring. He reached for his bedside water glass, drained its contents. "In the sense of having noticed him take an overdose of sleeping pills earlier."

"I imagine she or one of the other ladies in bed with him would be able, under sympathetic questioning, to remember such an incident. Of course, such a witness might not be able to state categorically the pills she saw him take were in fact sleeping pills."

"A man that deeply involved in debauchery doesn't limit himself to sleeping pills anyhow. Were there needle marks on his arms, did he leave a written confession?"

"These are questions, Comrade General, I neglected to ask the officer in charge. He was in a state of shock, because he'd never before lost one of our consignments. I thought it would be charitable to excuse him temporarily from detailed interrogation. Also, he outranks me. I apologize for the oversight."

"No apologies are necessary, Vasili Yaklovovich. You too—I can tell by your voice and manner—are in a state of shock. As I myself would be if I hadn't somewhat anticipated this cowardly suicide."

"It occurs to me," Nikitin said, "the traitor Subotin was probably too drunk to write a full confession. It's not easy to write coherently when you're drunk."

"This is true, Vasili Yaklovovich. It's likely, however, that Subotin, overcome by guilt and remorse, volunteered an informal oral confession before he killed himself."

"What kind of information would such a confession be likely to contain, Comrade General?"

"Given his drunken condition, it wouldn't contain too much detail. I suppose he'd mention the icons he sold to foreigners, and how this led to his being blackmailed when one of his customers turned out to be working for U.S. Intelligence. He might mention the name of the Swiss bank where U.S. Intelligence opened a secret account for his benefit after it recruited him sometime in seventy-three, but he'd be too drunk, unfortunately, to remember the number of the account. And although he didn't know *our* Chessplayer's true identity, he could have warned U.S. Intelligence that a certain Ivan Glukhov, if he ever defected, was an empty vessel programmed to believe 'Chessplayer' was the code name for a certain David Belknap. This betrayal, too, might be part of any confession." Opening the aspirin bottle on the bedside table, Demichev gulped four tablets. "But I'm afraid most of Subotin's admissions would be too garbled and hazy for us, for anyone, to check their authenticity."

"I'll personally interview the ladies involved, Comrade General, to see if anyone remembers his talking in the hazy vein you describe. It's been my experience a man about to commit suicide usually tries to square his accounts. So I should have a transcript of his garbled confession on your desk by mid-morning."

"And let us hope it never has to be shared with General Pechenko. The man's dead, he should be allowed to rest in peace. But if the situation in Washington doesn't improve soon, Pechenko's paranoia will demand a scapegoat." He sighed. "It would become necessary to admit we'd succeeded in identifying Subotin as the traitor."

Behind him Natalia awoke with a start. "Goshenka, what's happening? Please turn out the light. My head feels as if it's been serving as the only ball in a Dynamos' soccer game."

He covered the mouthpiece. "Not even our magnificent Moscow Dynamos would dare abuse a head as lovely as yours. Nikitin's been telling me Subotin committed suicide during the night, though it's not impossible Nikitin arranged the death to prevent my discovering Subotin or Pechenko had subverted him. Since these matters are always so damnably complicated, particularly with a paranoid type like Pechenko hiding behind the curtains, it might be prudent to have Visko intensify his investigation of Nikitin's investigation of Subotin." He patted her shoulder. "The light will be out shortly. The bathroom, if you wish to use it, should be in the same place. But who knows, I no longer count on anything."

"Comrade General?"

Demichev removed his hand from the mouthpiece. "Yes, Nikitin."

"I thought we'd perhaps been disconnected."

"As far as I'm concerned, Vasili Yaklovovich, we'll never be disconnected. Now inform me, please, about the present situation in Washington."

"There's little to add. The whereabouts of Belknap remain unknown. U.S. Intelligence, according to sketchy information from Chessplayer, continues to be as anxious as we are to find and then eliminate him. Colonel Zalenin's men, acting in response to your theory Belknap might try to meet with or even assassinate Chessplayer, continue to provide unobtrusive protective surveillance when he's away from his office. Chessplayer has been advised to carry on his person a small constant-signal transmitter to make surveillance easier. General Lisovsky, because of his historic relationship with Chessplayer, because of the trust and friendship existing between them, will remain in the embassy around the clock until the crisis has been resolved. General Lisovsky requested, and I delegated in your name, authority to make, as events in Washington might require, immediate decisions without consultation with the *rezident*."

"I commend your initiative. The same initiative, Nikitin, I know you'll exercise when you conduct your investigation into Subotin's suicide. And don't forget to look at his arms. Thighs as well. It wouldn't at all surprise me if you found needle marks."

"Nor would it at all surprise me, Comrade General."

Demichev, concluding he needed to determine whether

the bathroom was still in the same place, said hurriedly, "Although I must detain you no longer, I'm compelled to share another small secret. After your promotion to captain has been approved and a modest interval has passed, I'm recommending you for promotion to major. As I observed yesterday, Captain, loyalty is like the pistons that drive a great ship's engines. It must travel down as well as up."

34

ON THE SHORT RUN into Washington from Freeway Airport, Belknap outlined for Brdnowski his duties after they put Myrt in a taxi at Dupont Circle. In the back seat of the Datsun, Vanessa worked at placating Myrt, who didn't like the idea of exile to Olga's any better now than when Brdnowski had first relayed the chief's decision.

It was seven-fifteen when the red station wagon turned off New York Avenue onto Massachusetts. Belknap, grateful to Brdnowski for shaving ten minutes from the time he'd expected the trip to cost, grateful for those ten extra minutes of daylight, said, "You're a good driver, Murph."

"A good arranger of weddings, too," Myrt said, "especially when it comes to package deals. License, ring, preacher, honeymoon cottage almost anywhere in the world."

Brdnowski sighed. Belknap studied the western sky. Sunset, according to the Friday *Post* he'd bought on the way in, would occur at eight-thirty-two. The sky was still hazed, but behind the haze the sun was bright enough to guarantee at least shallow daylight another thirty minutes after that. And without at least some daylight, his wild card was unplayable. Malkin had to be recognizable when the two of them took their last walk together.

"Dupont Circle," Brdnowski announced nervously, but Myrt had apparently resigned herself. She opened the rear door, stepped grandly onto the curb, and never looked back.

Belknap, taking her place beside Vanessa, told Brdnowski to swing onto P Street and park just before crossing the bridge into Georgetown. He reached for the bag of goodies acquired in the back room of the pawnshop on Eighth Avenue. He gave Vanessa her Colt Cobra, distributed the other goodies after Brdnowski had parked. A canister of Mace, tear-gas grenade, and smoke grenade each for Vanessa and Brdnowski. A walkie-talkie for Vanessa, another for himself.

"Before we start over the bridge," he told Brdnowski, "I'll get down on the floor, keep out of sight."

"Why's that, Fred?"

"The chief is afraid my cover's blown."

"And that the gentleman we've been ordered to take into custody," Vanessa said, "might have someone posted on O Street to watch his house, warn him if Fred shows up."

"Nobody'll be expecting you, though, Murph. Even if they were"—Belknap leaned forward to touch the dead-white skin where Brdnowski's beard had recently bloomed—"they'd never recognize you."

"Right," Brdnowski said without conviction. "What about Van?"

"Headquarters says her cover isn't blown. She'll concentrate on spotting unfriendlies while you concentrate on driving."

"And since our red Datsun's going to be quickly spotted if we scout the area more than once," Vanessa said, "give me enough time to check out all parked cars. Turn south on Twenty-sixth after we cross the bridge and when Twenty-sixth curves into O, continue west along O to Twenty-eighth. Then head north to P and park."

Belknap worked his body into the cramped space separating front and rear seats. The Datsun began to move. Brdnowski coughed officially. "We're entering historic Georgetown. On your left is part of Rock Creek Park. On your right you'll soon see Gun-Barrel Fence, built out of musket—"

Vanessa tapped his shoulder. "Brdnowski . . ."

"Sorry. Force of habit. Some fares, they want a guided tour. Some fares, they don't even want you to breathe."

"Breathe and drive. I'll handle tour bulletins."

Belknap, head against the far door, knees bent, smiled up at her. Foch at the Battle of the Marne. It didn't fool her, of course. She sought and clutched his hand. "Turning onto O, Fred."

"Jesus!" Brdnowski said.

"Yes," Vanessa said. "A visitor, Fred. Tell you when we're parked."

Belknap grimaced. It wasn't hard to guess what she'd seen. Not when Brdnowski was also reacting to the presence of the visitor.

"Passing Malkin's townhouse," she said. "Nobody on the street, nobody in any of the parked cars."

"Maybe he isn't home." Nothing had worked in New York. Maybe nothing would work here, either. There was always a symmetry to failure.

"He's home," she said flatly. "Otherwise there wouldn't be the visitor." The station wagon was turning, slowing. "You can get up, Fred. We're on Twenty-eighth."

He rearranged himself on the seat. "Acme Termite Control's the visitor?"

She nodded. "The van's parked a block and a half east of George's, facing west. How'd you know?"

"The visitor isn't entirely unexpected. It's not Malkin's style to panic, to order up protection. Malkin's a romantic. A romantic believes in the charmed life. The Soviets, though, are pragmatists. They've an investment to protect. They're also waiting for the moth to come to the flame." He took the Detective Special from his pocket and checked it. "How many men in the van?"

"Two in the front seat, wearing brown twill coveralls. There could be others in back. The little hood over the motor was up, with a white handkerchief tied to the hood insignia."

"The old automobile-in-distress dodge. Supposed to

reassure residents the parked van isn't a cause for concern. Only after an hour or so the audience starts wondering why no tow truck has put in an appearance."

"About then they probably move it, start over with a new audience."

"Well, the moth would get fatally burned if it now went into Malkin's by the front entrance. But then, we assumed all along I'd have to go in from the back. Get over to Wisconsin Avenue, Brdnowski. We need a liquor store and a florist's . . ."

When Brdnowski, following instructions, had parked on 27th at the corner of Poplar between O and P, Belknap glanced at his watch and was satisfied. It had taken twenty minutes to complete the purchases and the round trip. There should still be enough daylight.

He removed half-gallon bottles of Jack Daniel's whiskey and Beefeater gin from their two gift cartons. He nodded to Vanessa and they got out. He clutched the Jack Daniel's carton under his left arm, the Beefeater carton under his right. He gripped the six-pack of club soda and the Cinzano dry vermouth in his left hand. Vanessa placed two dozen blood-red roses wrapped in green florist's tissue in his right hand.

"Beware of Greeks bearing gifts." Her smile was forced.

"Which reminds me. Reach in the left back pocket of my trousers. There's a key there for Brdnowski."

She produced the key, studied it, her expression perplexed.

"Tell Brdnowski it opens a coin-operated locker in the Greyhound bus station on New York Avenue. Tell him that's where he'll find the hundred Eisenhower silver dollars. Tell him it's our wedding present."

She stared at him. "But you told John Littlejohn you gave the silver dollars to an old friend on *The New York Times*, along with a sealed letter to be opened if anything happened to you."

He laughed, pleased with himself, pleased with her consternation. "Hell, I don't know anyone on *The New York Times*."

This time the smile was unforced. "Unscrupulous bastard!"

"Ah, well. Beggars can't be choosers." He gestured toward the solid row of townhouses in the middle of the block. "I'd say the gray one's my target."

"I agree. And if no one's home?"

"I'll use my skeleton keys and picks. In any event, wait no longer than thirty minutes once I'm inside. I'll try to do it in less, but if I haven't made contact in thirty, take off. Because it'll mean George has someone with him and I was taken. And if that happens . . ."

"David . . ." Her voice was tremulous.

"Come on, no tearful farewells, okay? You're my girl." He touched her chin with the bouquet of roses. "Keep Brdnowski honest."

"Keep George honest."

"God knows, I'll try." He started toward the gray townhouse. Before climbing its steps he looked back and saw her getting into the station wagon. He rang the bell.

The man who opened the door was wearing a short-sleeved shirt and blue Levis. One arm was holding a crying, naked boy about a year old with a very runny nose. His other hand held an open can of beer.

Belknap took a step backward. "Sorry. I thought this was George Malkin's house."

"George?" The man inspected the Jack Daniel's and Beefeater cartons, then the six-pack of club soda, the vermouth, the roses in green tissue. "George lives on O Street. Just behind us."

"I thought this was O."

"This is Poplar."

"That son of a bitch of a taxi driver." Belknap turned to survey the street. "Too late. I let him go. My mistake. He told me this was the right place." He sheepishly indicated the gifts he was carrying. "These aren't actually for George from me. I hardly know George, though I hope he'll break open the Jack Daniel's for services rendered. They're from my father . . . college friend of George's. Dad lost a bet with him on an Orioles game. I had to come down here for a meeting, so Dad asked me to handle the payoff. Asked, *hell*! He damn well ordered me to. The booze and fixings are the payoff, the roses are supposed to show Dad has no hard feelings, but if you believe he has no hard feelings, I'll try to sell you the Washington Monument. Is your boy sick?"

"Weekend flu. He never fails us. How does he always know it's our two days off? I asked the pediatrician once, he laughed. Didn't think I was serious."

"Doctors are a pain in the ass. Well, sorry to have bothered you." Belknap looked at the street again. "Which way do I go to work my passage to O Street with this loot? Or can I get there by walking in either direction? Assuming I don't drop the goddamn booze before I arrive. Or drop from heat exhaustion myself. No offense intended, but Washington in summer isn't my idea of the perfect climate."

"No offense taken. My first wife used to say that living in Washington in summer was better than living in a hot tub of mashed potatoes, but not significantly better. Joyce was never entirely comfortable with Washington, though far be it from me to say it was just the climate. What'd you say your name was?"

"Fred. Fred Ryan. I'm with the Treasury in New York. Government hack, but safely removed from the major scene of confusion."

"You're lucky. I'm in Labor myself. There's an old joke, maybe you've heard it. I'm in Labor, but somehow I never seem to deliver. Anyhow, back to basics. Why fight your way around the block with all those packages? There's a lilac hedge with a trellised archway between our yard and George's. You can come through the house."

"I ought to give you the Jack Daniel's. You're saving my life."

He could see through Malkin's kitchen window that the kitchen was empty. He turned to wave reassuringly in case his benefactor might be idly watching from his own kitchen, but the lilac hedge was high enough to block the line of sight. He set his gifts down and went to work on the kitchen door.

When the lock yielded and he was inside, he drew his gun. He removed his shoes and carried them in his other hand as he padded through the dining and living rooms to the vestibule. He deposited his shoes on the marble refectory table and cautiously approached the open study door. But he knew from the quietness within it had to be empty.

The quietness in the entire house shocked him. Though Friday evening social life in the circles in which Malkin would travel usually began after eight-thirty, the evidence was accumulating the master wasn't in residence. Belknap found himself confronting the catastrophic possiblity Malkin was working late in Lafayette Square. Then he remembered Vanessa's flat assertion that the van on O Street wouldn't be there unless the master *was* in residence. Praying her reasoning was flawless, he started climbing to the second floor, testing each polished oaken stair for telltale creaks before he trusted it with his weight.

The walls of the upper hallway were papered with hunting scenes . . . huntsmen in red coats and black caps sipping from stirrup cups in a cobbled courtyard . . . huntsmen on mounts galloping through bracken behind the hounds . . . ahead the winded fox plunging through thickets and copses, then turned by the hounds toward the meadows and an inevitable cry of *View Halloo!* Belknap liked the symbolism and hoped the fox was truly winded.

From a bedroom came the faint sounds of a radio or TV. Since he hadn't heard those sounds downstairs, he was willing to hope his own intrusion hadn't been heard in the bedroom. Marginally willing. He kept the Detective Special very ready.

It was a gracious room. The carpeting was as lush as the meadows in the hunting scenes. The bed was a satin-canopied four-poster, which seemed out of sync with Malkin's style, and the drapes were a silky pale blue, almost feminine, but Belknap abruptly dismissed that wild thought. Most of the furniture was maple. There was a fireplace in which real logs rested. And there was a TV, the source of the sounds.

He found Malkin in the adjoining bathroom. Malkin was in a tuxedo. Malkin was adjusting his black bow tie in front of the washbowl mirror. Malkin was about to pick up two silver-backed hairbrushes when he discovered the new reflection in his mirror.

"David!" There was a hint of that wonderful boyish smile. "What a welcome surprise!" He turned slowly, looked disapprovingly at the gun. "But put that silly melodramatic toy away. After all . . ."

"I may have to kill you," Belknap said. "I may not have to. Why don't we adjourn to your study and try to decide?"

"Really, David. I'm not sure I care for that kind of nonsense." Malkin brushed lint from a satin lapel. "Even though you've put yourself in an extremely difficult situation, I'm terribly glad you're here. I might still be able to help."

"I appreciate that. Belated thanks; also, for your offer of the guest room at the institute."

"You entirely misread that unfortunate affair. I merely wanted to talk with you. It was so foolish, so unnecessary, to assault the poor fellow who was trying to look after you until I returned."

"Well, I can tell you one thing. My killing him was an accident, but since it's down in the books as murder, you'll appreciate I've nothing to lose by killing you."

Malkin shook his head in dismay. "You didn't *kill* anyone. Where did you get such a bizarre notion? The man broke some ribs, has a fracture of the right leg, assorted cuts and bruises, but he'll be out of the hospital in a week or less."

The man you assaulted, Littlejohn had said, *was pronounced DOA when the ambulance got to George Washington University Hospital . . .*

Belknap took three quick steps forward and delivered a stinging slap to the patrician face. Malkin gasped in disbelief, but his dignity was admirable. So admirable Belknap was infuriated.

"Lie once more and I'll pistol-whip you. There is no more Golden Rule, George. It's been repealed for the duration."

"But the man's not dead, don't you understand? Why should I tell you he's in a hospital if he's not?"

"What hospital?"

"Capitol Hill."

"You're lying again." He got ready to raise the gun.

"Phone the hospital, you idiot! The man's name is Sam Bowker."

The phone was on a stand beside the four-poster. Malkin hurriedly looked up the listing. Belknap did the dialing, asked for Sam Bowker's room number.

"Three-twelve. I'll connect."

Dazed, he replaced the phone. No sealed letter had been given to a *New York Times* reporter. Score one for David Belknap. Nobody had been killed last night on those basement steps leading to Malkin's guest room. Score ten for John Littlejohn and his demented game-playing. The books still have to be balanced, but whatever his own troubles, they didn't include a charge of murder. He suppressed a hysterical urge to cry, to laugh, to dance a mazurka.

"What happened to your shoes?" Malkin asked, as if mindlessly performing in a theater of the absurd.

"They're waiting for us downstairs."

"I don't have much time." Malkin, testing the waters, politely smothered his impatience as he might a yawn. "I'm booked for a dinner party. A reception given by the Horizon Institute. Allen Lundhoven's shop."

Belknap shook his head. "No, George. For you the party's over."

35

If THERE WAS A GUN hidden in the study, it would probably be in a drawer of the desk. Belknap took the precaution of directing Malkin to one of the tweedy armchairs. He sat in the other, crossed his legs, and aimed the Detective Special at Malkin's groin.

"David"—Malkin's sigh was exploratory, like a doctor's cautious probe of a massive abdominal wound—"I do indeed fear recent events have driven you over the edge. Extremely serious charges have been made against you by that Soviet defector—there's even an FBI dragnet out for you—but it's my opinion Glukhov's a provocateur. With your cooperation, I think I can expose him in short order."

"You're right about my being over the edge."

"I empathize. Who could blame you? Now if you'll put that gun away, I'll phone Hathaway, begin the process of straightening things out, agree to be responsible for you in the interim. By the way, how did you get in? An alarm would have sounded in my bedroom if you'd used the front door."

He wondered whether Malkin knew about the Acme Termite Control van on O Street and was expecting calvary to the rescue. "Maybe the alarm was on the fritz."

"That must be it. Whatever else fails, we can always count on Murphy's Law." Malkin started to get up. "I'll try to reach Hathaway."

"*Sit down!* Or I'll blow your balls off."

Malkin decided not to get up.

372

"I was in New York this afternoon," Belknap began, "talking to Mo Moore in his apartment on Forty-eighth. It took some persuasion to get his side of the conversation started, the man was courageous, I'll grant him that, but in the end—would you believe it?—he was literally on his knees, begging to talk. My problem was, I'd no one to guard him after I left, and in view of my own problems I obviously couldn't call on the police or FBI. So I had to kill him. It's odd, I thought I'd made my bones last night. Never realized I was actually making them this afternoon.

"Now, I can spare a little time, George, if you feel you have to go through the motions of denying you know of anyone named Mo Moore, who until today operated a stamp-and-coin shop on Forty-second, but you'd be missing the vital part of my message if you did. I don't care one iota about your denials. The vital part is, I wouldn't be sitting here confessing to killing a man if I ever expected you to be able to testify against me."

Malkin frowned over steepled fingers at his black patent-leather pumps. "I assure you, I've never heard of anyone named Mo Moore. Are we perhaps talking about another agent provocateur?"

"We're talking about the man the cabdriver picked up at the Library of Congress on Tuesday. Your postman, George."

He stared past Malkin at the bust of Mozart on the pedestal beneath the mullioned window. He thought of Malkin listening to Verdi in that Moscow January of '63 when he had been dispatched to Beirut to give Kim Philby a Spanish ring. Mozart, Verdi . . . and look at the magnificent books lining the shelves of this comfortable Georgetown study . . . Kant, Hume, Spencer, Montaigne, Balzac, Proust, Dante, Goethe, Tolstoi, Jefferson, Emerson . . . yet somehow music from a different drummer had been heard . . .

"I began wondering about you in Bonn, George. After the business with Fehler." He glanced at the rosewood table's inlaid chessboard, at the chessmen Erich Fehler had given Malkin on a birthday long ago. "If I hadn't gotten into trouble with those diamonds later on, I might have made my wonderings a cause. Instead, I got rid of the monkey on my back. Until you brought me down here to feed to the sharks. In the next few minutes, though, I'm getting rid of it forever."

"You weave an intriguing hypothesis," Malkin said impassively. "I always did admire the fecundity of your imagination, especially when it ran away with you. Do you mind if I smoke?"

"Why not? Might as well follow tradition. I can't supply a priest, but if you wish I'll hear your confession when the time comes."

"Your misconceptions appall me, but"—he reached inside his dinner jacket—"you do hold the gun."

"When you bring your hand out, bring it out very slowly."

Malkin ventured a wry smile. "A concealed weapon would ruin the cut of the jacket." He removed a Montecristo from the slender gold cigar case now in his hand. "Oh, dear, no match."

"Use my lighter."

Malkin arched his silvered eyebrows. "Really, David. If you're going to smoke a fine cigar at all, you light it with a kitchen match. I'd have thought you knew that by now. But never mind. I've matches in my desk."

Belknap uncrossed his legs, the better to watch the passing show. Malkin walked around the mahogany desk and opened a drawer. Belknap rose from his chair. *"Freeze, paisan! Don't move an inch!"* He circled the desk. There was a box of kitchen matches in the drawer. That was good. There was a long-barreled Mauser Parabellum in the drawer. That was bad. "You're being naughty, George."

"I'm afraid your paranoia's showing."

"I'm afraid you're right. But he who naughty is, must in the corner stand." He jabbed the gun into Malkin's ribs. "By your chessboard table would be fine."

Malkin returned the cigar to its gold case. That move was apparently over. "And do I have to face the wall, Teacher?"

He was gutsy, no question about that, and not a mad dog like Littlejohn. But he could still transmit his own brand of rabies and other fatal diseases. "Of course not. I don't want to shoot you in the back unless absolutely necessary."

Malkin positioned himself beside the rosewood table. "The diamonds always puzzled me, David. Did you really steal them?"

Hope springs eternal. Malkin was fishing, and what he was fishing for was a modus vivendi between a gentleman traitor and a gentleman theif. The true nobility in this vale of tears was always linked by an entente cordiale. Belknap obliged by taking the hook.

"Ah, George, in one way or another we all got corrupted, didn't we?"

Malkin beamed. "So you did steal them?"

"Shame on you for putting words in my mouth. Would you be interested in entertaining a certain modest proposal?"

"You still hold the gun."

"From the barrel of which grows power. Wasn't that in Chairman Mao's Little Red Book? Imagine getting deified for revealing that two plus two equal four. Aphorisms are absolutely where the money is. At least in great-power politics. Remember Stalin? *And how many divisions does the Pope have?* George, from vulgar curiosity only, are you a Maoist or a Stalinist?"

"I?" Malkin seemed puzzled. "Why, I'm simply the proverbial man of goodwill."

Belknap, irritated by the foppish mockery, thinking Malkin was getting too gutsy, suddenly understood that the man, my God, was serious. Maybe he wasn't a mad dog like Littlejohn, but his insouciant manipulation of lives was just as dangerous, just as evil. Belknap grimaced . . . to hell with pretentious moral judgments.

Malkin looked down at the chessman. "This proposal o
yours . . . ?"

"Simplicity itself." He closed the distance betwee
them. Malkin might be considering another move, also n
on the chessboard. "You're going home."

"Home?"

"Like Philby." He watched the color flow out of th
chameleon face and the shock of recognition flow in
"Think of it as a reunion with an old friend from Spain."

"But David"—fingers splayed like claws hung motion
less over an invisible piano keyboard in search of the prope
chord to strike—"that's preposterous. Moscow isn't m
home."

"Well, there's the other option. I shoot you first in th
balls for the sake of auld lang syne, then in the head for th
sake of Frank Willis. As well as for a detective who's dea
because of you. As well as for the Czech STB man you ser
me to meet during the Prague Spring. As well as for wh
knows how many others you've betrayed over who know
how many years."

Malkin stole a gulp of air and magically transformed i
into a conciliatory smile. But chameleons adapted. It wa
how they survived. "There must surely be a civilized wa
to handle these complicated matters."

Belknap returned the smile. The crossing of the Rubicon
"Let's at least give it a try."

"I've a flask of Wild Turkey in the first volume o
Proust . . . would you care for a drink?" Malkin reache
deep into repertoire for an expression of homespun sinceri
ty. "There's no concealed weapon in the Proust . . . why
don't you see for yourself?"

"No time for farewell toasts, George." And no stomacl
either, he thought. "Was Philby your mentor?"

Annoyance flashed in Malkin's eyes. "The trouble witl
your generation is, your only knowledge of the Spanisl

Civil War comes from reading Hemingway. The battle was fought between the forces of freedom and the forces of oppression. The politics was sideshow. We who believed in the forces of freedom were"—he hesitated, perhaps embarrassed by his grandiosity—"a band of brothers. There was Kim Philby, humanist foremost, Englishman only incidentally. There was Dmitri Lisovsky, humanist foremost, Russian only incidentally. You wouldn't remember, but I once introduced you to Dmitri."

"Oh, but I do remember. My only time in the Kremlin. Diplomatic reception in St. George's Hall."

Malkin dismissed the annotation with an impatient wave. "There were others beside Dmitri and Kim, of course . . . all of us sharing a passion for mankind. Long before it became fashionable, we foresaw the inevitability of another world war, and the inevitable aftermath . . . cold war and slow march to the edge of the abyss. True, we failed to foresee the atom and hydrogen bombs, none of us were scientists, but those discoveries confirmed the necessity of continued common action to prevent the destruction of civilization."

"So that's how you became a Communist?"

"*Communist!*" Malkin as horrified. "The last thing I could ever be is a Communist."

"I stand corrected. I'm not familiar with the dialectical niceties. So that's how you became a spy for the Soviets?"

"Your problem, David, is parochialism. You lack, I'm sorry to say, a world view."

"Don't be sorry. I can live with it. So when did you begin spying for the Soviets? In Spain?"

Malkin shook his head. "I despair of you. I've never been a spy for the Soviets."

It astounded Belknap that Malkin continued to insist on blowing smoke. Maybe he still expected to be rescued by those good Samaritans from Acme Termite Control. Or maybe trauma had zapped enough fuses upstairs to let megalomania and perseveration take over the switchboard.

"I'm a conduit, albeit a vital one, through which two unruly children disguised from each other as superpowers signal their tantrums, their fears, their intentions before the matches they're playing with produce an unmanageable fire." The tip of one shiny black pump traced an erratic circle on the Persian rug. "I'm the honest broker impartially attending the needs of both sides . . . yielding a secret here, collecting a secret there, it's always a judgment call . . . in order to keep the world stable."

"And naturally your friend Dmitri, equally dedicated to the noble cause of keeping the children in line, is the other honest broker. It sounds like a really nifty arrangement . . ."

"Kindly spare me your flippancy. If Dmitri and I were the only two involved"—exasperation, or a good imitation, brought the color back to Malkin's cheeks—"such an arrangement would obviously be a form of madness. But we, those others of us who first met in Spain, merely supplied an idea, and a nucleus of volunteers with which to test it . . . today there are more of us than are dreamt of in your philosophy."

Parthenogenesis, Belknap thought, also known as hogwash. It was time to lance the boil. "Lot of catfish in the river tonight. I met another of your old comrades in arms recently. The Sage of Alexandria."

"Choice name for John," Malkin said appreciatively. "Getting more eccentric each year, but in his prime a crackerjack mischief-maker." He bemusedly contemplated the chessboard. "Still sometimes comes over for a game after we've taken potluck at the Cosmos. Usually opens with Pawn to Queen Four when he's white. Just like Spassky. As a chess player, though, John isn't exactly Spassky. I've never had any trouble keeping several moves ahead of him." He lifted his head, uncertainty falling across his face like a shadow. "Recently, you said? How recently?"

"Earlier today," he replied vaguely. "Claimed I was in a lot of trouble."

"Well, isn't that what I've been telling you? And I intend to do something about it now that you've perceived the utter folly of this talk about . . . Moscow."

Belknap laughed mordantly. Hope springs eternal still.

"George, you're not only going home, you're going home with a departing gift from me. Littlejohn knows about your Soviet connections. The Lafayette Research Institute is a toy he created for your special benefit. He's controlled it, controlled you, from the beginning. All your jiggery-pokery's been for naught. Fittingly poetic, wouldn't you say?"

"Oh, dear." Amber eyes glinted with amusement and rationed challenge. "I do think you must be talking about Operation Trojan Horse."

Still reeling, conscious of a seepage of resolve, Belknap heard a crippled voice say, "I don't understand. I thought . . ."

"You don't have to understand. All you have to do is put your gun away." The words were almost a caress. "You became too obsessed by one instrument in the orchestra, David, its collectivity escaped you. You see, men like myself, men whom their governments can trust to exercise initative discreetly, to work for balance through contacts with the other side that are unique to them, have become the diplomats of last resort. We trade wares in a marketplace established not for personal or political profit . . . only for mutual national survival. So naturally there are people in higher positions than John Littlejohn, and of course in lower positions"—Malkin smiled ambiguously—"with an interest in keeping such initiatives alive. So naturally I'd be told about Trojan Horse at its inception."

Belknap felt distinctly better. Anger was always a fast-working tonic and a dead fish wrapped in semantical butcher paper still stank. But curiosity won out over presumed better judgment, and he danced on cue to the piper's tune. "Who told you?"

The diplomat of last resort wore a roguish look. "Who, indeed? Sybil Pruett, perhaps? A wonderful woman, absolutely thrives on duplicity. Did I ever tell you we had a brief affair in London during the war? But it couldn't last, she had no ideology. So she married Squadron Leader Pruett, who came home from one of those moonless bombing runs over the Ruhr with a V.C. and no legs. Sybil, faithful in her fashion, stayed with him until he was put under the churchyard sod. You might find it hard to believe that in her twenties she was a very attractive dish."

"But she unfortunately lacked ideology. What was your ideology at the time, George?"

"Mankind, of course. I thought we'd settled that."

"Of course." It was going to be easier to kill Malkin, if it came to that, than he'd supposed. "And because Sybil's faithful in her fashion, she told you about Trojan Horse?"

"Shame on you for putting words in my mouth. Perhaps, instead, it was someone on the Trojan Horse Oversight Committee. Or perhaps one of Brother Littlejohn's acolytes experienced a religious conversion."

Malkin gestured with one fluttering hand. "I must tell you, though, Trojan Horse did have its entertaining aspects. While Brother Littlejohn wasted resources creating product supposed to be misleading, but which in reality mapped the acreage where the disinformation specialists were planting their crops, I simultaneously wasted resources creating a bustling bureaucratic infrastructure, a bustling Potemkin village one could say, that existed only to complete the illusion his product had been accepted at face value. Yet worth the cost and inconvenience, because I was then able to concentrate—I almost said on good works, but have it your way—on the serious jiggery-pokery. And far more freely than I could have if John hadn't been kept so busy and happy." He cocked his head and said collegially, "What goes around, comes around."

Malkin's valedictory, Belknap thought. Mannered anomie and egocentric babble. "Was it you, or Frank Willis, who delivered Beowulf to Moore at the Library of Congress?"

Malkin smiled nostalgically. "What was always so endearing about Frank Willis was his childlike enthusiasm for the dark side of intelligence work. He aspired to be a spy the way devout first-born sons in Catholic families used to aspire to be priests. Of course, you yourself made this same useful discovery in Germany, and when the young man eventually reenlisted in Washington after the tragic collapse of his fried-chicken empire, he still retained that delightfully misguided innocence. He was a tabula rasa, a Galatea with sergeant's stripes . . . living clay waiting to be turned on the potter's wheel and emerge from the kiln a full-blown, red-blooded secret agent. So after he was detached to NSC guard duty I took a modest paternal interest in him—how could I resist?—and offered the chance to participate in Project Utopia, an operation established, I believe I told him, to unload bogus NSC documents on the unsuspecting Russians. Needless to say, the opportunity to join the Utopia Team, even to deliver the documents on occasion, appealed immediately to his baser patriotic instincts and he became a member in instant good standing of that bustling bureaucratic infrastructure I mentioned a moment ago.

"Are you following me? I didn't need Willis's cooperation to gain access to the NSC reading-room vault, nor did I need his occasional courier services. I recruited him to keep John happy, since he'd arranged Willis's assignment to NSC guard duty to encourage just such a recruitment. As to the Library of Congress, I've never been in it, I don't even like its architecture." He paused as though to measure audience reaction, always unpredictable at the first public tryout of a new script. "So it could have been Frank Willis. Or it could have been . . . John Littlejohn."

"What do you mean, Littlejohn?"

"Exactly what I told you earlier. I've never been under Soviet control, though of course the Soviets thought otherwise, we long ago made sure of that. I repeat, I'm a man trusted by my government to barter information discreetly, to work for balance, for peace, through exclusively personal contacts developed over decades. And I can say with a degree of pride that anything I've given up, any temporary losses, have been more than offset by what we've received over those same decades from those same contacts. Littlejohn's something else. Consequences never considered when he manipulates his puppets . . . look what he did to Frank Willis. Placed him like a Parcheesi counter in a game where the young man had neither the training nor native wit to hold his own. You seem determined to hold me responsible for his death, but disabuse yourself. John was the man who manipulated him. And more important, owned him. John's the man you want."

"Shame on you for trying to muddy the waters, George. First Sybil Pruett and the acolytes, now Littlejohn. I don't care about Littlejohn. I've got you."

Malkin's lips formed an absurdly defiant pout. "You used to be more perceptive. Before you embarked on your self-defeating vendetta. If I was actually under Soviet control, I'd have long ago told Moscow Center that our side had activated a deception exercise called Trojan Horse because it had learned of my 'Soviet connections.' The proof I didn't is self-evident: if I had, why would the Center go to such lengths after the return of Beowulf to deliver a defector with a story intended to divert suspicion from George Malkin? Since my supposed Soviet connections were already known, what could the defector accomplish? Besides, do you think someone as unstable as Littlejohn would be put in charge of a deception exercise like Trojan Horse if the exercise was serious? Trojan Horse was a charade, in a sense another Potemkin village."

His petulant voice trailed off and his eyes seemed to be wandering the room in search of the cosmic facts and figures that would explain everything. "It became apparent in recent years that Littlejohn was not only fanatically enamored of the far right's lunatic fringe, he was also decidedly paranoid. Nothing to be ashamed of, of course, paranoia and suicide are our occupational diseases, like black lung in the coal mines. But John saw Communists under beds in every branch of the government. He even thought the historic schism between the Soviets and the Chinese was a Politburo scheme to lull us into a fatal complacency. Worse, he cavorted with right-wing extremists wherever he could find them, passing on bizarre stories of alleged Agency coddling of crypto-Communists, liberals, and one-worlders.

"So why, one naturally asks, wasn't he quietly muzzled and put out to pasture? For the same reason that Lyndon Johnson once gave for keeping Hoover on as head of the FBI. Better to have him inside the tent pissing out than outside pissing in." Malkin grimaced at his own lapse of taste. Vulgarity, even borrowed vulgarity, was as alien to him as sincerity, but circumstances alter cases.

"Littlejohn, suddenly the Agency's number-one problem child, had to be diverted with busy work. Yet there was a horror of providing that busy work within an Agency framework. So he was given ostensible retirement and told to go after me, a maverick one-worlder playing footsie with the Soviets. The story I was a Soviet agent pleased him immensely, because in his catechism all advocates of coexistence were automatically suspect, and here was proof of the pudding. For anyone to take the next step and tell him I was in fact a double agent would have obviously exposed the whole Trojan Horse charade as the busy work it was, but no one would have dared take that step anyhow. Just as John always knew by way of divine revelation that an agent working for us on the other side was sure to have been doubled, he knew that a double agent working for us on our side was sure to have been tripled. For the ideological paranoid, life is simultaneously simple and complex."

"Is that the end of the speech, George?"

"Not quite. If I was actually under Soviet control, I'd have packed my bags as soon as I learned about Trojan Horse. And if I was actually under Soviet control, I'd never have learned its true purpose in the first place. My information had to come from the highest levels, because neither Sybil Pruett nor the acolytes knew Trojan Horse existed only to keep John from running amok."

Belknap experienced a twinge of uncertainty. "Littlejohn said he had two hundred people working under him to make sure you were led down the garden path. That's quite an investment just to keep a man from running amok."

"Delusions of grandeur. They go with paranoia, don't they? He'd no more than twenty, most of them misfits. For John, Trojan Horse was an obsession feeding on itself. He couldn't let go."

"You weave an intriguing hypothesis. I always did admire the fecundity of your imagination, especially when it ran away with you. But it's like trying to sell refrigerators to Eskimos, it won't make anyone rich." Belknap, concerned about remaining daylight, more concerned about the Acme Termite Control van, decided to close the inquest. "Any other last words?"

"My God, yes!" Malkin instantly seemed to regret his vehemence, but all his self-control couldn't quite suppress the quaver that crept into his voice. "I'm trying to save you from your own folly. Before you take a step you'll regret forever, let me phone the president's national security adviser. He'll confirm everything I've told you, everything."

"It's too late. Too late for you, too late for me. I've heard too many lies to know anymore what the truth is, or even if there is such a thing." He looked abstractedly at the Staunton figures on the chessboard. Truth at least existed on that field of battle . . . some strategies succeeded, some strategies failed, and truth was whatever won the game. "One final question before you start your journey: why was

I chosen, all those years ago in Moscow, to take the fall? Why me?''

Malkin, distressed, shook his head. "David, it was never personal. In the scheme of things, each of us is assigned roles. The Fates somehow touched the two of us in different ways. Who could have dreamed we'd someday stand facing each other, and you with that gun, as we are now?"

"That's your answer?" Belknap felt murderously calm.

Malkin sighed. "In restrospect, we perhaps should have made you witting. But if we had, you'd have been acting your part, not living it, and we both know the hazards along that road. Down through the years, however, you've never been in any kind of danger . . . until you ran amok yourself last night. Because of Glukhov's disclosures to the FBI, we did intend, it's true, to go through a pretense of arresting you, it was the only way to convince the Soviets their plan to protect me had succeeded. I'd even begun the job of keeping the Bureau from upsetting the apple cart by telling Hathaway I was sure I could turn you. In actuality, you'd have been a hero and those of us privy to the true story would have been standing in line to shake your hand.''

"I'm touched.'' Belknap reached into the breast pocket of his jacket. "I almost forgot. I've a farewell memento before we go.''

"*Go?*" Malkin bit into the word and spit it away. The façade of confidence he'd sustained during most of their time in this room was quite remarkable. But it was certainly showing more hairline cracks than a moment ago. "Although your vendetta mentality limits a free conversational exchange, isn't it time to talk realistically? You can kidnap me at the point of a gun, but there's no way you can march me to Moscow.''

"Oh, I agree.'' Belknap smiled. "That's why I'm only marching you to a way station. The Soviet Embassy on Sixteenth Street.''

Malkin, staring as if he'd seen his father's ghost, said, "You're quite mad, you know.''

"Probably." He held out the ring he'd removed from his pocket. "The farewell memento. Compliments of your executed Spanish cell mate and Kim Philby and all the old gang at the KGB. I thought it might have sentimental value on your journey home, and it'll definitely guarantee safe passage."

Malkin took the ring, disbelieving. "Where did you get it?" he whispered.

"Maybe you're not the only one with KGB connections."

Malkin seemed dazed. He read the Spanish inscription silently, then translated in a frail voice, " 'Every man is the son of his own works.' " He brushed his face, as though entering an attic thick with cobwebs and the must of old steamer trunks. "Cervantes."

"Ah."

"You can't do this, David. You're making a catastrophic mistake." His chin trembled. "I'm not a Soviet agent."

"I know. You're the proverbial man of goodwill."

Malkin blinked and shook his head. "My God. It's enough to make the angels weep."

It was enough to make Malkin weep, too. Those were genuine tears in his eyes. Belknap remembered another time he'd heard those same words from this same man . . . and remembered *Rigoletto* playing in the background on a small phonograph expertly rigged to jam Russian electronic surveillance.

"Enough, yes. But Ecclesiasticus was right, George, and so were you when you quoted him before you sent me off to deliver that ring to Philby. There is a time to every purpose under heaven."

Belknap stepped forward and drove his left fist into Malkin's stomach. Malkin bent over, gasping. Belknap kneed him in the groin and considerately supported him as he fell forward in an attitude of salaaming prayer. "No more Golden Rule, George."

Hoping the fox was truly winded, he reached into a

pocket for his walkie-talkie, extended its short antenna. "Fred to Mobile Unit, package ready for pickup at front door. Sixty seconds and counting."

Vanessa's answering voice was unsteady, charged with apprehension. "Read you, Fred. Sixty and counting."

Belknap glanced at the package. It was obvious the package hadn't recognized Vanessa's voice, because the package wasn't recognizing much of anything. The package was too preoccupied with inner pain.

He dropped the walkie-talkie in a wastebasket and put away his gun. He helped Malkin to his feet, dusted his dinner jacket, and dabbed the beadings of sweat on his forehead and the spittle running down his chin. His eyes were glazed, his complexion pasty, his breath sour.

Belknap gripped Malkin's upper arm and steered the unresisting body toward the vestibule. "We're going to get into a Datsun station wagon. We're going to park opposite the embassy. Then you and I are going to walk across Sixteenth to the embassy gate. You're going to press the buzzer and when someone answers on the intercom, you're going to say. 'This is George Malkin. I have to come in, it's a matter of life and death.'

"From the time we park you have exactly ninety seconds to get through that gate. If you don't make it through by then, I'll shoot you. If you call out for help or try to run, I'll shoot you. And if you so much as look at the Executive Protective Service cop, MPD cop, whatever he is, on embassy duty in the middle of the block, I'll shoot you sooner."

"There's no way"—the hoarse, enervated voice sounded as if it came from a sepulcher—"you can succeed. I told you that. You wouldn't listen."

"Ninety seconds," Belknap repeated. He opened the front door and forced Malkin ahead of him. Daylight's fragile wash was fading into night, but there was afterglow enough for Malkin to be recognized at the gate.

Belknap's overloaded optic nerves registered fragmented

images . . . a woman watering a window flower pot
. . . two helmeted bicyclists . . . the station wagon pulling to the curb . . . Brdnowski hunched over the wheel
like a machine-gunner in an old war movie, or a bulldog
with a toothache . . . the Acme Termite Control van a
block and a half away, hood still up. Its occupants, once
they realized why the station wagon had appeared out of
nowhere, would perhaps lose another few seconds getting
that hood down before they could give chase. Hope springs
eternal.

Vanessa had already opened the rear door. Belknap gave
Malkin a hard shove and piled in behind him. "Take off,
Brdnowski! Left turns on Twenty-ninth, Pennsylvania, L,
Fifteenth, M, and Sixteenth, then park near L in front of the
old National Geographic building." Heart beginning to
race, he said to Vanessa, "Pull the pin on one smoke
grenade, one tear-gas grenade, and drop them in the middle
of the street. Brdnowski, make an omelet with your two
eggs just before turning onto Pennsylvania."

"Right."

Belknap glanced back when they reached 29th and saw a
reassuring dirty yellow cloud billowing in front of Malkin's
townhouse. The cloud, as the man in the back room of the
pawnshop on Eighth Avenue had promised, temporarily
obliterated the view of anyone on its far side. The man had
also promised that anyone driving through the dirty yellow
cloud would be incapacitated to some extent by tear gas.
But put not your trust in princes or pawnbrokers.

Brdnowski scrambled his omelet and headed southeast on
Pennsylvania. Belknap watched the beginnings of another
dirty yellow cloud. Malkin sat leaning forward, head in his
hands, apparently still in pain. Understandable. And apparently he still hadn't recognized Vanessa. Also understandable.

Without looking up, Malkin said, "Your father will
certainly appreciate this betrayal of him."

Belknap hastily revised *apparentlys*. Vanessa caught her breath.

Malkin straightened himself and sighed. "It wouldn't surprise me if your father kills himself. A proud man can stand only so much shame. But you've thought all that through, I'm sure."

Vanessa closed her eyes and looked away.

"Why are you doing this to her?" Belknap asked helplessly. "Have you no decency left?"

"But I'm not doing anything to her," Malkin said equably. "You're the one doing the doing. I'm merely trying to help her understand that fact." He languidly pulled at the sleeves of his tuxedo, as if to correct a sartorial defect that impaired his credibility. "Oh, dear, it seems I've managed to return that monkey you were getting rid of forever. I must have thought you'd be lonely without it."

The green roof of the four-story gray mansion bristled with antennae. The upper two rows of windows and the second floor's three small pedimented balconies were masked by nondescript gray shuttering. Trees and shrubbery behind the seven-foot-high fencing of ornamental iron substantially obscured the first door. A bored policeman wearing a luminescent orange vest tried to make himself discreetly inconspicuous in the open area between the Soviet Embassy's north wall and the adjacent University Club.

From the sidewalk in front of the National Georgraphic Society, Belknap watched tensely as Malkin got out of the Datsun. If the son of a bitch had a coup de main in reserve, this was the moment he'd probably produce it.

Malkin, standing erect but still somewhat wobbly, said, "You'll regret forever what you're about to do."

Belknap indicated the embassy across the street. "Your ninety-second clock's running. I want you one pace ahead, my hand's on the gun in my pocket. Gives a cleaner shot if need arises."

"All right, David. Your funeral, not mine." As Malkin stepped off the curb, he reached inside his jacket and brought out his slender gold cigar case. "My parting gift . . . there wasn't time to arrange something more appropriate, you'll understand. Accept it, please."

Astonished, Belknap took the cigar case. "But now that we're enemies, I thought . . ."

"Even enemies"—Malkin favored him one last time with that engagingly boyish smile—"can afford a modest beau geste."

Belknap put the case away. "You won't find it easy to replace an item like this in Moscow."

"What makes you so sure I'm going to Moscow?"

"I'll have to take my chances, won't I?" Belknap was pleased Malkin was dressed formally. It made him extremely respectable as they crossed the street, extremely non-threatening to the security of the embassy if you happened to be a bored policeman wanting not to get involved while on duty with bomb throwers or other disturbers of the embassy's peace. Belknap was even pleased with his own moderate respectability, bought off the rack in Silver Spring a hundred years ago.

They reached the embassy's grillwork gate. Belknap stood directly behind Malkin. "You know the drill."

Malkin did not move.

"Fifty seconds and counting." He nudged Malkin's spine with the muzzle of the gun in his pocket.

Malkin pressed the buzzer. A guttural voice came through the intercom box above it. "We are closed for the weekend. You must come back Monday."

"No, this is George Malkin. I have to come in."

"Matter of life and death," Belknap prompted in his ear.

"Matter of life and death," Malkin said mechanically.

"Once more with feeling," Belknap whispered savagely.

"Life and death. Urgent, urgent, *urgent*."

"The embassy is closed for all business. Monday. Come back Monday."

Belknap renewed the pressure against Malkin's spine. "Twenty-five and counting, George."

Malkin seized the iron bars and rattled the gate frantically. "*This is Chessplayer!*" he shouted to the heavens, loud enough for the policeman up the street to hear, loud enough for any FBI observers nesting in a borrowed National Geographic aerie to hear. "*This is Chessplayer, let me in!* Tell General Lisovsky. Dmitri Lisovsky, tell him for God's sake. *Chessplayer is here!*"

No one responded on the intercom. Belknap didn't dare look toward M Street to see if the policeman was considering intervention. By his watch, Malkin's time on earth had expired. He pretended the guard inside was consulting superiors, even consulting Dmitri Lisovsky. Friend from Spain, like-minded defender of civilization and Caspian Sea caviar, and actually present, it was asserted, in Washington. Malkin couldn't have been bluffing about that. Almost paralyzed by the uncertainties, Belknap struck a bargain with Hope, said to spring eternal. He'd wait another fifteen seconds before deciding whether to shoot or throw away his gun.

As he watched the seconds vanish, he heard the click of a latch-release. Malkin almost stumbled as the gate swung inward under his weight. He caught himself, half-turned as though to deliver an apologia. Or perhaps a Parthian shot. But something changed his mind and he walked proudly, head hight, toward the embassy door.

Chessplayer was home. *Ave atque vale.*

The door opened and an avuncular, white-haired man stepped out. He embraced Malkin, then looked at Belknap and winked mischievously. "Games," he said in mellifluous Oxbridge. "Children disguised from each other as superpowers. Other children diguised from each other as intelligence agents."

The door closed.

Belknap, trembling, at last glanced furtively at the policeman and almost laughed at his own timidity. Cowards die, what, a thousand times? The policeman was temporarily hors de combat. The policeman was absorbed with the antics of two mini-skirted lesbians passionately kissing on the other side of 16th.

He breathed deeply, savoring the magic and mystery of things. With a sleeve he wiped the tears forming in his eyes, precious tears celebrating joy. He was free. Free, he thought, and a sob began to rise in his throat.

He turned and smiled weakly at Brdnowski and Vanessa. He raised two fingers in an unsteady Churchillian victory sign and started to cross the street. From the station wagon's rear window, Vanessa blew a kiss. My Lady of the Bower, he thought, half-drunk on euphoria. The Tourney is Done, My Lady welcomes Her Knight.

He saw the Acme van then, hurtling down 16th toward them. In the same instant, he saw the submachine gun poking from an open window on the passenger side and his brain registered *Uzi*. "Get down!" he cried and took cover behind a car parked in front of the embassy. He heard the splatter of bullets as the Uzi raked the street's west side. Then the van flashed past and was gone.

In shock, he staggered into the street and saw the two mini-skirted lovers, entwined still as they lay in death, one missing part of her head. The policeman, his left trouser leg stained with blood, was trying to get to his feet; the driver of the van must have been taking random shots from his window with a handgun he couldn't possibly have aimed.

Passing cars had begun to stop. Someone was already helping the policeman. Belknap, seeing jagged holes in the metal of the station wagon and no occupants, charged across the path of an oncoming pickup, reaching the Datsun as Brdnowski's head and shoulders reappeared.

"Are you hit?"

Brdnowski shook his head, but his eyes were vacant and both hands now gripped the steering wheel as if they'd found their only link to life. Belknap opened the rear door, stared at Vanessa's body on the floor. Blood gushed from a terrible wound in her throat. There was a gaping hole in the left rib cage near the heart. He dug his fingers into Brdnowski's shoulder. *"Nearest hospital!"*

Brdnowski sat motionless, suspended in time, frozen by fear. Belknap slapped him with all his strength. Brdnowski whimpered and stirred the engine to life.

36

BELKNAP WAITED with Brdnowski in the small room next to Emergency for the decision of the triage team. Even this early Friday evening it was apparent the incoming flow of patients was nearly overwhelming the doctors on duty. He looked up, frightened, when the middle-aged triage nurse appeared.

"The surgery will take at least five hours. Perhaps you'd like to get something to eat . . . I know you don't feel like eating, but there's nothing you can do for her here, and believe me, it's better to get away."

"You're a kind woman. The truth, though, would be better than anything else I can think of right now. What are the odds?"

She hesitated. "A slim chance . . . otherwise she wouldn't have been selected for surgery."

But she was avoiding his eyes, and he knew what that meant. Hospital euphemisms never change. Then, hardly aware of what prompted him, he took out Malkin's slender, cleverly constructed cigar case. It wasn't difficult to take apart and within minutes he'd found the miniaturized constant-signal transmitter the case concealed.

He stared at the dismantled mechanism. Explanations could change nothing now, but the transmitter explained why the Acme van had come, not in hot pursuit from M Street onto 16th, but down 16th from the north, above M. The smoke and tear-gas grenades, as promised, had sufficiently confused the hunters. They'd lost the quarry

. . . until the van, probably making haphazard sweeps, had once more picked up the transmitter's signal with whatever homing equipment it carried.

Malkin's beau geste, he thought, and let the tears of rage and anguish come streaming down his face.

Brdnowski touched him awkwardly. "Fred?"

"Alexandria," he gasped at last. "Take me to Alexandria. To her father."

As they drove down Washington Street past Christ Church, Brdnowski spoke for the first time since they'd left the hospital. "Van was your girl, Fred?"

"My life, I think."

"How are you going to break it to her father?"

"I'll tell him what happened, then I'll shoot him, once in the throat, once in the heart."

Two state police cars, the play of their flashing lights bathing the night with a kaleidoscopic glow, were parked in the driveway of the house half-hidden by climbing ivy and wisteria. A trooper, sitting on the edge of the front seat, one foot resting on the ground, was writing on a clipboard. An unmarked Ford sedan was parked in front.

Belknap, taking in the scene from forty yards away, anticipating the questions the trooper would surely ask when he saw the damaged left side of the Datsun, had Brdnowski turn it around and park. "That's her father's house. I'll find out what's happening."

The trooper didn't look up from his clipboard until Belknap was twenty feet away. "Good evening, Officer."

The trooper squinted at him, flipped through mental file cards of muggers, bank robbers, and car thieves at large in his sector, then sent a squirt of chaw onto the lawn. "Neighbor?"

Belknap shook his head. "I'm a good friend of Mr.

Littlejohn's daughter." He somehow got the next words out.
"Her fiancé, in fact."

The trooper nodded condolingly. "You've heard then?"
"Heard?"

The trooper tugged uncomfortably at an earlobe. "I had
this idea you'd been crying. So I thought you'd heard. Mr.
Littlejohn, his Chris-Craft washed up in the cove down by
Belle Haven Country Club about two hours ago. Not
carrying a wallet, but he was a member, someone recognized the body. My captain's in there with the wife,
explaining. Mr. Littlejohn, according to first reports from
the scene, shot himself behind the ear." He waited for a
reaction, but didn't seem concerned about not getting one.
"Funny thing is, there was no gun in the boat and there's no
way I know of a man can blow a hole in his head and then
toss away the gun. His daughter with you?"

"She couldn't get away from Washington tonight."

"Just as well, she probably couldn't go in. These two
government men have put the whole place off limits. Even
kicked me out. They're stuffing papers into cartons like
there's no tomorrow. What did this, uh, Littlejohn do for a
living?"

"What two government men?"

Another squirt of tobacco almost reached the unmarked
Ford sedan. "Them."

"From the Agency?"

"Agency?" The trooper laughed bitterly. "In these parts,
the Agency don't exist. Just two government men, obstruct-
ing an investigation of . . . suicide."

Belknap got into the station wagon. "You know this area
of Virginia?"

Brdnowski pretended to be insulted. "Do you know how
many years I've been driving cabs, Fred?"

"Take us down to the Potomac . . . as close as you can
get by using back roads."

"Right."

"You're a good man, Murph."

"You too, Fred."

"Not too many of us around anymore."

"I guess."

"Myrt will be a wonderful wife."

"Cross your fingers when you say that, Fred, then knock on wood. One thing I got to tell you. I was sure taken with Van."

"I think a lot of people were."

Brdnowski drove the station wagon down a narrow dirt road until underbrush made it impassable. Belknap got out. "I'll be a while. You'll wait?"

"Aw, hell, Fred. I'm your partner now, right?"

"Right."

Belknap struck off through the night-mantled woods and came at last to the river. Through the light mist that lay over it he could see the faint, twinkling lights of Maryland. He walked blindly along the bank as water lapped against the rocks below and the timeless currents traveled to the sea. His heart was nearly breaking when at last he defiantly raised his fist and shook it at the sky.

Author's Afterword

THE PRINCIPAL EVENTS of this story took place in 1975. Information concerning subsequent circumstances of some of the persons involved in those events, not all of it verifiable, has recently become available.

The Belknaps

Through the long medical recovery of Vanessa Belknap, her husband nursed her and loved her. There was cardiothoracic surgery to repair damage to the pericardial sac and left lung. The spleen was lost. Later there was reconstructive surgery on the pharynx and larynx, followed by a fistulectomy to correct abnormal communications involving food and saliva between the trachea and esophagus. Excising of accumulated scar tissue from the vocal cords. Cosmetic plastic surgery on throat and neck. Eight operations, in all, by the end of 1977, when the doctors officially pronounced her "recovered."

Not totally, perhaps, but certainly enough for the Belknaps to take, without arousing undue interest in their activities, a meticulously planned tour of the Far East and Europe they casually described to friends as an overdue combined honeymoon and business trip. To complete the essential misdirection, Belknap told senior associates of his industrial-security business that the time was ripe to consider possible expansion into such related activities as the gathering of economic intelligence for international clients through a worldwide network of listening posts.

While abroad, he would conduct appropriate feasibility studies.

The Belknaps arrived in Tokyo in February of 1978, and if any intelligence agency had them under precautionary surveillance, the surveillance was wasted, because at the end of their first week there they disappeared. In a letter to his senior associates postmarked Manila, Belknap explained that he'd decided he could more effectively conduct feasibility studies by traveling incognito, particularly since he had no consuming desire to alert competitors to the possible expansion. He of course did not mention the collection of counterfeit passports, painstakingly acquired over the thirty months his wife had struggled to regain her health and nearly normal speech functions, that they would be using to guarantee their incognito status. Nor did he mention the carefully selected world capitals where, if the gods, like conscientious auditors, approved of the settling of outstanding accounts, the two of them would try, first in Bangkok, then in Rome, Madrid, and Bonn, to lend the gods a helping hand.

The Brdnowskis

After the success of their chain-letter operations in Chicago and several other cities, the Brdnowskis used their financial wind-fall to start a new life in a small midwestern town, where Brdnowski bought a drive-in near the Interstate and renamed it The Home Run. A year later he bought the adjoining gas station and feed store.

The Brdnowskis have a four-year-old daughter. Brdnowski is a member of the American Legion and Kiwanis. His wife bowls every Tuesday with the Amazorenes, top women's team in the county league, works every Thursday as a volunteer in Community Hospital's gift shop, and runs the three-card-monte game at the annual fund-raiser for the fire department.

* * *

Ivan Glukhov

After several years of intermittent interrogation of Glukhov at Camp Peary, Virginia, the CIA debriefing team reached the conclusion he was a bona fide defector. He was provisionally made a consultant at a five-figure salary and assigned to translate *Krokodil* and other Russian humor magazines for a renowned academician admired within higher echelons of the CIA for innovative approaches to applied psychology, and in particular for his classified paper postulating that humor magazines best mirrored underlying stresses in a totalitarian society.

Upon learning of his new status, Glukhov made a down payment on a Volvo and became engaged to a former East German gymnast he'd met in the PX at Camp Peary. She has a husband in Leipzig, but this is thought to be no problem, since Glukhov has been promised that, if he performs well in his new job, arrangements will be made for East German security forces to come into possession of information establishing that the husband works for West German Intelligence. East German law provides that the spouse of a person convicted of espionage can unilaterally dissolve the marriage by filing an affidavit of renunciation with the judge who presided at the trial.

Recently Glukhov was told he might be given the opportunity to work for the East German desk. It may never happen, the operation hasn't yet been approved topside, but a few cowboys in the Eastern Europe Division who sometimes have had fairly decent luck with similar operations are intrigued by the damage they could do if Glukhov and his gymnast were sent East posing as redefectors.

Colonel Igor Demichev

As a result of the failure of the Chessplayer rescue operation, Demichev was demoted and transferred to Vladivostok as assistant director of security for the eastern terminus of the Trans-Siberian Railroad. To some extent, he took his exile stoically, willing to wait for a change in the Moscow weather, or for someone else at the Center, with luck even Pechenko, to make such a shambles of things he would be dispatched to relieve the disgraced assistant director in Vladivostok. Besides, Vladivostok was better than Bratsk, and a railroad system was better than a hydroelectric plant.

Occasionally Demichev flirted with the idea of defection, but he had enough insight to recognize the pathetic motivation behind such a Draconian remedy: continued depression over his wife's threats to leave him. Without Moscow, she said, she could not survive. Without Moscow, neither could he, yet somehow he did. Barely.

Natalia Demicheva

When Demicheva divorced her husband in 1977, she returned to Moscow, underwent another face lift, and reestablished her celebrated salons. She had a brief, unsatisfactory affair with her husband's former aide, Lieutenant Nikitin, in part because she was sorry for the young man. Gosha had promised, she knew, to make Nikitin a captain, and soon afterward a major, but things had happened too quickly in that nightmarish summer of 1975 for Gosha to complete the paper work.

By the spring of 1978, Demicheva was again ready to undertake a concert tour of European capitals . . . ready to be overwhelmed with flowers by adoring audiences, with elaborate receptions by wealthy social climbers, with extravagant gifts by amorous impresarios. Demicheva subscribed to the theory that concert pianists and opera singers performed better after sex in the afternoon.

During the tour, two of her impresarios, working unknown to each other for intelligence services of different NATO countries, chided her about her long absence from Western Europe. She patiently explained to each—on rare occasions she seemed to have a bookkeeper's orderly mind—her husband was no longer a custodian of secrets and consequently there was nothing of value she could share on this tour. She'd had an affair of sorts with a lieutenant on his staff, but the poor fellow had been transferred to a meaningless job after her husband's fall from grace, and anyhow he refused to discuss KGB business in bed. She promised to seduce someone better informed after her return to Moscow, then teasingly hinted she had a prospect in mind.

General Anatoli Pechenko

In the immediate aftermath of Demichev's departure for Vladivostok, Pechenko pondered the appropriate reward for young Nikitin, who during the Chessplayer crisis had secretly reported to him on most of Demichev's desperate twistings and turnings. Such reporting convincingly demonstrated the lieutenant knew how to put distance between himself and disaster, but it would be unwise to reward that kind of treachery too quickly. Besides, there was no way Pechenko could satisfactorily explain to his own staff the sudden addition, as well as the sudden promotion, of his former archrival's key aide. There would be revolution.

Pechenko, resigning himself to the necessity of first testing Nikitin's loyalty by deprivation, arranged his transfer to the Liaison Office for the Training Command. There would be time enough after this seasoning by adversity to call on and reward his talents. If, that is, he survived the seasoning. Pechenko, not entirely happy with this even-handed resolution of a complicated problem, consoled himself with the thought Nikitin was lucky not to be inspecting freight trains in Vladivostok.

Pechenko's star continued to rise and, after swallowing whole most of Demichev's former empire, he had so much patronage to dispense he sometimes lost track of who was worthy, who was not. By 1977 the situation had become intolerable and he decided to reward Nikitin by transferring him to his personal staff to straighten out the confusion. The lieutenant had established a fine reputation for ruthlessness in the Liaison Office. Before Pechenko could act, however, not only did Natalia Demicheva return to Moscow from Vladivostok, she also took Nikitin—according to quite reliable rumors reaching Pechenko—as a lover.

Devastated, Pechenko abandoned any thoughts of trying to rehabilitate Nikitin. He didn't know Natalia well, he could count on the fingers of one hand the times he'd been invited to her overrated soirees, but it deeply offended his sense of the fitness of things that she would choose her husband's trusted former aide—in the bargain a treacherous opportunist—to make her husband a cuckold. Of course, her husband was technically no longer her husband, but this was a quibble. The principle remained. Pechenko, feeling personally betrayed by her capricious choice, slept poorly for weeks.

Then, not long after Natalia's return from her triumphant European tour in 1978, Pechenko ran into her at Marshal Rogov's annual reception for Bolshoi principals. He was intrigued by her mature beauty, her teasing wit, and as she chattered gaily about her tour, spicing the chatter with intimate gossip about Europe's leading politicians, he began to realize she was flirting with him, outrageously and delightfully. After several agreeable excursions around the marble dance floor, she hesitantly asked if he'd care to attend a salon she was holding the following week.

Pechenko retired that night a happy man. His former archrival languished in Vladivostok, and there was nothing wrong with that. But to cuckold well was the best revenge.

George Malkin

Upon arriving in Moscow, Malkin received the welcome exclusively reserved for champions of peace. The ceremonies and celebrations had of course no public aspect, and not until twelve months later did the first Western correspondent catch sight of him.

The correspondent was interested in obtaining an interview with Philby and, knowing that Philby frequently came to the International Post Office to pick up his airmailed London *Times*, decided to try to intercept him there. The day he spotted him, Philby entered the post office with a male companion. By the time the two men reappeared, Philby with several issues of the London *Times*, his companion with several issues of *The New York Times*, the correspondent had grasped the extent of his good fortune and tried to zero in on Malkin instead.

Malkin was unwilling to talk and brusquely walked on. But Philby seemed to find the situation amusing and spent perhaps ten minutes with the excited correspondent. Philby's celebrated stammer was as pronounced as ever; so was his penchant for the outrageous. He freely admitted his companion was Malkin, who he said liked the Russian winters no better than he did. Malkin now held a KGB rank slightly lower than his own—here Philby smiled impishly—and was at his desk daily, lending his experience and analytical skills to the solution of problems always occuring in a troubled world. Malkin, as far as Philby knew, had no use for Communism, he was simply a man unshakably dedicated to the cause of peace. He had a pleasant dacha in Zhukovka and shared a Moscow apartment with an attractive older movie actress. Philby, impish again, refused to reveal her name, on the ground he wasn't going to do *all* the correspondent's legwork.

Malkin missed Washington, missed the cherry trees, missed the restaurants, although in his own days in Washington, Philby added, the restaurants were something anyone ought to appreciate missing. New York had good restaurants, San Francisco had good restaurants, but Washington had edible food only in certain embassies, and it was the same depressing story in Moscow. That was one of the reasons he himself still missed London.

When Philby began to ramble, the correspondent, horribly afraid almost nothing he had been hearing about Malkin would turn out to be true, thanked him profusely and raced to his office to get the story on the wire. Yet without regard to the literal accuracy of all of Philby's remarks, independent evidence accumulating in the last months of 1976 did confirm their substance. Malkin had become a respected senior adviser to the KGB and possibly to the Ministry of Foreign Affairs.

Malkin's influence continued to increase throughout 1977, but sometime in 1978 disturbing indications he might not be exactly what he seemed began to trickle into the Center from sources around the world. The information was usually vague and never satisfactorily documented, yet it had a unifying thread: U.S. Intelligence believed it had successfully placed a dispatched agent in the highest levels of the KGB during the summer of 1975.

The acutal name of the reputed agent never appeared in these frustratingly imprecise reports, yet once more there was a unifying thread: his alleged KGB code name always seemed to be connected with chess. A Bangkok source said it was *Grandmaster*, a Rome source *The Sicilian*, a Madrid source *Ruy Lopez*, a Bonn source *Chessplayer*. The Bonn source, it is fair to say, attracted exceptional attention.

From the standpoint of the counterintelligence ferrets, there were only two explanations for this worldwide feedback. Either U.S. Intelligence was orchestrating a campaign to destroy Malkin's usefulness by falsely claiming him as one of its own, or the KGB had taken an asp to its bosom. Such were the problem's uncomplicated parameters; the problem itself was another matter. The *gospodin* from across the sea by now had many friends at court.

When the ferrets at last could no longer safely avoid transmitting preliminary findings to higher authority, a certain Captain Gusin, heartily disliked by his superiors, was selected for the honor of briefing General Pechenko about the possible presence of a U.S. spy in his far-flung empire. While Gusin on the appointed day nervously pulled together the incriminating threads and his superiors sat well apart from him at the conference table to establish they weren't necessarily endorsing his presentation, a scowling Pechenko drew daggers and gallows on a note pad, concealing his delight only by superlative self-discipline.

If Malkin was in fact tainted, then for more than a generation a corps de ballet of strutting buffoons led by Igor Demichev must have been either collaborators of dupes. As for himself, Pechenko told Natalia with great good humor that evening, his skirts were clean; he had had no involvement with Malkin until after his arrival in Moscow. So he'd almost decided to mention the Malkin rumors in his next private luncheon with KGB Chairman Andropov. It would have to be done with tact of course, since Andropov too would be in an embarrassing position if the rumors were true. It was Andropov himself, after all, who had pinned on Malkin's chest the Order of the Red Banner and the Order of Lenin. But Pechenko felt he had a solution that should appeal to everyone's enlightened self-interest.

In 1980 there would be a presidential election in the United States. He would propose to Andropov that Malkin immediately be given a staff of specialists, preferably former exchange students, and be directed to monitor the U.S. press with a view to preparing appreciations of all prospective candidates and their foreign-policy philosophies. Andropov could even host an intimate private dinner in Malkin's honor—perhaps another medal could be presented during the toasts—and personally emphasize the strategic importance of the undertaking. But in reality, and Pechenko could not resist slapping his thigh as he shared his plan with Natalia, Malkin would be administering the affairs of a hastily constructed Potemkin village until the ferrets had completed their investigation.

If the investigation ultimately cleared him, no harm had been done. He could be restored to good standing in the KGB by a stroke of Andropov's pen, never even knowing he had been under suspicion. But if the investigation seemed to confirm he was a dispatched agent—and such a finding was for all practical purposes inevitable in these cases—there would be nothing to gain by looking for scapegoats or embarrassing dedicated senior officials. It would be disastrous to execute him, because execution would openly signal that the Center had been penetrated with such ease U.S. Intelligence wouldn't be able to resist trying again. It would be insane to attempt to turn him, because how could it ever be known where his true allegiance lay? So why not instead let U.S. Intelligence wrestle with the problem of true allegiance? Pechenko slapped his thigh again. When the proper time came, Malkin would be sent West posing as a redefector.

What did Natasha think of the whole idea?

Laughing as she led him into her bedroom, Natalia confessed she was always hopelessly confused by the bold initiatives, the daring gambits, of generals. But as a woman unschooled in intrigue yet not without intuitions, she didn't see how a plan so brilliant could fail. And the concept of a Potemkin village was, well, fascinating. So original.

When she finally stood before him wearing only the pendant he'd bought her to celebrate his day's good fortune, she poured two jiggers of vodka from the bottle on the bedside table. *"Za vashe zdorov'e, mon général!"*

Pechenko downed the vodka and gallantly unbuckled his belt. He had bored the lady long enough with secrets of state. Now it was time to reward her patience.